Praise for The Black Swan Files

AWARDS

GLIMMER, Winner
IPPY Gold Medal
Best Young Adult E-book, Independent Publisher Awards

GLISTEN, Winner
Best Young Adult Fiction, Pinnacle Book Achievement
Award
The Write Touch Readers Award

GLISTEN, 2nd Place
Best Young Adult Fiction, eLit Book Awards
Best Young Adult Romance, Book Buyers Best Award
Best Young Adult Paranormal, YARWA Athena Contest

GLISTEN, Finalist
Best Genre Fiction, North Street Book Prize
Best Paranormal, The Daphne du Maurier Award for Excel-
lence in Mystery/Suspense
Best Young Adult, The Maggie Award for Excellence

The Black Swan Files
001: GLIMMER

"*Glimmer* is a thrilling adventure set in the near future and it completely took me by surprise! I highly recommend it!"
~Sarah Palmer, **YA Love Magazine**

"I loved this story. If you love books with telekinesis, secret government agencies, and superhero powers, then this book is for you…*Glimmer* is like James Bond meets X-Men!"
~Benjamin Alderson, **Benjaminoftomes** Booktube Channel

"*Glimmer* was super intense. So fast-paced you did not want to put the book down. A gripping novel…it will keep readers on the edge of their seat. You will not be disappointed!"
~Nicole and Marija, **Let's Talk Books** Booktube Channel

"HOLY FREAKING MOTHER OF GOD! IT WAS AWESOME. Spy story + Prison break + Science Fiction = Best combo ever!"
~Uma Shankari, **Books.Bags.Burgers.**

"Great, innovative storyline with edge-of-seat action while still managing to tug on the heartstrings. A dystopian gem!"
~ **USA TODAY Bestselling Author**, Lynne Marshall

"Incredible! It will leave you begging for more!"
~Maureen Moyes, **MoMo's Book Diary**

"YA readers will love this book. The plot is full of twists and turns, conspiracy theories, and lots of action. Written with snappy dialogue and thrilling action sequences, *Glimmer* kept me hooked to the very end."
~Melanie Thompson, **Librarian**

The Black Swan Files
002: GLISTEN

"*Glisten* had me laughing out loud and on the verge of tears. It is a hard novel to put down! Just as enjoyable, thrilling and emotional as its predecessor."

~Sarah Palmer, **Confessions of a Lit Addict**

"Fast paced, exciting and emotional! *Glisten* is the perfect sequel to *Glimmer* and will have readers rooting for the brilliantly written characters."

~Uma Shankari, **Books.Bags.Burgers.**

"This fast-paced adventure features a uniquely gifted young woman whose power is enhanced by the bonds of friendship."

~USA TODAY Bestselling Author, Maureen A. Miller

"Ms. Cerrone packs action, adventure, and intrigue into the second installment of The Black Swan Files, *Glisten*—balanced by friends, family, and first love—a winning combination."

~ USA TODAY Bestselling Author, Lynne Marshall

THE BLACK SWAN FILES

003: SHIMMER

TRICIA CERRONE

mystic butterfly

Published by Mystic Butterfly, Inc.

The Black Swan Files is an official Trademark.

ISBN: 978-1-938258-18-3 (trade paperback)

ISBN: 978-1-938258-17-6 (ebook)

Cover design by Mark Harris, Harris Graphic Services

DEDICATION

For Jim and Tom

Thanks for being my loyal fans, beloved brothers, and the voices in my head when male characters are cracking jokes.

ACKNOWLEDGMENTS

Thank you to my trusted story editor, Janet Maarschalk—who always has insightful comments that make my stories stronger. Thank you, Mark Harris, for the cover design. Many thanks to my early reviewers, beta readers and early adopters.

I especially want to thank all the readers and fans who support this series, and the many who have generously posted positive reviews.

WHO'S WHO
IN THE BLACK SWAN FILES

Jocelyn Esperanza Albrecht (Marques): a.k.a. Sunnie Cashus, a.k.a. Project Sunday, a.k.a. The Black Swan—TOP SECRET

Georgie: College freshman, super sleuth, and crusader for justice

Brittany: Georgie's best friend, expert "maker" and sustainable fashion designer

Lena: Passionate cryptologist, budding hacktivist, and pie connoisseur

Graeme: Software entrepreneur, softhearted protector, and tenacious truth-seeker

Seth: Social outcast, smooth-talking survivor, and a former experiment at Camp Holliwell

Alastair: Georgie's cousin, former Army Ranger, and general badass

Richie: Al's Army buddy, mechanical genius, and Holliwell survivor

Evie: Project W: 017 human experiment, ghost-horse whisperer, trained killer

Morgan: Graeme's foster sister, entitled heiress, and Jocelyn's real sister

Benny: Graeme's foster brother, Jocelyn's real brother, and an unabashed charmer

John: Dedicated cop, devoted dad, and silent gun collector.

Kymber: Head nurse, protective mom, and anxious muncher of sweets

Sabrina: Medical doctor, determined researcher, Benny's aunt and last hope

Dominique Wicker: A.K.A. "Wicked," ambitious geneticist, ruthless power-seeker

Jerry Ramstein: The President's top advisor and Secretary of Information of the United States of America, or SOI

Camp Holliwell: Camp Holliwell is a United States Government, Science and Military facility located in the Virginian mountains, specializing in solutions to humankind's most significant issues. The New York Times Square Office is an East Coast branch and secret location. Holliwell West compound is in Colorado. Other sites to be revealed. Holliwell's motto: *Science, Technology, Service.*

TABLE OF CONTENTS

003:
SHIMMER

CHAPTER ONE

𝒯ime. It was her most precious commodity.

Jocelyn gazed up at the night sky. The last remnants of dusk were gone. Clouds blocked out the stars. Temperatures dropped by the minute. A person without a heat-activated suit wouldn't survive more than thirty minutes.

Benny had fifteen minutes left on his suit—if it still worked.

Ice crunched under her boots as she trudged up to the last restaurant on the hill. Her chest burned from tension, and she breathed cold air to clear her head before entering the boisterous, overly warm, Irish pub filled with skiers, noisy families, beer and hot cocoa. The first day here with the Rochesters she had loved this—the energy, the chaos, the fun.

Now she scoured the room, desperate.

Be methodical. Stay calm.

She turned away from the large clock on the wall.

Time. It haunted her, whispering the future in her ear.

Jocelyn started at the bar, showing a picture of eleven-year-old Benny on her phone.

Lots of sympathy. No luck.

Quickly she made her way up and down the tables and finally to the back of the pub. The music faded out and conversations were more easily heard. The smell of French Fries

1

wafted through the space. A girl at the back in a bright orange ski hat eyed her curiously. She was about Benny's age. *Maybe?*

"Excuse me." Jocelyn interrupted the three girls at the table, her eyes on the youngest. She was about ten with straight black hair in two short ponytails and dark brown eyes.

The girl's hand paused, fry mid-air. She peeked at the two older girls as if to see what they would do.

"I'm looking for a boy your age. He didn't return from the slopes tonight." Jocelyn stuck her phone in front of the girl. "Do you by chance recognize him?"

The girl blinked, put down the fry, and took Jocelyn's phone, expanding the face with two fingers on the screen. She blinked up at Jocelyn. "Yeah. I saw him today. He was behind me in line at Eagle's Nest, and I saw him again at Timberline."

She reached into her pocket and pulled out a map. "Here. But I took the green path, and he went cross country with his dad to North Basin." She handed the phone to the eldest girl. "That's him, right?"

Jocelyn's heart picked up a beat.

The older girl in black took the phone. Nodded. "Yeah. He was cute. Chatty. The older guy, not so much."

"Can you describe the man?" Jocelyn asked.

"Six-foot. All black ski-suit. Goggles. They both had helmets, so obviously more serious than we are."

Jocelyn nodded. The man was Ellis, Benny's security detail. But why would they have gone to the back of the mountain so late in the day?

"You can keep that if you want." The younger girl offered the map. "I hope he's okay."

"Thank you so much. This helps."

Jocelyn folded the paper and hurried off, pressing numbers as she ran. Graeme answered immediately. His voice was warm and comforting but there was no mistaking his tension. Her feelings for him swirled with guilt. This was her first trip with him and his family. The summer had been busy, to say the least – capturing a serial killer bent on killing her, infiltrating Holliwell New York, and trying to grasp the basics of dating. Now this. So much for her chance to warm the relations with his family. She shivered from the cold.

Benny was missing.

And she knew in her heart it was because of her.

This was supposed to be a joyful time. Benny's last big ski trip. He was already struggling to keep his neuro-motor disease at bay. Graeme's exo-skeleton had been the one thing that kept him upright. The thought that someone might have harmed, frightened, or kidnapped him made her insane with fear…and rage. *Her little brother. And she still hadn't told him. What if she never could?*

"Jocelyn. Where are you?"

"Graeme! I got something. Some girls saw him going to the North Basin at the end of the day."

"That doesn't make sense."

"I know. But can they check?"

There was a pause.

"Graeme?" His silence triggered the knot in her stomach. She huddled, self-protective.

"They're shutting down. The storm is coming in, and there's no visibility. It's too dangerous for helicopters."

"But he's out there!"

"I know. My parents are a wreck. My mom's calling the National Guard. My dad's calling private companies. Ellis can survive in the snow."

Ellis was trained for all weather conditions. The fact that they hadn't heard from him either didn't inspire confidence at the moment.

"But what if—" Jocelyn didn't trust anyone. "What if he was a target or kidnapped. Has your mom received any ransom requests?"

"Nothing. The police said it sounded like bad judgment."

A gush of icy wind nearly froze Jocelyn in place. "Bad judgment?" She was almost at the Rochester's large chalet at the foot of the slopes. "Graeme, you'd be able to find their phones if they were on."

"I know."

"Something bad happened," Jocelyn insisted.

"I know." His voice was husky. "I'm barely hanging on, Joss."

"I know." Jocelyn felt her eyes burn.

She waved to the two security details on the street then entered the code for the garage. The door opened to a six-car garage partially used to store snowmobiles and other ski equipment. Jocelyn took stock.

"Graeme," her voice was soft. "I—" She couldn't tell him. He would worry more. "Will you tell them to go to the North Basin as soon as it clears?"

"Yes," he promised. "I'll be at the chalet in an hour."

"Graeme…" She hesitated to reveal her plans.

"I adore you."

She squeezed her eyes against the emotion, her throat as tight as her stomach.

"Same," she said.

Jocelyn hung up. She gathered her energy with a slow breath and checked her watch. The clouds were low, the mountains obscured, and snow fell fast on the street. Benny's fifteen minutes of suit protection were up. If he was still on the mountain, she had less than thirty minutes before he died of exposure.

Time was against her. Again.

Evie worried.

She and Tatiana had been summoned to Wicker's tower of torture. Their mission had not gone as planned, and on top of that, she'd hallucinated out on the mountain. The gray horse in the snow had been a hallucination, right? Probably a combination of side effects from Wicker's experimentation and being raised on a reservation. She'd grown up on horses. It only made sense that her subconscious produced one in times of stress. And no one else had seen its disapproving stare or heard it neigh before she'd pushed that kid over the side. When she turned the gun on the man, the horse vanished—a positive outcome at least.

They entered the control center for the maze. It had windows out to the giant warehouse from three sides of its hexagon shape. Evie had been here only a few times before—to watch experiments be terminated. Wicker knew the art of terror and made sure everyone understood the consequences of their actions.

Which was why entering the tower now made Evie's anxiety spike and her mouth go dry.

Dr. Dominique Wicker turned and smiled pleasantly at her and Tatiana—the cold smile of success. Evie repressed a shiver. Wicker's triumph usually meant someone died or was about to die.

Evie had learned not to show any expression in success or failure. A wrong turn could send her back to the maze. Few experiments survived the maze, and never when it was used for punishment.

"It seems that Keisha was successful. Our target is following the bait. Good work." Dr. Wicker continued to smile as she set her gaze on Tatiana.

Evie's stomach clenched.

"Twenty-one. You had some trouble?"

Tatiana didn't answer. It wasn't really a question.

Evie jumped in. "No trouble, Dr. Wicker. We accomplished the mission."

Wicker tilted her head slightly at Evie. "You did. But I explicitly ordered Twenty-one to handle the agent."

It was their first mission, and they both had nearly failed. No matter their loyalty to Dr. Wicker, no matter the powers she had given them, the life she had saved them from—some things weren't natural to do. Killing was one of them.

Kind of a problem when that was now their life purpose.

Tatiana finally spoke. "I didn't think shooting him was necessary. He would freeze soon enough. It's less messy and harder to trace."

"I see." Dr. Wicker tapped her pen loudly thrice on the control panel. Metal on metal echoed unnaturally loud in the room. She motioned to Chang.

The commander joined their circle with two guards at the ready behind her. Chang partnered with Wicker on the base leading the military while Wicker led the science. On their own, they were smart and competent. With the might of a well-funded government behind them, they seemed unstoppable. Evie only recently understood that might be a bad thing. Control was a drug. And drugs made you unstable.

"But the problem, Twenty-one, is not the mess." Wicker's voice hardened. "The problem is that you didn't follow a direct order from me. This was a test. If you can't pass the very first, most simple of tests, how can you possibly be of use in difficult situations?"

Silence.

Evie could feel Tatiana's rebellion radiating off her. Her friend had been questioning their destiny for a while. Questioning the ruse that had lured them here. Questioning the testing on the children. Questioning the methods of termination. And now, questioning their purpose. Tatiana wanted to leave. Only they both knew there was no way out.

"Maybe you need to fine-tune your skills in the maze."

Evie didn't breathe. She tried not to move. Wicker motioned to the guards, and they came for Tatiana. Her friend acquiesced. The only failure of protocol was when Tatiana touched Evie's arm and gave it a brief squeeze. Blood rushed to her stomach. Her heart raced. Evie understood the sign. It meant goodbye.

"Come join us, Seventeen."

Evie followed obediently, stepping deeper into the Maze control room where Freddie, the gamemaster, worked the controls. The maze was a vast, four-story warehouse of shipping containers, each fitted with game software to train memory, dexterity, math and logic skills. Each container was a different challenge, but all the challenges required at least two people to survive. If you solved one container, one of the four doors would open to send you to the next one. Sometimes the containers would lift, go sideways, or drop, so that the game could play out longer than you thought. On days when Dr. Wicker culled the experiments that were not successful, a container would simply explode. They used gas originally, as it wasn't as messy, but Dr. Wicker felt the visible sign and sound of failure was important for all experiments to recognize.

Tatiana entered the first container and disappeared inside. She showed up on the monitors above the viewing window.

Tatiana examined the room, waiting.

"Set it to three players, Freddie, with a ten-second solve."

Evie glanced at Freddie. She hoped he didn't see the fear in her eyes. He was brilliant but a coward. And even though he was equally trapped, he would do whatever was necessary to cater favor from Wicker and Chang.

"I think she's fully capable of doing this. Let's see." Wicker folded her arms over her chest comfortably.

The first challenge was easy—a series of colored buttons flashed around the room. When it stopped, Tatiana replicated the pattern. The following rooms got progressively harder. She needed to use hands and feet to hit the buttons in time. Evie finally took a breath when she realized Wicker didn't want Tatiana to fail. This was just a lesson. A hard one, but a survivable one.

Tatiana finally reached the last container.

Dr. Wicker pressed the intercom at Freddie's table. "Last one, Twenty-one."

It was a musical challenge and there were a lot of choices. Memory was key. The order played out. Tatiana didn't move.

Evie stepped forward. *Tatiana!*

The sequence repeated. Tatiana stared into the camera.

"What is she doing?" Freddie spoke, slightly concerned.

Wicker pressed the com. "Last chance."

"Tatiana?" Evie lunged, hitting the intercom. "Tatiana!"

Chang's minions grabbed her before she could say more.

Evie stared at the monitor, fighting to control her reaction. Emotion was not allowed. Teamwork was required, friendship was not. No one could be trusted. Orders must be followed. Fire seemed to burn her insides. She knew what was coming. The seconds counted down in bright red. The clocked ticked loudly in the room. The red light flashed behind Tatiana in warning.

Three.

Two.

No!

Tatiana smiled, lifted her hand and made one last act of rebellion into the camera. She held up her hand using sign language. *I love you.*

One.

The camera cut off with the explosion. It echoed inside the warehouse.

Evie gasped—for control, for courage, for her wits. She must maintain control.

The group was silent, watching the destruction.

"Well." Wicker turned to Evie, "that was surprising."

Evie felt ice cold where seconds before she'd been on fire. "It was." She matched Wicker's pleasant smile. "I didn't know Twenty-one had a thing for Freddie."

Freddie sputtered.

Wicker laughed.

Evie lifted her hands helpless. "There's no accounting for taste."

"No. There's not," Wicker said.

"May I return to the bed hall?"

Wicker studied her, waiting. "You threw the boy off the cliff?"

Evie nodded.

"You shot the guard?"

Evie nodded again.

Wicker handed Evie a detonator from Freddie's work console. "Then finish the job."

Evie took the device. "Gladly."

Freddie turned to her, breaking the tension. "Actually, it's just a remote for the computer," Freddie said. "I thought it was more dramatic. Like you know, a big red button."

Evie stared at the thin, long-nosed guy. He'd been sweating since Tatiana entered the maze—not because he hadn't seen death before, but because he was afraid of her. She could tell. She'd always had a good sense of smell, but with her powers she was like a wolf. And he was cornered prey.

"We hacked into the resort computers. Easy really. They already had safety detonations planned for a controlled avalanche later this week. We're just speeding up the process."

His eyes shifted away.

She pressed the shiny red button.

And didn't feel a thing.

CHAPTER TWO

*I*t was slow going up the mountain. Snow flew into her goggles violently, making visibility nearly impossible. Jocelyn pressed her watch for the time and took off again at a slower pace. It was 6:35 PM. Benny's heat suit batteries would have been done fourteen minutes ago. The night was black except for the light from the snowmobile. She didn't know this terrain and a wrong turn could send her off an edge. Doubt filled her.

What if the girl in the pub was wrong?

Jocelyn stopped, lifted a flashlight toward a structure, and spotted some signage. Relief filled her. She was at the turnoff. Only the basin was blocked with orange fences and avalanche warnings. Benny wouldn't have gone here.

She kept the headlight on and sat, listening. Wind. She blew the whistle around her neck. The wind seemed to whistle back.

"Benny!" she called out.

She'd come this far. Jocelyn had to look. She parked the snowmobile, grabbed her pack and threw the rope over her shoulders. The first thirty steps were a struggle. Then miraculously, the wind started to die down. The snow fell in silent beauty as she trudged. She took a breath.

Then tripped.

A log? Tree root?

Her heart lurched. An arm. She fell and dug urgently. A man. "Oh, God. Oh, God." Her flashlight revealed the truth. "Ellis. No." Her heart broke. She pushed emotion down. *No time. Think.*

A bullet through his head. She searched for his weapons. They were gone.

"Benny! Benny?" Jocelyn grasped in the snow, searching. Had someone killed her brother and left him for dead? He didn't even know he was her brother. She'd never told him. Now it was too late. He would never know her. He'd never know she'd been alive all this time.

She dug deeper, searching for Benny's body with one hand, terrified of what she might find.

The wind whistled.

She searched both sides of the mountain path. It was impossible to tell. The drop was steep on each side and snow covered everything.

"Benny!"

The wind swirled around the basin, teasing her. Whistling. She fought for control, slowed her breathing, and tuned her hearing. If he was here, she would find him. If he'd been taken, she'd find a clue. But she wasn't going back without answers. Her suit had eight hours on it. She had until 2:00 AM.

She took her whistle and gave it three short blows.

Silence.

She pressed her heart, holding back emotion.

Whistle. Whistle.

She lifted her head in that direction.

Whistle.

"Benny! Benny!" Hope surged. Jocelyn hurried toward the sound, stumbling as she traversed toward the repeating sound further around the basin.

"Benny!"

"Here!" It was faint. Then another three whistles.

She followed the sound to the edge, laid her body flat, and looked over the side, searching with her light, tracing the snowy mountain methodically, until finally, a small figure in a snow-covered red suit revealed itself.

"Benny! I'm here. Are you okay?"

"No!"

She had a better view of him now. He was in a ball with one leg bent out awkwardly. His skies were missing. He still wore his helmet, but the mask was open as he searched upward.

Jocelyn didn't waste time. She grabbed his extra heat jacket, zipped a water inside a pocket, and lowered it on the rope. His pants would have to wait. Benny grabbed the new jacket and struggled but eventually got it on. She tied the rope to a large tree. It wasn't going to be long enough. She took it off the tree and tied it around herself then sent the looped ending down to Benny. He put it under his armpits.

Jocelyn dug in and began to pull, grateful for her super-strength.

"Halfway!" Benny called out.

Then an explosion. And another. Faraway it seemed.

Jocelyn froze. The sound echoed. Then silence. She gazed upward at the other side of the basin—a crack.

Jocelyn pulled faster.

She counted the seconds until the crack became a quake—then thunder. They weren't going to make it.

Terror erupted from Benny's throat.

"Avalanche!"

Ski patrol headquarters thinned out as rescue crews were on standby until the weather cleared. Graeme gave his foster sister, Morgan, a hot chocolate and brought his parents more coffee. They wouldn't sit down—as if standing they would be ready to do something quickly.

His older brother Rex grabbed his arm and pulled him into the hallway.

"Where's your girlfriend?" he asked.

"At the house."

"And do you believe what she heard?" Rex asked. "That Benny would have gone to the backcountry to ski the Basin?"

"We won't know until morning," Graeme said.

"Don't you think it's a little suspicious that crazy stuff keeps happening to Benny and our family ever since she showed up?"

Graeme knew what his brother was getting at. And yeah, he knew Jocelyn came with baggage. "We've always had crazy things happen to us." He lightly kicked one of his brother's prosthetic calves to make a point. "We get through it."

Rex shook his head, about to say more when screens flashed an alert in the patrol monitors.

A patrol technician at the monitors spoke up. "Our detonators went off. That doesn't make sense." She typed urgently. "Sir, I think someone accessed our system."

"For what?" Rachel Rochester stood over the other woman, her body tense.

"An avalanche," the tech explained. "We do controlled avalanches, only—"

A sudden disquiet came over Graeme. "Where?"

His family froze, silent, in fear. Coincidence did not exist in their lives.

The Patrol Chief frowned. "The North Basin."

Seth took two large oatmeal cookies and passed the plate to Maddie. She took one and passed it to her brother, Max. It was game night at the Morrows. They were playing *The Game of Life*. Seth was losing, and the irony was not lost on him.

"Don't worry. You'll be out of the hospital soon," Maddie comforted.

From what he could tell, John and Kymber used game night to get into their kids' heads and brainwash them. It wasn't a bad technique. But coming from a science and military testing facility where humans were toys, he didn't much like games.

Kymber poured him milk along with the kids, while John cracked open a beer.

"You were saying, Seth?" John encouraged him to continue.

Yeah, the adults were trying to get into *his* head too.

"That Jocelyn isn't careful. She thinks helping people will make a difference in the world. How does helping one person matter when the world is so screwed up?"

"Well—" John started.

"I know! I know!" Max interrupted. He was the youngest at six and a half. "Tell him dad. Tell 'em. About the starfish."

John sipped his beer and smiled. "You tell him."

Max jumped out of his chair. Apparently, the story required it.

"Okay! Okay, so this man and this boy—like a teen boy—like you, are walking on this beach, and all around"—Max spread his arms to emphasize—"are a gazillion starfish. A gazillion! And this old man is just walking along tossing them back in the ocean."

15

Max bit into his cookie and chewed. Everyone waited. He eyed his mom and chewed more, then swallowed really big before continuing.

"Can't talk with my mouth full."

Kymber nodded, approving.

Seth grinned. "I thought it was for dramatic effect but go on."

"So there's a gazillion! And he's just throwing one here or there, and the boy, the one like you, goes up all angry and says, 'what are you doing?' or maybe it was 'you're wasting your time,' or something. And—"

Long pause.

"I think I forgot the rest."

Maddie rolled her eyes and shook her head. "He said, 'you can't make a difference!'"

"Oh, yeah! Oh, yeah! Yeah, so there's a gazillion, and the boy's like you. You can't make a difference! And the old man picks up another starfish and throws it in the water."

Seth snatched the glass of milk just before Max knocked it in the demonstration.

"And the old man says, 'Made a difference to that one.'"

Seth put the milk back and looked at the kid a long time. He nodded with respect. Lesson learned. "That's a good story."

Max took his seat. "I know." He started eating his other cookie.

Seth turned to John and Kymber. "You're brainwashing them."

Kymber smiled, proud.

John just folded his arms over his chest, cop-like, since he was a cop, and said, "We prefer to call it psychological indoctrination. But, yes."

Seth was about to say more when the doorbell rang.

John went and got it. It was his partner, Tim, who lived on the street. John glanced at the kids then Kymber and stepped outside. Kymber immediately got up, alerted. Seth followed. He found John leaving a message for Jocelyn to call him as soon as she got his message.

"What is it?" Seth felt his skin turn icy. He'd told Jocelyn not to go to Colorado. Holliwell had a facility there. They could kidnap her, and no one would know. But she had to be with Graeme. Learn to ski. Spend time with Benny and Morgan.

He punched a name on his phone.

"Graeme? Is Jocelyn with you? What happened?"

"Seth." Silence. "Benny went missing on the slopes. I'm at the chalet but Jocelyn's not here. I think…I'm not sure. There was no visibility. They had to call off the search teams."

Seth's heart pounded in his ears. "And?"

"One of our snowmobiles is gone. I tracked her phone."

Seth heard Graeme's inhale of breath.

"It's in the avalanche zone."

CHAPTER THREE

They weren't going to make it.

Jocelyn dragged Benny up over the edge and into her arms. She ran, stumbling near her goal. The giant tree was their only chance. Otherwise, they'd be swept off the side of the mountain.

Benny cried out in pain. She ignored it.

She shoved him face forward into the trunk, wrapped the rope around him and the tree, and again around him, tying him off. She couldn't hear anything but the approaching thunder. It was like a herd of angry cattle about to trample them.

"Hold on!"

She knotted one end of the rope around her wrist. If they survived the beating then suffocation was the next likely scenario. She needed to create a pocket.

Tearing off her gloves, she turned and faced the tidal wave of snow. It hit before she could take a breath, but she was stronger than she was last year. She thrust her hands out to block, energy ripping from her body, beating back the onslaught and sending snow around them.

Only it kept coming.

Icy rocks, sheets of snow as tall as buildings, relentless waves of it.

She cried out, sending a stronger force outward. She took a breath, closed her eyes, and focused. Soon. Soon it will stop.

Her feet slipped. Benny screamed. She didn't have infinite energy. She was losing. She needed to be strategic.

Jocelyn whipped around, wrapped her body over Benny's, and gripped the rope on either side of him until her hands bled.

It still wasn't enough.

Evie watched with curiosity. *This was the real target.* A girl. Only she was like them. An experiment—an experiment with extraordinary powers.

Evie didn't care. Tatiana was dead because of this girl. She and the boy would die along with the bodyguard. That made three lives. A big day for her. Three lives.

The Apsaalooke believed all things were connected. This would come back to haunt her—if she still believed such things. She didn't. She'd left the reservation with no intention of ever returning.

Only…three lives.

Finally, the snow stopped. The deep basin was now a flat surface. Where trees had been, treetops were obscured. There was no movement. No life.

Evie put the detonator on the table. Freddie scrambled to recover it like a hungry rat.

"May I return to the dorm now?" she asked.

Wicker nodded, satisfied.

Evie left. Chang escorted her with two guards, their uniform steps echoing hallow in the white-tiled hall. The officer left her at the dorm entrance.

The girls were still awake. They stood as she passed. She and Tatiana had been the first chosen for a mission and Tatiana had not returned. They wanted to ask questions, but they also knew they were monitored.

Evie gave some nods and smiles, then a few mindless fist bumps. She was a hero now.

A hero or a villain? It was questionable. Evie understood the country was at war with itself, but she hadn't understood how deeply. Children were being weaponized, information controlled, and the dissenters eliminated. She had to believe she'd done something important today that would turn the tide for the good. If not, then she was just as responsible for Tatiana's death as Dr. Wicker. And she couldn't live with that.

Keisha waited at the end of the bunks. Her expression told Evie that she had heard the news. Keisha took a step forward. Evie shook her head, admonishing the younger girl. *No hugging.* The kid needed to learn. They were not sisters of any kind. Emotional bonds and sisterhood put you in danger.

Keisha pulled on her beanie and rolled under the bottom bunk. Evie heard the scratching sound of rock on concrete. Keisha kept count. Twenty-nine. Tatiana was number twenty-nine.

Evie climbed onto her top bunk bed and stared at the ceiling. Thanks to Dr. Wicker, she was faster than a horse, stronger than ten warriors, and could leap further than the mightiest mountain lion. She wasn't Evelyn Broken Shield anymore.

She was Project W, subject seventeen.

And she would fulfill any mission they gave her.

Silence and frigid cold enveloped her.
And darkness.

Jocelyn's goggles tangled around her neck, but she still had her hands on the rope. She released slowly, giving into the whimper of pain as she slid her hands free.

They needed heat. That was easy. She could radiate heat and create space. Her body warmed instantly. She pushed snow away from her face. Benny wasn't moving. She pressed into him, sharing her energy. Soon there was a cocoon of temporary warmth.

"Benny?"

"Are we alive?" It was a whisper.

"Yes. Alive."

Precious seconds ticked away. They needed oxygen. She turned and spit on the wall of snow next to her. It slid on a diagonal telling her which direction was up. She pushed her fist through snow then summoned a shot of power through the ice. Heat swelled in her chest from the effort as a path of ice cleared, and snow exploded upward, before gently falling free.

Fresh air returned downward.

She pulled Benny backward as much as the rope allowed to give him access to air then reached for his helmet and lifted the mask.

"Breathe."

He gasped hard. Then his body started to heave.

Oh no. "Do not throw up. Benny. Slow down. You're okay. I've got you. Slow your breathing. There's no room—"

His body shook violently as vomit came up inside his helmet.

"Okay. It's okay. It's okay, Benny. I'm sorry. Can you move your arm? Wipe it with your scarf. I'll clean it up once we are out of here. Just hang on."

"'Kay."

It was a pathetic response. She dug toward the sky, creating more space.

"What's the plan?"

That was better.

Jocelyn exuded optimism. "I'm gonna tunnel us out of here. We're going to climb up, get our bearings, and get warm."

"My leg is hurt."

"I know. I'm sorry." She rested her chin on the back of his helmet. "We'll deal with that after we're safe. Okay?"

"'Kay."

It was painstaking. She widened the hole big enough to pull him up with her, created footholds in the packed ice, stepped them up, and repeated. Creating successive spurts of energy to clear the path became increasingly difficult. They stopped midway and shared a granola bar in her pocket. She found the water bottle she'd zipped into his jacket and they drank a little. She had a few more bars along with matches and random supplies in her pockets but her pack, first aid, heat blankets and water were lost with the snowmobile. She'd have to improvise.

They reached the top. Snow blew in their faces.

"I hate snow!" Benny shouted into the night.

"Shhh!" Jocelyn hugged him. "Let's not start another avalanche. All right?"

"All right." She pulled him all the way up to the surface. He leaned into her lap, exhausted. Neither of them moved for a while. "Are we going to die?"

"Die?" Jocelyn sat up, moved him carefully and sent heat into his legs and boots. "We just survived an avalanche! Did you see it? A giant avalanche! And we crawled out. And—" She reached into her pockets for granola bars and candy. "We have food. Which means I don't have to eat you tonight."

He laughed. Part hysterical. She laughed with him.

Minutes later, neither of them laughed. She had him on secure ground but tending to his injury required digging his supporting exo-skeleton out of his flesh with a pocketknife and mini-flashlight. She used the unbroken exo-skeleton from his other leg to make a splint for his injured one. "I'm not sure if it's broken. Maybe cracked. Let's be safe, okay?"

He nodded, wiping silent tears.

It took her an hour to build a snow shelter in an area she thought was safe. It was impossible to tell where there was solid trail and where snow filled formerly empty space. She slid her heat pants on Benny while he explained what happened.

He had joined a girl to ski the Basin. There were several girls in the area skiing. Then one ran into him and knocked him over the side. But no one helped him! He called for Ellis for he didn't come. Then he heard a shot. Everyone left. He knew Ellis was dead because he would have rescued him.

Jocelyn wiped his tears with her scarf and adjusted the heat pants over his feet. He'd been through a lot. Just being alone in the dark for so long was frightening. Heck, she was scared right now.

She searched the sky for a hint of light. The pants and jacket had a few hours of heat left. Then her heat would need to be enough. She cleaned his helmet and tucked him into the shelter. She would let him sleep until then.

Graeme sat on the sofa, unmoving. He wasn't sure if he was in shock. He heard the front door. It was Rex and Morgan.

"Where's Jocelyn?"

Graeme didn't know whether to lie or tell the truth. He opted for in between. "Out looking for Benny. Trying to get more leads."

Morgan didn't speak. She just hugged her stomach and walked in circles, self-comforting.

"You were supposed to be with him." Graeme said. He didn't mean to accuse but he couldn't help himself. "What happened? Some guy?"

Morgan spun around at him. "No. No! He was supposed to head back. I was just doing another run. He was with Ellis!" Tears welled up. "He's my brother! Mine! I wouldn't let anything happen to him."

Rex enfolded her in his arms. "It's okay, Morgan. This is not your fault. We're all just upset." Rex glared at Graeme and shook his head. "We're family. Everyone is scared."

"I'm sorry." Graeme got up and joined them, hugging his brother and foster sister. "I can't drink more coffee. How about a mocha?"

"I'll start a fire," Rex offered. They made a silent truce.

Graeme was about to join Morgan and Rex by the fire when Seth called back. He went to his room for privacy.

"Can you talk now?" Seth asked.

"Yes. She was out of cell service, but I was able to track the phone. It didn't move for two hours. Then it disappeared. I'm pretty sure the battery died or it froze."

"Right," Seth said. "Here's the deal. There's a Holliwell location near you. That's why I didn't want Jocelyn to go. But ya'll were caught up in the sno-mance. This is not a coincidence. It can't be. Unless someone really kidnapped Benny for ransom, but there's been no call or threats, right? No wacky terrorist groups related to your mom being a Senator or your dad selling pharmaceuticals to foreign nations?"

"No. Nothing."

"Then it was a set up. They found out she was there. They used Benny."

"Why Benny?" Graeme pulled at his hair.

Silence.

"I don't know. He's the cutest. Most vulnerable. It would obviously play with a woman's emotions."

Graeme couldn't respond. He had nothing left.

"Benny might be safe and secure somewhere. It might just be Jocelyn out there. And they tricked her. She could survive. She did a training mission in the cold weather. Though, I don't think there were mountains, but—" Seth stopped.

"It's a lot of what-ifs." Graeme sat on his bed. "We're keeping an eye on the weather. As soon as there's a break, we can send a patrol."

"Call as soon as you know something. John and Kymber are worried." Seth added awkwardly, "They said to tell you, 'they're sending prayers'."

"Thanks," Graeme said. "We need them."

CHAPTER FOUR

*D*ominique got the urgent call at 4:30 AM. It was 6:30 AM in Washington D.C.

The Secretary of Information wanted to conference her. Her boss. And the man who ruled the "free world." Freedom was an illusion with government tracking and the SOI used of that.

Early calls were never a good sign. But she'd been expecting it. She broke protocol by not telling him. Better to ask forgiveness than permission, right?

She took the connection in her personal office and was put on hold. Of course.

SOI Jerry Ramstein had gambled early in his career on technology. Each gamble had paid off. Now he ran the government for the obedient party. Presidents had come and gone in peaceful elections, but their role had become less leader and more social media celebrity and comforting spokesperson. In difficult times people hungered for a voice of reason and compassion.

Dominique played the game. The compassionate angle had enabled years of research and test subjects she wouldn't otherwise have had. Compassionate laws gave parents the right to decide their child's destiny. Compassionate science meant that legal government subjects would help millions of suffering citizens. Everything she did was legal, approved by the nation, and taxpayer-funded. She succeeded where others failed. It gave her power and she intended to keep it.

Secretary Ramstein's face flashed on the monitor.

"Sir. Good morning."

"Dominique." He shook his head. "I thought your goals were clear. Develop the next-level formula. Maintain security. Win a Nobel Prize. Is that still the plan?"

"Of course."

"Please do not interfere with civilians."

"Sir, I found Project Sunday. She's traveling with Senator Rochester."

"Exactly."

"You knew?"

"Of course. I've had tabs on her for months. I don't want her touched unless absolutely necessary. She's leverage."

"For what?" The question was out before she realized it. Senator Rochester was in play. "I see. She's probably not leverage anymore. There was an accident."

The SOI scowled. Before he could speak, Dominique updated him.

"We don't need her, sir. I have seven levels of experiments. I've diversified the genes to enhance unique skills in each group."

"With what life span?"

"We are still measuring that. My full report is nearly ready. The more kinetic the skills the shorter the life expectancy. What will be curious is how long groups five through seven last. We also have our twin experiment as a follow-up to the New York test. Were any of those subjects recovered?"

"Sadly and strangely, no," The SOI said. "But we do have your Holliwell test, Seth Johnson on the radar. He survived the crash, it seems."

"I knew it!" Dominique would hunt him down and dissect him alive—the bastard.

"He's in New York. Apparently, he followed Project Sunday."

"Sir, he can't have more than a few months. May I acquire him for follow-up and close-out? The knowledge would be invaluable. It could—"

"Fine. Fine. But have Chang handle the acquisition. I don't want a public spectacle. It could put our work at risk. You need to be more discreet. There's speculation about all the fresher test subjects. Let's not get into a sympathy battle, Dominique. You understand the consequences, I'm sure."

"Yes, sir." She knew the consequences. But she did not appreciate the veiled threat.

"My apologies regarding Project Sunday. I thought I was doing something helpful."

He waved a hand. "Just communicate. You don't have all the information. There are much bigger plans. And I want you to be part of them."

"Thank you, sir."

The monitor flashed off and was replaced by the White House emblem. Dominique turned off the monitor. Something akin to joy leapt inside her—a rare feeling of delight and expectancy.

Seth.

Jocelyn carried Benny away from their brick building. It wasn't just the lab that was on fire. It was the whole building—their home. Flames lit up the windows at the top floor where Morgan and Jocelyn had their bedrooms.

Jocelyn hurried down the alleyway toward Morgan, to the street with neighbors. She dumped baby Benny in her sister's arms then spun and bumped into a woman. She wore all black and an oxygen mask. Morgan screamed as the woman took Benny and tried to grab Jocelyn. Jocelyn grabbed her mask and fought free, exposing a woman with red hair and a grim expression. Jocelyn kicked free of the woman's quick hold and ran back to their home. She had to find her parents. She vaguely heard screams from Morgan and others behind.

The voices faded away when blue smoke and heat enveloped her. She ran downstairs to the lab, not sure what way to go. Finally, she saw her dad, relief filled her. He was standing, swinging something. Then she saw the man in the green glasses holding the gun. It exploded. Once. Twice. Her father fell. Someone called her name. Jocelyn couldn't move. The man aimed at her. Her mother knocked her over. Gas filled the room. Her mother stabbed her arm with something then crawled to the corner of the room, dragging her. She shoved a little bottle into the safe. Pressed a button. "Save Benny."

Jocelyn promised that she would.

The man in green glasses had come and killed her father. He and the woman did this. Destroyed the lab. Destroyed her parents. Destroyed their last chance to save Benny. Jocelyn had to save Benny herself.

"Jocelyn. Jocelyn!"

She felt cold. She was never cold.

"Jocelyn! Wake up!" Her cheek stung. She opened her eyes, drowsy.

"Benny?" Where were they? "Did you slap me?"

"You fell asleep. You wouldn't wake up. I got scared," his voice went up, defensive.

She propped herself on an elbow, alert, remembering. "I'm okay. Your alarm went off?"

"Yes. Every fifteen minutes. Only this time, you were sleeping. I got cold. Our igloo is freezing."

"I know." She pulled him close, took a breath of cold air, and forced heat through her body, through her skin, into him. It hurt. She didn't have much energy left. She pulled out the last half of a chocolate peanut butter bar. "Benny, I need to eat this. Do you have anything else?"

"No. That's it. Are you okay?"

"Yes." Her voice was faint. She didn't even want to talk. She ate the remains of the protein bar and hoped it would be enough. Enough to keep him warm and get him to safety. She put snow in her mouth, craving a long drink of water.

Benny shivered. She took his feet and put them into her stomach. They were cold but not icy. She hadn't slept too long. "What time is it?"

"Five-forty-five. It will be light in maybe an hour forty-five."

A lifetime.

She handed him the bottle of water. She'd melted ice in it while he slept but it had started to freeze again. "Benny, I wanted to tell you." Her lids drooped. "So many things."

"Like?"

"I'm not who you think." Would there ever be a time when she could tell him she was his sister?

"Well, I know you're not a ninja robot. Or even a robot. Or a cyborg."

She smiled. "That's good. How is your leg?"

"Sort of numb but throbbing."

30

She turned toward the outside of their shelter. Fallen snow covered her back and created a wall around her where she blocked Benny. Moonlight crept through an opening in some clouds.

"Look. You can see some stars, Benny. The storm is clearing." She closed her eyes and laid her head down on the folded rope.

"You have to keep some heat for yourself."

Jocelyn opened her eyes.

"What?"

"I know you've been making heat for me. Your body gets warm, like a fever, then I get warm. When you fall asleep it gets cold, doesn't it? Igloos only work if there's a fire. We don't have a fire so you need to stay warm too."

"It's just a little longer."

He nodded and snuggled closer, rubbing his hands on her cheeks. Then he covered her head with her ski mask and pulled down her goggles over her eyes, protecting her. "It's okay, I think I might know."

Jocelyn stared at Benny, certain he couldn't see her eyes burning through the dark goggles. She squeezed him, rubbed his back vigorously then his legs and feet, careful of his injury. "Put your stinky helmet on then I'll help you with your boots. We might be able to see a way back if the moon holds. I need you to tell me where we are."

Benny scrambled to obey, but his movements were hampered by injury and cold. He moaned in complaint—a good sign that he'd stayed warm. Jocelyn got up and stumbled. Concern shot through her. She must keep going. It didn't matter if she was weak. Iron will trumped a weak body all the time. Fight yourself. That's what the military had taught her at Camp Holliwell. The enemy is sometimes yourself.

Clouds moved again, revealing shadows of mountains and shimmering snow. She wasn't exactly sure if they were on actual ground or on unstable snow over the basin. Once they were near a ski lift, far from the avalanche zone, she would feel better. But she didn't have much strength left. She needed to move Benny to safety before another weather change.

"Benny, I'm going to wrap this rope over your chest and under your arms, then through the arms of my jacket, I think you can lay back on my jacket and I can drag you."

"No. You wear your jacket. You can drag me in my ski suit. We used to do it all the time."

Jocelyn considered. "Okay. But I'm going to tie your legs together. It will secure your broken leg in case it starts to dangle. Then I'll wrap it around your chest. If your hood fits over your helmet that will help keep snow out. We'll keep your arms free so you can hold the rope, okay."

Together they plotted a moonlight course across the basin. From there it would be a short but steeper hike to the top ski lift. The clouds drifted over them, and the mountain turned dark again. Jocelyn hesitated. If she veered off course, she risked burying them deep in snow or dropping them off the wrong side of a mountain.

As if sensing her hesitation, Benny sat up a little and directed. "That way."

"Okay, boss. Let me know if you get too cold."

He laid back down and gave a thumbs up.

Jocelyn trudged slowly through the deep snow, checking on Benny. He seemed comfortable and at rest. Though he might be frozen and dead.

Just when she thought they'd gone off course, she saw shadows. A treeline!

"Benny! We're close!"

He opened his helmet mask. "Cold."

"Almost there." She got up, stumbling, her only focus moving one leg after the other, Planting and lifting in the snow.

The avalanche covered a lot of territory, but the tree line marked a turn-off from the basin. She'd made it to a legitimate path. Clouds move again, and this time moonlight illuminated the slope. The lift was near. She could imagine the warmth of the lift cabin…

Her eyes closed.

She fell. She pushed a hand away.

"Jocelyn! Jocelyn!" Smack. Smack. "Jocelyn! Wake up. Please…wake up."

"Benny?" *Let me sleep.*

"We're almost there. You fell. Are you okay? I thought you were dead. Don't leave me here. Don't fall asleep. We're almost there."

He had crawled on top of her. His panic pierced her cozy dream.

"Sorry. I'm sorry. I won't do that again."

"We can make it. Stay awake."

Jocelyn got up with renewed energy. It lasted ten steps. She needed to get up the incline. Only five hundred yards. Just over a quarter mile.

One foot, then another.

CHAPTER FIVE

"Sir!" A ski patrol agent called out urgently. "We have someone!"

Graeme, Rex, and Morgan stumbled from their sleep on the hallway sofa outside ski patrol and ran into the office. Graeme's parents were already on their feet crowding a monitor of the slopes.

His mother leaned into his father, clutching his hand, silently heaving in shock.

Graeme saw the monitor and pressed forward. His stomach clenched. Someone was dragging a small body across the snow toward the ski shack. The body was wrapped in rope. It was a child.

The Chief pushed through, forcing some space.

Morgan saw them next. "Oh, God! Oh, my God. Benny. That's Benny." She gasped, tears coming out. What happened? Who is that?"

Rex put an arm around her as they watched the person feebly try to get into the shack, leaning on the door as if giving up, then finally stepping back, seeing a window and breaking it before crawling inside.

"Can we get lights on the chair lifts?" the Chief commanded.

"Yes, sir. One moment."

The door to the shack opened. The person brushed off snow from the body and pulled it inside. Benny's body. Graeme wiped his cheeks.

"Got it." The tech said. The outside of the shack illuminated a little more. "I've opened the channel. They just have to turn on the equipment from their side, sir."

The group waited. Morgan wept silently, gripping Rex.

Suddenly a desperate voice crackled over the monitor.

"Hello? Hello? Is anybody there? Over."

"Copy. This is Ski Patrol Headquarters. Who is this? Over."

"Turn on the lift at North Basin." She gasped for breath. "Please. Turn on the lift at North Basin. Over."

Graeme recognized Jocelyn's voice. His gratitude for her life was mixed with his torment over Benny's. But she had found him. And he had never heard a voice so exhausted or weary.

His father turned to him in question. Whatever he was going to ask would wait. Jocelyn spoke again.

"I have Benjamin Rochester. I need an ambulance."

Ford grabbed the intercom and pressed. "This is Ford Rochester. Is Benny alive?"

"Ford." Her voice choked, thick with relief and emotion. Then silence. Graeme thought she might be crying too.

"Dad!" Benny's voice sounded over the intercom.

"Benny!" His mom cried out.

Cheers went up. Suddenly everyone was hugging and moving around. The Chief quieted everyone.

"I'm okay! We were in an avalanche then had to dig out, and made an igloo, and ate chocolate, and it was freezing, and—" Benny sounded like he'd been on a grand adventure but was cut off before he could say more.

35

Graeme guessed that Jocelyn didn't want details out.

"Ford, I think Benny's leg is broken. His Exo cut into his thigh when he…fell. I think I can get him on the lift. But…I'm not sure I can get him off and onto the lower lifts. I'm sorry…"

"We're sending help to meet you. Just get down that top slope," Ford said. "Hold on."

Ford turned to the Chief and they looked at the map on the wall. "How long before you can have a rescue squad?"

"I'm going too," Graeme said. "I have a snowmobile."

The Chief took the intercom. "It will take about twenty minutes. There should be a first aid kit and a refrigerator with water and some supplies. Drink something then grab an extra blanket and head out. By the time you get off the lift, our team will be there. The wind is blowing hard on but it will get better about halfway down. Just hang on."

"Copy. Thank you." The voice was breathless. "Over and out."

The intercom cut off.

Rachel grasped Ford's hand then turned to Graeme, a question in her eyes. "I don't care how she did it. Go get them."

Jocelyn helped Benny across the snow to the ski lift. The wind picked up again and the moonlight disappeared. Thankfully ski patrol had turned on the lights at the lift, and the area was illuminated enough to get through the snow safely.

Benny's leg made walking difficult, but they hobbled three-legged and she managed to get him in place to hop onto the moving lift. It was awkward, and she fumbled, but she got the safety bar down and pulled the blanket over their heads to protect them from the elements.

Benny was in good spirits. She put her arm around him and hugged tight. He would be safe. She closed her eyes, grateful for her ski mask and goggles. Her gear was mostly frozen and hid a frightening view. She'd seen her skin in the patrol shack and a brief look in a mirror revealed eyes that would make Benny freak out.

She was blue.

From her hair to her toes.

The whites of her eyes were streaked with blue, and the tired bags underneath her eyes seemed to have an aqua glow.

She couldn't be seen like this. Only who could help? Graeme? He didn't need this. She leaned weakly on the edge of the lift. Graeme was the only one that she could trust.

Sounds of engines got closer the lower they got on the lift. Jocelyn pulled the blanket from over their heads. The wind and weather were in fact better. They were off the highest part of the slope. A sense of relief filled her. She could see snowmobiles in the distance. Benny waved. She summoned the strength to finish her mission.

There were six people. Four wore ski patrol suits. The other two were Rex and Graeme.

She and Benny were pulled off the lift in a synchronized effort. She stood, unmoving, nodding when asked if she was okay. Graeme immediately saved her. She leaned into his arms. She could sleep now.

She heard Rex's voice greeting his little brother with love and relief before carrying him to the emergency sled. EMTs wrapped Benny up and quickly transported him down the mountain.

Graeme helped her to his snowmobile. He gave Rex a wave that they were okay.

"Can you make it?" Graeme reached for her goggles to see her, but she weakly pushed him away.

"Take me home."

A patient medical technician, intervened. "We need to have her checked out."

She shook her head. "Graeme." It came out like an urgent gasp.

Graeme declined the offer, got her on the snowmobile, tucked in her feet, strapped her to the backseat, and wrapped her hands around his waist.

It was the last thing she remembered.

"What do you mean she's blue?" Seth asked.

Graeme's heart raced. Jocelyn laid still on the floor of Graeme's bathroom. She was probably going to die there because he didn't take her to the hospital. His phone was on speaker as he hurriedly ran a bath. "She's blue. Everywhere. I don't know what to do. Her pulse is really weak. I'm running a warm bath. I'm getting more blankets for the bed, but she's unconscious. Or not responding. Her skin is icy. And she's blue, Seth. Like—"

"A corpse?"

"No! I mean, I wouldn't know. Like aquamarine and midnight blue, but blue. All blue! I opened her eyelids and—"

"Okay, okay. I got it. Don't panic. That sounds really bad. Hold on."

Graeme worked to get Jocelyn out of soaked leg protectors and long underwear.

"Graeme? It's Kymber. What are her symptoms?"

Pause.

"Besides blue," she said.

"She's icy. I can barely feel her pulse. She's not responding to anything."

"Graeme, she needs an I.V. I'm pretty sure she's dehydrated. She must have some form of hypothermia, and—"

Seth interrupted. "I just got a text from Georgie. She said sometimes when Jocelyn expends a lot of energy her eyes get a little blue."

"This is A LOT blue!" Graeme yelled.

Seth yelled back. "She pulled your brother out of an avalanche!"

"Enough!" Kymber intervened on the speakerphone. "You need to get fluids in her and keep her warm. Don't put her in the bath if you can't submerge just her core. Put her in the bed with covers and get next to her. But if she is not responsive soon you have to take her to a—"

"Holy—!" Ford pushed opened the door wider in the bathroom.

"Dad!"

"Uh-oh." Seth's voice came from the phone on the toilet seat.

"Geez, Dad! Some privacy."

"Hell." He bent and took Jocelyn's pulse. "No bath. Let's get her into bed."

Graeme didn't move.

"Move it!"

Graeme jumped.

Ford put a warm blanket over the mattress sheet then they lifted her onto the bed. "Get the rest of her clothes off. You can leave the bra if it's dry. Get some flannels and socks. Have you given her anything?"

No." Panic receded a little with his dad's confident instructions.

His dad disappeared. Graeme hurriedly followed directions. His dad returned with a large plastic box and began pulling out medical equipment. He took Jocelyn's hand and inserted a needle on the top, taping a tube for an I.V. He unfolded a portable metal stand then attached a bag of fluid before looking at Graeme.

"I was a scientist before I was a businessman." He smiled then explained. "We keep this for Benny. In case of an emergency."

"Of course. I didn't know."

"We always hope we don't need it, but—" Ford covered Jocelyn up to her neck with the blankets, adjusting her arm. "Let's add a cap. The head is important to keep warm."

Graeme scrambled for a knit beanie and slid it over her short soft hair. He touched a small curl that poked out. Her hair had grown back nearly black but glinted midnight blue in some lights. "I know it looks bad."

"Ya think?" His dad's brows lifted sarcastically.

"Kymber said it might be a form of hypothermia."

His dad pressed his lips tight and gazed at him, openly skeptical. "Not sure about that. But if she doesn't improve in the next five minutes, we move her to the hospital." His dad checked the flow of the bag, then his watch.

Graeme nodded, noting the time. He stared at Jocelyn in the bed, willing her to move.

Ford broke the silence. "She shouldn't have gone up the mountain on the word of a stranger."

"I know," Graeme said.

"It seems like it was a trap. Did she say anything about Ellis?"

Graeme shook his head. "She barely made it here."

"Benny would have died even without the avalanche. She's incredibly brave."

"Yes." His stomach still hurt from worry.

"But," his dad was matter-of-fact, "she's probably going to get herself killed trying to save people."

The remark got his attention. A warning? He met his dad's eyes. They were sympathetic and concerned. Yeah. His dad didn't want to see him hurt. He got it. He took Jocelyn's free hand and warmed it between his.

"It's curious how she keeps saving Benny."

"She helps everyone," Graeme said.

"We never found the Good Samaritan who rescued Morgan. The blonde."

Graeme's attention perked. "There are lots of good people in the world." *Did his dad know it was Jocelyn?*

"Anyway, blue isn't a terrible color on her, overall."

Jocelyn's mouth opened, her chest expanded with a breath. Her skin seemed less blue. Then her body settled with an exhale, as if sleeping.

Ford touched her cheek and forehead. "Warmer. Huh." He noted the time. "Interesting."

Graeme waited until his dad looked up.

"I think she's going to be okay.

Graeme exhaled with relief. Her color did seem to get better. He touched her cheek. *Not icy.* His throat constricted. Gratitude and anger battled. *What were you thinking? You could have died.*

Ford nudged him. "I think you're being called from the bathroom. I'll come back in fifteen minutes."

The phone! Graeme ran and grabbed it, explaining what happened.

"Wow. A dad with skills," Seth said. "Ouch! Haha. John just whacked me. Okay, text me in fifteen minutes. You might as well include Kymber and John. They're super parental."

Graeme hung up. He checked Jocelyn's pulse. It was easier to find this time. He touched her cheek. She was just a girl. Right now, a pale blue girl.

He gently laid Jocelyn's hand under the covers. He worried about what his dad had said, because it was true.

Jocelyn just might give until it literally killed her.

CHAPTER SIX

Seth sat up on the MRI machine at Sabrina Albrecht's lab in A & R Technologies. She'd been working late and missed all the drama with her nephew Benny. He was glad of that. There was nothing you could do from across the country but worry. At least Sabrina had been spared.

She waved at him from the other side of the window, smiling—a good sign.

He winked back. She was probably ten years older than him, but he didn't care. She was hot. The white lab coat over her dress and red high heels made science a lot more interesting and doctor appointments a lot more fun. She had the same blue eyes as Jocelyn. Apparently, they ran in the Albrecht family. Only Sabrina was fair-haired and fair-skinned like Jocelyn's dad, where Jocelyn had dark hair and light olive skin from her mother's side. But the bone structure in both said Albrecht. Strong. He wondered if Sabrina ever noticed it.

He joined her in the MRI control room. "Good news?"

"Progress," she answered. "Want to see?"

"Not sure."

"Don't be a chicken. Get dressed and come back out."

"Or you could get undressed, and we could stay right here."

43

Her eyes widened. Then she laughed. But her cheeks turned pink. The same way Jocelyn's did when she was embarrassed or emotional.

"Let's stay focused on what's important."

"I am." Seth gave her an admiring look over.

She shook her head, stern. "Jeans, shirt, shoes. Don't make me get a chaperone." She turned to the machine and began pulling up images, but she was smiling.

"Sorry. Just trying to take my mind off things."

"And there are healthier ways. Go." Her eyes had compassion. That hurt worse than rejection. He didn't even have a chance.

Obedient, he dressed and rejoined her. He was anxious. The idea of dying was not one he accepted yet, despite evidence otherwise.

"The good news is that the inhibitors are working. You've had fewer seizures, and which also puts less stress on your heart."

"And the bad news?"

"No bad news. More good news. The formula I gave you last month looks like it's working. Your measurements have shrunk."

Seth straightened his back and gave his jeans a tug. "Trust me, Dr. Albrecht. My measurements have not shrunk."

She laughed out loud. "Stay on track, Seth."

"I am. I like playing doctor with you."

"Seth!" This time hands hit her hips.

"Too far?" He held back a grin.

"Yes. Now show some respect. I'm trying to save your life. And you can call me, Sabrina."

He grinned into her bright turquoise eyes. "I get it. It's my brain that you're fascinated with. What's the news?"

"I pulled up the last four weeks of images. In the last two weeks there's been a change."

"Honestly, looking at my brain makes me a little—um." He shook his head, queasy.

She grabbed his head with two hands and turned it to the screens. "This is good."

"You can barely tell."

"It's measurable. That's exciting and hopeful. It's a good sign. I think I can stop the progress and maybe reverse most of it…eventually. I'm working on an idea. That sample you gave me was invaluable."

Seth didn't make eye contact this time. "Good."

"Any chance I can get more?" She kept her eyes on the screen, keeping it casual.

"No."

That sample had been Jocelyn's blood. He wouldn't ask her for more. "That's all there is. If you're going to find a clue, you need to get it from what you have."

He grabbed his worn cowboy hat, ready to exit.

"Okay." She studied him.

"I should head out."

"I'm working on something with the sample. You said it was from the prototype?"

"Doc, don't fish. I'm okay dying. It sucks, but I'm not going to put anyone else at risk."

"You're not going to die," she insisted. "We're going to figure this out. I'm close to something. I can feel it. Just don't give up, okay?"

He tipped his hat. God help him. He loved optimists.

Jocelyn groaned. Or was that her stomach? Something called to her.

Bacon?

"Bacon," a voice confirmed.

She opened her eyes. Graeme sat in a chair near her holding a tray of food—pancakes, eggs, bacon, toast, and jam. She could smell Graeme too. He was freshly showered and used the wintergreen shampoo. She inhaled the comforting scents, taking in his tousled brown hair and gentle green eyes.

She moved carefully. Her body felt stiff but okay. She yawned and reached for the bacon, smiling. He brought it close, and she leaned up for a kiss.

Then she remembered and sat straight up.

Heads bumped and the tray jostled. Lights flickered from her energy.

"Benny?"

"He's doing great." Graeme laid the tray on her lap. "He's in the kitchen with the others having brunch. I saw you move finally, so I thought you might be ready to wake up."

"Actually, I think I have to—"

He picked up the tray as she scrambled to the bathroom. After a quick look in the mirror, she did her business. Everything seemed to work fine. Her skin looked normal. She was a little pale, but she'd been asleep. She returned to the room and started on the bacon.

"The official story is Benny was holed up at the ski lift tower with a friend of the family until the weather broke."

Jocelyn felt relief. "That's a good story."

"Benny told us what happened. A woman threw him into the basin. He heard a shot."

"Ellis." She stopped eating. "I found him. He had family."

"A wife and daughter."

Her hand shook. More death and pain on her plate. She moved the pancake around aimlessly then put down the fork.

"He said you were buried in the avalanche."

That was a story for another time.

"I think the snowmobile and Ellis won't be found until spring."

"I think that too," Ford said, popping his head in the door. "You look much better."

Jocelyn touched her face. *What did that mean?*

"I can tell your security detail everything." She assumed he wanted answers. "Ellis was murdered. Shot in the head."

Ford's somber expression turned angry. "I've already reached out to his family. I'll have to let them know this. Security will come this afternoon. Right now, everyone wants to see you."

There was another push at the door. Benny wheeled in.

Jocelyn scooted off the bed in shock. "Benny." She hurried to him, kneeling at his feet. "What happened?"

"Well, I have no exo-skeleton." His voice shook a little. "And according to the doctors here, who my dad said, 'don't know nuthin,'" I've had a 'deterioration in my condition.'"

"No." She pressed her head into both his hands. "I kept you warm."

"His body dealt with significant shock," Ford said. "As did yours. Physical effects are bound to happen, Jocelyn. You kept him alive. We owe you so much."

She shook her head. The heaviness on her shoulders worse.

What if someone had used Benny to get to her? He was dying faster because of her. She wiped her eyes quickly on the flannel pajamas she seemed to be wearing.

"When can you get out of the wheelchair?"

"My leg has to heal. But maybe when there's a new Exo." He trailed off. "Maybe. Anyways, I'm just glad you're finally up. I got home from the hospital last night and Graeme's like, 'Still sleeping. Can't go in.'"

"Last night?"

"You slept thirty-one hours," Graeme said.

Jocelyn's mouth dropped. That wasn't natural for her. "Well. That explains why I had to pee and eat bacon." She wanted to make Benny laugh. "At the same time."

Success. Ford laughed too.

"I should probably shower. Then I'll come out."

"Of course." Ford wheeled Benny around. "The others are waiting more politely but are anxious to see you."

Graeme remained. "I have a bunch of messages from Georgie, Brittany, Lena, Seth, and the Morrows. Everyone is grateful you didn't freeze or suffocate in the avalanche."

Jocelyn smiled. Again with the avalanche.

"And it's a miracle you and Benny were able to keep warm after losing all your supplies."

He sounded suspicious.

"Body heat," she said. "Plus, I had matches and power bars in my pocket."

"Uh-huh."

Jocelyn bit her bottom lip, anxious. Communicating in relationships was hard when you were hiding things. She sat on the bed. He had an expectant expression, waiting for her to confess or something.

"Are you asking me a question or lecturing me?"

"Both. Mostly, I want to know why you were blue and how you recovered."

CHAPTER SEVEN

*J*ocelyn wiped down a table in the corner of Cravings. Her server job had been a blessing and she was unofficially acting as an assistant manager now. But they really needed more servers, and she preferred to keep moving. She moved to the next table and sprayed organic disinfectant. Wiping was meditative and strangely comforting.

The lunch rush thinned out. Now it would just be random students and professionals working and hanging out. That gave her a little free time for a break when her friends arrived.

It had been a week since the ski trip, and things had settled outwardly since the Thanksgiving holiday. Inwardly, her energy charged—decidedly unsettled.

She probably wasn't the only one.

The gang debated whether she or Rochesters had been the real target. And if it had been because of her...then Ellis was dead because of her. Another girl had lost a parent because of her. And Jocelyn knew what that loss meant. She lived it. Her stomach felt a little sick when she viewed the family photos in the online news with the Rochesters all in attendance at a memorial. She felt like she should have been there. But it would have been for her. And her feelings really didn't matter in the big scheme.

Benny's health had accelerated for the worse. A series of doctor appointments meant her little brother would be poked and tested for any hope of sustaining or improving his current condition—though improvement sounded unlikely. Of all things, she didn't want him to become a test subject as she had been. She had to find a solution for him. Her mother had a cure. Jocelyn just didn't know how to find it—yet.

Graeme's family acted friendly but guarded with her. *Suspicious.* She couldn't blame them.

Jocelyn straightened and sighed. There were no more tables to clean.

She checked on the girl in the corner and brought her more water and a soda refill. Jocelyn had studied Native American tribes and languages at Holliwell. The languages were standard spy school requirements but she hadn't met anyone her age that looked a hundred percent Native American. It was hard not to be curious.

The girl ate a burger and fries then ordered more fries. Jocelyn was all respect. The fries here were good.

"What tribe are you?"

The girl lifted confused dark eyes. She had brown skin and a long nose that was perfectly straight. The short hair didn't suit her. She'd been a little gruff at first too.

Since serving at Cravings, Jocelyn learned a lot about people and the real world. This girl wasn't very open and hadn't responded to Jocelyn's friendliness. Her demeanor seemed angry or sad. Maybe both. Jocelyn had been there. It made her want to reach out.

"What?"

"You're Native American, right?"

"Apsáalooke."

"Crow."

"Yes," she answered.

Jocelyn slid into the booth, sitting across from her. "That's so cool. Where did you grow up?"

"Montana," the girl reluctantly answered.

Jocelyn thought a moment. "On a reservation?"

She nodded. The girl was attractive but in an intense, piercing way. Jocelyn smiled. She decided she would get a smile out of the girl too. They both needed a pick-me-up.

"What was it like? What are you doing in New York? Going to school? Do you miss it?"

The girl stared at her like she had said something wrong. Jocelyn figured she had asked too many questions at once. It happened. She reached her hand across the table.

"I'm Jocelyn."

The girl blinked, stared at the hand, wiped her fingers on a napkin then studiously gripped it, warm and strong.

"What's your name?" Jocelyn asked when the girl didn't offer.

"You ask a lot of questions."

"Just curious. People are interesting. Don't you think?"

"Are you in school? Or college?" the girl asked.

"Not yet. I'm saving. I want to study music."

The girl laughed.

"What?"

"I don't know." The girl stared at her. "That just seems so... useless."

Jocelyn thought about it. "Everyone says college is useless these days so if I studied something I loved, it would be useful. And music makes people happy. Wouldn't you want to have a talent that made people happy?"

"You're very strange."

51

The bell to the restaurant rang, and Jocelyn saw Brittany and Lena enter. She got up. "Strange is okay if you have friends. It was nice to chat. Hang out as long as you like."

Jocelyn welcomed her friends with long hugs. Especially Lena whom she hadn't seen in three weeks. She grabbed them some sodas, yelled to Josh she was taking a break, then joined them at a booth.

"Where's Georgie?"

Brittany plopped into the booth. "With her *new* friends." She swished her dark, heavy mane dramatically. "Saving the world."

Lena slid in after her then balked, but not fast enough to avoid the hair whip. She pulled strands of Brittany's hair out of her face, disentangling a piece from her glasses before adjusting studious frames on her winter-pale face.

"Oh." Jocelyn glanced at Lena for insight into this mood.

Lena shrugged helplessly. Georgie's new friends were from a leadership club she had joined. Brittany was suspicious of anyone who dressed badly, and apparently, this club needed a stylist and a better attitude.

Brittany saw their shared glance. "It's not like I'm jealous. Or I don't want her to meet people and have the"—she made air quotes—"full college experience."

"Uh-huh." Lena sipped her soda and opened her laptop. Her laptop was an extra brain appendage but mostly protection in social situations. She ducked behind it for cover, tipped her white-blonde bob over the keyboard, and shoved light gray glasses over her light gray eyes in an attempt to be invisible.

"I'm not jealous!" Green eyes flashed. "It's just she's acting all weird and self-righteous and 'miss know-it-all.' It's annoying. You'll see."

"See what," Seth asked. He squeezed next to Lena and checked out what she had open. "Writing a paper?"

"Yes. It's on the death of privacy."

"Sorry." Seth put up his hands.

"No, you can look." She laughed. "That's really the topic."

"Oh." Seth relaxed and adjusted his cowboy hat back over sandy blonde hair for a better view. "More important, what are you eating?"

"I'm on a diet," Brittany said.

"It's making her grumpy," Lena warned.

Brittany stuck out her tongue. "Oh, here's the leader of the free world now."

"See," Lena mumbled, sinking lower in her seat.

Georgie entered the restaurant with a wave, taking off her scarf and coat while juggling her backpack.

Jocelyn grabbed the pack and tossed it in the booth. She hugged Georgie and complimented her on the new purple highlights on the tip of her fro. Her hair had grown out—bigger—and was perfectly round but in a stylish, sixties way.

"Brittany did the tint. She likes purple. I think maroon next time," Georgie grinned. "I'm glad to see you safe. We were all worried." She squeezed Jocelyn again then slid into the booth.

Jocelyn let Georgie get in first so she could stay at the end of the booth and keep an eye on things in case it got busy.

Georgie's backpack took up half the seat. She pulled out a folder, excited, and slapped it on the table. "Okay. I'm recruiting."

Silence.

"Don't all jump at once." Georgie opened the folder.

More silence.

"Don't you even want to know what it's for?" Georgie asked.

Jocelyn gave in. "What are you recruiting for?"

"Thank you for asking." George gave her pitch. "I'm signing people up for a march. You get one thousand dollars per march, and if you do six marches, you get free health insurance for a year. Who here doesn't need six grand and free insurance?"

Brittany scowled. "What are you marching for?"

"Money and free health insurance, obviously." Seth smiled encouragingly. Jocelyn knew it didn't mean he was on board. More often, he was setting someone up.

"For free education, free health insurance, and parents' rights," Georgie clarified. "And to stop obstructionists from taking over the government."

"Who are obstructionists?" Jocelyn asked.

"Politicians and their followers that are not adhering to the compassionate laws of our country."

"Georgie…" Jocelyn swallowed.

"I need cake," Brit said. "Jocelyn. Cake."

"But your diet."

"Then diet cake! I'm hungry. And pie for Milk. Can't you see she's white from hunger?"

"I'm not hungry," Lena said. "This is my skin tone. But… pie would be okay."

Jocelyn scrambled to get her table some food and put in for three orders of fries. She grabbed a pitcher of soda on her way back and poured.

Seth took his hat off. "I'm not as educated as the rest of you, so maybe I missed something. How is everything free?"

"The government pays for it."

His brown eyes narrowed. "Who pays the government?"

"Taxes," Georgie said.

"So," Seth reframed the scenario. "Not free. We pay for it, but we don't control it?"

Georgie jumped in. "It's not like that. People don't know how to save and spend. This is a way to help them manage our combined resources."

Seth nodded with a contrary note, "Cause they're all too stupid to do it themselves?"

"Lots of people make me claustrophobic," Lena inserted.

"Who's funding all the marchers? What do they really want? And do you *really* think "parents' rights" are a good thing?" Seth continued. "Parents make all the life and death decisions for you until you're eighteen. What if you get too expensive, or depressed, or difficult? Or what if parents wanted a girl instead of a boy? Yikes. Do they get to commit you to "treatment" or donate you to science? Which is basically allowed, right? Until age eleven, you're not granted 'personhood.'" Seth started to sip his soda, then added, "Or what if people just start having babies for the money? To sell them. A one-time payout from the government. That's technically permitted by law. Have babies for the tax-funded government slave program." Seth turned it over to Georgie for a rebuttal.

Georgie frowned. "First. You sound very angry. The law is so parents can choose life. The only thing the law doesn't do is let parents choose treatment if a hospital says their kid is terminal or vegetative. Then the state doesn't allocate resources that someone else might need."

Lena interrupted. "But it veers on the side of disposal and efficiency. The department of children encourages parents to support a more "robust population" by turning their kids over up to age eleven if they are not likely to be productive contributors or are damaged in some way—as determined by psycho adults, it seems. So, if we are not perfect or loved by our parents by age eleven then a human can be 'optioned' under the guise of a more 'robust' child?" Lena slapped her laptop shut and sat up. She didn't like the law.

Georgie nodded. "Yes. I'm surprised you know that."

Lena froze, stared across the table at Georgie. Jocelyn knew about that law too.

"What?" Georgie asked. She glanced around. Seth shook his head.

Lena's voice was tight. "The original law was passed right after Cashus made Jocelyn his legal ward. It allowed him to control all the testing on her—legally through age eleven. Remember?"

"It's not related to this."

Lena opened her laptop and typed furiously. Her white bob of hair jiggled frenetically.

"Wait for it..." Seth smirked.

"Here. The new law extends the rights to age eighteen and 'retro-actively absolves all parents and legal guardians for decisions prior and up to thirty-two years ago." She slammed her laptop in a rare dramatic display. "That means they've been experimenting on kids knowingly for thirty-two years and are covering themselves with this new law. Or trying to."

"Conspiracy theory." Georgie dismissed. "Seth, I know you need the money."

He blocked her with his hat. "Talk to the hat. I'm anti-government. For obvious reasons."

"Georgie," Jocelyn spoke softly. "When we went after the Butcher, Seth found all those boys. Kids."

"Probably criminals like the rest."

Jocelyn gasped. Seth's face tensed. They both felt sure the kids had been victims of experimentation. It didn't matter if their parents had donated them, if they had volunteered, been trafficked, or ended up in juvenile detention. Testing on humans and kids was wrong. Jocelyn felt sure of it. But the government kept saying it was good and honorable and for the country's best interests. To be fair, a lot of people believed that, so it was confusing.

Jocelyn took a breath. "Even if they were criminals, do you think experimenting on them is okay?"

Georgie tapped her pen. "I don't know. If their parents turned them over, then the experimenting was legal."

"But is it right?" Jocelyn felt her throat tighten. What was Georgie saying?

"If unproductive members of society can serve the greater good, and help us cure Parkinson's, and Alzheimer's, and diabetes, then I think we go with the greater good."

"So I should just give up my life, so you all don't have to worry about suffering in your old age?" Jocelyn felt rage. And hurt. Georgie was her best friend. How could she think that?

"I don't mean you, Jocelyn. Just hypothetically. Some lives are more important than others."

Brittany gasped. Loud. Then gasped again. She pressed a hand to the table as if unable to breathe. After a dramatic pause she lifted the hand of purple-polished nails. "Excuse me, *black girl*. Fellow descendant of *brutally enslaved* ancestors. Daughter of civil rights activists. Isn't *that* exactly what evil, self-serving slave owners said?"

Georgie pressed her lips. "Yes. That's out of context. But yes, they did act that way. But this is a new world. And this march is to bring attention to things that aren't working, and to promote love and compassion and understanding."

Jocelyn glanced at Seth for support. He gave her a slight shake to be quiet.

Brittany studied Georgie for a long moment, as if reading her soul. Then she softened, lightened up. "Okay. If it's after finals, I'll go, but only to make sure you don't get trampled. I'm not registering on your crazy list. The next administration might hunt you down you know."

"But then you won't get the money."

"I'm going as a friend, not as part of your pyramid scheme." Brittany squeezed Lena's hand briefly. "We're not fighting. We're discussing. Friends can disagree and still be friends."

Lena nodded, subdued.

Georgie explained. "I'm trying to make the world a better place for all of us."

Brittany sighed dramatically. "I know. And we love you for it."

"This is important to me." Georgie absorbed herself in organizing her notes.

The others exchanged worried looks.

"I know." This time Brittany reached across the table and gave Georgie's hand a squeeze. She shot Jocelyn an understanding glance, then changed the subject. "Help me eat this diet cake."

"It's not really—" Jocelyn cut off at Brittany's glare. "I'll get some extra forks."

Jocelyn checked with the Crow girl on the way to get forks. "Can I get you anything else?"

The girl glanced over at Jocelyn's friends. "Sounds like a tough crowd. What were you arguing over?"

"Oh, nothing. Truth, justice, the usual."

"That's usual?" She laughed. "Just the check, please."

Jocelyn grinned, whipped out her check pad and tore off the bill. "You have a nice laugh. Come back soon, Miss Crow."

"I will." The girl offered her hand, only this time with a genuine smile. "Broken Shield. Evie Broken Shield."

CHAPTER EIGHT

Sabrina joined her team in the new lab, checking on progress and making plans for next steps. The blood samples Seth had given her from the "prototype" had spurred a new direction and potential solution not just for Seth, but for Benny. Sabrina also knew that the technology she'd been privy to was the product of her sister-in-law, Illeana Marques Albrecht. Illeana truly was the premier geneticist of her generation. Sabrina's brother, Grayson, was the perfect complement—a neuroscientist and nanotech engineer. According to Ford, they had a cure for Benny and were making plans to implement it.

Sabrina felt grossly inept at replicating their genius.

The explosion in their private lab released chemicals from Grayson's work into the lab. Illeana and Jocelyn suffocated. Grayson was shot. Their bodies were quarantined by FEMA until they were released for burial. At least that's what she'd been told. But then, Sabrina had only been sixteen—about to have her next birthday. Morgan's age now.

Sabrina shivered. The idea of her brother shot in the head had been too much to ever process. The genius of who he was, but even more, the warmth and anchoring love her brother provided was taken forever. Wiped off the earth. And in one night her only family and way of life completely changed.

The Rochesters included her in family events, and they had their rituals, but it had never been the same. Little Jocelyn had been a joy. Curious, funny, kind—always asking questions and eager to please. Morgan was equally cute but cranky from day one. Thankfully she had improved with age…a little.

Benny had arrived, and even in the womb, Illeana knew her purpose in life had changed. She became determined to save him.

Sabrina pressed "Enter" to start the last test she wanted to do. She'd accessed the A & R Technologies genetic database. Ford approved it, but he didn't know why she'd specifically asked for it. No one did. It might not tell her anything, but if it did—.

"Seriously focused," Rex said. He pushed open the door a little more, his eyes asking permission to enter.

She smiled, a tingle of pleasure warming her core at his intense gaze.

"It's okay. Come in." She moved away from the computer to a safer zone—an empty meeting table in the center of the room. She stayed on the other side of the table. She practiced discipline around Rex. Visual separation and distance meant he wouldn't inadvertently get too close. They finally developed a friendship. She tried not to bring needless emotion or impossible hopes for more into that reality. Too much had happened in their lives, and they had changed too much as a result to ever go back.

"How are you?" she asked. "Anything new on Benny? He was supposed to get his blood work back today."

"Yeah." Rex took a stool and rested his elbows, propping up his chin. "As we suspected, the shock of everything in Colorado accelerated his disease. They don't think he will be leaving the wheelchair. Even with an exo-skeleton."

Sabrina's eyes burned. She turned away, nodding that she understood. She couldn't think about losing Benny or she would never be able to focus on saving him.

"I understand you're working on something," he said.

He fished for information. She knew Ford hadn't given him details.

Margaret Little entered from the other side of the lab. Despite the name, she was a tall woman. "This is the most interesting thing I've seen in over ten years. We might get a Nobel Prize!" She grinned with excitement, pushing up her reading glasses.

"Really?" Rex asked, curious.

Margaret stopped at the sight of him. "Rex. I didn't see you."

"Dr. Little," he greeted.

She covered her excitement. "I have to go." She left the report next to Sabrina. "Lots of shopping to do tonight, getting ready for Christmas."

"It's coming quick." Rex accepted the small talk.

To Sabrina she added, "I submitted the next set of tests on our shared drive."

"Thanks. I'll review it before I leave."

Rex surveyed the lab that had been set up. "This is a leap from what you've been doing."

"I know. But..." She didn't know what to say. "I need time. I know I can find the answer—"

"But not in time to save Benny." He nodded to the door. "Didn't she work with Illeana?"

"Yes. Very closely. She's been helpful, but not as much as I hoped. And yes, I'm in charge of the team, and I know the least."

"I didn't say anything."

"I have a clue. A big one, Rex. And if I can deconstruct it, I think I'll have a map. But reconstructing a cure might still take years. I don't know how easy or simple any of it will be. But it usually takes longer than you think.

"Yeah." He got up and came around the table, giving her a hug. "In the meantime, you need to pace yourself for the long-haul. You're here all the time now. How are you managing your residency?"

She craned her head up at him then stepped out of his arms, moving toward her desk. "Um. Well. I quit the program."

"You what?" His volume went up then he caught himself. "Sabrina. You worked so hard. That was your first-choice program. I want you to save Benny, but realistically it's out of our hands."

"What if it's not? Anyway, they wouldn't accept my resignation. They gave me a leave of absence for personal reasons."

"Good!"

"Don't lecture."

"I'm not. Work on this for a few months, but if you don't get anywhere, go back."

"I will."

"I just want you to be happy."

Then why did you bail on me, sleep with another woman, have a kid and never explain yourself?

"I need to wrap this up for the day." She tried to give him a pointed exit.

"I'll wait for you. 'Wanna grab some dinner?"

Yes.

"No. Thank you." Wants were not a priority. She needed to check her last search results in private—and she needed distance. "I'm going to do some reading and crash." She glanced at her monitor. The search had finished. One match? What? Her heartbeat picked up.

"Okay. Off you go." This time she sincerely wanted him to leave.

He gave her a sad, disappointed expression that used to work instantly on her. She shoved him playfully out the door. "Seriously. No. Maybe next week."

Sabrina hurried to her chair. The genetic makeup of Seth's "prototype" had been altered significantly, but it wasn't unrecognizable. She identified markers that were distinctive in the integumentary system—the skin.

She opened the results. A probable match. *Morgan?*

That didn't make sense. Or did it? Morgan was exposed to the chemicals in her parents' lab. They had tested her extensively afterward, especially when she seemed to be capable of some interesting parlor tricks. But her new power had not become very powerful. And the genetic change to Morgan seemed to be related to an unpredictable reaction to one of Grayson's experiments, not Illeana's. So either Morgan was the prototype or...

Related to the prototype?

A chill went down Sabrina's spine. What did that mean? She got lightheaded. It wasn't possible. They had buried Jocelyn. And sure, it was a coincidence that Graeme dated a girl named Jocelyn Marques, who was part Cuban and Mexican, but Sabrina had searched the Internet, and there were more than a couple thousand girls named Jocelyn Marques. Jocelyn was a popular girl's name during those years.

Her hand shook as she moved it over the trackpad. Jocelyn had blue eyes like Grayson. Didn't Sabrina think when they first met that she looked familiar? And how had she survived the avalanche and fought off the Butcher when he attacked Benny last summer?

She shook her head. Her niece could not be alive. It was almost too terrible to imagine. And too unlikely. She took a cleansing breath.

She needed a DNA sample from Morgan first to see if it had altered. Maybe someone was using Morgan's blood samples? Yes. That was the more likely scenario.

But that would mean whoever took Benny's antidote was experimenting on people. Or A & R Technologies was the one doing it. And that meant she couldn't trust anyone.

She took off her exotic necklace and copied the search and results to her personal backup drive then put the necklace back on. Then she carefully deleted the test and the search results from her machine, the shared drive, and the backup server. She needed to keep this quiet for now.

And she needed to get Seth to tell her the truth.

Who was the prototype?

CHAPTER NINE

*J*ocelyn pressed the code for Graeme's house. It was a giant mansion and former union hall, but he had plans to make it homier and functional. That meant people would be tearing out the kitchen area for a while.

The workers were gone for the day, and she found Graeme in the living room. He had Thai food laid out over a tablecloth on an ottoman by a burning fire.

Her stomach flipped. It was romantic.

She took a deep breath as he folded her into his arms. "Feet tired?"

"Not so bad," she leaned upward. His head came down, but he didn't kiss her. His whiskered cheek caressed hers. Strong fingers brushed the short hair back by her ears then trailed down to her shoulder. He slid her coat off and tossed it over the sofa with a grin before returning to her neck, his lips hot on her skin.

"I'm glad your skin recovered. The blue version was icy cold."

She stiffened self-consciously.

He cupped the back of her head and pressed his lips on hers, but she stepped away. She needed to see him. What was he thinking?

"It was hypothermia," she said.

"Definitely." He took the cue, smiled, took a seat, and cracked open some sparkling water. "Let's eat." He sat on the floor and waited, patting a pillow next to him.

She hesitated, unsure of his mysterious smile, but the aromas called to her stomach. She sat and scooped a little of everything onto her plate. Then they talked about their day.

"I think Georgie is brainwashed."

"It happens," Graeme said.

"She thinks everyone who disagrees with her is evil or an 'Obstructionist.' I don't even know what that means. She loves the President, but I know the President is in on everything at Holliwell, right?"

"We don't know for sure, but probably." Graeme stayed neutral.

"Graeme, she's turning into the people who…she helped me at Holliwell and now she's helping them. I'm so—"

"Mad, angry, scared?"

She smiled. "Yes. All that."

He leaned in and kissed her. This time she accepted it. It felt affirming and life-giving, and…she sighed. It made her want more. She pulled Graeme down to the floor. He went willingly, his hand sliding up her shirt, his lips distracting her effectively as she felt her bra unsnap in the back. He hadn't done that yet, but she wanted it. She wanted to feel his hand there.

"Ah," she sighed. "Yes."

"Definitely."

A low growl in his throat vibrated through her, serving to heighten her excitement. She felt energy shoot up her body, heat manifesting in her core and spreading out. Her skin glistened in the candlelight.

Graeme lifted his head, a wicked smile curving his lips. "I confess. I love it when your body does that." He snapped her bra back on and took a deep breath.

"But?"

"You're seventeen. I'm twenty-one." He drank some water. "Our lives are complicated."

She sat up. "I know."

"And I wanted to talk through some stuff tonight."

Her stomach tensed—this time not from excitement.

He recognized the change and kissed her nose. "Don't stress. I adore you. I just want to make sure we're…that I know everything I need to know so that I'm prepared. I was not ready in Colorado. You might have died."

"I would have woken up," she assured. "Eventually."

"My dad saw you. Blue."

"He did?" What did he think? Was he having her investigated? Did he take a blood sample?

"He gave you an I.V. Surprisingly, he hasn't said much since." Graeme leaned against the sofa and pulled her into his arms in front of the fire. "I made a list."

Jocelyn pulled back. "A list?" She offered hopefully, "Of how cool I am?"

He laughed. "Something like that." He pulled a notebook and pen from under the ottoman. "Don't worry. There's nothing else under there." He folded open the pad. "Okay. Here we go. One. Skin changes when you're excited…by me."

"Is this a sex talk? Cause Kymber gave me a book."

"No. Pay attention. Two. Skin heats and can generate heat. Three. Runs fast. How fast?"

"Is that a question or a note?"

"Both."

"I don't know. Fast. Faster if it's urgent."

"Humans can run 22 miles per hour."

"Faster than that."

"Jumps long distances. I haven't seen that, just assuming based on previous experience."

She nodded. "I don't know how far or high. Again, depends how freaked out I am."

"Wow. You're actually sharing."

"It feels a little bit like a relief."

He nodded, approving. "Honesty is therapeutic." He scribbled something. "Okay. Fighting skills. Karate, Judo, Taekwondo, Boxing...other?"

"Kung Fu. Krav Maga. Hapkido, Brazilian jiu-jitsu, Jeet Kune Do. I did Sumo once."

"Sumo?"

"Yes," she grinned. "I totally lost. Weight disadvantage."

"Yeah, I get that. Did you wear the little loincloth?"

"A mawashi?" She laughed, "No. Just shorts and a t-shirt. It was more educational than fight training. If you're in a real fight, you just try to knock them out quickly. The training is to recognize moves and be able to counter quickly."

"Not sure I want details, but I won't be getting into a ring with you."

"You wanted to know."

"Yep." He made a note. "Next. Seventeen weapons and nine vehicles. We never listed them out."

"Because they're classified. I can operate plenty of known weapons and artillery.

"My list is getting really long. Recon experience. Drafting skills." He reviewed a note. "What languages?"

"Almost all."

"That's a lot."

"I would have to make a list. There are a lot of dialects. I learned languages and fighting until I was twelve. Then they expanded to history, science, and other things. But I think in other subjects my—" She almost said her uncle. It was habit. "Cashus selected information that was useful to manipulate me." She shrugged off the memories with a cheerful facade. "But it's amazing what you can learn on the Internet."

"It is." Graeme kissed the top of her head. "What else?"

"Music." Jocelyn was proud of that one.

"I missed that."

"It's the most important!"

"Learning the cello." He spoke as he wrote. "And I have this other one we haven't discussed."

She waited.

"Moves objects."

"What does that mean?"

"Not sure. You tell me."

"I don't think that's a thing."

"Not a superpower?" he questioned. "You can't, like, deflect?"

She went silent. "I don't think you should write things like this down."

"I'm not writing any of it." He showed her a blank paper. "It's too dangerous and you know it. Plus, Seth would rip my limbs off."

"I'm not indestructible. I could freeze and die. I could get hit by a bullet and die. Any number of ways. I can die. Just like everyone else. I can get a disease and die."

That was her more likely scenario. She couldn't tell him that. Her life had a time limit. She never thought Benny would die before her, but that was the inevitable truth unless she found her mother's cure or Sabrina could find a new one.

Her memories had started coming back since Kymber discovered one of her Holliwell medications was a memory suppressant, but she still worked at piecing together the bits she remembered.

Trapped in her parents' lab, her mother had stabbed her with a blue syringe. She thought the serum might be the last of its kind. The cure for Benny. She'd promised her mom to help Benny, but the man with the green glasses who shot her dad took everything. At least that's what she thought. What if her mom had hidden some vials? She kept remembering a safe her mom used in the lab, like a small refrigerator. And Jocelyn didn't know what was in the case the man took. She just remembered he smiled at her when he took it and trapped her and her mother in the lab.

Graeme pretended to write on the paper. "Avoiding deflection power. Ironic." He smiled at her. "I saw you move something once. I'm pretty sure it's a thing."

"You might have hallucinated. Stress can cause that."

"Yep."

"Can we talk about something else? Besides, Seth is listening. He's rude that way."

A shout from the other side of the house echoed toward them. "You're both too boring to listen to!"

"That's what happens when you give refuge to people with superpowers." Jocelyn lifted her hands, helpless.

Graeme pretended to add another note. "Super hearing. Noted. Come on. Let's see what our super freaks are up to."

They gathered the food remains and dropped them in the fridge before joining Seth, Brittany, Richie, and Lena. Lena was in a black suit that Brittany had sewn together. It was a fabric-based exo-skeleton. Lena, at only ninety-five pounds wet, held Seth in her arms.

Jocelyn laughed at the picture. Seth rested his head on Lena's shoulder like a baby.

"Wow! That's amazing! And really funny." Jocelyn observed that Richie didn't think it was quite as funny. *Interesting.*

Richie liked Lena, but so far had kept a safe emotional distance. Jocelyn knew Lena liked Richie a lot. He was a wiry, high-energy engineer and a genius with software and hardware. He gave Lena the intellectual balance and challenge she needed to thrive. Brittany didn't think it was a good idea because of their age difference, and background difference, and because Richie still had some PTSD issues after his experience at Holliwell—but who wouldn't? Jocelyn could relate. As far as Lena and Richie, she couldn't imagine two minds melding better. The rest might or might not happen.

The door to the mansion sounded but instead of a ring, a loud crashing of thunder reverberated throughout the first floor.

Brittany jumped. "What the—"

Lena dropped Seth. He landed on his feet.

"You have to change that, Graeme." Jocelyn admonished him.

The guys laughed. "It scares off door-to-door salesmen," Graeme joked.

"I think the 'killer dogs' sign does that sufficiently," Brittany said.

Graeme disappeared into the foyer then came back with his mom and Benny.

"Hello, Senator." Jocelyn gave Rachel a hug. Then she re-introduced everyone since it had been a while. Benny navigated the room in his wheelchair, driving up to Lena in the exo-suit.

"And this is Lena Bell." Jocelyn introduced Graeme's mom to Lena. "I don't think she was around when you met everyone before."

"No, you weren't." Rachel shook Lena's hand, curious.

"It's nice to meet you, Senator."

Lena smiled politely but had her usual anxious face at meeting new people. Jocelyn added, "She goes to M.I.T. so sometimes it's just weekends when she can visit."

"Excellent," Rachel said. She released Lena's hand, still staring at her. "I'm sorry, but are you by chance Kitt Bell's and Greer Ferguson's daughter?"

Lena blinked pale gray eyes, confused. "Yes. How do you know them?"

"Ford and I just had lunch with your mom two days ago when she was here for the U.N. summit on genetics technologies. She said you were at M.I.T. and doing very well. You're studying software engineering and cryptology, right? She was very proud." Rachel added, "We go way back because of her connection with Ford's work and projects at A & R."

Jocelyn saw a wave of pink rise on Lena's neck. Lena hadn't mentioned her mother in months. Jocelyn was pretty sure she didn't know her mother was in town.

Rachel seemed to realize her mistake too. "It was a fast trip, of course." Rachel backtracked. "With all the important work she's leading in Geneva…"

"If you'll excuse me, I'm going to change out of the suit so Benny can try it." Lena turned away, stiff.

Brittany started to go after her, but Richie already had an arm around her. Lena tripped and he caught her, whispering something that made Lena nod and relax a little.

Rachel turned to Graeme and Jocelyn. "I'm so sorry. I didn't realize they didn't connect on this trip."

"It's not that," Jocelyn informed her. "They never connect. I think she's shocked."

"Oh." Rachel sighed. "That's tragic. Greer is very private. I didn't know."

"What does her mom do?" Jocelyn asked. And did her mom know Jocelyn's parents too?

Rachel hesitated. "She runs an international science and technology firm. Ford sees her more than me."

Graeme took his mom to a seat. "Why don't you wait here, and I'll help Benny with the suit. Brittany's going to tailor it for Benny."

"Thank you, Brittany." Rachel relaxed in a chair.

"Of course." Brittany waved. "How is the bulletproof wig working out?"

Rachel smiled. "No one has guessed, so very well. Thankfully big hair is coming back, and a little extra poof isn't noticeable."

"That's what I hoped," Brittany said. "But I'm working on a Big Brain 2.0." Brittany referred to her bulletproof wig concept. "I'll call your office to schedule a fitting. I think I nailed the hair better."

"I'll look forward to it."

Brittany grinned. "No problem. But when you survive the first assassination attempt, mention my name."

"The first? You think there'll be multiple?" Rachel laughed.

"Well, I hope none. At least not successful, but it's really good advertising." Brittany shrugged as if stating the obvious. "Sorry. That's a bad thing to hope for. I'm not that mercenary, I promise."

"I forgive you. Politics has become fairly dangerous." Rachel stood up when Benny rolled out in the black exo-suit with the others following. "You look like that bad Spiderman."

"That's what I—" Benny swallowed. "Said." He pushed the joystick on the arm of his chair to go over to Brittany. Graeme helped him stand but then he pushed Graeme's arm away. "Is it going to—"

Jocelyn's stomach tensed as Benny struggled again to speak.

"—work? I can't feel anything yet." Benny flexed his jaw as if it needed loosening.

Richie adjusted the top of the suit around his neck. "We're going to make it work, little man. In the meantime, keep exercising your muscles."

Benny gave a thumbs up.

Brittany continued to work.

"Where's your friend, Georgie?" Rachel made small talk.

Brittany answered without looking up. "Fighting evil Obstructionists."

"Obstructionists? You mean people who disagree with the President?"

"Yep," Brittany said. "Don't ask."

"She's exploring political activism," Jocelyn explained. "She's organizing marches and stuff."

Rachel nodded. "My alumnus is known for that. Is she part of the Work for Good Org?"

"Yeah. That's it." Brittany said. Then she looked up. "Are they good?"

Rachel sighed. "Americans have the right to assemble peaceably. Are they good?" She shrugged. "I believe there are a lot of good people that they've recruited. They just got a permit to hold a rally in front of my office at the end of the march."

"They did?" Jocelyn swallowed hard then glanced at Graeme. He seemed to understand already. "Why?"

Rachel comforted her with a smile. "It seems I'm an Obstructionist."

CHAPTER TEN

*E*vie couldn't believe she'd told Jocelyn Marques her name. Thankfully she hadn't had a comm device on. The girl had super hearing, so they didn't risk it. But if Chang had heard Evie, it would have been suspicious. She told herself it made her likable. Jocelyn was gullible. She thought Evie was just another girl needing a friend. It worked in her favor. Now she trusted Evie—a mistake that might actually payoff.

Evie sat at the counter of Cravings where Jocelyn was stationed today. It wasn't long before Seth came in. Jocelyn introduced them.

Perfect.

Seth scooted next to her, and Jocelyn shared a list of specials she thought he would like. He called her Sunshine, teased her, and asked a ton of questions. They were annoyingly cute. And cheerful.

"You can have anything except the Ultimate Burrito, the Rice 'n Bean Bowl, or the Vegetarian Chili—it's all beans today."

Seth closed the menu. "I assume that means you want to crash at my secret lair tonight."

"Yes." She smiled at him with confidence. "I'm working late. It's closer and safer."

"Of course. But I'm not allowed beans?"

"You don't really like them that much anyway."

He turned to Evie. "I don't know how she can say that. It's a major food group, incredibly versatile, filling, and nutritious. Who doesn't love beans?"

"Bad for keeping friends while in close quarters," Evie said. "I wouldn't risk it."

"Two against one." Seth threw up his hands, defeated. "Okay. Chicken bowl it is."

Jocelyn took his menu. "Good choice. Coming right up."

Evie wasn't used to small talk—or really any talk. It wasn't a thing anymore. Someone was always listening, and the only purpose of talking was to connect with people. In her business, the less connection the better. These two were already elevating her nerves with their banter.

The sound of trotting hooves caught Evie's attention. A strange chill went up her spine. She turned to the windows. *Not again.* A horse. *That* horse. The one from the mountains back to haunt her. She turned back to Seth, checking. *Does anyone else see the horse?* No one else noticed. A giant horse pressed its nose to the window or a restaurant in the middle of a New York City street and no one noticed? *A beautiful giant horse.* The silver-gray horse nodded like it knew her thoughts. Then it waited and stared right at her—and spoke.

Don't.

Evie panicked. Horses can't talk. This is not real. This is a delusion caused by experimental drugs, stress, guilt, and trauma. It's normal to see things considering what she'd been through. Just focus on reality.

She spun on her stool, turning away.

The horse neighed for attention. She continued to ignore it. Finally, the sound of hooves leaving was replaced with horns and traffic.

Evie swallowed and gulped her soda. Sweat beaded on the back of her neck. She could not let hallucinations interfere with her mission.

"Hey. Are you okay?" Seth touched her arm.

The gentle touch and concerned tone were her undoing. She yanked her arm away. "Stomachache. Stay away from the beans."

Evie excused herself to use the restroom. When she came back, the situation was more complicated. The albino-looking girl had shown up. Lena. Evie sighed. The girl's pale gray eyes stared at her thoroughly and without welcome. Time to make her move.

"It was nice to see you all again. Seth, enjoy your afternoon sport."

"I always do." He winked at her.

Evie paid and left. She took her post down the street and waited. Seth was getting ready to leave. He should walk right by her. Then her work here would be done.

Jocelyn waved to Seth as he left, then put a menu in front of Lena.

Lena opened her laptop. "What did you say her name was?"

"Evie Broken Shield."

Lena typed expertly. "Very little on her. Fell off normal channels three years ago. Why is she in New York?"

"She lives here. Why?"

"I don't know. I don't trust her. You said Benny was lured by a bunch of girls, right?"

"Yes, but that was to trap me. And that was Colorado."

"But Holliwell is everywhere." Lena typed some more. "Last known address—Colorado." Their eyes connected. "I have a bad feeling."

Jocelyn felt her heart thrummed. "But Evie is so nice. And I can tell she's lonely." She pulled out her phone and called Seth. It rang and went to voicemail. "He just left."

Lena shoved her laptop into her bag. "Watch my backpack. I can catch up with him. Just in case."

Jocelyn nodded as Lena hurried out of Cravings. She texted Seth: *Heads up. Lena thinks Evie might be a Holliwell agent. Crazy?*

Jocelyn stored Lena's backpack then found her boss. "Josh. Something's up." She took off her apron. "Can you manage with the staff here until I'm back?"

"Yeah, it's the slow time. Everything okay?"

"I'm not sure."

Jocelyn closed her eyes and tuned her hearing, sorting through the sounds, the traffic, the bus coming to a stop. She couldn't track Seth's voice. She pressed his number again, stepping outside on the sidewalk. There was no sign of Seth or Lena.

Then she heard Lena's voice amidst traffic. She ran in that direction.

"Follow that van!" Lena ordered.

Tension flashed down Jocelyn's spine. Everything was not okay.

Graeme gave her the coordinates. "I'm two minutes away."

"I see you." Jocelyn ran toward the Porsche and hopped in.

"Richie is on speaker and tracking Lena and the van." He updated her with a concerned glance. "We lost Seth's phone."

She nodded, too worried to speak.

"G." Richie spoke over the car speakerphone. "It looks like they're headed toward a private airport east of LaGuardia."

"I know it," Graeme said. "We're ten minutes behind." He raced around some cars. "Buckle up, babe."

She locked in. Graeme maneuvered around traffic. Jocelyn felt her skin electrify beneath her hoodie. It made a flash that was hard to detect in daylight but Graeme sensed it. He glanced over again.

"We're going to get him."

"I should have suspected. I'm so stupid." She was a royal idiot.

Lena's voice came into the car. "I'm here. They're loading a big box onto a private plane. I think he's in it. They are preparing to go. I'll get closer."

"Stay back," Richie warned.

"Copy. Over."

"She's not going to listen." Jocelyn tensed.

Graeme gassed it onto a sidewalk around an accident. They saw the airstrip.

"Just get close to the runway," Jocelyn said.

Graeme drove through a parking lot, up over a curb, across a field of grass, and spun to a stop. Jocelyn jumped out and leaped the fence in two moves. She spotted Evie at the foot of the plane's steps, guarding the aircraft as they loaded equipment. Jocelyn raced, power building up around her.

By the time Evie turned and recognized her, Jocelyn had her in range. She rammed Evie with speed and force. They skidded, rolled and locked arms, wrestling as they tumbled twenty feet to a stop.

Jocelyn punched hard.

Evie defended. She was strong. And trained.

They took a step back. She had underestimated Evie. She waited to see what moves she had. Kung Fu? All right.

Jocelyn defended and struck at the same time. Evie fell back, surprised.

"You fight decent for a girl."

"You're an embarrassment to the Crow." Jocelyn insulted. "Is that why they kicked you out?" Jocelyn had training but learned the art of fight chatter from Seth.

Evie's momentary shock gave her the opening. Jocelyn smashed her nose, cracked a knee, then threw her with fury away from the airplane.

While Evie recovered, Jocelyn ran to the plane. A woman in uniform stood at the top of the stairs and fired. Jocelyn deflected forcefully, more with anger and less with finesse. The bullets ricocheted back at the plane, sending the woman on the defense.

Two more women came out. Girls. One had a knife strapped to her leg. The other appeared unarmed. They skipped the stairs and leaped to the tarmac.

Jocelyn watched them. Behind her security had come out from the building. She didn't know whose side they were on and didn't care. Everyone was guilty.

The girls came at her together.

Jocelyn jumped high and face-kicked both. They stumbled back in surprise then grounded themselves with renewed focus.

When they came back, she shot energy at them that knocked them into the oncoming security line up.

She heard the orders to shoot and turned, prepared to defend. Bullets, tranquilizers, it didn't matter. She felt a fire burning anger so strong that they were the ones who needed to watch out.

"Get to the plane up! Go! Go!" Their leader shouted to the pilot.

The stairs for the plane started to move. One of the girls helped Evie hurry toward the plane. Evie stopped. She wasn't giving up.

Neither was Jocelyn.

Jocelyn leaped onto the edge of the open jet door. Her success was short lived. A shot from a power blower sent her flying backward, flipping and tumbling onto the tarmac. Evie jumped her then, stabbing.

Jocelyn flung Evie back like an irritant then ripped the syringe out of her arm.

No! The drug hit her hard. Her eyes blurred. She got up. The girls ran up the stairs. The plane turned for the runway.

Jocelyn stumbled to her feet. The guards around the building stood back, waiting. Jocelyn saw Evie's face in a window.

She ran.

The landing gear was within reach. She jumped and hugged it as the plane took off, shaking her head, angry at the drug attacking her body.

She swung her legs up and pushed against the plane, ripping the landing gear from its position enough to disable it. She kicked the body of the plane with force, letting them know she was there. She wouldn't give up.

Graeme's voice called from far away. He'd made it onto the runway and raced toward her as the small jet escaped.

They gained altitude. She kicked the underbelly again and again while fighting for breath. Frustration erupted as one last effort failed and her bones melted to jelly. She tried to hold on.

Her arms gave up.

Darkness continued to grab at her.

She couldn't let go. She couldn't let them take Seth!

She kicked again. The kick landed weak on the belly of the plane. Darkness flickered in and out. Her hands loosened and her muscles felt like jelly. Slowly her body unfolded from the landing gear.

Then she fell.

CHAPTER ELEVEN

She was going to die.

Air rushed by Jocelyn's ears in crushing waves. She opened heavy lids, dimly aware of the ground racing to meet her. She must remain conscious, focus on the tarmac…just a few more seconds.

The ground seemed everywhere, moving toward her at an impossible speed.

With all that was left, Jocelyn shot energy blindly from her body. Her skin seared from the pain of so much power.

Then the ground froze. Still. She reached out to confirm it was real. She gasped, then plopped the last two feet to the grassy field. Her hands clawed the earth.

Blackness descended.

Evie and the other experiments sat anxiously, feeling the threat pounding at the underbelly of the plane. Then it stopped. She assumed the girl passed out and fell to her death. They couldn't see her, but she was dead for sure.

Evie's heart continued to race. She didn't want to die. The others were equally scared. They'd been taught they were strong.

They were amateurs.

Words finally worked their way out of her dry mouth.

"What the--? What was that? What is she?" Evie demanded of Chang.

Chang shook her head. She didn't know either.

"I thought she was going to take down the plane," 053 said. "What if she's still alive? What if she finds us?"

"She's just one person," Chang said.

"She must really care about this target," 053 added, confused.

"They're friends," Evie told them. "People have friends there."

Chang knocked her nose with a bag of ice. *Hey!* That hurt. But you couldn't cuss out an officer. Evie took a breath not moving until the pain alleviated. Project W experiments weren't allowed to believe in sentimental things like friendship—or that they even existed.

But they did exist.

"That's a restricted word," Chang reprimanded.

Friends. Jocelyn and Seth were friends and Jocelyn just did everything possible, even giving her life to save a guy who was going to die in a few months. It made no sense.

081 spoke the same thoughts. "It doesn't make sense."

The technician on board gave Evie a shot in her knee then wrapped it for the journey.

"You all did well." Chang encouraged them. "This is what adversity looks like. Next time you'll be better prepared. You need to work together. Outsmart those who want to destroy us. But you're here, and you accomplished the mission, 017. Well done. Dr. Wicker will be very proud of you."

Evie nodded. Dr. Wicker owned her. Intellectually, she didn't care if Wicker was proud of her. She turned her gaze out the window. But for some sick reason it made her feel good.

Jocelyn stared into Graeme's eyes. He smiled, but only a little. More like his lips moved.

"Your eyes were a little blue from exertion, but nothing like Colorado."

She frowned, confused.

"Should I add leaps thirty feet and flying skills to the list?"

"The list?" Then she shot up, "Seth!" She took her bearings, frantic, grasping the arm of the sofa. They were at the Graeme's house—in the "war room." Richie, Brittany, Georgie and Georgie's cousin, Al, were there too.

"Yeah. That was three hours ago," Graeme informed.

"Three hours!" She cursed and stood, wobbling. Graeme let her wobble. "How did I get here? What's going on?"

"I carried you to the car. We drove here. I alerted the troops. We've been planning. You've been sleeping. Or recovering I suppose. Your superpowers seem to come at a cost."

Jocelyn didn't speak. Graeme didn't sound happy. More like tense. *Angry?* She assessed the room. *Al!* She smiled. Brittany was right. He was sexier than ever—all six foot six of him. "Hi, Al." She went to him. "We missed you."

Georgie's older cousin enfolded her in a hug. Warm strength squeezed her tight. "Seems like you've been too busy to miss me."

"Never."

Georgie slid some food across the table. "Chicken, broccoli, sweet potato, rice and a mango smoothie." She added a fork and paper towel. "I figured you'd be hungry, and we need you focused."

Jocelyn glanced covertly at Richie. He had his arms folded over his stomach and bobbed forward and back staring at a screen. Jocelyn swallowed. Definitely a setback. That's probably why Al was here.

"Where's Lena?" As soon as she said her name, memories came back, along with a strike of panic. "Is she okay? What did I miss?"

Richie pointed at his screen. "She's there."

Jocelyn joined him. Lena's phone beacon moved rapidly over Kansas and into Colorado. Her heart flipped in outrage. "They took her? They took Lena! They can't do that!"

"They didn't," Georgie said.

"Milk stowed away." Brittany informed her with a helpless shake of the head.

Jocelyn swayed. It felt like she was falling from the plane again. She slid on a stool, speechless. Finally, she turned to Richie. He raised his head to her. She didn't disguise her fear quick enough. His bobbing got faster.

She stood and inched closer. She didn't know how to do these things. She put her arm around him. "We're going to get her back."

"You know what they do," he whispered.

"I know. She's strong for a string bean." She spoke quietly so the others didn't hear. "And if something happens, Richie, you'll be able to help her. You're the only one who could. I know it. You're a genius and you're kind. It's exactly what she needs. You understand her, and if something happens, your strength and experience is what will save her. I know it."

Richie stopped bobbing. He met her eyes and nodded in agreement. He knew a thing or two about overcoming.

Jocelyn got her food and brought it to his side of the table, sliding the smoothie at him. "Drink this. I have too much food."

He obeyed. Finally, he took a cleansing breath. "They're landing. We'll have coordinates soon."

Al joined them and patted her back. Was that approval? He generally liked her because she was likable, but he had never approved of her—mainly because she was the source of danger for his cousin Georgie and their friend, Brittany. Maybe he was warming up?

Brittany filled Jocelyn in on the rest. "Lena texted that she was hiding her phone on board, on mute, in case they found her. She said to call her dad. We did. He's on his way.

"My dad approved me to use the jet for a new ski trip," Graeme said. "Since our last one was interrupted. We can leave tonight."

Jocelyn stood up and shook her head. "You can't go."

Graeme stiffened. "Excuse me?"

"This is not your battle. Your mom is a Senator now. You need to watch out for Benny."

Graeme pushed his stool back from the table. A loud scraping on the floor made her pause. The scowl on his face made her panic. Everyone froze. He was angry and getting angrier.

She added more reasons to help him understand. "You have a business to run and renovators tomorrow…"

"This is not my battle?" Graeme's voice raised in Jocelyn's direction.

Richie and Al looked down and away. Brittany stared mesmerized. Georgie winced.

Graeme turned around and paced, as if fighting for control. She had no idea why he was so mad. He should be happy not to do something stupid and dangerous.

"I can go in alone."

Georgie shook her head at her, as if to say, 'shut up.'

"This is not my battle?" His voice got louder.

She tried to grasp why he was getting so angry when he repeated the question again. *Yeah. Definitely fixated.* And by everyone else's expressions she was the only one who didn't know the answer.

He finally came over to her, grabbed her upper arms firmly, as if to hold her in place, and continued to question and berate her with passion.

"You've cornered the market on friendship? Is that it? Or you think it's *okay* to go in alone and none of us should be concerned? Or what? We're not supposed to be there for each other?"

Her skin shimmered dangerously from the tension. Items on the table vibrated tellingly.

Richie began to bob again.

"It would be better if you weren't concerned." She had to agree with that point. Graeme froze. Georgie closed her eyes and shook her head—wrong answer.

"You're going into danger. I'm *in love* with you. And this is not my battle?" He paused for a cleansing breath. "How does that work?"

Jocelyn gasped. All the objects froze.

Silence.

A pen rolled off the table.

Brittany gasped. "Lena is going to be so pissed she missed this."

"You…what?"

"I love you."

She stared at him blankly and he shook his head, clearly exasperated with her.

"What did you think I meant when I kept saying 'I adore you'?"

"That you really, *really* liked me. And liked kissing me."

"Oh, God." Al grabbed Richie to make an escape.

"I was waiting for you to tell me first." Graeme said.

"You were?"

"You're the girl!"

What did that mean?

"So sexist," Brittany quipped, disgusted but riveted. "Where's the popcorn?"

"Lena would have the statistics if she were here," Georgie explained this life moment to Jocelyn. "But yeah. For whatever reason, girls do seem to say it first. But it's not a requirement." She pulled on Brittany's arm. "We'll give you guys a moment."

"I think I should stay and interpret—" Brittany resisted.

Georgie didn't let Brittany finish.

Their friends wandered off, probably to the half-built kitchen or living room.

Jocelyn didn't know what to say. Graeme didn't seem to have anything else to say. They were at a standoff. He was sincere and he cared about her. She understood that. She cared about people too. But love? She vaguely remembered her parents using that word. Then she learned it had an entirely different meaning—one that meant pain, sacrifice, obedience, and finally, humiliation. It was how her uncle—not her uncle—Cashus, had brainwashed her. She didn't trust that word—or anyone who used it.

"Okay," Graeme finally spoke. "So…nothing?" He threw up his hands.

"I don't know what it means—what you mean when you say that."

"When I say, I love you?"

She nodded. Miserable. He looked disappointed—in her. And sad. She had let him down in a big way. He wasn't even mad anymore.

"Haven't you ever said those words? To Seth? Or even Benny?"

She shook her head. "Should I?"

"Benny loves you."

Her eyes filled up. "I would die for him. You know I would."

"But you don't know if you love him," he stated, trying to understand.

"I don't…" She struggled to tell the truth, he deserved it. "I don't believe in love. I don't think it's a real thing. I can't. Because if it's real, it's horrible. And I hate it. I hate hearing the sound of it. I hate the word. And hate anyone who says it. I hate *you* for saying it!"

The words burst out of her with more anger than she realized. Words that had been trapped for a long time. And she knew then, no amount of revenge for her past would ever make a difference. She would never love anyone, nor did she want love. Love had stripped her of her identity, her family, her hope, and her spirit. For love she had endured lies, solitary confinement, and scientific experimentation—with a smile—all to receive love.

"No sane person would wish for love!" She screamed at him, backing away. The tears fell and her body shook. She couldn't stop it. Her teeth began to chatter and her stomach twisted with nausea. She closed her eyes and took a breath.

Then another. She couldn't look at him. And she didn't want him to look at her. She wanted to disappear.

The silence seemed forever. She felt a light touch on her arm.

"Okay. It's okay."

Graeme carefully took her into his arms and held her while her body fought to recover. "Clearly, I'm not sane, but we can explore that another day," Graeme joked. He held her tighter. "It's going to be okay. Don't worry about this. All right? No one has to put names on things."

"I would die for you, too."

"I know baby. I just don't want you to. I got used to having you around."

She nodded and finally put her arms around him, emotionally spent. "Me too. That's why I don't want you to get hurt helping Lena and Seth."

"I understand, but they're my friends too. You don't get to corner the market on helping people. And I'm allowed to worry about you and want to protect and help you. That's part of relationships—friends, family, etcetera. You're going to have to figure that out."

"Okay." She relaxed into his warm chest, comforted. They stayed like that.

Al walked to the entrance of the room with a piece of pizza in his hand. Brittany tried to come in and he put his free hand on her head, holding her back. "Natives are restless. You two ready to do some damage?"

Graeme and Jocelyn separated.

"Let's do this," they said in unison.

Al grinned. "Trouble averted."

Brittany slapped Al's obstructing arm and entered the room again.

Jocelyn relaxed a little, grateful for Graeme and her friends. But it wasn't just her and Seth in danger. It was Benny and now Lena. How many people would continue to be at risk because of her?

If she really had died ten years ago everyone would be a lot safer now.

CHAPTER TWELVE

*D*ominique studied Seth and the twiggy blonde girl in the first box of the maze. Seth had needed a second shot to keep him down and was finally coming around. The skinny one had been a feisty irritant. Dominique shook her head—bad news for blondie.

Chang debriefed Dominique in the Maze Control Room. "She's Lena Bell. She goes to M.I.T. and her dad is an FBI agent."

"That's unfortunate." Dominique couldn't let a potentially dangerous witness go free. "We'll have to dump her near her university. Coeds disappear all the time. Plenty of unsolved murders."

Chang nodded. "Shall we handle it tonight?"

Dominique didn't think so. "Let's see what their relationship is. She might be useful to us before disposal. But tomorrow for sure. How is 017?"

"They did a total knee replacement, but it will be stronger than before. With the new healing drugs, she can be training in a week," Chang informed.

"Make sure she works the upper body in the interim, and don't let the girls spread any rumors from their mission. I understand they had a challenge, but if Project Sunday is dead now, they have nothing to worry about."

Dominique turned to Freddie. She'd forgotten he was there. He jittered in his chair. She wondered if their discussion had him worried about himself.

"Turn on the maze," she instructed. "Level 3. Let's see what an M.I.T. student and high school dropout can do."

Freddie wiped sweat from under his glasses. "Uh…for two players?"

The two subjects on the monitor screen stood and looked around the room expectantly.

Dominique pulled a fresh piece of licorice from Freddie's console table. "Yes. I don't want to kill them—just yet."

He nodded eagerly and obeyed.

The game narrator spoke through the speakers. "Welcome to the box maze. Complete each puzzle correctly to move onto the next box. Fail, and you die. Good luck. And don't forget. Smile! You're on camera."

Seth searched the box, found the camera, and lifted two middle fingers.

Dominique smirked. It was good to have him back.

Seth and Lena stood in the small room, waiting.

"Are you okay?" Seth asked.

She nodded. "They're listening. But I stowed away on the plane when they kidnapped you. The authorities are probably on their way now."

"Outstanding. I'll look forward to that."

Two spots in the room lit up. "It's set for two players. You go there," Lena ordered.

On the wall in front of each spot were four large buttons, each a different color.

The room darkened, then different colored lights were projected, raining down toward the buttons. Lena figured it out quickly. "It's like that old game, Rockstar. Hit the right-colored button when it's over the button."

"Got it."

Twinkle Twinkle Little Star played out in the room. When it was over, shooting stars were projected overhead then the lights came on and the door opened.

"That wasn't so bad."

"It gets progressively harder," Lena said. "Go. Same thing."

"Oh, man. Is that Somewhere Over the Rainbow?" Seth moved faster as the song got faster and more complicated. They had to use both hands instead of just one. When they messed up wind rushed the room like a tornado. He panicked. "We're definitely gonna die."

"We're not gonna die," Lena said.

They completed the song and exited at the end of a pro-jected rainbow, hurrying to assess the next challenge.

"Okay, I'm getting the hang of this."

Lena pushed the hair behind her ears as they entered the third room and the setup was different. "This one is a memory game. We have to remember the order of the colors."

They played the game, completing three sequences of fifteen, twenty, then thirty colors. Seth's memory saved them. Two doors opened this time.

"Do we separate?"

She grabbed his arm. "Never. It's an I.Q. test. Part of in-telligence is the ability to survive and groups always survive longer than individuals. It's non-intuitive but true.

They hurried into the next room. Seth glanced over at her. "Is now a bad time to ask how you know all this?"

"I designed this game. It won a software competition." She shouted to anyone listening, her face turning pink. "You perpetually, pubescent pathetic piece of—" Lena took a controlling breath. "I even patented the design!"

"Oh." Seth ran to his new spot. "Death by irony. Outstanding."

"I'll figure out who it is. Egomaniacs steal but they always try to add in their own pathetic designs so they can say it's theirs or they changed it, or to showcase their genius. Which is really about showcasing how pathetic they are."

"You must be pissed. You never talk this much."

She glared at a camera. A countdown projected on the wall and the next game began. They continued advancing. In the eighth room there was a spiral design decorating the walls and a horizontal line of buttons on each wall.

"This isn't mine."

The first button lit up five times. The second one lit up eight times. Seth stepped forward when it was their turn to press the third button. "Finally, something easy." He ordered Lena to press hers thirteen times. "It's that sequence. Fibonacci."

Lena blinked, turned bright pink then spun to a camera. "Freddie! I know it's you! You slimy, stealing, murdering, scum. I'll get you for this. You never had a creative idea in your life. You—"

"Shut-up!" Freddie's voice sounded in the room. "The box explodes if you fail. Putting you on mute now."

"Lena," Seth called to her. "Stay with me!"

"He called himself Fibonacci." Her face heated to red as she turned back to the camera. This isn't even an activity! A high school student could have the sequence memorized."

"A high school dropout!" Seth emphasized to the invisible game thief.

"A dropout!" Lena shouted the insult.

"Hey now." Seth winked at Lena. "Not sure I liked how you said that."

She took a breath, connecting with him, and focused.

They finished the sequence and left the spiraling room. The next room was smaller. They moved to their spots. When they succeeded, the room started to move down.

"It's an elevator," Seth said.

Lena nodded.

They waited for the doors to open. One more box. In it were six chairs. Two lit up across from each other, indicating where they should sit. Reluctantly they did so. The lights went down and the game started. In the arms of the chairs were small screens with six buttons, each a different color. Seth and Lena's chairs then lit up with a pattern of colors, each chair a different pattern. They each repeated the pattern for their chair into the touchscreen.

Electricity shot up Seth's legs. Lena screamed. He assumed she felt it too.

"Switch," she cried, then explained. "You put in the pattern you see on my chair. I'll do your chair."

It worked. Except Lena messed up her pattern.

Seth swore violently. Lena screamed again, shooting off her seat.

"Sorry! Sorry!" Lena panicked. She sat back down.

Another pattern played. This time they both got it right. After two more patterns, lights flashed in the room. They stood up.

Seth hugged Lena and whispered in her ear. "Get ready to run."

The door to the box opened and they burst out.

Then they slid to a halt. Lena slid and fell on her ass to the smooth finished concrete. A guard grabbed her and pulled her away. Seth moved to help her. Then twelve other guns at the ready, turned toward him.

He lifted his hands slowly.

Near them, doors from other mazes opened, and individual escorts guided the groups away. Groups of children. They had to be under five.

Seth froze. Lena paled. She had just seen too much. They both knew what that meant. They weren't going to let her out alive.

Her normally pale eyes flashed dark gray at him, helpless. Her body shook as they pulled her away.

The last group had two cherubic children that were barely toddlers. They literally toddled out. One fell over. The baby redhead with short wild hair helped the smaller one. Then she looked up at Seth curious and smiled knowingly. Her handler took her away, but she turned back to him with a last intense gaze that burned his insides.

He turned to the box they just exited. The warehouse was stacked with containers, some moving and reconnecting. At the other end of the warehouse, high up in a tower, was a glass-enclosed room. That's where the Fibonacci guy must be.

Before he could look away, a box exploded.

"Clean up, aisle seven," someone called.

A giant foam spray shot down, encapsulating the box. The box was lifted out with an overhead crane and another fit into its place.

"Where are we?" Lena asked.

A click of heels on cement redirected Seth's attention. A deep sense of doom overwhelmed him as the woman entering smiled at him with genuine satisfaction.

He answered Lena with the truth. "Hell. Level two."

As if this day couldn't get worse, his nemesis, Dr. Dominique Wicker, approached them in blood-red heels and a black dress, her white lab coat flapping casually at her sides. She wasn't pretty but she did the best with what she had. She might have been attractive if her hair wasn't in a tight ball and she hadn't threatened to dissect him while his heart still beat. But then Wicker had a way with words.

"Welcome home, dear." She ignored Lena entirely, her focus on him. "It was inevitable. And your termination date is near, so this is the best place for you."

Lena spun to him in shock.

"I came down to share some news. Apparently, Project Sunday tried to save you."

He didn't respond.

"Right?" Wicker continued. "Who knew? She attacked the plane after getting stabbed with a tranq. It made the landing difficult when you arrived, but eventually she blacked out." Dominique smiled at him. "And fell a few hundred feet to her death. At least that's what I'm told. She might be on life support. You never know. That girl seems to have nine lives. But, umm." She pulled out her e-pad and scrolled to show him. "According to this blog report. Splat. The End."

She showed him the report.

Lena turned violent and got loose. She attacked Wicker and knocked her to the ground, grabbing her lab coat by the side and rolling her, apparently trying to strangle her with the garment. Guards dragged her free. It took two guards to hold her off. Chang helped Wicker from the floor and when Wicker gave her a nod, Chang approached Lena and quickly gave her a left hook in the temple and an upper cut in the stomach that made Lena gasp for air.

Lena steadied her feet, and glared Chang, ready to spew more curses.

"Lena!" Seth warned. "Save your energy." He couldn't resist casting an insult to Chang. "You're wasting your time with robots. They're programmed to obey."

Lena gathered herself.

Wicker, back to her orderly self, albeit hair pulled out of her bun, continued. "As I was saying." She smiled. "Sunnyside down."

Seth didn't react. He wouldn't give her that satisfaction.

But in that instant, hope died inside him.

CHAPTER THIRTEEN

*J*ocelyn, Graeme and Al waited in the SUV outside a coffee shop with a lucky horseshoe nailed over the entrance. She noticed a few of them in this town. This one had a splash of red paint on the bottom part of it.

They had arrived at Eagle Regional Airport around midnight then drove twenty-five miles to the town of Little Eagle, population 840. It had been a short night of sleep.

Lena's dad, Kittrick Bell was with them. Thanks to him they had the directions to the Holliwell compound, and plans used by the building contractors including all their building information models. Richie could use the models to guide them around. Only it wasn't just one building. It was a two-by-three-mile complex with a mall, a food court, housing, laboratories, and some other unidentified warehouses. There was also an adjacent airstrip.

They'd left Georgie in New York. Al didn't want her coming and he said it was her or him. He was army ranger trained and she was "gas range trained." Georgie had hit him hard for that comment. He also threatened to tell her parents she was skipping class and working with criminals.

Brittany didn't want to do any military maneuvers either. Physical conflict was not her strength. But she agreed to drive

Richie's communications van as long as she was back for class in two days.

The communications van turned out to be a Mini Cooper with tinted windows. Richie only needed his laptop and phone, so a van was overkill anyway. The two were playing honeymooners out for a hike and were currently scouting the vicinity of the Holliwell West compound for the best location.

Kitt exited the coffee shop and hopped into the front passenger seat of the SUV. Brittany had done a double take when she'd met him. It was clear where Lena got her coloring—or lack of color as Brittany said. Kitt was just under six feet, slender but attractive with very fair coloring—military short, white hair, white skin, gray eyes and a hard gaze that was surprisingly intimidating. There was little to no body fat on him. He hadn't turned into a donut-eating Fed. He moved as if ready for battle.

He had summed Jocelyn up pretty quickly. She wondered what Lena had said.

"The Sheriff here is on the take," Kitt said. "He provides security for all ground shipments and has a fairly large staff of thirty-five."

"For a town of three thousand?" Graeme scowled.

"Not all of his staff are loyal. There are some moles, passing on information when it's possible."

"Passing to whom?" Jocelyn asked.

Kitt turned his stony eyes to her and Al. "There's human trafficking in the area. Word is there's also an underground network that intervenes and rescues victims then finds safe homes. But there was a standoff earlier this year that resulted in several deaths—the victims and their rescuers."

"I remember that," Al said. "They said a group of Obstructionists were enslaving illegal immigrants to make bombs."

"Yeah. That's the story," Kitt said.

Jocelyn wondered at his tone. "But not the truth?"

"Truth is a lost art, kids. Hate to break it to you." Kitt leaned back in his seat.

"It's important to Lena," Jocelyn said.

"I know." Her dad sighed, resigned. "She hasn't been given a lot of it. Not her fault." He instructed Graeme. "Turn at the next light. There's a garage at the end of the street called Turner's. Our team is meeting us there."

"Platoon, I hope." Al said.

"Don't worry. They're the best of their kind." He turned back to Jocelyn. "Are you sure you're up for this?"

"Of course. I'm not leaving without Seth and Lena. I promise you that." She leaned forward and patted him on the shoulder. "I'm the best of my kind too."

Graeme straightened Jocelyn's light brown wig. She had brown contacts, a brown plaid skirt and a schoolmarm cream blouse. The worn-out pumps and tortoiseshell glasses completed the costume, but they had also changed her nose, and aged her with makeup. She definitely resembled the woman across from her, a member of this mysterious underground who was scheduled to do reconnaissance today at the Holliwell Complex in the guise of a county safety inspector.

Jocelyn would go in the woman's place as a county inspector, approving the fire safety systems and emergency kits in three new buildings they were preparing to open.

"Where will you go?" Jocelyn asked the woman.

"I have a new location and identity. This was my last mission here. It's a young person's game. But I have hope that things will change. We must all hold onto hope."

Graeme walked Jocelyn to the beat-up Ford Taurus the woman owned, and he and Kitt double-checked she had all the proper information. Kitt ran through the plan one more time.

Graeme felt anxious. The last time they had done something dangerous, they had gone together. This time she was alone. He promised her that they would be right behind. Today Graeme and Al were local FBI agents escorting a concerned colleague and dad who was looking for his daughter. The Sheriff hadn't wanted anything to do with it. Until they had procured a warrant. Graeme had no idea how Kitt had gotten a warrant, but he had, along with official FBI IDs for Graeme and Al. Unfortunately, the search warrant was limited to the plane where her phone had been located.

He kissed Jocelyn lightly on the lips. "Be cautious. Don't draw attention. We will search methodically then deploy the team when we've marked their location. Okay?"

"Yes. Okay. I adore you."

He smiled. "Ditto."

"And you look really cute in that suit."

Kitt turned his head to them. "It's not a fashion show."

"Yes, sir." Jocelyn erased her smile.

Kitt was anxious too. His only daughter's life hung in the balance.

Jocelyn drove the Taurus toward Holliwell West. The road was in and out of mountains, then a flat valley of snow before she spotted the outer buildings. They weren't hiding the complex. There were dozens of building, an airstrip and hangar, and a tunnel into the side of the mountain. She also knew from the BIM model that everything was connected underground to guard against the weather.

What did surprise her was the line of service vehicles at the gate waiting to get in. Most of them were food trucks, milk trucks, and gas or utility vehicles. Her little Taurus was comically dwarfed by comparison and after the cursory check on the computer she was let in without question. A little too easy. After a quick survey, she realized there was a whole other layer of security past the first one.

Jocelyn smiled at her escort when she parked. The young woman wore a dark suit and flat shoes.

"I'll just slip on my sneakers before we start," Jocelyn said. "I've done this a long time. Need to save these little dogs."

The woman nodded politely. "Just this way. I thought we'd start at the top floor and work our way down, then up the next and down the last."

"Sounds like a plan." Jocelyn followed her, making small talk about the cold weather.

They reached the top floor.

"Are you staying, or do you have anything else to do?" Jocelyn asked.

"I'm scheduled to escort you for the next six hours."

"Perfect. Hopefully we'll be done before that. I have a very efficient method." She pulled up her inspection list, checked the first hydrant then moved to the next. "It looks like this one is missing a screw." Jocelyn pointed to the hydrant casing. The woman walked over to inspect.

Jocelyn choked her from behind. Her body struggled valiantly but she eventually succumbed. Jocelyn gagged and tied her, locked her in a closet on the top floor, and took her phone, badge, and TASER. She also took a photograph of the location to send out later so someone would find the young project manager.

Jocelyn hurried down the elevator and searched for the main artery. On the plans, the artery was the underground path that connected all the buildings but each building could cut itself off from the artery if there was a security risk. She found an artery lobby, used the woman's badge and entered. She immediately went to a fire hydrant system and checked it, dutifully marking it off in her booklet.

A guard stopped her.

She showed her visitor badge and county inspector I.D. "I'm just doing the annual check. It's a formality."

"Who's your escort?"

"Today? They are different every time, But today it's Ms. Clydesman. She got called off but promised to meet me in fifteen minutes. I'm trying to wrap this up quickly. I have a date. We met on the Internet in the dog club."

His brow raised.

"For people who like dogs! Don't you like dogs?" Her voice raised with a hint of outrage.

The guard handed her badges back to her.

"She said to wait at the end of the artery. It's not very far from here."

"Go ahead." She walked on, going to the next system. She did her physical inspection then marked her list, continuing until she was out of sight. Other people continued walking by barely noticing her. She used the time to listen, piecing together conversations, clues, and sounds. With any luck, she'd hear a familiar voice.

"Evie is in the therapy ward until next week."

Jocelyn's heart skipped with excitement. She turned at the approaching voice.

It was a ten-year-old with dark eyes and dark hair. Only she didn't sport the ponytails today. She wore an athletic beanie with her hair sticking out the back. She walked in unison with five other girls and a soldier or handler leading them. Jocelyn looked up as they passed and the girl eyed her, her head turning as she walked.

Jocelyn made notes in her check list, pretended to check the station for an I.D. number then wrote it down, hiding her anger and careful not to look back.

That cute little ten-year-old had been the messenger. Benny had been the bait. Did she even care about human life?

At least Evie was out of commission for a bit.

Jocelyn typed a message, not sure she was in an audio-safe zone.

Reaching the end of the artery.

A message came back. *T2 are at jet.*

Team Two—Al, Graeme and Kitt—were in. That meant Team Three were in as well, smuggled in via the 'FBI' SUV.

She needed to get into the heart of the complex.

But there was another underground security checkpoint with guards and x-ray machines and some very large dogs. She had no doubt that even the dogs were being brainwashed.

Tense, Jocelyn huddled into her nerdiest slouch. She offered her badge but when she was about to press her hand to the biometric scanner she looked to the ceiling and gasped, pointing and sending a very focused blast to a cable. It made a warning sound.

The guard turned at the noise.

"Something just sparked there!"

Jocelyn pressed her hand to the scanner and flooded the device with power.

The lights went off.

She had five seconds before the emergency lights would power up. She pushed past a guard with a believable cry of fear, then ran.

Graeme, Kitt, Al, and the Sheriff were on the small jet. The Sheriff hung out with a soldier near the cockpit having a coffee. The arrogant lawman didn't expect they would find anything. Graeme wasn't sure they would either. Likely, when the Holliwell team found Lena, they searched her for a phone… but she had two phones.

Luckily, she'd given them some info to go on. She'd hidden herself in a food container. Graeme pulled out the three serving containers on board and searched. Something caught his eye when he lifted the second cart.

"I think I got something." He turned over the cart and banged it. Nothing came out, but it loosened the object. He grabbed a utensil from the galley drawer and flicked it. A small phone shot out at Al who snatched it up midair and opened it. It was dead.

"It needs to be charged."

An escort made a grunting sound of concern.

Graeme pulled out a charger and plugged it in. They all stared at it waiting—except the Sheriff. He got on his phone and spoke to someone with babbling urgency.

When he hung up he advised Kitt. "If that's your daughter's, she was trespassing. And if she's somewhere in the complex, no one here knows about it, but it's breaking a lot of laws. I'd suggest you get a lawyer."

Kitt stepped up nose to nose with the fat Sheriff, his voice low and hard. "I suggest you find my daughter before something happens to her. Because if one hair on her head is harmed everyone involved is going to meet a very deadly shadow in their sleep."

The Sheriff laughed albeit uncomfortably—in part because Kitt Bell was so pale and in part because Kitt was scary. Graeme had never seen a darker expression. The puffed-up lawman twitched, realizing the danger and huffed in outrage. "Don't threaten me. Your daughter, if she's here, is breaking federal laws."

"Bob, you're a big man in a really, really, small pond. I break men like you every day. You know why? Because you're the ones breaking the laws. Do you want me to investigate your financial accounts? 'Cause a lawman with your size county doesn't have a Swiss account with quarterly deposits of five hundred grand. You've done well for yourself. Don't you want to live to enjoy it?"

The Sheriff paled. "You don't know who you're dealing with."

"Trust me. I do. They're the ones who will be cleaning up,"—he waved a hand at the Sheriff—"the mess. So, I suggest you start producing results, or I'm coming after you."

Wow. Graeme swallowed. Al's eyes widened and his mouth made a small 'o'. Lena described her dad as a sweet, doting father. Graeme decided to make every effort to stay on his good side.

The Sheriff made a call.

"Commander Chang is coming to meet us. She'll be able to follow up."

"Much appreciated, Bob." Kitt smiled, approving.

Lena's phone blinked with an initial charge. Graeme opened it and discreetly pressed a code. That's when he found a text message that didn't go through.

Chang is in charge. She's been watching us.

CHAPTER FOURTEEN

*B*rittany opened the back of the Mini and set up a pseudo lunch scene in the frozen picnic area in case anyone found them. Then she poured some coffee. It was nice and hot. Hard to believe they were on a covert rescue mission. Truth—she was in denial that she was involved in anything this athletic, let alone dangerous. She just needed to pretend long enough and it would be over. Their last mission cured her of secret agent work.

Richie spoke on his headset directing Jocelyn. "Joss, there's only two sections on the model that could be detention facilities. They are on opposite ends. I don't have the tech to do a heat map. But if you can, get me into the system."

Brittany listened curious.

"Yes, maybe the escort's phone has something. An App?"

Richie saw Brittany listening and handed her a set of earbuds.

"It doesn't have the detention facilities on it," Jocelyn said. "Likely she doesn't have that clearance."

"Call this number from that phone and I'll create a link where I can hack the phone and see if there are options."

Brittany waited as a call flashed up on Richie's computer.

He went to work, calm and grounded. He'd been a mess when the news of Lena had been shared. But Jocelyn had known what to say—one survivor to another. And now he seemed to have his head together. It was like getting an insight into him before he'd ever heard of Camp Holliwell. Still the same funny Richie, but she saw a steadier person underneath instead of a mentally fractured soldier. Maybe he could heal from the PTSD caused by Holliwell. It would be a sign of hope.

"I got something, Joss. One is for military personnel, the other for science use. What do you think?"

"Seth will definitely be at the science one. I just hope Lena is with him."

Richie started to bob forward and back—a sure sign of panic.

Brittany put a hand on his shoulder and squeezed hard, getting his attention. "It's only been eighteen hours. They are likely together or close by. They would use Lena to manipulate Seth, right? She has some value to them, at least temporarily. It's sick but logical."

Richie stared at her. Oh, dear. Had she lost him? He didn't move. Dang, and just when she was thinking she might be wrong to call him crazy…and brain-fried…and a few other unkind thoughts that she hadn't vocalized.

"Richie?"

He stopped bobbing. "Yes. You're right. Joss, go left at the next main artery. In about 400 feet is an elevator lobby. If you can get on, go down one or two floors. Both have cells. Don't get caught."

"Got it. Send Graeme and Team 2 a visual of where I'm going."

"Already done." Richie nodded to himself then turned to Brittany. He patted her shoulder.

Brittany grinned. She was starting to understand the guy. That pat meant more than just 'good job.' It meant 'thank you.'

Graeme slid lower in the driver's seat of the car, FBI glasses on. "That must be Chang. If they had spies watching us, hopefully it's only been the last week. Maybe they don't know you."

"Probably not." Al waved at Chang.

Chang waved back and smiled slightly, checking out their vehicle and giving a final nod to Al before hopping in her own vehicle.

Al turned to Graeme, smug. "Asian chicks dig me."

Graeme laughed. "Of course they do."

Kitt hopped in the back seat. "Commander Chang is going to take me and the Sheriff to a security surveillance room. She says if Lena's here, she's hiding but she'll let me look."

"I think Lena would have found a way to contact us by now," Graeme said.

"Me too. They're going to open the next security gate to let us in. I told them you'd wait

in the car. Find a spot where my friends can exit."

Graeme obeyed. Kitt's 'friends'—Green, Red, and Brown—were the three scary soldiers hiding in the back of the SUV. Not very interesting code names, but apparently simple was best. They were going to go through the same security checkpoint that Jocelyn had malfunctioned. Either they would get through or be detoured. They were supposed to be a distraction as soon as Jocelyn found Seth and Lena. Kitt's job was to link Holliwell's surveillance to Richie's feed so Richie could feed the team information.

The goal was to get everyone out quietly. He prayed Jocelyn could do that.

Seth held Lena to keep her warm in the concrete chamber. They would be coming for them today. Either they would torture Lena or dispose of her quickly. He worried about either option, not to mention his own fate. Only she was innocent and here because of him. Courageous and damn stupid. Same as Jocelyn. His throat tightened. He couldn't believe she was gone. If she really was, that was his fault too.

"Lena," he said. "Lena, are you awake?"

"Yes." She sat up bleary-eyed and reached for her glasses. "What time is it?"

"Don't know. That's deliberate in these situations. No night, no day, no time. It messes with you." He helped her sit up. Her left eye was bruised and a little swollen. "How's your head and ribs?"

She touched her cheek and then moved her core. "Surprisingly, nothing broken, and I think no concussion. I must have a harder head than I thought."

"Determined too. I wish you hadn't come after me. You don't deserve this. I don't think I've ever been sorrier about anything."

"It was your only chance. They knocked you out and stripped you of all tracking options. I found your phone on the street crushed. When I saw them load the plane, it was easy to get on. I know my dad will get us out. And Graeme was able to track my phone for sure. They didn't find my secure phone."

"Lena." Seth appreciated the optimism, but he also knew it would be too late for her. As if to prove it, their cell door opened, and Lena was instructed to get up and enter the next barricaded room. It was a safety measure. Two guards were on the other side. He took both her hands and held them tightly. "Lena, fight. Delay. Escape. Hide. Do anything necessary. But you know they aren't letting you out alive. You and I already saw too much. Do you understand?"

Lena's gray eyes went dark with fear but she stood calm and ready.

"I understand. Take care of yourself, Seth."

She hugged him. "You're a good person. In case no one ever told you. I'm not sorry for trying to save you. You're worth saving."

"Other than cussing out Wicker, Chang and the mysterious Freddie yesterday, I think that's the longest speech I ever heard out of you." He held her longer. "And the sweetest." He wanted to believe her. But he knew he wasn't worth dying for.

"Let's go," a soldier shouted. "We'll use the TASER if you don't move it."

They released. Lena held his hands, squeezed and smiled softly into his eyes. "I won't give up. Don't you."

She turned, lifted her head high and walked into the chamber. The door began to close on Seth. He stood watch. This might be the last time he saw Lena. He struck the wall. His eyes blurred. The heat of fury and regret unleashed something. *This can't happen.*

The door wasn't closed yet.

"Not today." Seth launched through the opening into the secondary chamber, squeezing through. "Get down!"

Lena dropped.

He kicked hard at the glass. It shuddered and flexed but didn't move. The guard outside shook his head and pressed something. Gas filled the chamber.

"Hold your breath."

Seth kept at the glass. He pounded until the skin on his fist bled, but he made a crack. And another. Soon air filtered in. Lena sucked in air at the opening. The guards stood back, guns ready.

"Lena," he gasped, coughed. "Fight." He fell to the floor as they opened the chamber and dragged Lena away, her nails scratching his arms as she fought to hold onto him. Then he just heard her screaming and fighting for her life.

Jocelyn continued on her course, passing busy workers, scientists, soldiers, and assistants. It was a large operation, but everyone seemed to know what they needed to do and were in a hurry to do it. She made progress without question. Everyone assumed if she was there, she belonged there.

Her escort's badge worked in the elevator lobby and Jocelyn got off in the detention center. Helpful signage directed her to the security office. Two officers manned the desk and surveillance.

She knocked on the door. A woman's voice came on the intercom.

"Yes?"

Jocelyn shuffled her stuff awkwardly and pressed the intercom. "Hi. Um, I'm inspecting the fire safety equipment. Annual inspection. I just need to look at the one in there quick." She lifted her checklist on the pad to the glass window in the door. "And check it off."

"It's good," the guard said.

"Well…I understand if there's a reason I can't come in, but could you give me the four-digit number on the outside of the frame." She held up another picture to show where to find the number.

The guard looked, nodded, then got up to go to the fire extinguisher. She didn't find anything.

"No number."

"Maybe the upper right? Sometimes they install the frame upside down."

The soldier went back then said something to her partner. He looked over and Jocelyn shoved her glasses up her nose and squinted a smile. He indicated to let her in. The female guard opened the door.

"Oh, thank you. This will just take two seconds." She hurried to the fire extinguisher, dropped her backpack and opened her pad and checklist, squinting at the metal. "Sneaky little sucker. Found it. 6-3-7-4." She put her stuff in the bag, adjusted her supplies and started to walk back out.

And there it was. The emergency panic button within their equal reach. She needed to pull both away from the panic button simultaneously then subdue them. She considered her options.

"Thanks. Have a nice—" She tripped a little, dropping her stuff between their chairs. "Oh. I'm so clumsy sometimes." She pushed her glasses up her nose and huddled her shoulders as if embarrassed.

The male soldier shook his head, exasperated. He reached toward the bag.

She grabbed the back of his collar and plucked the other soldier's uniform just as quickly, yanking them back and off balance then knocking their heads hard.

It stunned them both, enabling her to do it again.

Jocelyn winced at the crack. "Sorry."

The woman went down. The man required a choke out. She secured them to a steel console with zip ties then took control of the detention center.

"I'm in. Checking cells now." She pressed buttons methodically. Her heart leapt, elated when she found Seth. He was alone in a cell, face down, not moving.

Where was Lena?

She searched the camera views. Two guards gripped each of Lena's arms. She fought hard, even stabbing a guard in the throat with something—a pen? She got free for a moment then two hundred pounds of soldier caught her and took her to the ground. Jocelyn could barely see her friend underneath the bulky body.

"Team! I got Seth and Lena. Richie, they're taking Lena away. What's on the north side of the cell block?"

Richie's voice crackled in her ear. "Hospital ward. Is she okay? Why are they taking her there?"

Jocelyn heard the panic in his voice. She couldn't tell him. Her best guess was she needed to hurry.

"Copy. Moving. Get me a path out from the hospital ward. I'll be there in…"

She looked at Seth not moving. If she had to carry him that would slow her down.

"Three point five minutes." She swallowed, not sure what to expect. "And I might need backup."

CHAPTER FIFTEEN

*G*raeme waited with Al in their 'FBI' SUV, tapping his fingers on the center console.

"I brought the plane to the party I should get to do something. You know."

"It's better this way. You're not military trained or anything. Even when you are, you don't know how you'll react under different circumstances. And this isn't a place you want to get stuck. If you got caught, they'd blackmail your mom and own her politically. You want that?"

"No." He tapped some more. "I'm just worried."

"Lena is tough. And Jocelyn—has some skills."

"I know. I thought I was watching her death when she fell from the plane. If she had been unconscious a second longer, she might have died. It gives me nightmares."

"She doesn't know her boundaries yet," Al said. "Only by stretching does she discover them. But she also—"

"Kills herself doing it."

"Yep. That's why she needs us." Al's tone changed to a more arrogant one. "I saved her life once, you know."

Al wasn't arrogant, so Graeme expected a good story.

"You saved her life? When?"

"The first night I met her." Al lifted his fist to show him. "With my bare hands."

Graeme smiled a little, curious, concerned, and hungry for information. "We've had a lot of beers and you never told me."

"She has a lot of secrets. But now that you've seen her blue and fall from the sky, this isn't so bad."

"Not exactly reassuring, but okay, tell me."

"It was a stand-off. Freakin' soldiers everywhere, helicopters, drones—"

"Drones?"

"Yeah, I figured out you were the Porsche guy."

"Does Richie know this story?"

"No man, I keep my secrets. And it would have freaked him out more."

"Yeah." Graeme thought Richie had been afraid of Jocelyn at first.

"So anyway, I see this skinny, bald chick. Georgie was determined to rescue her. I was just making sure my cousin lived another day. But like, the entire army base went after her—and us. And, honest—I was freaked out but maintaining for Georgie's sake. Somehow, we reached Jocelyn and she headed for freedom. But then my truck exploded nearly killing Georgie. Soldiers were everywhere, drones circled us overhead, and I thought no one would ever see us again."

Al paused, remembering. "But then she came back. I have to credit her for that. She had a chance to be free and she came back for a couple of strangers. I couldn't see what was going on. But one by one these soldiers, man, they were dropping like flies around us. Total stealth moves. Scary. And I'm like—I'm with her, but the drones...Anyway, when she was done." He turned to Graeme. "There were no drones left and this helicopter—"Al started laughing. "It was all tweaked, blades sideways and stuck in a mountain. I thought she was an alien. No joke. The bald head didn't help, you know what I'm sayin'."

Graeme nodded.

"Anyway, she passed out after that. Dead. No pulse. No heartbeat. Nada. Total blue face. Blue eyes. Very alien."

Graeme didn't find this funny anymore.

"Georgie was screaming. We did CPR. Nothing worked." Al lifted his fist. "Then in desperation, I used the fist of fury."

Graeme sputtered. "The fist of fury?" His tension eased a little. "I didn't know your fist had a name."

"It gives life, and it can take it away. Beware."

"Okay."

"And I pounded her chest." He swung the fist of fury onto the console. "Again, and again. I don't know how many times. And Georgie was crying and screaming. And I thought one… last…time." Al nodded with pride. "She gasped for air." Al leaned back in the passenger seat. "The rest is history."

"So what you're saying is,"—Graeme carefully interpreted his story—"you want to be godfather to our first born—should the occasion ever occur."

Al grinned and adjusted his dark sunglasses. "Hell, yeah. Without me…"

Graeme gazed out into the parking lot. "I'm glad you saved her. She's worth it."

"I guess."

Graeme punched his arm. "Come on." He changed the subject. "There's something going on over there. I wanna check it out."

In the detention security room, Jocelyn opened all the access doors, grabbed badges and weapons from the guards, and ran fast. A guard on duty sitting outside the cellblock stood from his seat, curious but not panicked by a woman in a skirt coming at him.

"Fire!" she shouted. "Get out!"

He looked around, and she continued running until her fist was within reach. He fell, unconscious.

She took his chair and rolled it down the cell block to Seth's chamber. The door was open but she didn't want to risk entering and being trapped. She grabbed his feet, dragged him out of the glass chamber and flipped him over. The smell of gas warned her that something had happened. She slapped him. Then again. Hard.

He blinked.

"Hey. Do I know you?"

"Seth! It's me."

"Hi Me."

"What the—" She shook him.

He made a funny sound then brushed her away before leaning forward, curious. "You remind me of someone."

"Okay, let's go." She lifted him and put him in the chair. He slid off.

"Seth!" She slapped him again. She wanted to punch him. "I'm trying to get you out of here and we need to get Lena."

"They took her."

Jocelyn put him back in the chair. "Just hang on. We're going for a ride."

"Yay!" He stayed in the chair and lifted his feet.

"Seriously. I don't have time for this." She pushed him at top speed toward the hospital ward.

"Weeee!" Seth giggled with delight and stuck his hands in the air. "Faster!"

Richie's voice came over her comm device. "Is that Seth?"

"Later!" She tried the door to the hospital wing. None of her stolen badges worked.

She cursed, then pulled out one of the guns and shot the system. Electrical stuff exploded. Seth threw his hands up, defensive. "What the—you have a gun! Why do you have a gun? Who *are* you?"

"Seth! I'm in disguise." The wires burned as she reached in and pulled. It remained locked. She swung Seth and his chair behind her for safety then shot again and again, this time blasting an actual hole in the door. It remained unmovable.

So much for being covert. She whipped the skirt from over her leggings and tossed it.

Seth cheered.

She stepped back again, then ran hard and kicked the steel door off its hinges.

The door flew. It slid to a stop inches from the steel-toed boot of a shocked guard standing at the entrance to the medical wing.

Not taking his eyes off her, a shaking hand reached and pressed the panic button just as she blasted more energy at him. He sailed backward, hit a wall and fell unconscious. It was too late. A loud siren alerted everyone in the medical wing.

"I said you could take the boy. What the hell went wrong? Chang is better than this. Didn't she understand the situation?"

The SOI was pissed. Actually more than pissed. He looked uneasy. Dominique's unshakable self-belief stuttered a moment. What didn't she know? And where was Chang? It didn't matter. Dominique wasn't taking the fall.

"Chang hasn't led these types of soldiers before. It seems we need someone here with more special ops training. But her team did get Seth exactly as planned. Somehow Project Sunday was alerted—probably by Ms. Bell. We didn't know the girl stowed away until halfway through the flight. Her actions are illegal. She needs to be handled. We have a plan to return her to Cambridge. There's been an increase in crime in that area for a long time. It's all set up."

Dominique saw the formidable looking Mercer behind him hand over a digital file. She'd become his right hand. Mercer seemed to know what was up as well. Jerry glanced down at the digital pad and scrolled before glancing up again.

"And, this stowaway. Lena Bell?" Jerry smiled like Dominique was prey he was about to eat.

She shifted in her chair. "Yes, sir. It's a little unfortunate. Her father is Special Agent Kittrick Bell. He's a top researcher for the FBI. She doesn't list a mother on any of her records. Her father and mother divorced before she was born. She's lived with him. I'm waiting on additional details."

Dominique's unease grew. They'd only gotten the two subjects yesterday afternoon. With the time change on the east coast, they'd pulled the girl's information very quickly. But not quick enough to fill in the blanks.

"Hmm." Jerry nodded. "Yes, well, Greer Ferguson led a colorful life. Obviously, her attempts to shield her kid from it have failed. Like mother like daughter."

Dominique's mouth went dry. She sipped some water on the table quickly. She knew Greer. The current deputy director of the International Science and Technology Foundation was second in charge of the largest and most powerful lobby in the world—one whose perspective on humanity's evolution was still backward compared to her own. The organization protected scientists and their work—at least those who committed to supporting their antiquated ethics.

What concerned Dominique was the rumor of a black ops division that worked around the world to protect and support their league of scientists and thinkers. Less than a third of her American colleagues belonged. Funding in America for science and innovation was largely a government endeavor. Jerry was the government, and he didn't have any rules except one. Obedience.

"My sources indicate Deputy Director Ferguson left Geneva yesterday afternoon. I would avoid direct contact if I were you." He scrolled further then tapped a file closed. "And a blog post indicating a woman fell from a plane yesterday at LaGuardia Corporate Runway turns out not to be true."

Dominique swallowed. "I see."

"Project Sunday is very loyal if I recall. It made keeping her in control very manageable for a long time. She has very different loyalties now." He leaned forward about to disconnect her. "If you're still alive tonight, I'll expect an update after the dust settles."

"But you agree, Lena Bell must be handled?"

"Well…at the end of the day, *everyone* is expendable."

He pressed the button and the emblem of the White House flashed on the screen to end the communication. A siren went off outside her office and she turned, her cold blood turning to ice—icy determination.

Graeme and Al walked through the busy parking lot to where a truck was unloading boxes from a local bakery. The sign on the side had pictures of bread, rolls, pastries, and the words Lulu's Cocina. The driver had been talking with one of the Holliwell workers checking off supplies.

The covertness of their conversation had caught his eye. Did Holliwell not want the locals to know what was going on? As they got closer he noticed in the back of the truck a small drawn horseshoe with a red strike on it. Interesting.

Then he saw the worker sign for the delivery and slip something on the clipboard.

Payment? Or a message?

Graeme wanted to find out.

"Hey." The two people jumped then looked at him and Al suspiciously. "FBI. We're here on routine business. I was just interested in the local bakery. Do you have a shop or is it strictly catering to large customers?"

The young Mexican American driver was Graeme's age or younger. He had a casual smile but wary eyes, checking them out.

"We have a shop on second. Come by. Good coffee, fresh bread and muffins Monday through Friday. We're open Saturday, but only half day. Everything in town is closed Sunday."

"Cool. Thanks. I'll definitely come by."

Al stood silent, looking cool.

Graeme noted the clipboard. "Do you get paid on delivery?"

"Naw. Everything is electronic."

Graeme nodded. "Much more convenient."

The young man agreed, getting into his truck.

"Just one more question." They guy tensed. He clearly wanted to get away. "On the back of your truck, you have the horseshoe. On the bottom right. What does that represent?"

The guy relaxed and smiled a little. "Good luck."

"Sure. I know that, but the red strike? I saw it somewhere else. Like a splat of blood."

The driver nodded. "Through blood and luck." The driver studied him. "Blood means hard work and sacrifice."

"Ah." Graeme nodded. "I like that. Thanks. Have a good one." He waved for the guy to carry on. He and Al climbed back into the car.

They had just closed the doors when Kitt spoke from the back seat. "Let's go."

Graeme sucked a breath. "Geez! I didn't see you." The man had a way of sneaking up on you.

Kitt buckled his seatbelt and Graeme saw the Sheriff waddle to his vehicle.

"Now?" Graeme asked, a little surprised.

"Now," Kitt said. "A siren went off while we were in the perimeter surveillance room. Chang had to leave. Richie, did you get my link?"

"Yes, sir. Busy now."

"What is it?"

"Jocelyn made contact. Things are in motion. We need to evacuate."

Graeme gripped the wheel. "I'm not leaving without Jocelyn and the others."

"Graeme," Kitt leaned forward. "Lena is my only daughter. Green is the only one I would trust her with. They are on the way. We will be a liability if we don't leave now. I need you to trust me on this."

Al nodded to him. He trusted Kitt. Graeme had to as well. He put the car in gear, reluctant, and they left the facility.

"Richie," Kitt called out. "Update."

"Prepare." Richie's voice sounded over the comm. "Seriously weird and wild."

CHAPTER SIXTEEN

*E*vie sat on the hospital bed, locked in the room, but at least not locked to a bed. A compression machine squeezed her calves rhythmically. Keisha and two of their dorm mates sat in chairs, visiting her while their science handler took measurements and made notes.

Keisha was still innocent enough to show concern at the double black eyes from the broken nose, and her bandaged knee. Evie shrugged off the concern. Evie didn't want the handler to think she had a relationship with anyone. Everything they did was reported, and every hint of sympathy noted. Sympathy, empathy, and compassion had no place in a soldier's life. It was beaten out of them by whatever methods necessary. She didn't need another beating.

Movement caught Evie's attention and they all turned when the skinny blonde girl from New York was dragged into the large clinical room by two guards. Their handler went to assist, leaving the door open.

Evie knew what would happen. Lena wouldn't feel a thing. That part was merciful. The syringe would prick a vein, the poison was injected, and dreamless sleep would be followed by death. They would incinerate or dump the body. Evie guessed they needed to dump the body and give the family closure.

Lena fought valiantly, even getting in a face kick to their science handler. Evie smiled, quietly enjoying the payback.

Then the siren in the ward went off.

She heard a hard thud, then a gunshot. Evie dove for Keisha and pulled her down. A few seconds later the siren stopped.

Keisha took a relieved breath.

Evie tensed. She had a bad feeling.

She stopped the machine and pulled her legs free, quickly strapping on her brace. Keisha went to investigate but Evie called her.

"333! Stay here. I need your help."

Keisha came back and Evie pulled her firmly to her side, letting the older girls go.

Evie heard Lena's warning. "You're in trouble now. I suggest you run while you can."

The doctor in charge smiled, pretended to glance around as if scared, then tested the syringe with a squirt before bending over her victim. Evie felt a little sick at the doctor's ease. As if killing was everyday sport. She swallowed hard. *It kind of was.*

Just as she was about to feel unwanted emotion, crazy entered. Swinging doors burst out and Seth flew in on a rolling chair with a loud shout.

"Cannonball!"

The force of him on the chair knocked the nurse into the doctor. Evie hobbled to her door, holding Keisha back as their science handler pulled a weapon.

A woman entered with light brown hair, black leggings, and a homely cream shirt. She seemed out of place but she shot with precision. Their handler's hand took the first shot. She dropped the gun. Their two friends bravely assisted, getting close, but the woman shot one in the knee and foot and the other in both feet. Apparently, the lady didn't want to kill.

That was a mistake. A serious one.

The girls could still throw.

And they did.

Until those objects stopped midair and the woman swiped her hand sending medical equipment right back at them.

Evie straightened and swore. Then she realized Keisha was no longer with her.

"Seth, get Lena!" the woman shouted.

Seth saluted the woman, but Evie recognized the voice, if not the face.

She was alive. How?

"Jocelyn!" Evie called her name. The girl spun to her, missing Keisha crawl under a gurney to get close.

Seth looked over too. "Evie? What are you doing here?"

Evie approached slowly, limping with exaggeration, though her knee did hurt.

"Weren't we going somewhere together?" he asked.

"We shared a ride," she smiled at him. He was disoriented. He must have gotten a good dose of the nitrous oxide trying to break out of his cell.

"Seth! Pay attention! Get Lena!" Jocelyn had her hands full.

The doctor and nurse got up, both attacking Jocelyn at the same time. The medical staff had military and martial arts training and moved fearlessly Jocelyn now had two guns, one in each hand and used them effectively. Both were shot in the knees and kicked away with an easy swipe as Jocelyn advanced.

Keisha scrambled under Lena's gurney and unlocked the wheels. When Jocelyn was distracted, she pushed the gurney toward Evie. Seth ran after the gurney, stumbling into Evie's reach. She gave him a hard punch in the face.

Shocked, his mouth dropped. "I thought you liked me?"

"I do." Evie said.

He smiled, recovering.

"For punching practice." She swung again. Seth deflected. Confusion marked his face but something must have come back.

"Where are we again?"

"Holliwell West, Little Eagle, Colorado." Evie informed him, pleased with the result. He literally froze, shocked.

She got another punch in.

Jocelyn dealt with two more guards that tried to enter the ward, then tossed the guns. At the same time, Keisha found the syringe on the floor and leapt at Jocelyn.

"Keisha, no!" Evie panicked.

Jocelyn maneuvered with ease, deflecting Keisha, snatching the syringe, and bringing the room to a standoff with Keisha in a chokehold and the deadly poison meant for Lena in one hand.

Evie grabbed the gurney. "I can kill her in one strike."

"Try it, bitch!" Lena shouted red-faced and furious.

Jocelyn smiled patiently. "I'm faster than you, Evie. I think you know that. Your friend here will be injected, and I'll send you flying through a wall. Go ahead. Which wall do you want to visit?

Seth cracked his neck and straightened his shoulder. "Make it the hardest one."

"The thing is, Jocelyn. I just saw you fight. You don't have it in you to kill. That's poison. Keisha's only ten. Would you kill a ten-year-old? You did everything possible to save Benny, I think I got this one."

Jocelyn stabbed Keisha hard without warning.

Keisha cried out in fear, fighting against Jocelyn's hold.

"I can be persuaded." Jocelyn didn't flinch. "Believe me, I intended to take down that entire plane because I knew Seth could survive a crash. I didn't care who else was inside. I kill when it's necessary. Not on demand. Not because I'm ordered to. And not because I have no choice—unlike you."

Evie struggled. Letting these three go free would be a major failure. Punishment was possible.

But Keisha was worth it.

She pushed the gurney toward Seth.

Seth unstrapped Lena and she scrambled to her feet, hurriedly running behind Jocelyn.

Seth turned to Evie. "I'm sorry it had to be like this between us."

Evie's mouth dropped at his arrogance. Then he grinned and joined the others. Finally, Jocelyn removed the syringe and Keisha ran to Evie. The others in the room were witnesses to it all. Seth pulled a gun from a guard.

"For the record, I kill everybody." He shot the gun toward a guard in the corner, sending the man into nervous fits. "Don't come after us. I'm *hurt* by y'all's behavior. I feel betrayed by you, Evie." He shook his head at her. "And I'm getting really pissed about this headache I suddenly have." He shot the gun toward the doctor before walking over to her. "You actually do deserve to die today."

The doctor was in pain from the gunshot wound but furious. He stepped hard on her knee. Evie heard the crush.

"Seth! Let's go!" Jocelyn called out.

With no time, Seth shot the doctor in the arm. Evie guessed it would be in a spot where she could never do surgery again. That might be a good thing for all of them.

He flipped the pistol around his finger like a Hollywood gunslinger, surveyed the room, and winked. "Later babes."

The guy had swagger. She'd give him that.

Jocelyn pulled Lena along according to Richie's direction. She didn't know if the entire complex was alerted or just their wing, but they were in dangerous territory.

"Right behind you," Seth called.

"Richie, get us out of here."

"Turn left. There should be an elevator. You need to get two floors up."

They hurried left, took the elevator, exited, and were halfway down the hall when a deployment of soldiers in combat gear faced them, jogging down the hall in unison, their steps a menacing threat.

Jocelyn guessed about thirty total. She slid and reversed with Lena, running the other direction. Seth shot his gun, deterring them briefly. They backtracked to a five-way intersection and froze.

"First right!" Richie shouted over her intercom.

They turned. Three black armored, helmeted soldiers faced them, striding with terrifying purpose while pulling their weapons in sync.

Team 3!

Jocelyn grabbed her friends' arms before they could freak out. "They're with us. Hurry!"

Seth and Lena hesitated but Jocelyn didn't give them a choice. They had to keep up. As soon as they were close enough she commanded her friends. "Slide!"

The three friends slid across the floor toward their back-up team as guns fired. Jocelyn looked up as the soldiers jumped over them creating a barrier. She spun on her stomach and saw them deploy some kind of hand shields that covered their entire body.

The shortest, and the leader, turned back and shouted at them. "Go!"

Jocelyn didn't waste time. One of Team 3 had already shot a gas grenade and she didn't have a gas mask. She pulled Lena to her feet. They needed to get off the main arteries.

"Richie, I need something new."

"Got it. Got it. Go down two floors. Left. Take the first right. It looks like a large warehouse. Not sure what's there but it's a clean shot out the other side then into the next one. After that there's a mini artery to an outside parking lot with lots of vehicles. Improvise from there?"

"Our specialty," Jocelyn quipped.

Seth's head cleared. With it, the magnitude of the risk Jocelyn and others were taking. He hoped for a path out, but if not, they were all going down in a fiery blaze.

Jocelyn swiped the warehouse door with the doctor's badge. *The doctor that had just tried to kill Lena.* She had been seconds from death.

Slowly they opened the door, readying themselves for anything. Then Jocelyn gasped and started shaking. He knew her well enough. She fought to keep her control.

Seth shivered, not from the temperature, but cold was the only word that pierced his mind. Cold as in cold-hearted.

He saw Jocelyn gather herself mentally while Lena stepped forward, outraged. She took Jocelyn's phone from her frozen hand and snapped pictures as they walked in silence through the warehouse, monitors beating away on every side. There had to be nearly two hundred cribs—with babies.

He followed behind until Jocelyn finally touched a digital chart, searching for information. She made a choked cry. He came up behind her and read: Project Sunday, Batch 11.

"Geez." Seth felt sick.

Jocelyn didn't move. Her lungs made a gasping movement.

"This is not about you Jocelyn. This has *nothing* to do with you." He pulled her firmly.

"We need to keep moving. We have to get Lena out."

Jocelyn nodded and obeyed.

A voice came over a speaker. "Identify please."

Jocelyn spoke firmly, reading the badge in her hand. "Dr. Elaine Ryman, Security ID 764357. Accompanying guests."

"Thank you," the voice said.

They neared the end of the ward. There were twins. He'd read somewhere that twins were valuable for testing. Some of the boys in New York that he'd help to free were twins.

Lena and Jocelyn marched forward, exiting then crossing a hall to the next ward. Seth covered the rear. This time they knew what to expect. Only this was the toddler ward. It was noisier. His chest hurt but he pushed the girls along. Jocelyn again identified herself as Dr. Ryman and they were given a pass. Maybe the rest of the complex hadn't been alerted to the breach? Were they on different systems?

That question was answered a minute later when two of their black soldiered buddies burst into the warehouse and shouted for them to move it.

They ran past Seth and grabbed Lena, practically carrying her. The little kids in the bed-like cribs seemed to understand something was going on. A few started to cry.

"Oh, man. Don't cry. It's okay," Seth said.

He ran behind the team, glancing sideways as one toddler stood in her bed. She leaned on the edge staring at him intently as he got closer. It was the little redhead from the box maze.

Then she did the most extraordinary thing.

She lifted both her arms.

CHAPTER SEVENTEEN

*G*as filled the hallway. Dominique pressed the code for an emergency kit and grabbed a gas mask. Confidence that her team had things handled dropped when she turned a corner and saw a fallen troop of nearly fifteen—not dead, but definitely disabled. Three soldiers in unfamiliar, high-tech combat gear stood over them, collecting weapons and devices.

Dominque stopped short. They slowly unfolded to their full height.

Dominique lowered her gas mask. "I'm just a civilian. I don't know what's going on. I…"

The smaller of the three soldiers motioned to the two big ones. They left. The third stepped over soldiers toward Dominique. Small was not the right description. He was still about five-eleven and walking with deadly intent. Dominique decided not to learn more.

She took off.

A second later, she was taken down, and it was a lot harder than when that slip of a girl knocked her down. This was a hundred seventy pounds of man and gear. Her body lifted and her back slammed to the hard floor. A knee jabbed her stomach so hard it felt like a rib cracked. She couldn't move.

Then the soldier touched the side of the helmet and a face mask cleared revealing her worst nightmare.

"Dominique."

"Greer." *Oh hell..* "I didn't know. She stowed away. I didn't know she was your daughter! I swear!"

The first punch hurt. Her nose broke.

"Too late." Greer punched her again. And again.

Dominique couldn't see. Her vision blurred.

"You were going to kill her!"

Dominique spit blood, trying to breathe. "It's the rules! I don't control that." It was the wrong thing to say.

Dominique felt her throat crush. Air stopped flowing. The bitch was going to kill her. Then just as quickly, she stopped.

"Tell you what old friend."

They were never friends. But they had been friendly at one time.

"I'll let you live if you call off security. Let us all out, and no one else has to die. Not you, not your staff, not your precious experiments."

Dominique knew a deal when she heard one. "What about the publicity?"

"I won't say anything. And my team won't. I can't guarantee anyone else. Lena is stubborn. That said, this perversion of science is probably too hard for anyone to believe."

True. She could play that up.

Face bloodied, and breathing through her mouth, Dominique nodded agreement. She felt Greer reach into her lab coat pocket, grab her phone, and press it to her face.

"Chang?" Dominique spoke into the cell. "Call off the troops and kill the security. Let them exit peacefully. We're not murderers after all." But this wasn't over. "We will pursue justice by legal means."

The knee in her stomach crushed a rib.

"If necessary," she gasped. "Yes. I'm fine."

Greer cut the line and kept the phone.

"You messed with the wrong family this time, Dominique. If you ever hurt a hair on my daughter's head, there will be no place in this galaxy you can hide. Are we clear?"

A troop of soldiers hurried down the hall and stopped just short of Dominique and Greer.

She slammed Dominique on the floor and shouted. "Are we clear?"

"Yes." Humility sucked.

Greer stood and dragged Dominique to her side. Dominique put up a hand to stop the soldiers.

"It's okay."

Dominique's body was airborne a moment later. She landed just short of the troop's leader. When she turned around, Greer was gone.

Seth took one look at the serious child with arms lifted to him, and for once in his life, didn't hesitate.

"Don't make a sound." He picked her up, grabbed the blanket in her crib and covered her like a little ball. With all the babies in here, they might not notice one missing—at least not right away.

He hurried to keep up with the others and scrambled into the back of a large SUV. Seth awkwardly maneuvered into the far back, the girls took the middle, and the two soldiers were in the front. He put the girl on the floor and bent over to adjust the blanket. Big brown eyes matched the spray of freckles on her cheeks. He held a finger over his lips and she smiled. Then she curled up in a ball and he covered her again.

"Where's Green," Jocelyn leaned forward and asked.

"Coming," the driver said. He didn't sound confident about it.

"What about Kitt and the others?" Jocelyn asked.

"Already out. Meeting your Comm team."

"How are we getting out?" Lena asked.

"Not sure yet. Maybe blow a hole at security, a gunfight, a dance-off." Their driver, Red, had a sense of humor. "Lots of options."

A bang on the window made them jump then Green hopped in next to Lena, squeezing her into the middle.

"Go." Green pointed to the exit then communicated privately with her team. If Seth didn't hear nearly as well as Jocelyn, he wouldn't have heard the rest.

"It's taken care of."

Jocelyn turned to glance back at him. Apparently, she was surprised as well—not just by the information, but that Green had a female voice and a Scottish brogue.

The security gate opened, and guards stood back. They didn't look happy. Seth slunk down anxiously. He expected someone to shoot any moment.

No one spoke—in or out of the vehicle.

The car rolled forward, and Lena let out a breath of relief when they were all the way through. Seth looked back. No one came after them.

"How did you do that?" Seth asked.

Jocelyn glanced at the soldiers, suspicious. "Where are you taking us?"

"To the airport. Stop panicking," Red said.

"But they aren't following." It was too weird for Seth to leave alone.

"We got a pass," Red said. Then after a moment he added, "Don't try this at home."

"I won't. Thank you," Seth said. He touched Jocelyn's shoulder and squeezed. "You shouldn't have, but I'm really, really glad you did. For Lena's sake especially."

Lena nodded.

He reached forward and gave her a little hug from behind. "Are you okay?"

She shivered and it didn't stop. "I think so. I'm cold. And hungry."

Green turned, grabbed Lena's chin and examined her. "Delayed shock," she told her buddies privately through their internal comm devices.

Seth took a chance and handed up the little girl's blanket. "Here, I took a souvenir." He wrapped it around Lena's shoulders. "Check the glove compartment. Maybe there are snacks."

"Chocolate bar, gum, and an apple," Brown said from the front passenger seat.

Lena took the chocolate bar.

Jocelyn put an arm around Lena and squeezed her, fixing the blanket. "You're safe now. You're still crazy and we should get you psychiatric help, but I promise we will get you some pie ASAP."

Lena laughed. "As long as I'm alive, your pie is on me.

"Green turned toward the window. The soldiers kept their faces covered in their helmets to protect their identities, he assumed. Red glanced in the rearview mirror. "You okay?" It was directed at Green. She nodded.

A woman of few words. Interesting.

"Your disguise is good," Lena told Jocelyn.

"Your dad helped with it," Jocelyn informed. She pulled off the nose and chin.

"I knew he would." Lena's voice got husky. "I knew he'd come for me."

They rode the rest of the way in silence. When they pulled into the small private airstrip the others weren't there yet. Green's flight team hurried to assist them.

Lena got out and thanked them, but they just nodded and began taking off some gear, packing it in special cases while their flight team assisted.

"I'm going to wait here until we're ready to go," Seth told Jocelyn. "It's cold out." He took the blanket Lena left on the seat and covered his 'souvenir.' He checked out Green, Red and Brown in their all-black combat gear. Something was up. Thankfully everyone was busy and preoccupied. Eventually they all left the vehicle.

"Hey there," Seth alerted his little friend. White chubby cheeks smiled innocently at him. "We'll get going soon. We're going on an airplane, okay? But I need to leave you here until it's time. I'll be just a few feet away, okay?"

She nodded like she understood. He didn't know if she even spoke English but she didn't cry and she was agreeable so he figured he could get out of the car. Graeme and the team arrived. He owed some thanks.

Lena ran into Kitt's arms first. Seth watched as Richie took a step back. Then stepped back some more, then he decided maybe he should just turn around and leave. The poor guy sucked at this. Brittany hugged Lena next. Graeme went immediately to Jocelyn and kissed her thoroughly. First things first. No judgment there. But then Graeme came and gave him a strong bear hug.

"Hey, man." Graeme said.

Seth hugged him back. A little shocked. They didn't really hug, but it seemed appropriate. "Thanks. More than I can say. Thank you."

"Of course," Graeme added. It got awkward. Brittany jumped him and made it cool again.

"I can't believe it!" she said. "I'm like a hero again!"

Seth laughed. "*And* you look amazing!"

"I know." She smiled then embraced him again. "I love you, Seth. I'm so glad you're alive."

His throat got tight. "I love you too. You guys are the best. I'm…lucky."

Richie gave him a fast, awkward side-hug and pat on the back. Then Lena joined them. She waited for Richie to turn-around. He did, then immediately ducked his chin in his chest, eyes glancing up.

"You okay, Lena Bell? Looks like you were in a fight."

"I'm in one piece."

Richie held out his hand, palm up. She took it and he squeezed gently. Then Lena took the two steps needed to hold him. She held him tight and finally Richie rested his chin on her head and held her.

Seth nodded approval of the embrace. "It took me being kidnapped. But we got there."

Richie and Lena parted, laughing, but Richie kept hold of her hand.

"Did you meet my dad?" Lena smiled, proud.

"We did," Al said. "He's a badass."

Seth found Kitt and shook his hand. "Thank you, sir. Sorry about the trouble."

"Don't thank me. Lena's mom is the real badass." He turned to the combat team. Green froze, about to get on her jet. Red and Brown looked at her waiting for a cue.

Lena turned, confused.

Brittany spun to Green then Lena, then to Green. "Her mom? MIA mom?" Brittany reconsidered. "Okay. Not the best description."

Kitt waited then encouraged. "Greer."

Green debated. Finally, she took off her helmet. Red waves fell over her shoulders. She turned to Lena with a sheepish smile, as if not certain of the welcome, her eyes searching her daughter's for understanding. "Hey, honey."

"Mom?" Lena dropped Richie's hand. She stepped backward. Shocked.

Kitt nudged Lena forward when she didn't move. "It's probably time for you two to talk."

Lena's mom handed her helmet to Brown and took a step forward.

Lena shook her head. Greer stopped.

Seth swallowed at this homecoming, wanting to support Lena. Her eyes filled. She seemed confused, hurt, and as uncertain as her mom. Curiosity won. She took one step forward. "What are you doing here?"

Greer came forward again. This time Lena met her and was enveloped in a careful embrace.

"It's starting to make sense now," Seth said. "I thought something was going on."

"Me too," Jocelyn answered.

The unusual hardness in Jocelyn's voice made Seth turn. "Oh! What now?" He put his hands up as Jocelyn chambered a bullet.

Brittany gasped. Graeme spun. Seth backed up. He knew better than to mess with an angry woman wielding a weapon.

Jocelyn commanded, her voice loud and angry. "Lena, step away." Jocelyn aimed the gun at Lena's mom, and she looked ready to use it.

CHAPTER EIGHTEEN

Jocelyn's heart pounded. She knew this woman, and she was dangerous. It didn't matter who she was to Lena. To Jocelyn, she was part of the team that killed her parents ten years ago. It made sense that Greer Ferguson was the head of a science and technology organization.

Kitt made a move on her, and she flicked a hand up, halting him with a snap of force that made him blink in surprise.

"Sorry, Mr. Bell," Jocelyn offered. "Please don't interfere."

"Jocelyn," Kitt said. "Whatever you think is going on, it's not what you've been told."

"I wasn't *told* anything," Jocelyn emphasized. "I saw you." She spoke to Greer. "With my own eyes."

Red took off his helmet and stepped in front of Lena and Greer. Jocelyn's heart rate and confusion increased. It was her old guard from Camp Holliwell.

"Ruben?"

"Hey, the cop," Al said to Brittany.

Brittany spun her head back and forth from Ruben to Jocelyn. "What is going on? I'm so confused!"

"Me too," Graeme chimed.

"Jocelyn?" Ruben put his hands out to calm everyone. "I know this looks strange."

"You said you were a double agent," she accused.

"What?" Seth wiped his brow. "This is intense. And cool. But maybe time for more communication?"

"I work for deputy director Ferguson at the International Science and Technology Foundation. We're based in Geneva but have locations around the world. We used to be the same organization as Holliwell, with the goal to protect scientists and their science, and ensure that human endeavors are only used for good."

"Well, you're failing!" Jocelyn shouted.

"There was a rift that began fifteen years ago," Ruben explained. "Leadership changed in America. The split became final. I was at Holliwell to protect our mutual friend."

Jocelyn knew whom he meant. Sergei had been her savior and mentor, helping her survive.

"You left me there."

"I had to inform headquarters. But I helped you in the end. Remember?"

She nodded.

"We're not perfect, but we are *not* the bad guys." Ruben put his hands down.

Greer stepped out from behind Ruben. "Please, if you'll give me a chance, I can explain. Privately. Come with us and we can talk. I promise to answer any questions that I can."

Jocelyn struggled. This woman had likely killed her parents or had something to do with it. But she also might have known them. She might have a clue that could help her or Benny.

Graeme watched her, concerned. "Jocelyn? What's going on?"

She couldn't tell him. Not now. Not like this. Al shook his head at her, warning her as well. He knew she was hiding her identity, even if he didn't believe it was the truth. But Al seemed to think the same thing. Now was not the moment. But too many thoughts slammed inside her head.

A memory of Greer flashed in her mind. She was in the alley by their home, holding Benny and calling to Jocelyn. *Warning her? Or trying to kill her?* It hurt to remember. She could smell the smoke. Heard the gunshot. Saw her father crumble. Her hand trembled.

The gun in her hand wavered.

Lena left her mother's side and walked over to Jocelyn's. She didn't touch her. "Joss. I'm here. Whatever you want to do, I'm with you. I want the truth too."

Jocelyn took a breath, and lowered the weapon. She handed it to Ruben. Lena hugged her.

Brittany let out a big sigh of relief. "I am all in on the truth!" She pulled her scarf over her head. "But in the warmth of somebody's private jet? It's freezing, in case y'all didn't notice, and—" Brittany frowned, tilting her head as she gazed past Kitt to the SUV. "Oh-mi-gosh! There's something moving in that car!"

Seth ran to the vehicle. "It's okay! It's okay. Don't panic. I can explain."

Kitt shook his head at the teens. "What now?"

"I don't know." Jocelyn followed Seth with the others behind her.

Seth climbed into the SUV then pulled out a bundle in a blanket. Two little hands pulled at the blanket and a bright red head popped out. She grinned charmingly at Jocelyn then at the others. Seth lifted her and she cuddled against his shoulder, studying the surprised expressions with innocent delight.

Ruben's mouth dropped. Kitt rubbed his jaw. Greer cussed. Richie laughed.

"Don't panic?" Al sounded panicked. "That's a baby. And it's alive. You know they poop, right?" Suspicious, he smelled the girl. She touched his cheek winning him over instantly.

Jocelyn couldn't speak. Her life was already complicated. Holliwell West was testing on children—because of her. Now she had to stare face to face with the evidence. Wicker would come after them for sure. She and Seth weren't even safe yet. How could they protect a baby?

She glared at Seth. He knew he was in trouble, and if he thought he could charm his way out of this one he had a lot to learn.

He shrugged as if helpless and brought the child closer into the circle. "Everyone, I want you to meet Starfish."

They had been in flight an hour. Everyone sprawled, silent, emotionally and physically exhausted—except Brittany. She was in the back of the jet fashioning a little girl's dress with scissors and a traveling sewing kit she kept in her purse.

Graeme stared at the baby asleep in Seth's arms. She didn't seem to have a care in the world. Seth looked kind of the same. He smiled at Graeme, his face unusually content. Graeme wasn't sure if Seth actually liked kids or if he was just pleased at getting one over on Holliwell.

They had fed her apple juice and a granola bar. Richie had gone on the jet with Lena and Jocelyn. It was just Graeme and Al staring at Seth and the sleeping baby.

Seth seemed to make a decision. "Will you guys be her godfathers? In case I'm not around?"

Al laughed. "I can barely take care of myself. I'm not raising a kid."

"Trust me. I wouldn't let you guys raise her. I have other plans. But just check in on her."

"Maybe she can be our mascot," Brittany piped up from the back.

"If it all works out, I'll do it." Graeme didn't want to say anything in front of the child. She probably couldn't understand, but it seemed like a bad idea to suggest Holliwell would likely come after her.

"I'm going to ask Richie too. Three godfathers are solid."

"All right." Graeme agreed.

"Perfect. Graeme, you'll have to pay for her college. Would you commit to that? Even if she wants to go to an expensive private school? And any school after that too. I think she's probably going to be one of those smart ones."

"You know this after having her for an hour?"

"I know women." Seth winked.

Graeme shook his head, laughing. "Okay. I'll set up a college account for her. She won't have to worry about anything."

Seth relaxed in his chair. "That's great. Thank you. It means a lot."

"Of course."

"And thanks for coming for me." Seth nodded to them both. "I don't deserve friends like you, and I know you know it."

"Wow. Having a baby has mellowed you." Graeme took a drink of his beer. It still hadn't taken the edge of the last twenty-four hours. Only getting a download from Jocelyn would do that. But the little girl switched up the vibe on the airplane. Babies made you soft. Mostly in a good way, he hoped.

As if on cue, she yawned and stretched. Blinking her eyes a few times, she smiled big and Seth turned to mush. "Hey, Starfish."

Who knew the guy had a baby voice.

"You can't keep calling her Starfish."

"It's better than"—He read her hospital bracelet—"Seven hundred. Hey, that's 007 backwards. It's a sign!" He kissed her creamy cheek then put her on his knee and began to inform her about her future. "I talked with Graeme and Al, and they agreed to be your uncles and godfathers. I'm going to ask Richie too. I'm sure he'll agree. He's the smart one."

"Hey," Graeme said.

Seth smiled and ignored him, pointing to Al. "Uncle Al is obviously the good-looking one but he's also the strongest and can scare off anybody who bothers you. Uncle Graeme is rich but nice."

"Huge endorsement," Graeme said.

"I don't think she really under—" Al stopped when the toddler reached out to him for a hug.

"Oh. Okay." Al took the baby and she squeezed her arms around his neck then kissed his rough cheek. Al went to mush too and hugged her again.

Starfish turned to Graeme and put her arms out. He took her and she repeated the hug and kiss. "I think her superpower is charm."

"She gets that from me," Seth bragged.

Al choked on his beer.

"And you have very good manners," Graeme said. Starfish's cheeky smile got bigger. Graeme sighed. Yeah. That's what mush felt like. Totally not fair.

She finally crawled down and did a little up-and-down bob in front of Seth.

"I warned you, buddy." Al noted the diaper.

"Oh! Okay. Hold on." He took Starfish to the back of the jet where Brittany worked away. She looked up.

"Can you take her in?"

153

Brittany examined the girl carefully. "Are you potty trained?"

The toddler bobbed again.

"Oh, okay. Let's go."

Brittany took care of her then came back out and announced, "Potty trained!"

"Yes!" Seth pumped his fist. "I'm so good at this!"

Brittany rolled her eyes then turned her attention to the girl. "I hope you like blue. And I apologize for the material, but at least it's something you can wear when we get off the plane."

Graeme looked at the simple blue dress. Something looked familiar. "Is that my ski jacket?"

Brittany gave him an outraged expression with a hand on her hip. "You would begrudge a baby? And it's not like I had much to work with. And these conditions—" She waved around the luxury jet. "Well, in other circumstances they're very nice, but I'm trying to create here."

Graeme lifted his hands helpless. He'd lost control a long time ago. Starfish stared at him. "It's okay, sweetie. It will look better on you, and Brittany actually does have some talent."

"Pfft." Brittany got back to her creation. She measured the toddler's neck quickly. "I'm The Fabulous Brittany Walsh. With a capital T for your reference--when you learn to write. But you may call me Auntie Fabulous." Brittany held the dress up to the baby. "I think this shade of blue is going to be a very good color for you."

The little girl nodded agreement then climbed on a seat nearby and curled up. Seth wrapped her in blankets and gave her a kiss on the head. Brittany observed. She peeked up at Graeme and bit back a smile.

Graeme grin back and shrugged. Maybe this was a good thing. Seth needed something to live for. The little carrot top might be just the answer.

CHAPTER NINETEEN

*J*ocelyn waited while Lena and her mom spoke privately. Lena had a lot of questions, and Jocelyn couldn't help but to listen to the answers. She tried to assess if Lena believed it all. When the conversation turned to all the things Greer missed in Lena's life, Jocelyn deliberately shut her brain off and focused on food and Richie. She'd tried to talk with Ruben but he went back to being an ice-cold super spy and pretended to close his eyes to sleep.

At one point she waved a hand over his face. He caught her hand.

"Let it be. You'll get your answers soon enough."

And so she waited, staring at the ground below, thinking about the Underground group in Colorado and how they might help her; thinking about Benny and how she might help him; thinking about Sabrina and how she might help Seth.

"You have a lot on your mind." Greer stood in front of her, a regretful smile. She nodded for Jocelyn to join her.

They took a seat in Greer's office. The jet was bigger than the Rochester's and had two bedrooms, an office, a conference room, and a main lounge.

"Were you able to hear me and Lena," Greer asked.

"Yes." She didn't lie. Ruben would have already shared Jocelyn's abilities with her. "But I tuned out when you spoke about private stuff. Out of respect for Lena."

"You can do that?"

"It took discipline, but I learned how. I needed it when I moved to New York. It would be too much otherwise. But the bulk of my missions for Holliwell were as a listening device and translator."

"I'd love to hear about them."

"They're top secret. Holliwell might be evil, but it's still national secrets. And the soldiers and ops teams I worked with were good people. I don't think they knew someone evil was running the show—at least not right away."

"And you think Holliwell is evil?"

"You've spoken to Ruben. What do you think?"

Greer sighed. "When we were building Holliwell and developing the network, we thought it was our greatest hope for humanity. Holliwell. Can you believe it?"

"No."

"It started off good. When things turned sour, the Chairperson of Holliwell—U.S., in Virginia, was coerced to turn the operation over to the federal government. That's when the military moved in, and it became Camp Holliwell. It was an open campus before that.

"I can't imagine it."

"I guess not."

"Do you know who I am?" Jocelyn asked.

"I know who you think you are."

Jocelyn didn't speak. It wasn't exactly supportive. Greer was interesting. She wasn't soft or easily swayed; otherwise, she wouldn't have given up Lena all these years to keep her safe while she was off watching the world and "making sure humans survived their own brilliance and stupidity." At least that's what she heard Greer tell Lena before she tuned them out.

"You can't prove who you are Jocelyn. That's the problem. When you left Holliwell—"

"Escaped, you mean."

"Yes. When you escaped they shut down Project Sunday—you—and destroyed all the files, evidence and project notes. While I believe there has to be something hidden somewhere, my people have yet to find it. Ruben acquired only a couple things the night you escaped. There wasn't much time. We told him to find you first. The evidence was secondary. I'm sorry."

"There was a morgue. With bodies of all the other tests. And—" she didn't want to say it but she did. "My parents' bodies are there. Do you think they destroyed them?"

"I don't know. I can try to find out."

"I saw you the night they died."

"I tried to stop a little girl from going into a burning building. Do you remember anything else from that night?"

"A man with green glasses shot my dad. I saw him. He shot my dad in the head. My dad fell dead. Instantly. Then he tried to shoot me. My mom stopped him. He left and locked us in somehow."

Greer took a breath. "That's a hard one. I'm so sorry."

"What did you know about my parents? Did my mother have a cure for Benny?"

Greer took another breath. Jocelyn knew she was calculating how much to tell her. No one ever revealed all their secrets or told the whole truth—not until they had to. Greer had played in the black ops world long enough to become like that. Lena wanted to believe her mother and be loved by her, but Jocelyn had enough experience to know half-truths would eventually crush her friend and destroy her relationship with Greer. Some things were inevitable. Jocelyn couldn't trust Greer, but they could use each other, and that might be enough.

"Your mother believed she had a cure for Benny. Her work was cutting edge long before any of her children came along. When she tested Benny's genetic makeup she discovered the neuro-motor disease. That's when she began applying her work to find a genetic cure—a way to locate and replace defective genes with healthy ones. Not just healthy…better. Using the smallest human tissue, cells and DNA material, she re-engineered new genes. Everyone in the world has been working on this, but she was more deeply motivated. She just needed a way to administer it. That's where Grayson came in. His expertise in physics and nanotechnology made him the kind of bioengineer that could solve this problem. He created infinitesimal computers that would carry the new genes into the DNA, searching and replacing. Then they would just be absorbed into the system and excreted as gas through the skin.

Without this system, the risk of injecting someone with a treatment could send them into shock, possibly heart failure as the transformation happens so quickly. The nanotech could slow down the pace of transformation so that the genes recover at a more natural speed allowing other systems to catch up as they are affected."

Greer took a breath. "All of it was new, and bold, and transformative. They were going to put Benny in a hospital and do the testing, but the FDA wouldn't approve it. Once the government understood the possibilities, they wanted it for themselves. Illeana and Grayson weren't amenable to that. Neither was the company that they started with Ford and Rachel Rochester.

They built out a hospital room in the Astoria location. It was finished the same day as the explosion.

The news fed the public a story that the home lab did not meet safety standards and the family was fined by the government and FEMA and HAZMAT for the clean-up and labor costs—Illeana and Grayson were dead, and the government sent a strong message to the science community."

Greer paused. "I don't know what happened to you that night."

Jocelyn filled in the blanks.

"My mother injected me with something. She said it was the only way I would live."

"That explains a little. I think something else happened that we don't understand. Grayson's experiments were destroyed that night and evaporated into gas. Somehow you breathed in a mixture that, instead of expelling from your skin, transformed it into a very different organ. Morgan was affected similarly, but in a significantly minor way. She can bio-transmit small objects, but other than that she was unaffected."

"I thought so," Jocelyn said.

"Do you know where your mother kept her safe?"

"Her safe?" Jocelyn asked.

"When I warned your parents of the danger, your mother told me they had a safe. She kept test samples there as back-up. She joked that no one would ever find it.

"Did they?"

"Not to my knowledge. I'm sure Ford would have used the samples or told me. All of their notes were destroyed. The building was nearly gutted but nothing was found."

Jocelyn didn't say anything. She didn't know Greer that well. Or how much of her story was true. She wanted to believe her, even trust her, but if her own mother hadn't told anyone then there was a reason.

"The man took one of my mom's cases. It had Benny's cure. I'm sure of it."

"And I'm sure he thought he could get it replicated, but so far they haven't been successful."

"So what? They're just trying to create a bunch of super soldiers, or child spies, or are all those kids in Colorado just human lab rats that will never see the outside?"

"I don't know."

"Did you know they were there?"

"Not exactly. We knew Dr. Wicker was purchasing un-wanted babies. It's legal, so there's nothing that can be done. But we had no idea the extent of the testing going on until today."

"How can it be legal?"

"That's a chat for another day, Jocelyn." Greer reached into her refrigerator and grabbed two waters. She handed her one.

Jocelyn didn't have time to waste. "I'm going to die in a few years. Maybe less. Hard to say."

"I know. I'm sorry." Greer didn't sugar coat it. "If you want me to take a sample of your brain tissue, I could have our scientists study it."

"No, thanks. But Benny doesn't have to die too. His cure is out there. If you're really sorry, tell me who the man is that wanted the formula and why was he willing to kill my father for it?"

"The man with the green glasses?"

"Yes," Jocelyn waited. Greer had to know him.

"Are you going to go after him?"

"Yes."

"That's a bad idea."

"I have a lot of bad ideas. He's not the President. How bad could it be?"

Greer took the digital pad off her desk and searched for a file. She held up a picture. "Is this him?"

Jocelyn's heart raced. Her throat tightened. "Yes."

"This is one of the last photos taken of him. He doesn't do press conferences or photo shoots."

"Who is he?"

"Secretary of Information, Jerry Ramstein. He runs the NSA, the CIA, the FBI, Homeland Security, the Pentagon, the IRS, the National Healthcare system, and a few other organizations that control science and technology—like all the American Holliwell locations. The deputy secretaries report to him. He's an information junkie. He's strategic. He requires very little sleep and most of the world leaders are in his pocket or at least leery of him."

Greer let that thought sit with her for a moment.

"But it's also very likely that he gave a sample of your mother's serum to Dr. Wicker. My guess is that's the source of her experimentation, along with your blood samples."

Jocelyn looked out the jet window. "Back there."

"Yes."

Jocelyn thought it through. If there was a cure for Benny it could be in three possible locations. She could hunt Jerry Ramstein and find out where he kept the formula. Figure out where her mother had her safe and hope something survived the explosion and ten years of neglect. Or go back to Holliwell West. She thought back on the plans they had of the complex. There was a science wing and a vault. She'd been so close.

"Tell me more about this Jerry Ramstein."

"He's the man who directs the president, and the last one as well. And probably the next one. He's the most powerful person in America. And he's virtually untouchable."

CHAPTER TWENTY

$\mathcal{D}$ ominique put down the ice pack and adjusted the gauze in her nostril as she shared her version of the story.

"Greer and I agreed to walk away from the incident. She got Seth and her daughter. I'm not at all happy about it, but there's still a chance to acquire the body for an autopsy at a later date."

"That would be the easier method," Jerry agreed. "Let's not rock the boat before that.

Everything else is secure?"

"Yes, sir." Dominique stiffened her spine and smiled. Not a chance in hell she was telling him she had a missing asset. It appeared Seth had taken experiment 700 but the surveillance footage of the moment was vague. They'd been cheap in their video quality. She needed to fire somebody for that. It was still possible the asset was simply on the loose, toddling around. Possible, not probable, but better to do a discreet search first.

Holliwell Colorado was her dream—but just the beginning. Today she felt a little unraveled. And she didn't like it all. She would not go back to being under anyone's command, and owning the science gave her that security. Despite playing by the laws she had helped to make, there were a lot of people who didn't like the laws. And the few lies that she told today, even by omission, were at risk of being revealed. She needed to clean up her mess quickly and discreetly. She did not want to be on Jerry's bad side.

Jerry finished his call with Dominique and was about to do his daily briefing with the President when Mercer interrupted.

"Deputy Director Ferguson, sir. She said it was important."

"I'll take it in here."

Jerry went back to his desk. Greer's lovely face flashed on the screen but with the expression of a highland warrior.

"Deputy Director Ferguson."

"Secretary Ramstein."

She didn't say anything else. But the threat was blatant.

"Busy day," he said.

"Not so bad. A little house cleaning." She smiled. "Are we good, Jerry?"

"Yes. I called off the dogs."

"No one is going to follow up in New York?"

"No. It's done." Jerry was honest. He had other plans for Jocelyn. Seth was never an issue. He could acquire Seth's body when it was time. Patience was one thing he had in spades.

"Dominique is a liability. You're going to be exposed."

"I think we're good, dear. Don't worry your little head about it."

Her lips curled upward, but this time something slithered down his spine in warning.

"What?" he asked. He mentally cursed. He didn't mean to fall for that.

"Nothing. I can control my team, Jerry. But I have no control of these kids today. They're crazier than we were."

"I miss the good ol' days too." Jerry adjusted his glasses on his nose, then caught himself over that long-forgotten nervous reaction.

She smirked. "Just a heads up. I worry about you."

He laughed out loud. "I used to miss you too, Greer. But that was a long time ago."

He pressed the End Call button and sat back.

It wasn't often he thought back on what might have been—the friends he had betrayed, the lovers lost, the choices made. He attained success by being focused and determined. Through information, he obtained leverage to control the leaders around the world and the financiers who elected them. He was chairman of the most elite group in the world. He led them. He made them successful. And together they controlled the world's resources, wars, and world news. Yes, there were still some Obstructionists, some rebels, some true believers that wanted a different world. But that world was one of chaos and naiveté. That world was one where everyone was allowed to do what they wanted.

He wouldn't allow that. Order required hard choices. He had learned that early. But it also required him to have control of the cutting-edge science and technology that everyone needed, and which continued to be his leverage.

Jerry adjusted his glasses and let out a rare sigh. Saving humanity from their own supreme stupidity and lack of discipline was a lonely job.

But he slept well, knowing he was the good guy.

Jocelyn, Lena and Richie waited on the jet, sipping soda and finishing a coconut pie. Apparently, Greer kept pie on the plane in the event it would ever be needed. Jocelyn wondered if she secretly had hoped to share her real life with Lena someday. Keeping secrets about your real life for so long wasn't easy. Jocelyn knew that better than most people.

They got up when Greer came out of her office. "We have a truce. The government will not come after anyone at this juncture."

Lena shook her head. "That's not enough! We have to let the public know. They're experimenting on and manipulating kids. They stole my own game software too. That's a crime we could go after. And I have pictures—"

"Lena!" Greer shook her head. "Leave it."

Lena wouldn't. "If people knew the truth, they would do something."

Greer raised a brow of doubt then relented. "Maybe. But let's not start a war. It's more complicated than all this."

"This is pretty complicated," Jocelyn said.

"Other forces are working to change things," Greer revealed. "But it takes time, building consensuses, and playing by the rules at hand. Today is a huge victory—for you, Seth, Jocelyn and whoever that child was that Seth"—she searched for the right word—"liberated. That could have been a disaster. Lena, Jocelyn. Please don't upset the balance. You all could be dead. That's no joke."

Lena finally acquiesced. "I know. I'm sorry."

"It's easy to be brave when you have the upper hand," Greer warned.

Richie reached his hand out in appreciation. "Thank you, ma'am." He nudged Jocelyn.

Jocelyn shook Greer's hand. "Thank you. If I think of anything, can I contact you?"

"Of course. I'm sorry I can't help you more. Everyone has been working on a cure for Benny. There's still hope. Don't give up." Greer released her hand.

The jet door opened, and Jocelyn led the way out. Richie followed. Jocelyn peeked at Lena. Her mother held her tight for a long moment. Whatever her job really was, it must be dangerous because she definitely cared about Lena. She even said she loved her.

Jocelyn shrugged that off. Love meant you couldn't see your daughter? *What kind of love was that?*

She looked out onto the jetway and hurried down. Georgie waited, arms open and a wide smile. Graeme and the others had landed just before them, and Seth carried the little toddler with him. She had on an adorable blue dress with a big blue bow tied around her head. Brittany waved a hand over the creation. Jocelyn nodded approval with some claps.

Graeme waited for her to greet everyone. Then she went to him and rested in his arms.

His fingers threaded through the back of her hair. "Did you find out what you needed?"

"A little."

"Can I ask how you recognized Lena's mom?"

Jocelyn pulled back, considered her answer then met his searching gaze. "I saw her, before I started doing missions for Camp Holliwell. I misunderstood the circumstances. It was chaotic at the time."

He nodded, accepting that answer—for now.

Everything she said was true. But she knew she deliberately let him think Greer was part of her Holliwell life, not her original life. Greer made it clear that any proof she had of Jocelyn's identity was only through third parties. Her DNA had altered enough to cause confusion, her fingerprints had been destroyed, and her baby teeth were gone. In a court of law, it would be one person's word against another.

Only Jocelyn didn't believe that Cashus, who had invested ten years of his career in her, would have destroyed everything. He was too possessive. He would want options. Even if Camp Holliwell had been ordered to destroy records and evidence, there were individuals who kept back up. Just like her mother and father had.

She leaned her head back for a kiss. Graeme's lips caressed hers lightly before taking possession.

"I love you," he whispered against her cheek.

She squeezed him before pulling away. "We have a lot to celebrate today." All her friends were here and safe.

"Yes. We're the lucky ones," he said.

"We are." If he only knew...

CHAPTER TWENTY-ONE

*S*eth knew he had to do the hard sell.

They were at the Morrows. John must have heard them as he rushed in from the backyard. He froze midstride then turned from Seth to Jocelyn to Starfish and back again.

"That's a baby," John said.

"That's what everyone keeps saying," Seth grinned. "The decorations looks great. Are we trimming the tree soon?"

Maddie jumped in, excited. "Friday night. You and Jocelyn are supposed to be here for dinner. Right?" She wanted to confirm everyone was on the same page.

"I wouldn't miss it," Seth said.

"You asked if you could keep something *small* here." John stared at the baby.

"I told you," Jocelyn chastised Seth for not being clear.

"She is small. And she doesn't eat much and she's already potty trained."

Starfish smiled engagingly. Seth introduced her. He had already prepped her that it might be a surprise to everyone.

"This is Starfish. She's an orphan. I couldn't save all of them, but I saved this one." He smiled proudly. What could they say to that?

Max gasped, his head jolting up to his frowning dad, then back to Seth with a smile.

Seth took advantage of the moment. "This is Max."

Starfish struggled to get down. She wanted to meet Max and Maddie. She waddled a

couple steps and hugged Max around the waist. He was the only one short enough for her to do that.

"Aw. She's cute." Max hugged her.

"And this is Maddie," Seth introduced. "She's the best big sister anyone could ask for."

Maddie flushed at the compliment, then picked Starfish up. "Wanna color with us?"

The baby nodded. Seth wasn't a hundred percent sure she understood as she pretty much agreed with everything. Maddie winked at Seth and took the little bundle to their crafts table.

"So, um…" Kymber led them to the kitchen where all the important conversations took place. She put an audio scrambler on the table, a precaution they were all used to in case the government or other organizations were listening. "Are you two planning on raising her?"

Kymber opened a jar and put some cookies on a plate, then added two glasses of milk for Seth and Jocelyn.

"We're orphans too. We don't know anything about raising kids," Seth said.

Jocelyn nodded agreement then turned back to Seth, expectant. He kicked her under the table. She was no help at all.

"But you two know everything. I never met better parents." It wasn't just flattery. It was true. He wouldn't leave Star with anyone else.

Jocelyn nodded her head, agreeing with Seth.

John shook his head 'no'.

"I'll put on coffee," Kymber said.

"Make it a beer," John said.

His expression to Seth indicated—*no way in hell.*

171

Kymber grabbed her husband a beer with an anxious glance and put it on the table. Then she put on coffee, standing at the ready and eating a cookie nervously while it brewed.

Seth heard the kids doting over Star in the living room. He hoped they would be his ace.

"All right. Let's get the story," John said. "Where did she come from?"

"I think we all know how babies are made." Seth smiled at his joke.

The joke didn't fly. *Smile gone.*

"Seth," John's hard voice warned him.

"Okay, three days ago I was kidnapped by my former government-funded scientific captor who wants to dissect me while my heart still beats. When I escaped, I ended up running through warehouses full of babies, even younger than Star, and some older kids too. There's probably upward to a thousand kids being tortured and experimented on there, but you know. Nobody cares. And while I was running for my life, 700." Seth explained, "That's the name they gave her. She stood up in her crib and lifted her little chubby arms begging me to save her. So I did."

Silence.

John's chin went down, and he rubbed his entire face.

Kymber cleared her voice. "Coffee's ready."

John finished his beer in one take. "Okay. I'm afraid to ask but—is that the real story?"

Seth nodded.

"And how did you get out?"

Seth turned his head to Jocelyn.

"Don't bring me into this." Jocelyn grabbed a cookie and dunked it studiously. "But it's true what he said, and the rest is just more complicated and unnecessary. But now we have her. And knowing what we know we can't send her back."

"What if they come for her?" Kymber asked.

Jocelyn helped him again. "A high-level official agreed to let us all go if we don't blow any whistles or cause a public nuisance. They are cutting their losses. It's a big break for us."

Seth jumped on that. "We just need someone to watch her until after the holidays. Nobody is doing any business the rest of this month. It's Christmas. By New Year's she'll be out of your hair. There are lots of families that want kids, right?"

The Morrows were silent. Seth took another cookie and dunked it, his stomach a little uneasy. If they didn't take her, he didn't know what he would do.

The kids came back in with Maddie holding Star's hand.

"Can we keep her?" Max asked.

"Children aren't objects," his mother said.

Star went to John's chair and tried to climb up on his lap. He finally relented and picked her up. She gave a cheeky grin then studied him and her smile went away. With a concerned face she touched chubby hands to his temples.

"Yes, I have a headache," he told her.

She nodded. Then he turned her around, seating her on his lap, facing the others. Max got her a cookie.

"Can she have one?" he asked Seth.

"Just half. I don't think she's had a lot of sweets," Seth warned.

"Well, is she staying?" Maddie asked. "'Cuz we already gave her a Korean name,"

Max jumped in excited. "Star Mi-hi Morrow."

Yes! Thank you, Max. Seth winked at the kid. "That sounds beautiful."

Kymber finally sat, accepting their fate. "It means beautiful joy," she told Seth.

"Aw. That's a good name," Seth said. "Do you like it Star?"

Star grinned and nodded, this time looking right at Seth. Yeah. He was pretty sure she understood a lot, even if she didn't talk.

John held the cup of milk up to Star's mouth so she could have some. She slurped and he wiped her face. Then he broke the cookie into a smaller bite and gave it to her.

"Through the holidays is fine," John finally said. "We'll need to get her a stocking."

"And a highchair and clothes, and—" Kymber jumped up and grabbed a notepad and pen from her junk drawer. "Just a few things."

"And she can sleep in my room," Maddie said.

John nodded. Then he looked back up at Seth and shook his head like he would get him back for this. But his body language relaxed and Star snuggled protectively in one arm.

Seth took a mental photo of them and smiled. He was pretty sure he'd finally done something right.

Jocelyn had her new cello with her at Cravings. She still couldn't believe it. The smooth wood, the vibration of the strings, the new bow, and a traveling case as well. She wanted to have enough songs so she could play on the small stage there in the evenings. She showed Brittany and Georgie the instrument.

"The Rochesters gave it to me at dinner last night. It's a thank you for helping Benny."

"You mean saving him from an avalanche?" Georgie clarified.

"Yeah." Jocelyn said. "I told them it was too much, but Mr. Rochester insisted."

"Well," Brittany lifted her hands. "What can you do? He's a multi-billionaire. I'm sure it's okay."

"Apparently Graeme was going to give me one for Christmas! Which is too much anyway, but they asked him for ideas and now I have one! I already learned three Christmas carols from a teacher on the Internet. And I know this amazing music teacher, but I can't afford him yet. But I'll figure it out. I need an apartment first."

"Graeme screwed himself," Brittany said. "That was a good gift idea."

"You're going to get an apartment?" Georgie asked.

"Yes. If Holliwell comes after me, they already know where to find me. It's not like I can hide, but I don't want the Morrows to be in danger."

"Why don't you just stay with Graeme?" Brittany asked.

"That's his place."

"I'm pretty sure he wants you to live there. It's big enough. You can have your own suite," Brittany added.

"I need to come and go as I want. And I want to do something on my own."

"Feeling trapped?" Brittany asked.

"No!" Jocelyn wanted to be with Graeme all the time, but she didn't want him to know what she was up to all the time, and was afraid she would slip and tell him something about her family before she was ready. "I've never had my own place. Even something small—which it would have to be in New York and with what I make. I need a third job."

"I think it's good for you to have your own place," Georgie supported. "I can help you look on Sunday if you like. Saturday is our march. There's still time if you want to come."

"I don't think protesting outside the office of Graeme's mom would be cool. She's a friend."

Georgie didn't look at her. "The Senator understands politics."

"And I'm working all day." Jocelyn added, "But be safe."

Brittany jumped into the awkward silence and held up a picture on her phone of herself in a retro outfit. "I made a special Rosie Riveter ensemble."

"I like it." Jocelyn approved.

"I have to get going." Georgie packed her stuff. "I'm meeting the organization team this afternoon. We're compiling a list of Obstructionists."

"A list?" Jocelyn asked. "What for?"

"You know, mailings and social media. And we can do protests at their offices."

Brittany smirked. "Throw paint, yell at them in elevators, you know—general harassment, nothing life-threatening."

Jocelyn frowned. "What if really crazy people *accidentally* get their address?"

"'Cuz that never happens," Brittany quipped.

Georgie snatched her purse from the table abruptly. Her voice had a slight edge. "Legal tactics only. It's about persuasion."

"Talking is about persuasion," Brittany argued. "But don't worry, I'll be there Saturday to watch your back."

Georgie nodded and hugged them both but didn't meet their eyes. Jocelyn knew she was irritated. There was nothing she could say or do to change that. She didn't understand why Georgie was doing this or how she could have changed so much. Maybe Jocelyn was wrong? Maybe these Obstructionists really were bad? But they were the only people fighting the government. And if they were bad, did that mean you hunted them down and harassed them? Isn't that what the government had been doing to everyone who disagreed with them?

Jocelyn shook her head. She was over-reacting. Georgie wanted to be more involved with public discourse. That's what she had told Jocelyn. It just felt like Georgie was separating from their group—from her. And Georgie was her anchor. The one that kept her grounded when she thought she might lose it.

Jocelyn put her new cello in the back office. It was the nicest thing she'd ever owned. She couldn't wait to play it again. Even if her fantasy of being a musician was stupid, she still loved the touch, and feel, and sound of the bow on the strings.

But guilt gnawed at her that saving Benny didn't make her worthy of the gift. He'd been hurt because of her.

Maybe separating from the group wasn't a bad thing. Jocelyn needed to be her own anchor, make her own decisions. And when she acted on those decisions, the further away everyone was from her, the better off they would be.

CHAPTER TWENTY-TWO

*J*ocelyn brought Italian food to Seth's secret lair.

Seth wanted to hang out, but she thought something else was on his mind. He hadn't updated her lately on Sabrina's work and she knew he had been in the Astoria office today getting a follow-up exam.

She wanted to talk about something too. She needed his help. He wouldn't want to go back to Colorado, but she knew despite what they had promised, she eventually would have to go. Project Sunday would haunt her if she didn't end it. They might have destroyed her records, but now there were hundreds of children, maybe more, being experimented on because of her, her DNA, and her ability to survive as long as she had.

Thinking about the medical chart she'd seen made her blood run cold all over again. How many "batches" had they mixed for testing?

Jocelyn pushed the emotional element aside. The logistics were key. She'd never planned anything this big. Moving out all the children, assuming they were willing, and getting them to safety under the nose of scientists and the military was seemingly impossible. And then, even if successful, what to do with them afterward. John and Kymber couldn't take care of a thousand kids.

She laughed at the idea. John would have a heart attack and Kymber would choke eating sweets.

She had an inkling about the Underground though and how to contact them. If she could coordinate with them, there might be deeper support. She suspected they might already have a way into the Holliwell complex and people working on the inside. She wouldn't be starting from scratch.

She hated to include her friends, but Graeme, Lena and Richie would be invaluable technical support. She would leave Al, Brittany, and Georgie behind. Though, Lena and Richie had already been through a lot. That might be asking too much. She sighed. That's why she needed Seth.

At the door, Jocelyn gave the secret knock that Seth insisted upon.

Seth opened the door about to welcome her then paused. "Uh-oh. I know that look. What's up?" The smell of garlic distracted him only a moment as he grabbed the bags of food, let her in, then dug into the garlic rolls. They were heavenly belly bombs of flavor, and she had a dozen of them. He shoved one in his mouth and grabbed another.

"I was thinking about Christmas presents," Jocelyn offered.

Seth's latest sanctuary was another studio about half the size of Graeme's kitchen. It had a queen-sized bed, a dresser, a desk and media stand, a separate kitchenette with a round table and four orange folding chairs. Nothing matched but it worked. On the wall, it looked like the owner either painted or had friends who painted. She didn't think they had much promise. The picture of the man by the sea was horrible.

"It's a paint by numbers," Seth said. "They all are. The owner was an addict and painting helped to distract him."

"Oh." Jocelyn focused back on the food. "I also need a Hanukkah gift for Lena. She said they celebrate both, so I'm confused about when to give it to her."

"Considering your luck, go with the earlier date. Or when you see her. Is everyone going to their parents for the holidays?"

"Yeah. It will be just us again." Jocelyn pulled out all the food and carefully opened it up.

"Umm." Seth was noncommittal.

She'd expected a joke. She glanced up, still holding plastic forks. She put them on napkins neatly. "What did Sabrina say?"

"The brain deposits are caused by a protein. I had shrinkage last check-up, but now they are growing again. 'Two steps forward, one back,' she said."

"Oh." Jocelyn grabbed two waters from the mini-fridge while Seth piled up his plate.

"She thinks treating the protein is not good because it can shapeshift and adapt, but she said my DNA has the blueprint for making the protein and my RNA is setting it in action. If we can cut off the RNA before it goes to work we can stop any of the effects. She's in touch with several doctors around the world who do similar work, but said she might need a year to develop a solution for me—which is fast, apparently."

"That's outstanding! You're doing well. The other drugs have helped the seizures. And if she can slow the proteins even a little that will help. We got this." Jocelyn felt encouraged.

"I'm not staying, Jocelyn."

He blurted it out.

"I knew when I was in that cell with Lena, it was my fault. I stayed too long. And it's not just about putting others in danger. I want to see a little of the world, be a beach bum, visit Zihuatanejo. I don't want to die in a big city, a number—or in a lab as a statistic and permanent experiment. I want sunshine and cool breezes. I want to play cards, learn to surf, maybe sail a boat. I need to go while I still can. I don't think I have a year. And I don't want to always be looking over my shoulder."

Jocelyn tried to breathe and stay calm. Her skin shimmered giving her away.

"Don't freak out."

"Wicker and Cashus won't bother us anymore."

"I really don't believe that. Wicker is relentless. She'll be back."

"What about…" *Me.* "All your friends here. And Star?"

"I know. But what about me? Seriously, you want me to live my life to make other people happy?" Seth shook his head. "That's what you do. That's not what I do."

"Don't be mean." She stabbed her lasagna three times in a mini-temper.

"I'm not. If you're happy that's fine, but I haven't even lived yet. Let me make my own choices without getting upset."

"How can I not be upset about it? You won't have medical treatment! Are you just giving up?" She glared at the beach picture on the wall as if that was the cause of all this. She wanted to send that ugly picture through the window.

"No. I'll take stuff with me and arrange shipments if needed and when there's a cure, I'll make arrangements. But I can't do this without your support."

Jocelyn's chest tightened. Of all the things to ask her. He knew how important he was to her. She nodded, fighting back tears.

"Don't cry."

"I'm not."

"I just want to be free. And there's only one way I can do that."

"I know."

181

"Then you'll support this?"

This time she blurted out the news. "I think there's a cure. Hidden in my parent's lab."

"The one that was destroyed?"

"Yes, but Greer said no one ever found my parents' safe. There are things I remember. I think I can find it. If there is a cure for Benny, then our cure is right around the corner."

"Great. Call me when you get that."

"Seth—"

"Are you going to support this?"

He was determined to leave. She could see it. She understood his desire to roam, to not be trapped, not be afraid anymore. He only ever wanted to be free. Free from his past and now free from his present. But free meant breaking their connection permanently.

"Can we at least have a party? And Christmas? I never had a Christmas—at least not in ten years. Kymber said it's her favorite time of year."

He relaxed. "Sure. I can leave after. But I need to start planning."

"Okay."

"Thank you," he said. He covered her hand and waited for her to look up. "You'll always be my Sunshine."

It was a truth and a joke. But right now, it seemed heart-felt.

She smiled, albeit with watery eyes. She couldn't tell him about her other plans now. It wasn't fair. She would move forward on her own. But she would do this first. She would say goodbye to Seth, and make sure that he really was, finally free.

Sabrina's excitement mixed with trepidation. She had a solution for Seth but couldn't shake the uneasy feeling that there was something in front of her that she was missing.

"Hi, Aunt Sabrina." Morgan entered the lab. Her security escort waited.

"I'll see her out," Sabrina told the escort. "Thanks."

Her niece was more subdued than usual.

"Everything okay?"

"Ugh. Not really. Benny had an episode this morning. Then he refused to see anyone, even Poem. She left crying. And with his one coherent movement of the day he threw his lunch plate at me." Tears welled up but Morgan brushed them aside. "And I have PMS."

Sabrina hugged her and brought her to a chair in her office. "I think I have chocolate."

"I don't want to break out." Morgan plopped in a chair. "But a little piece? You wanted a blood sample?"

"Yes. When did you last give one?"

"I don't know. Maybe eight years ago. Mom and Dad don't let the doctors take blood."

"But have you given any to A & R?" Sabrina asked. "Or anybody at all?"

"No."

"Okay." Then the blood sample she had was very likely not Morgan's which was her assumption. However, she needed to prove it decisively.

"Does this have to do with what you're working on for Benny?"

"Yes."

"Do you have a cure?"

"I have a clue. And I have an idea. It's based on the work your mom and dad did. I'm trying to recreate it. But they were years ahead of all of us."

"Dad says you're as smart as my first dad." She held out her arm.

"I hope that's smart enough." She wiped the vein inside Morgan's elbow and inserted a needle with a tube attached. "I'm taking four samples."

"Okay."

"How are your friends?" She tried to distract her niece.

"Fine. Meghana is great. I'm trying hard not to be so bossy and stuck-up. It helps overall with people. But the nicer I get the more annoying Jenna becomes. It's like she's trying to dominate just because I do something nice, and then I have to crush her, and I feel bad—a little."

"I noticed you've been different. I like it." Sabrina grinned. "It's hard when you're so awesome." She switched out a tube.

"I know, right? But I never felt *bad* about it before."

They laughed. Sabrina took the last tube of blood, withdrew the needle and pressed a cotton ball to the spot.

"And then Jenna said she's not going with me and Meg to the concert in January because she got better seats and VIP passes. And I'm like, whatever. We have backstage passes. My mom got us right in the front. She's stupid for showing off."

Sabrina never had these problems. She'd had her head in studies for so long. "So who will you take instead?"

"I don't know." Morgan held the cotton ball down. "I thought, maybe…Jocelyn? Would that be weird since she's Graeme's girlfriend?"

"Of course not." Sabrina taped the cotton ball.

"She's always nice to me. Even when I was mean. But don't you think she's a little weird?" Morgan opened her purse digging around.

Sabrina glanced up from marking the vials. "How so?"

"I don't know. She saved Benny from an avalanche. Who does that? Who knows *how* to do that?" She pulled out some lipstick.

"Didn't she grow up on a military base?"

"Still. I would *not* do that. Then she gets all this attention from everyone, and I get—"

"Insecure?"

"Thank you. But my therapist said to call it out and own it. Jealous. I start getting so jealous. It's like I can't stand it." Morgan put on a fresh coat of lipstick and smacked her lips before snatching a tissue from the desk and blotting. "And I say something mean, and she still acts nice, and I feel bad, and it's this whole vicious cycle!" Morgan summed it up with a helpless shrug. "I'm super grateful she saved Benny but now I'm jealous of how much Benny loves her."

"He loves you the most," Sabrina assured. "You're his one and only. You two have an unbreakable bond."

Morgan's eyes filled up again. "But now he's breaking."

Sabrina pulled her niece's chair to her and reached in for a hug.

"You must save him, Aunt Sabrina. You're the only one who can. I know it's impossible and I won't blame you if you can't. But will you promise to do everything you can, even if people think you're crazy?"

"Yes," Sabrina said. "I promise. No matter what it takes."

All she had to do was slow down time.

CHAPTER TWENTY-THREE

*G*eorgie pressed forward with her sign for a Free America as the crowd settled in Bryant Park and spilled into the streets.

The marchers gathered, their chants echoing within the valley of buildings. "Be a constructionist, not an obstructionist!"

Dougie, one of the leaders she worked with in the Student Union office, yelled to her over the chanting. "They estimate over twenty thousand! Not bad for our first run!" He high fived her.

Behind him, Brittany shook her head at his multi-colored striped shirt over jeans and bright yellow jacket. She snapped a picture. "I think I found a market with a need!"

They were waiting for the first speaker when something caught Dougie's attention. He turned and four guys in olive shirts with swastikas on them had climbed a nearby statue and were shouting obscenities randomly at the crowd. Everyone ignored them—mostly. Brittany pulled Georgie away from them, shaking her head.

Georgie searched for security. Only marchers were supposed to be allowed in the park, but in a big space it was easy enough for people to hop the barricades and cause trouble.

One of the neo-nazi guys eyed Dougie. Georgie thought Dougie inclined his head. He must have done something to piss off the guy, because he jumped toward Dougie over the crowd.

Georgie pulled Brittany back but the dense crowd gave them no room to hide. The guy landed on a bunch of girls, knocking them down and starting a wave of people falling and losing their balance. Then the other guys jumped the same way and ran across fallen bodies, trampling them and throwing fists to clear a path of escape.

One of the crazed-looking guys got near Georgie and stopped. He stared her in the eye, as if debating whether to hurt her. She stood her ground but moved her banner on the wood stick into an offensive position, squeezing the stick harder to fight her trembling.

He moved as if to push her and she shoved the stick in his face, surprising him and cutting him off. He got wild and started puffing up, cussing at her, and raising his fist in intimidation, but then other people put their signs in the same position as Georgie. Ready to strike. His buddy called him, and he took off.

"Someone stop them!" Georgie shouted. But the four jerks knocked down a barricade and took off down the street.

People lifted the fallen—a girl was bleeding at the mouth, another had a broken nose, others cried from their injuries.

Georgie spun as someone grabbed her shoulder. It was Brittany. She wasn't happy.

"I guess not everyone wants free education, free healthcare, and a free world."

As if cued, a new chant began, and even the wounded were buoyed by the hyped-up energy.

"Free books, free school, stop obstructing, it ain't cool!
Free health, free fuel, don't let losers rule!"

Dougie came through the crowd, high fiving everyone for overcoming and jumping up and down, shouting louder than ever. "Stop obstructing. It ain't cool!"

Brittany rolled her eyes and focused on snapping photos of the more ridiculous outfits.

After a while the crowd settled, and the speeches began. There was a California Senator, a Congresswoman, a former Secretary of Education, and Teresa Mercer, who emceed it all. The last was a graduate of Barnard and a formidable black woman. She had a fierce smile and she seemed to know everything about everyone. She never raised her voice and had a poise that indicated a quiet power you didn't mess with. Georgie aspired to that, if not the same career path. She had researched Mercer, though very little was available. The woman graduated from West Point then Barnard for graduate school. She had a software engineering degree, a law degree, and had been a researcher at the CIA before becoming Assistant to the Secretary of Information.

The woman also had the right sense of levity, remarking on a few of the hostile outbreaks in the crowd.

The rest of the rally went perfectly and everyone left to the sound of energizing music. Most dispersed down streets others hung out and supported local park vendors. Brittany motioned to her stomach, ready to bail and get food. They headed out and were several streets away when Georgie spotted Dougie. He was alone.

She was going to call out to him when he ducked with a covert glance into an Irish Pub.

Curious, Georgie pulled Brittany in that direction. "Let's go here."

Georgie walked inside the dark pub and stopped. Brittany walked into her from behind and complained.

"Sshh. Back up." She pushed Brittany outside. "Wait here. Give me your cap."

"I don't want to. My hair—"

Georgie grabbed the cap and snuck back into the pub. Sure enough, Dougie was at the table with the four neo-nazi troublemakers. They had different shirts on now. She saw him slide four envelopes across the table to each guy. They put the envelopes away, but one opened it and pulled out a bill, calling to the server. He ordered Dougie a beer.

Georgie hurried back out.

Brittany huddled against a wall, freezing. She snatched her cap back. "You owe me big for today. Or at least a good lunch."

"I know. Let's go. There's a better place. Not far," she promised.

Georgie didn't think she'd be able to eat. She needed to tell her leaders about Dougie. He was a mole. And he was working with the opposition.

Jocelyn played her new Christmas carols for Benny. He smiled appreciatively.

"You learned," he struggled to say the next word. "Quick."

"I know. It's like the only natural talent I have—other than languages. Supposedly my mom was really good. She played in an orchestra before she—" Jocelyn almost forgot herself. "Got a real job." Jocelyn ate one of his gluten-free cookies. "But, I met her cello instructor. Well I didn't actually meet him. I saw him then I stalked him. I don't have the guts to introduce myself yet."

Benny shook his head, eyes chastising.

"I want to be a little better first. He only takes the top students."

"You've only played for…three…days."

"Still, I might only get one shot at asking him. But enough about me. What song do you want me to learn?"

"Um. How…about…" He sipped his hot chocolate. "Grandma Got Runnn…over by…a Reindeer." He took a breath.

"That's not a song."

He laughed and nodded vigorously.

"It sounds sad. It's a Christmas song? I don't remember singing that when I was little. But, if it's a song. I'll learn it tonight."

"It's a happy song." Benny breathed easier for a moment.

"I guess they didn't like the grandma." She changed the subject. "How's Poem? What are you getting her for Christmas?"

Benny shrugged.

She knew there'd been some conflict between them. "Don't you like her anymore?"

Benny shook his head and rolled his eyes.

"Okay, so she doesn't like you? Or she doesn't like your new wheels? Or she's not a real friend, because a real friend sticks with you through the hard stuff. But if say she's a loser, I can take care of her. A big wad of gum in her hair, then honey on her face near a wasp's nest and—"

"No." Benny waved for her to stop.

"No wasps? How about ants? I hate ants."

He laughed again. "No. She's not…" His face changed. "A loser." He put his face in a hand, and waved the other for her to stop.

She put her cello bow down and knelt in front of him.

"Do you miss her?"

He shrugged.

"I'm pretty sure she misses you. You two are pretty close. It's got to be hard on her."

"I'm…" he put his head up. "Like this."

"Cute?"

He smiled.

"Okay, I get it. You feel awkward in a wheelchair?"

"Sometimes…I can't talk. Or eat…by myself."

"I guess," Jocelyn considered. "I would feel embarrassed if it was me. And I think I'd get frustrated and want to throw things."

He nodded.

"But there are still games and things you two can do together. Even watch a movie." Jocelyn took one of his little hands in both of hers and kissed it. "She might just want to hold your hand like I do. Don't give up on life yet, Benny. You need to fight for every moment."

He sighed then nodded.

She was pretty sure he missed Poem.

"You should text her. Want me to do it? I can write something juicy." She lifted her eyebrows with exaggerated inspiration. "Dearest Poem, your eyes are like black ink blobs. Your hair…the color of a worm that never saw light. Your smile—"

Benny shook his head vehemently, his expression one of mock horror. "I'll do it."

Jocelyn laughed. "I'll put my cello away." Jocelyn packed while Benny typed. Poem responded immediately.

"She wants to come over," Benny said.

"Of course. She's a good friend." Jocelyn made light of things, but she needed to tell him the serious stuff too. "John and Kymber taught me that when people care about you, you have a responsibility to them. Benny, there might be a time when you can't communicate with her or talk to her like you can now. And if you don't want to see her then, I won't blame you. But for now…do everything while you can. I'm not good at these things either but I think seeing her will make you happy. And you should be happy. It's Christmas after all." She enclosed his smaller hands with her own, getting even more serious. "I'm even learning a homicidal carol for you."

Morgan froze in the doorway. "Did I just interrupt something?"

Jocelyn straightened and smiled. "I told Benny I would learn the dead Grandma song for Christmas."

"Oh." Morgan nodded then entered. Apparently, she knew the song too.

Her sister looked beautiful as usual. She wore a lot of makeup up, but it was always the latest eye color, brow design, lip technique and cheekbone highlights. Jocelyn had watched her at Cravings in the restroom one night before her shift was over. She'd used lip liner, two colored sticks, and a gloss to create the perfect lips. Morgan was as expert as Brittany with makeup—maybe more so. As if knowing her lips weren't perfect right now, she pulled out some gloss and freshened them.

Then she went to Benny and smacked her lips on his cheek.

"Ew!" He smiled and rubbed it off.

"What did I miss?" Morgan asked.

"I'm just heading to work."

"Poem is coming over," Benny said slowly.

"She is?" Morgan perked up. "That's great. I miss her."

Benny gave a little head bob of agreement.

Morgan glanced back at her. "I'll see you later, Joss. I'm working a half shift tonight."

"You are? That's great. I thought you'd quit after you didn't have work anymore."

"Me too." She shrugged. "I find the people interesting sometimes. And it's a good experience in case I ever open my own chain of stores."

Jocelyn agreed with a wide smile. Not a store. A chain of stores. *Always going big.*

She gave Morgan an awkward one-arm hug that was more of a pat. Jocelyn had her cello in one hand and they weren't at the hugging stage yet anyway, but she also didn't want makeup on her clothes before work. Regardless, Morgan seemed to be warming up to her a little.

Jocelyn navigated the large mansion and was at the bottom of the steps when she heard a sarcastic comment from a deep voice nearby.

"Nice cello."

It was Rex.

Jocelyn swallowed and nodded politely, waiting to see his intent.

He had always been suspicious of her, but it had transformed into active distrust. Graeme's older brother seemed to have been born a cynic. He was as handsome as Graeme, but the dark features were usually wrapped in a scowl when directed at her.

"Seems strange to give you a reward when Benny would have never been targeted if not for you, right?"

Jocelyn tried to read his eyes. What did he know about her? Was he fishing for information? She kept silent.

"Ellis liked music too. Word is they won't find his body until spring. When the snow thaws."

"I'm sorry." She couldn't say much more.

"Tell that to his family. And Benny."

Jocelyn felt her throat tighten even more. Rex had a harsh side, but he was in the right.

"Did you have a lot of missions in the snow?" he asked.

"I'm sorry?" She tensed.

"It was a joke. You grew up on a military base." Rex clarified.

"Oh." It wasn't a joke. He was testing her. "I should go. Nice to see you." It wasn't nice. The words just came out nervously.

She turned and left. Rex had something on her. She didn't know what, but he knew about her missions. He had been in the military. He might have checked her out or had friends check her out. Hopefully that was all. It wasn't illegal to serve your country, even under-aged if your legal guardian permitted it.

It worried her though.

Rex was right that she was the target. He was right that she didn't deserve a reward. And he was right that she should apologize to Benny. Only an apology wouldn't fix anything. The only answer was a cure. And with every day, she seemed to be making things worse instead of better.

CHAPTER TWENTY-FOUR

*G*eorgie entered the university offices of the Work for Good Org. The main space had a bunch of beanbags, colorful desks, and a Ping-Pong table. The beanbags were taken with students on laptops working on something, probably scouring political candidates for Obstructionists.

Dougie stood in an enclosed glass office in the corner giving a passionate spiel to a group of new recruits that spilled out into the doorway. When he finished, they cheered and dispersed to go to their workstations. Had she cheered that first day? And when did Dougie get an office?

She noted that the club's faculty advisor was in the adjacent office. There were four advisors in total that rotated supervising during the week, and three full-time workers that maintained the office. Everyone else was a volunteer. The place was packed with volunteers. Technically, most of them got free health insurance and money for every march so it was not exactly volunteering.

"Hey!" Dougie waved to her.

She went to his door, her stomach twisting with nerves at confronting him. "Can we talk?"

"Sure. Everything okay?"

She closed the door. "Not really."

"Take a seat."

He sat on the edge of his desk. *To be higher than her?* His demeanor was dominant and superior. It made her uncomfortable. She remained standing.

"It's about those four guys who disrupted the rally."

"Yeah?"

"I saw you with them after the rally."

"Okay." He smiled, as if to say, 'so what.'

"I saw you pay them, then have a beer with them."

"Yes. I did. Why?"

Georgie stared at him, frozen. A feeling of nausea spun up in her belly. "Who are you working for? Are you an Obstructionist?"

"What?" He laughed, at ease, genuinely surprised. "No! Oh, my gosh. Is that what you thought?"

"Then what is going on?"

"That was a setup. The whole thing is. Everyone was paid to march. Those guys were paid to look like crazy Obstructionists. You know, disrupting the pure-hearted students. It was on TV. Did you see it? A few bad guys make our cause more empathetic. The march got a ton of free coverage, and did you see our social media? The dive into the crowd was epic! Someone actually caught it on their phone and posted it. A million views in the first twenty-four hours."

"I thought we were bringing attention to needy Americans who need better healthcare and education."

"We are. But it takes money to do that. The march was less than fifty grand with speaker fees. A commercial would be a couple million. You get it?"

"I get the money part—"

"Look, it's a business for some, and a lobby group for others."

Someone knocked on the door. Georgie turned. It was their advisor. She came in.

"Georgie just found out that we paid the disruptors to show up."

Their advisor turned to her and nodded, then shook her hand. "You're now in the inner circle. Welcome."

Now she was part of it? And she was supposed to be flattered?

"People got hurt. It could have been worse if someone fought back or a bigger fight was started." Georgie's heart pounded at the deception.

"I understand how you feel, Georgie. I used to feel that way too." The advisor took her hand and seated her in the chair, then took the one next to her. "There's a battle taking place for our country that most people are unaware of. You're entering it at the halfway mark. But we must do everything possible to support the President and stop the Obstructionists from taking over the government and repealing the compassionate laws that we've worked so hard to pass in the last fifteen years. The young men we hired were paid actors but,"—she emphasized—"they *represent* the real thing. We must show the world what the dark side of democracy looks like."

Georgie nodded but didn't speak. Their logic was so twisted she needed time to consider. Was she the crazy one?

"Thank you so much for explaining." If she was crazy, she wasn't going to show it. "I thought Dougie was a mole," she joked.

They laughed. She laughed with them. *What the—? I am such an idiot!*

"All right then. We're good," her advisor said. "I'll leave you both. But if you're in town before Christmas, you should come to the salon at the Provost's house. There will be some amazing and powerful people there. Most of them women. I think you'll like it. And great future connections for anyone considering law or public service. Dougie, give Georgie the details."

"Will do."

Their advisor smiled and studied Georgie carefully.

Georgie felt the assessment and pulled out her biggest look of gratitude. "I would love to attend! Thank you so much for the invitation and being such a champion for me."

"Of course, dear." She winked at Dougie and left.

Dougie took a seat at his desk and pressed some buttons on his computer. "This is good Georgie. Trust me. You'll move up in the ranks really fast. All the key leaders are going to be there. The pay is good, but there are great perks in terms of networking."

"That's awesome. Thank you." Earnest and ingratiating— she never thought she'd pull off lying so well. She took the invitation he printed for her and noted the date. Then she high-fived him and said she needed to get to a class.

What she really needed was a shower.

It was three weeks until Christmas. Jocelyn wasn't completely sure what the excitement was about, but Maddie had assured her Christmas was the best. Lots of parties, games, presents, people visiting, and everyone was happy. They went to church. There was music and all her favorite carols—which Jocelyn had diligently learned.

Jocelyn tried to remember her last real Christmas. It popped into her mind now and again when she wandered the streets of New York and saw lights, a shop, a display, or heard a song her mom used to sing. But more often, she felt a feeling—one she hadn't felt in a long time—and it made her insides ache to the point of pain. As much as she tried, she couldn't pinpoint the source of the longing or grasp this intangible thing she seemed to desire so much.

"Jocelyn, baby. Help your daddy put the star on the tree." Her mother bounced Benny on her lap while Morgan slept in a big leather chair, wrapped in a fluffy red blanket, exhausted from decorating.

Two strong hands gripped under her ribs and Jocelyn felt herself lifted. She put the star on the top. Her dad lowered her then plugged it in. Magic.

Jocelyn clapped. "It's perfect."

"Yes, it is. And so are you." Her father enfolded her in his arms and spun her in a circle making her squeal. Her mother shushed them so they wouldn't wake Morgan and they just laughed instead.

"I have hot cocoa with marshmallows," Sabrina said, coming from the kitchen.

"Yay! I love Christmas," Jocelyn declared.

Jocelyn squinted, trapped by the memory. *Love?* She couldn't remember loving anything.

Ten years ago, she had spent Christmas in a hospital. Nine years ago, when she was eight, she'd spent four days in solitary confinement for complaining she wanted a Christmas tree. Four days had felt like a month. It took her weeks to recover. Before that, two days had been the most for a standard "time out" when she didn't behave perfectly—like when she didn't promptly tell her uncle she loved him for his latest test. He demanded she say she loved him after putting her fingers in acid. He had erased her fingerprints to hide her identity and he wanted her to kiss his hand with gratitude.

Jocelyn closed her eyes, released a breath to fight the attack of resentment.

The final eight Christmases at Camp Holliwell had been quiet. Everyone left for a few days, and she usually had a soldier or handler check in on her. She did her runs every day, but the rest of the time she was locked in the condo she shared with her "uncle," who was really her legal guardian for the purposes of scientific experimentation. He took the week off, but she was left with plenty of homework to do.

Holidays were the loneliest times of the year. This one might end up being the strangest.

Someone touched her shoulder. The firm warmth comforted her instantly.

Graeme.

"Are you okay?"

She stared at him confused. There was an ornament in her hand. She'd forgotten where she was. How did she get here? How long had she been standing there?

She blinked, getting her bearings, taking in the smell of pine, apples and chocolate before connecting with the subtle scent of Graeme's cologne and laundry detergent—definitely competition for favorite scents going on. Oddly, it causes stress and pleasure and confusion.

They were at John and Kymber's. Everyone was there—all her friends, Kymber's parents, and even little Star who was in Seth's arms drinking milk from a sippy cup. They stared at her, waiting.

"Sorry?" she said.

Kymber smiled. "The kids said you should put the first ornament on this year."

Jocelyn swiveled to the tree then to everyone. They had looks of expectation. She stared at the ornament in her hand. Maddie told her it was always the first one. A little baby in a manager. "I'm not sure." A pulse in her throat beat unnaturally.

She searched out John for help, ready to hand the ornament to him.

John lifted a hand toward the tree, reassuring.

She swallowed and turned back to the tree. The already looked pretty with just the colored lights. "Anywhere?"

"Yep," John said. "Plenty of space. You can't screw it up. Unless you drop the baby Jesus. That would be a family trage-dy."

Jocelyn quickly put her other hand under the ornament. She could feel the heat building in her body, even her toes were sweating. She took another step, not sure where to put the or-nament and avert a family tragedy.

"I think she's hyperventilating under the pressure."

Was that Brittany? Was she hyperventilating?

A strange buzz started in Jocelyn's ear. Just when she thought she might faint, something warm connected with her.

Graeme had an arm around her waist. He stepped her closer to the tree, his whisper tickling her ear. "It's supposed to be fun. There's no wrong choice."

She nodded, cursing herself for not doing Internet re-search on tree trimming. Just breathe. Stay calm. No one is going to punish you for not knowing where to put it.

Graeme stepped away.

She put the ornament hook on a branch, her hands trem-bled so hard she could barely secure it. Anxious, she took a breath and turned to the group.

"Is that okay?"

"I don't know. We can't see it." John teased.

She hurriedly stepped aside.

"Oompa!" John shouted.

Jocelyn jumped.

"It's a party," John declared, flipping on music and raising his drink. All the gang clinked glasses. Seth tapped his coke and to Star's sippy cup. Maddie and her grandparents clapped.

"Perfect!" Kymber told her, stepping over Max and giving her a hug.

"You can move it if you don't like it," Jocelyn said.

"Jocelyn. It's perfect." Kymber kissed her cheek.

Jocelyn finally smiled. The ornament was okay. Everyone was happy. She should be happy too. She loved parties. Nearly everyone she cared about was here.

She stepped back. Then another step.

The world closed in.

Star gave her a worried frown and reached out from Seth's arms but Jocelyn hurriedly ducked, turned, and scrambled through the kitchen into the yard.

The only thing she cared about was getting away.

CHAPTER TWENTY-FIVE

The cold air shocked Jocelyn but felt good. She took a breath, then another, not stopping until she reached the furthest corner of the yard and was blocked by the fence. Her attempts to gather herself failed. Definitely hyperventilating now.

"Jocelyn?" Graeme called out, coming toward her. "What is it?"

"Nothing. Go back! I'm okay." She pressed her back against the fence, trapped, desperate.

He kept coming.

"I'm okay. Go away!" Panic pounded in her chest again. *What was this?* She flattened her hands to the rough wood of the fence, focusing on the texture, trying to ground herself.

Graeme stopped about four feet away. They were in the darkest part of the yard, but she could see his face in the lights from the neighbor's yard.

"Talk to me."

"I'm okay. I just need space."

"You're scared," Graeme said. "It's okay to be scared."

"But I'm happy."

"Yeah. I get it."

"You do?"

"Everyone you love—or everyone you *care* about"—he corrected—"is here. Together. It doesn't happen all the time.

And nothing's wrong. We're not at a hospital or a burning building, or a train wreck. For one moment, the world is just right."

"Then why do I want to cry? Why is my heart pounding like I'm going to explode?"

"Well…" Graeme didn't move from his spot.

"Don't say it. You're wrong."

"Jocelyn, this. This night. These people are here because of you." He took a cautious step forward. "This is what regular people call love."

She wanted to scream. She nearly did. "It doesn't last!"

"These moments don't last. But caring for people does. You'll still care about everyone tomorrow, when you're at work, or in the shower, or saving the world. It's what drives us all— well not everyone. But most of us." He conceded. "You've had a different life."

"The last time I felt this, I was a child. I was tricked. And then everything was gone. I feel like my parents lied to me about everything. Otherwise, how could I lose…everyone? How could they have let all those things happen to me?"

"I don't know." Graeme's voice was soft. Truthful. He didn't have an answer for any of that. "But now you've gained so much. There are a lot of people who love you and care for you in a way you don't even understand yet."

"You can't just take away ten years."

"I'm not trying to. But it's okay for you to enjoy this. To-night. Embrace it. Let yourself feel what it's like to be…part of a family."

Jocelyn's eyes burned. "Even if it doesn't last?"

"Even if it doesn't last, it doesn't make it less good." Graeme took another step closer. "Some things are precious. You're supposed to be afraid of losing them."

She scrubbed her eyes roughly and nodded. He took the final three steps and embraced her.

"You're precious to me," he said.

"You're precious to me too." It felt good to say it. She sighed with relief and leaned into him, emotionally exhausted.

The lights in the yard started flicking on and off. She spotted Seth on the patio doing John's warning maneuver.

They went to Seth and Jocelyn hugged him, hard—so he would feel it for a while. He gasped for air.

"You're my family, Seth." She whispered in his ear.

He hugged her back. "Good. Cuz' you're the only one on the planet who would actually claim me." He leaned back and ruffled her short hair. "Come on. Star is worried. And we don't get to eat until the tree is trimmed. Kymber knows how to motivate people."

Jocelyn laughed. She joined the group. Tim and his husband gave her hugs on her way back into the room. Kymber handed her some drinks to bring to the girls. At the tree, Al covered the taller spots while Richie and Lena worked covertly in the back. Brittany debated the merits of ribbon, and Georgie did the middle. Star, Max and Maddie had the bottom branches covered. John had his feet up and occasionally directed.

Georgie handed her a box of ornaments. "You do these. Just spread them evenly around the front from top to bottom."

"How did your march go? You never said."

"It was very successful," Georgie said.

Something in her voice wasn't right. "Weren't you happy with it?"

"Well, there were some jerks, but it was okay in the end. I'm just not sure everything is what I thought. I need to do some research."

"Oh." Jocelyn felt bad. "I'm sorry if I wasn't totally supportive."

"It's a good thing you weren't there."

"But I support you, regardless. I want to make sure you know that."

Georgie hugged her.

"Don't crush the ornaments," Brittany said.

"We're not," Georgie answered.

"Slacking," Brittany added.

"How many have you done?" Al asked.

"I'm directing," Brittany voiced like a boss. "Now move that big red one a little to the left, Al." She grinned, softening her tone. "That's better."

Jocelyn hung her batch of ornaments, checking with John for approval. He gave her the thumbs up.

She smiled, remembering her father doing that. It was okay. This wasn't a replacement for what she lost—just something new. The music, the chatter, the food, the hugs—she liked it. A lot. Graeme was right. It didn't make it less good.

Even though she knew it couldn't last.

Evie shivered from the cold, watching the homey scene. Fools. She turned and left the holiday neighborhood. Wicker would want a report out. Seth needed to be taken quietly in an alley. She hadn't picked his spot yet. Wicker thought he might be willing to come freely. Evie didn't think so.

As if reading her thoughts, Seth looked out the window. She ducked behind a tree. There was no way he could see her, yet she felt his eyes on her.

An old warrior once told her he could tell when it was his time. Death followed him for days, picking the right moment. Death was merciful like that. Warriors were allowed to say their farewells then go off quietly into the woods to accept their fate. She remembered an old warrior that did that. They found him a couple of days later at his campfire. He had died in his sleep.

Seth had that look now. The multi-colored tree illuminated one side of him. A big black guy handed him something to drink. He accepted the drink and slapped the guy on the shoulder. He was making his farewells. He knew it was his time.

Evie disappeared into the night. Seth deserved his last days. Perhaps if she was merciful, death would show mercy to her when it was her time.

It was the only hope she had left.

CHAPTER TWENTY-SIX

Seth ducked behind a display of mechanical frogs and plastic toys. Someone was following him. He had felt it for days.

Today he led them on a little trip around Chinatown, in and out of streets, chatting up vendors, backtracking, and getting visuals. It was a girl. And she was pretty good. She mixed up her clothing several times, forcing him to find her again and again.

But he was better than most at hiding and seeking.

Finally, he went through the Wong's mini grocery store. The Wongs were the first people to give Jocelyn a job when she came to New York and had often kept her fed and Seth fed. Jocelyn still worked for them but more to make sure they had help unloading supplies. Seth came for the Mrs. Wong's noodles. The tiny, ancient woman gave him a headshake as he hurried past the cash register. He opened the back door into the alley and let it swing, then snuck up narrow stairs to the second floor.

The stalker came through the store, hurrying when she realized what he was up to. Mrs. Wong cut her off at the door in Chinese. Seth wasn't sure what the old lady said, but guessed it was something like people weren't allowed back there.

It gave Seth time to see his tail. It was Evie. He'd had a feeling—he just didn't want to believe she'd be back—that they'd be back.

Evie finally made it by Mrs. Wong and rushed into the alley. Seth jumped from the second floor before she could look up. Hearing him, she moved stealthily, spinning back for safety.

He landed, stood straight and waited.

"Hey, Seth."

All right, first name basis.

"Evie. I knew you had a thing for me."

She laughed out loud. "Thank you. For making me laugh. Not everyone can do that."

"It's a gift. Merry Christmas."

She inclined her head but didn't return the greeting.

"I was told there was a deal made," he said. "My friends and I are free and clear."

"Yeah. Good luck with that. Dr. Wicker didn't know you took 700 when she made that deal. So it's you or her."

"You came to negotiate?"

"Just making the offer. Your brain is more valuable to Wicker's research than the kid. But if you give her back, we can make a deal."

"No deal."

"I figured." Evie tucked her hands in her pockets. "Do you want to come back alive?"

"Hell no."

"Yeah. I figured that too."

"So we're at a standoff." Seth shoved his hands in his jacket, mimicking her stance.

"It's inevitable. I don't want to hurt anyone else in the process, believe it or not. I'm just trying to live another day myself."

"Runaway with me."

"Right." Evie smiled. It made her pretty in an exotic way.

"Seriously. We can make it. There's an Underground organization. They'll help us."

"There's no escape. There's only survival. And running just pisses them off. They are the least creative people on the planet until it comes to torture."

Seth laughed. "Yeah. But it's worth a try." So, she wasn't going to kill him right now.

"Why have you waited?"

"I don't know." She sighed. "I wanted to apologize first. Tell you I'm sorry about how all this had to go."

"Thanks. Believe it or not, I do understand more than you realize."

"Thanks."

"Will you shoot in the chest. Right here." Thumped his chest. "Since you're breaking my heart anyway. Leave my face alone so I can have an open casket?"

"Sure. Like I said. She needs your brain. One shot. In the heart. It will be over quickly."

"And the kid will be okay?"

"I don't have the power to guarantee, but if something changes, I'll do what I can to protect her. Would that be enough?"

"Does your word mean anything?"

"Not so much. Does yours?"

"About the same," Seth said, matter of fact. "I'd shake on it, but I don't think you'd be able to fight my magic touch."

"No doubt." She checked the time. "Two days, Seth. I can't hold them off longer."

He turned to enter the back of the shop, leaving her.

He had a lot of things he needed to take care of in the next forty-eight hours.

Sabrina was excited. They'd had a breakthrough. "Seth, it's an initial test, but it worked. We were able to take a slice of your DNA then repair it with the prototype's DNA."

Seth didn't respond. His mischievous brown eyes lacked their usual twinkle, and he didn't seem interested in anything, even his own health or recovery.

"Are you feeling all right? Have you had any seizures recently?"

"No. I'm good."

"This is exciting." She pushed the lab photo of DNA across the table.

"I'm not super smart or anything, but how would making my DNA more like the prototype's DNA help me?"

"The prototype's DNA has a self-repairing gene that searches and replaces broken or useless DNA. It essentially reads and reboots."

"And…" Seth shook his head.

"We just need to find the strand related to the proteins affecting your brain and apply the replacement DNA."

"What if there isn't a replacement DNA? And how would my body even do that? Change millions of cells or DNA bits everywhere?"

"I'm not exactly sure," she admitted. "There would be an incubation phase."

"Uh-huh. So what. A couple years of research?"

"Well."

Seth stood up. "Dr. Albrecht." He corrected. "Sabrina. The prototype has the same disease. It's just progressing slower. She's a goner too."

"She?" *That was a clue.*

"He. She. Whatever. This isn't gonna work."

"Is she still in New York?" Sabrina probed.

"Trust me. *He* is long gone. Last I heard, somewhere in Patagonia, looking at llamas. Before that, surfing in South Africa. Living the good life, while it's good." Seth grabbed his cowboy hat and plunked it on his head. "I just wanted to let you know I'm going out of town for a while. Visit the beach and stuff. Winter is damn cold here."

"Oh." If he left, Sabrina would lose access to Seth and the prototype. A feeling of hopelessness sucked the air out of her.

"Sabrina, focus on Benny."

"I am."

"For real. And give me your phone number."

"You're not going to send naked pictures, are you?" She was worried about him but knew not to show it.

"Only if you want me to."

He had his phone ready and she gave him the digits.

"That's my private cell. You can call if you need anything, or if you get worse while you're gone. Anything. When will you be back?"

"Not sure yet." He shrugged into a worn leather jacket. "I want to explore a little without a timeline."

"My friend owns a beach house if you want to stay there. Down in Florida."

"I'm okay. Thanks."

He lifted his hat and gave her a long hug. She hugged back. He certainly did have a nice, warm, solid body.

"I really appreciate everything you've done, and all you're doing. And I also really do think you're an amazing woman, not just a hot doctor."

Sabrina didn't like the tone in his voice. It was too sincere. "This isn't goodbye. Where are you going?"

"I have a loose plan, but I don't like to be committed." He patted her shoulder. "That's why it could never work between us."

She slapped his hand away with a laugh. "You're completely incorrigible."

He slid his worn-out cowboy hat back over tousled blonde hair and smiled. "Now and always, Doc."

CHAPTER TWENTY-SEVEN

*J*ocelyn hooked her arm through Seth's and guided him into the coffee shop. She was grabbing some hot drinks before they went into the Winter Festival at the Brooklyn Botanic Garden. She was excited to explore, but mostly because there would be music. She was more relaxed today, getting familiar with holidays and the warm, happy feelings she was having.

They ordered drinks and she opened the program to show Seth so they could plan what to do first.

"What's Graeme's ETA?"

"He said ten minutes." She checked her phone. "And Morgan is coming. She invited herself." Jocelyn was happy about that even if it was because Morgan had a crush on Seth.

"Don't look at me," he said. "I haven't encouraged it. I'm just friendly."

He took his beanie off and rubbed his temple. "I'm gonna sit outside for a second."

"Sure. I'll wait for the drinks. Are you okay?"

"Headache or something. Don't worry. It's nice out. Blue skies."

"Yes." She smiled wide. Her heart felt a little lighter today.

He kissed her on the cheek then went outside to a small metal table. The inside of the café was half full. Nobody sat outside. It was in the forties but with the breeze, it felt colder.

Jocelyn checked on Seth to make sure he didn't have a seizure. They called her name, and she picked up the cup holder with four drinks, and strolled outside. It was cold but the air was fresh and the sky clear—the perfect winter day.

A girl bumped her from behind, passing her on the sidewalk and Jocelyn quickly balanced the drinks, saving them. Seth had his head down and looked up.

But not at Jocelyn.

He stared at the girl in the green overcoat who just bumped her. Jocelyn expected to see him smile flirtatiously.

He didn't. He didn't even blink.

She saw the gun too late.

"No!" The drinks fell from her hand.

The gun exploded.

She shot energy outward, blindly, but it was too late.

Seth flew backward from the force of the bullet.

Jocelyn screamed, shock igniting every cell in her body. Her mind spun dizzily as she stumbled to the ground where Seth's body slipped from the chair. She vaguely heard other screams from in the café and people on the street taking cover.

Seth's eyes met hers, wide open. "Hurts," he whispered.

She touched his chest and pressed. Shock hit her again. Red moisture oozed over her hand.

"This was not the plan." Helpless tears fell. "Seth."

"Sorry, Sunshine." He struggled to take her hand. Pressing it to his jacket pocket.

"I know. I'll take care of everything." She kissed his forehead, lifting his upper body into her arms. "I promise."

Someone came near. Morgan! Her tanned olive skin turned pale. Her eyes dilated. "Seth?"

"Call an ambulance!"

"On the way!" Someone called out.

Jocelyn knew her scream bordered on hysterical. She bobbed forward and back, the same way Richie did when he was trying to hold it all together. She screamed again in anger and agony.

Graeme pushed through.

"Get away!" She yelled at him, holding Seth, protecting him. No one would touch him. "Get away!" And she wouldn't let anyone take him. Not without her. She wiped her face. She needed to see clearly. She needed to complete this mission. This was not the time for tears. She bundled up her scarf and pressed it to his chest, holding it.

"Jocelyn," Graeme knelt down.

"Don't touch him!" She choked on the pain. Seth didn't move. *This was not the plan.*

Graeme's heart pounded. Seconds before he'd been teasing Morgan.

"Are you going because you want to spend time with me, or you want to flirt with Seth?"

"I want to spend time with you, and I want to get to know your girlfriend better." She patted his hand as they drove in the Porsche. "Seth just makes the two of you more tolerable."

"Gee. Thanks."

"The coffee shop is just another block. I think I see Jocelyn, aaaand—" Morgan stretched out the word before adding, "She dropped all the drinks. Nice to know she's not—"

Morgan stopped.

Graeme turned, slowing with the traffic.

"Something happened!" His sister shoved open the car door with urgency. He braked before she killed herself. Morgan shot out of the car and took off at a run.

"Morgan! Geez." He drove onto the sidewalk to see better then parked illegally before jumping from the Porsche. A crowd formed ahead. Someone screamed. Panic made his legs move faster. *Jocelyn?* Jocelyn didn't scream.

His head got light. Jocelyn kept screaming—agonized, shocked, helpless screams. He couldn't take it in.

She curled over someone—Seth. Blood covered her chest and hands. It wasn't hers. She pressed a bunched-up scarf over Seth's heart as if to stop the bleeding.

His mind scrambled to understand. Greer's plan didn't work. They came back. One shot. Seth wasn't moving. It had only taken one shot. It didn't make sense. Seth was too strong. Too young. This wasn't right. If they killed him, then none of them were safe.

"The ambulance is here," someone called out. An EMT came over. Another grabbed the gurney.

Jocelyn lifted Seth's upper body. The medic and Graeme quickly grabbed his lower half. They had Seth in the ambulance in seconds.

Graeme stood helpless at the closing doors of the ambulance. Jocelyn simply shook her head.

The driver took off and the EMT in the back closed the dividing curtain between them. He gave Seth a shot and hooked him up to some monitors, communicating Seth's status to someone at the hospital who calmly gave orders. Seth's heartbeat began to fade.

The EMT pressed his lips, anxious. "If you have anything you want to say…"

Jocelyn nodded, clutching Seth's hand to her chest. She caressed his cheek lightly. His skin had become cool. She could feel his pulse, once so powerful, now a fading whisper. He'd challenged her, betrayed her, befriended her, and became a brother when she had no one else. She left Holliwell searching for her family, and instead, they had made their own—a little bit on the crazy side, sure, but no less powerful. She brushed his thick blonde hair.

He needed to be free. She just never wanted it to be this way.

Jocelyn sniffed hard and wiped her eyes. He didn't move. She leaned over him as close as she could, rested her forehead against his temple, and whispered close into his ear, wanting him to know so much that she had left unsaid. But she only had a few words.

"You will always be in my heart."

The ambulance doors closed on Jocelyn and Seth. Graeme stood there in shock until Morgan grabbed his arm. Black mascara streaked down her cheeks.

He hugged her. "Come on. We need to get to the hospital. Where did they go?"

"I don't know." She called to people to see if anyone knew what hospital the ambulance was going to. Someone said Kings County was the closest.

They raced to the Porsche and rode in silence to the hospital.

There was only one ambulance outside of the emergency room. He hurried inside ignoring directions for "visitors". It was surprisingly silent. But it was Sunday morning.

Two staff in scrubs came out of a curtained space followed by a young-looking doctor. Someone turned off a heart monitor machine. He hurried to them.

"Nineteen-year-old. Male." Graeme's throat tightened. He couldn't say more. There *he* was. Still on the gurney.

The doctor assessed him. "I'm sorry. It was a fatal shot. It was over before he got here." He closed the curtain on Jocelyn bent over the body. "I told her she could take her time. But you can't be back here."

"What?" Morgan trembled, shock taking over.

Graeme didn't move. Seth was dead? Just like that.

It didn't seem possible. He felt lightheaded. His feet stumbled for grounding.

"I'm sorry." The doctor said again. He didn't call security. He seemed to think they weren't a risk. He left. The rest of the staff went about their business cleaning up around them, working a desk, filling out paperwork and other random tasks while they stood there in shock, their world disrupted.

Morgan clutched his hand, convulsing quietly against him, choking on her cries. She started to go in, but he held her back.

"We..." Graeme's throat caught. "We should give her a minute." He put his arm around his sister and pulled her close, the two supporting each other as they stared through the curtains at Jocelyn's body thrown over Seth's, her arm over his chest, cheek pressed to his.

Jocelyn finally straightened, kissed Seth's cheek, then pulled the sheet over his head. Graeme went toward the bed. He wanted a moment with Seth too.

"Jocelyn?"

Her face was ravaged with tears.

She stepped on the roller brakes that kept the bed in place. "Hold that door."

"What? You can't—"

He and Morgan blocked the door to the hallway leading outside.

"We can't—" A million legal questions flooded his brain. And in a minute, the entire staff would notice.

Before he could consider his options, the door whisked open on them. A girl with a hooded green jacket entered.

"Hey!" Morgan yelled. "Hey! Stop! Graeme, she's the one who shot Seth!"

They all froze. Graeme's head spun between Jocelyn with a dead body and Morgan with the killer.

The shooter stared at the three of them, focusing on Jocelyn about to wheel Seth's body somewhere. Then she pulled a gun, shocking them and the nearby nurses.

"Gun!" Morgan screamed.

"Get away." The girl ordered a warning.

She didn't want to kill them?

Staff ducked. An alarm went off. People scrambled for cover.

Graeme stared at the barrel of the gun a few feet away. He moved slowly in front of Morgan pulling her behind him. A second later, the girl and her gun went flying backward, somersaulting uncontrollably.

When he turned, Jocelyn had already rolled Seth away. What she planned to do with the body, he had no idea, but he ran after her.

CHAPTER TWENTY-EIGHT

Outside, Jocelyn pulled the cigarette from the EMT's finger as he blew smoke into the cold air. He turned to her then stepped back as she maneuvered the bed.

"I need your help with this. We're transferring him." She shoved a thousand-dollars cash in his hand from Seth's wallet. "You drive."

His partner in the driver's seat came at her. "We don't do that—"

She held up her hand to send enough energy to block him. He stopped. Shook himself, then tried again. She blocked him again. The third time he ran at her. The block sent him backward, falling on the curb.

Morgan yelped as he landed at her feet, stopping her escape. Graeme pulled his sister away.

The first EMT decided to be on Jocelyn's side. He pocketed the cash. "For the record, I'm being forced against my will."

"Deal."

They got the bed in the vehicle, and he scrambled to the front. "Where to?"

Jocelyn reached for the doors.

"Jocelyn," Graeme interrupted. "Where—"

A van squealed to a stop behind them. Chang got out and lifted a weapon.

"Get down!" Jocelyn shouted.

Graeme spun then pushed Morgan to the ground.

Jocelyn shot a blast of energy at Chang's hand then pulled the doors of the ambulance. "Go! Go!"

Wheels squealed as the ambulance squealed took off.

Jocelyn moved to the front of the vehicle behind him, opening Seth's wallet. "Head to Brighton Beach. I have another thousand if you can get us up on the sand. My friend wanted to die at the beach. That's all I'm asking of you. I'm not going to hurt you."

The guy gave her a quick look. "Yeah. I get it. Hold tight. It's a straight shot down Ocean Parkway, but you don't want to alert any cops."

Jocelyn thanked him. Then she went to the back of the vehicle and tucked sheets around the body.

Graeme and Morgan squealed out of the lot. Graeme gave his sister a quick look. Her cheeks had gone from pale to flushed. She'd been in the line of fire twice. His parents were going to kill him. But he needed her help right now.

"Where's that van?"

"Right!" Morgan pointed. "What's going on? Why did they kill Seth? Why are they following Jocelyn? Where's she taking him? Is that legal?" She twisted her hair and pulled it. "I don't think that's legal." She panted with increased stress. "There! Ocean Parkway!"

Graeme made a hard left. "Seatbelt!" There was traffic, but not much in their direction. It was too cold for the beach.

Morgan scrambled to obey. Graeme pulled the console under his seat that Richie had installed and grabbed the gun, putting it on her lap with a warning. "Hold that."

She held it. Face tense. Then she sat up, pointing. "That's Seth's killer!"

The girl leaned out of the van a few cars ahead of them and aimed a weapon at the ambulance.

Graeme swerved to the far right and put his window down. "Give me the gun." He took it from Morgan and aimed. Morgan jumped when he shot. *Not good.* She should not be here. This was definitely not safe.

The shot alerted the girl. She ducked back in for safety then out again. He shot
another warning shot.

She shot one back at his bulletproof glass and seeing the result, ducked back in.

Morgan peeked from the low position on the floorboards where she had slid for cover.

"Morgan, I need you to keep a secret. Can you do that for me?"

She glanced up at him like she didn't recognize him but nodded, speechless for a change.

Between the cold weather and everyone at Sunday morning services, the road to the beach was fairly empty. A small win. He opened the center panel and pressed a code. "Nellie, activate missiles."

"Missiles? Missiles!" Morgan shot up in her seat. "Graeme! That's not legal!" She asked to be sure. "Right?"

"Neither is people shooting at us." He spoke to his onboard computer. "Nellie, left tire."

Nellie spoke back. "Left tire. Prepare to evade."

"Where's the missile coming from?"

"Under the headlight. Hold on!"

"Oh-my-gosh!" Her eyes widened to saucers. "Do mom and dad know about this?"

The screen blinked three times on the tire and kept a solid beep when it locked.

"Secret."

The missile fired.

"Remember."

Morgan stared straight ahead. "Secret. Got it."

The missile hit the van's back left tire. It exploded. The van skid and tipped. He swerved hard and fast around it. A glance in the rearview mirror revealed it flipping just as Seth's assassin leaped free of the tumbling mess.

Morgan's head swiveled back at him then back at the scene. "That girl jumped!"

The ambulance got away. He slowed down, keeping it in his sights.

Morgan twisted back in her seat staring out at the road. "Uh, Graeme." She grabbed her purse and dug frantically. "You better hurry." She opened the sunroof.

He caught sight in the rearview mirror and cursed. The girl gained on them. He put the Porsche in high gear. He debated the red light then ran it. Horns honked loudly.

The assassin jumped for the Porsche.

In the same instant, Morgan released her seatbelt, flipped on the seat and popped up from the sunroof meeting the girl head-on.

CHAPTER TWENTY-NINE

The Porsche swerved through the intersection with Morgan wobbling out the sunroof like an inflatable in the wind.

A fierce scream sounded from his sister. Whether it was from fear or to scare the assassin he didn't know.

A second later, their attacker rolled on the street.

Morgan took her seat and closed the sunroof. She took a breath and felt her head as if making sure all her hair was still there.

Impressed, he gave her a curious glance.

She held up the small device. "Supercharged pepper spray. Three different settings. Sprays up to ten feet. I used 'hostile hose.'" She put the spray back in her purse. "Very effective."

Graeme squeezed her trembling hand. "As Seth would say. Outstanding."

Shaking, she buckled her seatbelt. "Sorry for thinking you were such a nerd."

The ambulance stopped at the sand.

"We're here," the EMT said. "That van crashed somewhere back there. There's a Porsche following us, and not sure about that psycho girl. I think she got hit by a car."

Jocelyn nodded.

She jumped out the back of the ambulance and pulled the body. It was wrapped in white sheets. The EMT helped her and closed the doors.

"You should go now," she said. "Be safe."

"You'll be okay?"

"Yes. Thank you. And, yes, you were forced against your will and barely escaped."

"But I'm too stressed to remember what you look like. Good luck." He saluted, hopped into the driver's seat, and took off.

Jocelyn carried the body over her shoulder, across the sand—close enough to hear the waves. She lay it down. A cold breeze blew sand over the sheets. She took a breath. She wasn't sure she could do this—emotionally or physically.

The Porsche drove up. Morgan and Graeme got out. She held a hand up to Graeme. *Please don't come here.*

He understood. He told Morgan to stay back. Morgan paused, conflicted.

A moment later, a silver BMW jumped the parking lot curb, sprayed sand on Morgan and spun out near Jocelyn.

Evie leaped out. Jocelyn shot energy at her. Evie fell back, holding her hands in surrender.

"All I want is the body. Seth made a deal. His body for the little girl."

Jocelyn didn't believe her. And she couldn't do that.

"Sorry. He and I made a deal too. You're not getting his body."

"Jocelyn, I don't want to fight with—"

Jocelyn struck first. A fast leap from the sand, up into Evie's ribs. She took her down and they rolled. Jocelyn grabbed sand and shoved it in her face.

Evie punched hard, getting a strike on Jocelyn's cheek, but she didn't defend fast enough, and Jocelyn's elbow hit her nose. Jocelyn knew how to fight dirty. And she didn't like to waste time on pretty stuff.

Evie backed away, trying to stand but Jocelyn caught her leg and dragged her down, careful of the other leg kicking and squirming for a target. She quickly grabbed Evie's other leg and flipped her over. Evie cursed.

Jocelyn put her in a headlock.

"I can break your neck now, Evie."

Evie cursed again, her arms trying to reach and break Jocelyn's grip. Jocelyn adjusted and gripped her neck, tightening. Evie's body went limp and she blacked out. Not trusting the girl, Jocelyn waited a little longer.

Jocelyn searched for Graeme and Morgan. Graeme gave Morgan something for the sand in her eyes. Jocelyn held her hand up again for him to stay. She only had a few moments.

She ran back to the body and moved the sheet.

Anxiety coursed through her. And sadness. This was it.

She put her hands on the torso and concentrated, taking slow deep breaths of cold air and exhaling as she released energy. A portion of a sheet drifted free. Her eyes watered from the effort. A taste of salt dried in her mouth from the sea air. Her skin glistened, pulsing with energy. The earth around her vibrated softly.

It took energy to dehydrate a body that was ninety percent water and other squishy organs. She tried not to think about it. She sucked in salty ocean air and released again. This time she gave it more than she thought of herself capable. Her head got light, her vision blurred, and finally, the body shimmered one last moment in the sunshine before falling like dust into the sand.

Jocelyn gasped for air.

Evie did the same, finally moving, confused then furious.

Wind whipped up near the water. Jocelyn worked with it, twirling dust and sand into a small whirl and shooting it out into the sea. It caught flight dispersing in the wind, separating, then catching a wave out to sea.

Graeme ran down to them when he saw Evie revive.

"Jocelyn." He looked around.

So did Evie.

Where is he?" Evie asked.

"Gone." Jocelyn's voice was horse.

Evie nodded.

"Don't move!" Morgan stumbled in the sand, a gun aimed at Evie.

"Hell. Really not good." Graeme pushed Jocelyn back, she presumed so she wasn't accidentally shot by Morgan's wobbling hold on the gun.

"Morgan," Jocelyn spoke with a firm voice. "No." She shook her head to clarify in case her voice failed her.

"She killed Seth! I saw her." Morgan spun around, searching for the body. "What did you do with him?" She accused Evie.

Evie stepped back, silent, her hands raised.

Jocelyn moved closer to Morgan until she could reach the gun. She didn't take it.

"Morgan. There's been enough death for one day. Please. I don't want this. Seth wouldn't either."

"I don't care! She killed him!" Tears fell down Morgan's cheeks.

Jocelyn swallowed hard. "I know." Her voice cracked. "And I need to know not everyone is like her. I need to know you'll be there for Benny. Not in trouble with the police. And I need you to help me." Jocelyn took a shallow breath. "Because I don't think I can get through this alone."

Morgan looked at her. Really looked at her. Then she lowered the gun. She turned to Evie. "You should go while you can."

Evie didn't need another hint. There was nothing left for her here. She walked passed the BMW, wheels stuck in the sand, and headed for the street, disappearing into traffic.

"You're blue," Morgan's voice wailed. "Why are you blue?"

"It's nothing," Jocelyn told her. "She sprayed me with something during the fight. It will fade in a little bit. I need water. And maybe chocolate."

Morgan nodded believing her.

"But what happened to you?" Jocelyn gave Morgan a once-over. Her sister was a wreck—hair disheveled, makeup smeared everywhere, her shirt torn, and a layer of dust covered her everywhere. Graeme was the only one who looked sane.

"We were trying to—" She looked down at her clothes and tried to brush off, stopping when she realized it was useless. "I don't know what happened!" Morgan started crying in earnest. Graeme took the gun from her hand.

Legs weak, Jocelyn reached for Morgan. Morgan caught her and Graeme came up behind.

The three hugged each other for a long moment, clutching tight as if to ward off the pain.

Only Jocelyn knew this was just the beginning of the pain they would face.

But it helped her. It fed an anger inside her for justice. And she would use that anger to bring Wicker down.

CHAPTER THIRTY

*J*ohn didn't ever want to see those expressions again. They were kids.

Just kids.

Grim didn't look good on Graeme. It made him ten years older. His sister Morgan looked like a beat-up hooker that had just crawled out of a bar fight. Only she had a steady, silent stream of tears instead of curses.

Jocelyn gazed at him, stark, with bloodshot blue eyes and pale blue bags underneath. She hugged herself tight in a dark coat and gloves. Without it, he was certain he would see signs of unusual activity in the skin on her hands and arms.

Seth was noticeably missing. John swallowed. Took a step off the porch.

Graeme said something and Jocelyn shook her head. He waited with Morgan. Jocelyn turned to the house, her face rigid with control, her movements slow and even. She gazed at the windows then at John, unblinking, as if still reliving a trauma.

Dread filled him. He'd been a cop long enough to recognize these faces.

His steps got faster.

His blood ran cold. This was irreparably wrong.

He reached Jocelyn in the center of the narrow cement pathway. She simply stared into his eyes. Willing him to know. As if saying it would be too much.

He grasped her hands. "Tell me."

Her eyes filled with watery blue tears that fell when she blinked. "We were at a coffee shop. Seth was shot."

"And?" His voice rose, strangely unwilling to hear the truth.

She shook her head.

"Hey!" Kymber's cheerful voice sounded from the front door. "Come inside. It's freezing."

Graeme came to Jocelyn's side and put an arm around her waist. "It was one shot. In the heart. They killed him. He didn't make it to the hospital."

Assassinated? John vaguely absorbed that the loud cry of fury and pain was his. He grabbed his head with two hands, bent at the stomach, and tried to hold on. "No! No. No. No!"

He straightened to see Morgan burst into fresh silent sobs by the Porsche. *God, help me!* He needed to hold it together. "Were there witnesses? Is there a report? What the hell!" He spun in a circle, fury filling him, sorrow a distant second.

"We left for the hospital before the police arrived," Graeme said.

Kymber came up the walk, touched John's arm, anxious. "What is it?"

Graeme repeated the news.

Kymber covered her mouth then looked back at the house. They all knew this would be hard news for the kids. News John dreaded. His wife's eyes watered then she sucked it up. The kids needed them first.

"I need to tell Star," Jocelyn said.

John nodded. "We need to think this through. Tell us what you know."

Kymber went to Morgan, still crying silently by the Porsche and wrapped her arms around her.

"Do you have a secure room?" Graeme asked.

John nodded. That meant there was more to this story than a drive-by shooting. "Richie just did a new sweep and installed audio-video blockers. And we have a scrambler."

Graeme nodded. "I need to get Morgan cleaned up and on point."

"I got her," Kymber said. She guided Morgan inside. "I'll put on some coffee, tea, and cocoa."

John touched his wife's arm as she passed. "Let's hear everything before we tell the little ones."

"I'll ask Mrs. Jackson to watch them for an hour," Kymber said.

John reached for Jocelyn. She didn't want to make eye contact so he pulled her in and hugged her, squeezing hard so she could feel it. He felt her resistance then a hiccup of emotion before she pulled away, her expression closed. Jocelyn and Seth had become family to them—like a grown niece and nephew. The kids looked up to them. If he and Kymber admitted the truth, it would be that Jocelyn had become like a daughter. They were fiercely protective of her. But she came with a lot of past trauma and some dangerous baggage he still didn't fully understand—which was why she needed guidance. He hoped he could provide it this time.

Kymber hurried back out with the kids in tow, Star in her arms. The little redhead saw them, and her face turned serious. She seemed to understand something was wrong. She turned in Kymber's arms while his wife brought them to the neighbor's house, all the while staring at them with concern.

John followed her gaze. *She's one of them.*

Jocelyn, Seth, now Star. How the hell was he equipped to deal with this?

"How is Star doing?" Jocelyn asked. "Has she spoken yet?"

John shook his head. "She doesn't talk, but she says a lot. I think she understands more than an eighteen-month-old kid should."

"Oh." Jocelyn's shoulders fell.

"Weight of the world?" he asked.

She nodded. "It feels a little heavier today."

"Yeah," he agreed. "It does."

Graeme and Morgan filled in most of the details. Morgan had a way of telling a more dramatic story than Graeme would want, but at least she was cleaned up and looked presentable. She still cried on and off, but she coped.

Jocelyn called Georgie to tell her. Then she checked out, mostly looking off into space. Graeme texted Georgie right after to tell her to get everyone to his place. They needed to be together.

The hardest part was explaining what happened to the body. Graeme couldn't really answer that, and Jocelyn merely said it was gone.

Kymber wanted to have a funeral.

Jocelyn wouldn't allow it.

"He didn't want one. We knew he was sick. He only had a few months," Jocelyn told them.

"He was sick?" Morgan asked. "What was wrong?"

"It was a brain disease. We talked about all this. His only wish was that the government didn't get his body and dissect him. It's done. We should move on."

"The government?" Morgan questioned. "Why would they want his body?"

Everyone stared at Morgan in silence. She wasn't privy to this information. Graeme jumped in. "She just means that a lot of scientists would like to understand the disease more, but Seth didn't want to be acquired under the public safety act."

Morgan nodded trying to absorb this.

Kymber continued with her plans. "Even without a body, it's important to honor someone's life. And it's a part of the mourning process for those left behind—".

Jocelyn pushed her chair back, scraping the floor loudly. "Do what you want, but I'm not going to a funeral." She stood up and isolated herself in the corner of the kitchen, wrapping her arms around her stomach.

The doorbell rang. A second later, the kids came running back inside while John went and thanked Mrs. Jackson for watching them.

Star came to the table and tried to climb an empty chair. Graeme picked her up and put her on his lap.

"What's going on?" Maddie asked. "Can you tell us now?" The eleven-year-old stared at Morgan. She knew something was wrong. Morgan ducked her chin, avoiding eye contact.

Kymber took Max in her arms and John put an arm around Maddie.

"We have some bad news," John said.

Graeme felt his eyes burn. That had to be the worst first line of any conversation.

Maddie waited, tense.

John pressed his lips, turned his head away. He sniffed at the congestion building. "Seth—Seth…" He looked into Maddie's eyes as if willing the pain from her before it happened?

"Daddy?" Maddie panicked. "Did he have another seizure? Is he in the hospital?"

John shook his head. "Honey. Kids. Seth was shot earlier today. He was taken to a hospital, but he didn't make it."

Silence.

Maddie pulled away from him. "What do you mean?" Her face contorted, a mix of disbelief, anger and pure shock. "What do you mean?" She shouted her question again, her eyes on her dad.

Max stared at their father too, waiting. Not understanding. Waiting to hear something that wasn't this conclusion.

John didn't give it to them. He tried to pull Maddie back to him.

"He died very quickly, Maddie." His voice broke. "He didn't suffer."

Maddie pushed away again and hit John, furious. "No! You're lying. You're lying." She spun to Graeme and Jocelyn for the truth. Jocelyn looked away.

"I'm sorry, Maddie." Graeme held out his hand to her.

"Jocelyn!" Maddie shook her head, confused. "Were you there? Did you do something? Didn't you save him? He's your best friend!" The accusation pierced and hung heavy.

Jocelyn took a breath and kept her eyes trained outside.

Maddie wouldn't have it. She pushed Jocelyn hard. "Why didn't you do something?" John reached for her.

"Maddie—" Kymber said. "There was no time."

"I—" Jocelyn hugged herself tighter. "He was sitting outside the coffee shop. I walked outside, but I didn't see until it was too late."

Maddie shook her head, face red, eyes full and tumbling out tears. "I don't believe. You liar! You liar! You could have done something!"

"I'm sorry," Jocelyn said. Maddie hit Jocelyn in earnest. John grabbed her and held tight. Graeme watched Jocelyn withdraw inside herself. She turned and stared out the kitchen window.

Max hiccupped in Kymber's arms. Maddie cried in earnest, fists hitting her father's shoulder.

Only Star was silent. But a large tear rolled down her face. She watched Maddie until her new sister lost momentum, then she squirmed off Graeme's lap and toddled to John.

Star lifted her hands to be picked up.

"Daddy."

It was her first word. Everyone turned.

His eyes full of unshed tears, John bent down and picked her up. She wrapped her pudgy little arms around his neck and hugged him. Then she lifted her head to Kymber and reached out with one hand. "Mommy."

Kymber got up with Max and hugged her and John together. Graeme watched as John searched his daughter's face. Maddie nodded to him in the unspoken language of family and joined them.

Morgan smiled at the family, wiped her eyes and gave Graeme a squeeze.

Only Jocelyn stayed apart. Five feet away could have been five thousand miles. She stood alone, gazing outside like a frozen sentinel.

Graeme knew better. He knew this Jocelyn. The soldier.

She was hurting. But it was a hurt that would drive her to do something dangerous, and he didn't think the Morrows or their friends could lose someone else.

Morgan's phone pinged. She checked it.

"Oh, my gosh." Morgan shared her phone, restarting a video. "This just hit the internet. A government facility is testing on children in a rat maze or something. This child failed and was…" There was an explosion on the screen. She covered her screen. "Uh. Probably not appropriate for young viewers." She stopped talking for a moment. "It's posted by someone named Fibonacci."

Jocelyn spun, her eyes on Star with concern. "And so it begins."

CHAPTER THIRTY-ONE

*J*ocelyn rolled out the plans to the Holliwell West complex and studied them again. They were gathered at Graeme's house. Everyone was there—except Seth. He left a conspicuously empty space. Jocelyn smiled a little. He would have loved knowing that.

Al entered with two pizzas and opened them, grabbing a piece. No one else ate.

"What you are thinking of doing is not legal," Georgie said.

"They killed Seth." Lena was on Jocelyn's side.

Though no one spoke the words, they all knew Lena leaked the video from Holliwell West. Likely her old school mate, "Fibonacci," was in a lot of trouble with Wicker and Chang about now.

"And what they are doing might be legal, but it's wrong. The kids are trapped there and treated like lab rats—with real human-sized mazes that I originally designed as a game. For fun! And now it's been co-opted by evil idiots." Lena slammed her laptop shut. Fury contorted her face.

"Yes. That's an I.P. issue," Georgie said.

Jocelyn's mouth dropped open.

"I'm joking!" Georgie said. She threw up her hands. "What are you going to do with a couple thousand kids? Just let them loose into the freezing cold night?"

"We have a connection." Graeme finally spoke. "I'm checking to see what their resources are. We might have to move quickly. The news outlets picked up the Fibonacci video and are trying to validate it." He glanced at Lena. "Most are saying it's a lie."

Richie reached out and put his hand over Lena's before she could throw something.

Graeme continued. "I do know my mom was delayed in Washington. The minority party made a move to keep session open until the President can address if this is a human rights violation. She doesn't expect they will learn much, but she's working with other sources to confirm the Holliwell activity in Colorado."

"Is anyone going to eat while it's hot?" Al took another piece of pizza. "We think better with food in our bellies. Just sayin'."

"Too many carbs," Brittany said.

"We can't do anything in Colorado until we know if we have help," Georgie took a slice of pizza.

"But we can plan," Jocelyn countered. "And figure out options. We should be ready to go before Christmas if things… get volatile."

"I can't." Georgie put her phone in her brightly colored backpack. "It was different when they were harboring a serial killer."

"If you hadn't helped me, I wouldn't have the life I have now," Jocelyn reminded her.

Georgie shook her head. "I have to draw the line somewhere, or I'll be going down a path that will determine the rest of my life." She begged Jocelyn to understand. "I'm just not ready to make those decisions yet. I'm sorry, but I'm out." Georgie turned to Brittany to see if she was ready to go.

Brittany cut a slice of pizza, avoiding eye contact.

"I'll see you Thursday after exams," Brittany said. "Comfort food," she told Al, not watching as Georgie left them.

It was silent after they heard the front door close in the foyer.

Richie squeezed Lena's hand then went for pizza, observing the thoughtful faces as he ate. He smiled at Jocelyn encouraging her. "It's her right to make her own decisions. This is dangerous stuff. It doesn't mean she loves us all any less."

Al, Graeme, and Brittany gave head nods.

Brittany's phone vibrated. She checked the message. "Um. I'm out too."

"What?" Al folded his arms.

"Graeme's mom got me into the Capitol for the last day of session. We're getting a tour and everything. My mom has been wanting this for ages and now I've got an 'in'! It's her Christmas present. I have to go."

"But—" Al didn't have more to say.

"Come on," Brittany said, "we all know I'm only there to make sure…" She looked at Richie then quickly away. "That all the communication goes okay. Besides, if I say no to Graeme's mom, she'll be suspicious. She has that sneaky mom gene in spades."

"That's true," Graeme said. He turned to Richie. "What do you think? We can get you backup."

"I'll be fine." Richie smiled at Brittany. "Don't worry."

"It's settled." Brittany focused back on her work. "I can communicate any news from Congress. They're going to be debating a Federal Family Law to increase the age to eighteen in all states, giving parents ownership of children. I can't believe something like that would pass, but you know, the wording is tricky. Insane. But tricky." She smiled. "Don't worry. I'll make sure all your super-suits are ready." She held up a picture of a guy in a pink onesie. "Graeme, is this the right shade you were wanting?"

Graeme blinked at the bright pink.

Jocelyn laughed softly and gave Brittany a one-armed side hug. She relaxed a little, but thoughts returned to Georgie.

Georgie was the first person whose moral compass she trusted. She was the person who first took a risk on Jocelyn. Was she really supporting the government now?

She glanced up to see Graeme studying her and tried to give him reassuring eye contact.

Things were coming that none of them could help her with. Maybe that's why she was reluctant to lose another one of the team now. She liked belonging. She liked knowing someone was there to watch her back because they wanted to, not because they were paid to or were guarding her—even if it was as simple as showing her how to make scrambled eggs or telling her not to wear silk on a rainy day. She knew Graeme would say that was because her friends loved her and she loved them, but love and belonging weren't options for her anymore. Not with Benny being sick and her own days limited. She had to make the best use of her time to help her brother.

Which meant, it wouldn't be long before she would be alone again. Her path was clearer. Her friends wouldn't be able to help her. And this love that Graeme thought he felt would be long gone when he knew the whole truth about her, and more blood was shed.

Georgie pressed her hands down the front of her dress before entering the large brownstone. The holiday party to thank you all the key march organizers, and several high-level women from D.C. were going to be there.

Dougie waved to her, and she joined him, grateful for someone to introduce her around. Then she saw who he was with and felt lightheaded with excitement.

"This is Major Teresa Mercer. She's the chief of staff to the Secretary of Information." Dougie gushed. "She literally knows everything."

"It's an honor to meet you," Georgie said, trying not to gush herself. Ms. Mercer was a role model for Georgie and had a powerful sense of self. Her speech at the rally had been incredibly inspirational. Plus, she was successful, focused, and seemed to know exactly where she was going. Unlike Georgie who had no idea what she was doing let alone where she was going.

Mercer welcomed her, gracious with her smile but keenly assessing with her eyes. Georgie held her gaze despite wanting to squirm. Mercer finally nodded. Georgie felt officially approved.

"It's great to be back and meet so many bright young women filling the halls of Barnard. How do you like it?"

"Oh, I love it." Georgie gushed then she toned it down. "New York is great. The professors are stimulating, and the other students are really supportive. No complaints."

"What are you studying?"

"Pre-law," Georgie said.

A serious-looking black woman heard and joined them. "That's wonderful. We were just discussing the new Child Protection Laws being voted on in New York." If Georgie was right, she was the Congresswoman who had co-authored the law for New York.

"Well, I'm eighteen, so I'll be able to vote on it this year."

"Wonderful," the Congresswoman said. "I'll see you at the polls."

Georgie recognized the Congresswoman meant to dismiss her. Mercer noted it too and gave Georgie a wink, softening the rudeness of the politician.

Georgie joined Dougie back in the kitchen. He and some other students were glued to the TV monitor mounted on the wall. There was a press conference going on that had everyone's attention. A woman at a podium with an American flag nearby was answering questions. Georgie read the title graphics at the bottom of the screen. *Dr. Dominique Wicker, Holliwell West Research Facility.*

She blinked. *That was 'Wicked'? Seth's doctor?*

"Turn it up!" She called to the front.

They did. She heard the doctor's voice better.

"Their parents legally submitted them to the program and were fairly compensated. In return, the subjects have shelter, food, and healthcare. They are allowed to live longer than they were intended to live. There is nothing illegal going on. The majority of our subjects are brain-dead when they arrive. This is the epitome of compassion."

"Doctor!" A female reporter jumped up and called out her question. "A majority is only fifty-one percent. What about the other forty-nine? Are they brain-dead or conscious?"

"Aren't all children unconscious for the most part, dear?" Wicker joked.

The reporter offered a forced smile. Then another approved newsperson was called on.

"What kind of experimentations are being done?"

"Our program is about scientific advancement. We don't do anything that corporations aren't already doing. Our mission is to solve humankind's greatest challenges. Most of which require science."

"What about the video of the child exploding in the maze?"

Dr. Wicker laughed again. "Obviously, that was smoke and mirrors. Made up and mixed into the video to look real. These things are so easy to do these days."

"Can you produce the child?" the first reporter asked.

"Unfortunately, she had a terminal illness before she arrived here. We couldn't save her."

"What illness?"

"I'm not at liberty to share personal information."

The first reporter persisted. "Per your earlier comment, she is a legal ward of the government, and we're taxpayers, so we have a right to know."

Dr. Wicker nodded patiently. "U.S. Statute 8686 states that all experimentation for the good of the country's health, in relation to national security, is not bound by civilian oversight."

Georgie quickly noted the statute on her phone to research later.

"In Colorado, specifically, parental rights laws state that once the known parents forego ownership of a child, the child loses personhood, and the state can determine all decisions and uses for the cast-offs up to eighteen fiscal cycles. As you know in other states it is age eleven, but many states are now catching up to Colorado. Both laws passed by wide margins."

"Wait," a girl near Georgie spoke to her friend. "We're eighteen. Can they still send us away?"

Dougie nodded. "In Colorado. It's eighteen and under." He smiled. "I'm nineteen."

"That's not cool!" the girl next to Georgie said.

"No one would do that," Dougie said. "It's just so parents have choices if they're poor, or there's something wrong with the kid, or if a teen is depressed and wants to commit assisted-suicide—which is super rare."

Georgie felt weak. And a little ill. "But personhood is granted by our right of being human. You can't just take it away or give it away."

"Scientifically," Dougie said. "But legally you're not a person until twelve in most states and soon nineteen nationally. That way parents and the state can give people options if things aren't working out or they discover mental illness or worse."

"Option to…" Georgie led him to reveal what she did not want to believe.

"Clean out and start over."

Something triggered in her. "Laws are meant to be based on what we know. And we are meant to use reason to figure that out, not emotion. So if by science we know someone is human we are obligated to protect them not take away their freedom and future. Don't you think?" It had happened. She just channeled her dad. "And what if it's *the parents* who have mental illness or are just mean and not the kids? Or they just want the money?"

"I know it sounds harsh, but it's about the good of the country and world. After a couple generations of it, the population will be robust – no more mental illness, hereditary disease. Better resources for those who contribute with their labor. This is how we bring unity back to the country."

"Unity?" That's the first she had heard of that. "How will it bring unity?" Georgie questioned. Others turned and listened in.

"Love."

"Love?" Georgie thought back to Jocelyn's outburst. The grotesque use of love. But she didn't understand how Dougie could possibly be imagining it here.

"The parents who love their kids must apply to the government for personhood. And if the government doesn't give it…" Dougie smiled and shrugged. "It encourages the parents to follow the laws too."

"So what? A new department of personhood?" Georgie laughed. "What do they do? Take away your kids if they decide they don't like you. Or you didn't pay your taxes on time. Make us all wards of the government?"

The girl next to her squeezed her forearm, eyes urgent, fearful.

Dougie thought on that. "That's a good idea. You should suggest that. Great internship option."

"Totally," Georgie smiled, going along with him.

He turned back to the TV, unaware Georgie and the girl next to her cautiously glanced around in horror. *This was surreal.* This wealthy home, educated leaders, champagne and the finest food. She suddenly felt contaminated.

The news conference continued.

As if knowing the public's question, the first reporter added a comment. "No one imagined you would be using children as test subjects."

Wicker dipped her chin and gazed up at the audience with obvious doubt. "Surely you can't believe *that many* people didn't know what they were voting for?" She condescended. "I for one, have a lot more respect for our voters. Of course, if Americans decide they don't want cures for Parkinsons, Alzheimers, and cancer, we can absolutely return the test subjects to their previous status and dispose of the biological waste appropriately. Thank you for your time."

Georgie swallowed. The girl next to her shook her head then nervously checked to see if Georgie agreed with all that.

"It's chilling," Georgie whispered.

The other girl nodded. "I'm out of here."

Dougie hooted from the front. "That's how you handle Obstructionist reporters."

"But how many of those subjects are alive and aware?" A girl in the front questioned.

"None," Dougie assured. "It's another Obstructionist scam. But even if they're conscious, it's better to live and serve the greater good."

The girl from the front shook her head in disagreement. "What about liberty and justice for all? That's our right. We're free because we're human. Parents shouldn't be able to determine if we become slaves or experiments because of our age. That's stupid. Do you know how many messed up parents there are!"

Dougie confronted her, standing an inch from her nose. "If you're not with us you're one of them. Obstructionist! Obstructionist! Obstructionist!" He chanted until others in the room followed suit. The person pushed through the crowd to get out and they all cheered.

Georgie quickly navigated out of the kitchen and returned to where Mercer hung out.

A man in the living room smiled at her. "Sounds like it's getting wild in there."

She gathered herself. "We were just watching a press conference in response to the Fibonacci video."

Mercer turned to them, her attention caught. "Oh. That was terrible. Such propaganda playing on everyone's fears like that."

The man nodded.

"Yes," Georgie agreed. *I need to get out of here!*

Mercer gave her a sympathetic smile. "Don't worry. By Saturday evening the truth will be known." She winked.

The man excused himself, but Georgie paused, stomach-turning. "Major, what did you mean by that?"

"I work for the Secretary of Information. There's very little anyone can hide, Georgie. Including which side they are on."

Did she mean Georgie too? Had someone been watching her in the kitchen?

"But what does that have to do with Colorado?"

Mercer hesitated, then spoke quietly. "Obstructionists are going to bomb the facility. By Sunday morning they will officially be a domestic terror organization. Everyone associated with them will be rounded up, questioned, and incarcerated. I understand you have a friend who knows this Fibonacci?"

Georgie's blood went cold. Had they done a deep background check on her just to be in the club? Or was it standard for everyone attending the party because government officials were here? Either way, Lena was on their radar and a big red flag. And this supposed bombing was two nights from now.

"Yes," Georgie finally answered Mercer. "My friend and Fibonacci were in a game design competition together. That was his handle or something." She smiled to cover the sweat breaking out on her forehead and casually selected a glass of soda from the tray of a passing server. "But of course, knowing someone doesn't mean you share their political ideology."

"Of course not." Mercer studied her, serious. "But if you're not for us, you're against us."

Georgie struggled. "But everyone is for America, right?"

"So they say," the older woman demurred. "Excuse me, Georgie. I see someone I need to speak with."

Georgie gulped the soda, desperate to alleviate her dry mouth. Why had Mercer told her about the bombing? Surely the government would be taking precautions to prevent a terrorist act?

Was this a test or a trap?

And if it was a trap, her friends were walking right into it.

CHAPTER THIRTY-TWO

*G*eorgie flagged a cab outside. She texted the team with her secure phone, but no one responded. A sick feeling overtook her stomach. They had already started preparations and she'd been taken off the secure network. She just hoped they hadn't left town yet.

She tried Brittany's regular phone number—three times. Nothing.

She directed the cab to Graeme's house. She didn't know where else to try.

At Graeme's house she rang the doorbell twice, waiting for the scary thunder sound to end each time. Graeme really needed a more welcoming doorbell. She was about to press again in sheer frustration when the door was opened.

"Morgan." She pushed the door open and hurried in.

"Come on in." Morgan gave a sarcastic wave then shut the door.

"Is Graeme here?"

"Nope. Skiing."

"When did he leave?" Georgie entered the war room to see if there were any clues. "Who was with him? Is anyone still in town?"

"Who is everyone? Am I supposed to know all my brother's friends? I'm just waiting for the painter to leave." Morgan shoved thumbs in the pockets of her tight jeans. "What's going on?"

Georgie put her hands on the war room table and tried to think.

"Is something wrong?"

"No."

"Liar." Morgan scowled then relented. "Al, Richie, Lena, Graeme, and crazy girlfriend all went 'skiing.'" She held up finger quotes for skiing. "Obviously that's not the whole story."

"Brittany didn't go?"

"No. My mom got her and her mom into the Capitol for a tour and to sit in on the end of session. Apparently, Ms. Walsh senior is a fan of all things boring."

"Thank you!" Georgie felt some relief. "There isn't anything wrong right now, but there might be soon. I need to reach Graeme. Can we communicate with the jet somehow?"

"Sure. From the airport if he's not answering his phone." Morgan didn't offer anything else.

"Can you contact him for me? Tell him not to do anything until he reaches me. I have important information." Georgie pulled up her travel app and searched for flights. She could probably grab some clothes and get out tonight.

"So," Morgan spoke skeptically. "He shouldn't go skiing until he speaks with you?"

Georgie bit her lip. "Uh. Yeah. Basically."

"Where are you going?"

"Skiing."

Morgan sighed and crossed her hands over her chest. "You may not be aware of this, but some crazy, super strong girl attacked me and Graeme in the Porsche and I pepper sprayed her. I was almost shot like three times, and I would have killed that bitch if Jocelyn didn't wimp out on me." She raised a brow at Georgie. "Whatever *this is*, I think I can handle it."

Georgie shook her head. "Yeah. I heard about that, but your brother would kill me—not to mention your parents. And you're under-aged."

"I can provide transportation."

"Graeme already took the jet."

"Please." Morgan lifted hands to hips, ready to conquer. "We have more than one jet."

Graeme hugged his parka against the cold then lifted his face mask. He and Jocelyn were laying on the frozen ground of a mountain overlook. Holliwell West sat in the distance, a lone collection of structures built out from the mountain. It was twenty-six degrees, and he was grateful for heated clothing. It would drop to twenty Saturday night but all reports suggested clear skies and a full moon.

He put an arm around Jocelyn as she studied the front gate security of Holliwell West. "This is romantic."

She smiled and finally put down the night vision spyglasses. "The stars are outstanding. Right?" She rolled on her back. "They were like this in Texas when we were out of the city. I could look at them all night."

"Was that when you were with Seth?" Graeme asked the question casually, but he still harbored curiosity about her relationship with Seth.

"Yeah. We slept in this ancient trailer that the restaurant owner said we could use." Jocelyn closed her eyes. "She was kind. And she fed us but made us work. Seth never wanted to come to New York. He wanted to retire to the beach and lay in the sun drinking all these exotic drinks—piña coladas, dai-quiris, margaritas, Mai Tais. Really, he just likes beer, not sweet drinks. But he said you gotta try everything at least once."

"Good that he was open-minded. What else happened in that trailer?" He tried to put humor in the question.

"Nothing much. We worried about being found by Holli-well and planned escape options.

We talked about dreams we knew we could never have. I thought a little about you."

"You did? Did you know I was in New York?"

"Yes. Georgie helped me get information," she confessed.

He propped up on his elbow. "Is that why you came?"

She laughed. "No! That would have been crazy."

"Not that crazy." He talked it out. "Hot genius with a clas-sic Porsche equipped with bulletproof glass and missiles saves your life. You're intrigued. You know you must find him and thank him. And make sure he survived the ensuing attack."

"I said I'm sorry about that!" She ducked her head into his chest. "I didn't know. That was terrible. I did worry about you."

"I'm just teasing. Don't worry." He put his arms around her—more to keep them warm than anything else. "So then, why New York?"

She sighed and hesitated. Finally, she pulled away and looked him in the eye. The moonlight on her face illuminated enough for him to see her expression of hesitation.

"I had some relatives there. I thought maybe—" She rolled back onto her stomach.

"You have family?" Graeme tried not to say it too loudly. He was shocked. "What happened? Were they happy to see you?"

"Not exactly the welcome I dreamed." She raised the spy-glass. "More like one of those dreams I can never have."

He studied her profile, pressing further. "Want me to go talk to them? Tell them they're idiots?"

"No. It's complicated. None of it was their fault. Just…a lot of time had passed. And they don't really remember me anyway. I barely knew them. It's better this way. I have the Morrows now. And you and Georgie and the girls. It's enough for this lifetime—more than enough. John says you're lucky if you have one good friend in your lifetime. I've done really well, right?"

"Yes. You did. But if you ever want to talk about it."

"I won't," she interjected quickly. Then she snaked her arm under his and locked elbows, still facing the complex below. "I just wanted you to know why I originally went to New York. I know I keep a lot from you. I don't lie, but I know when you figure things out, you probably feel like I'm lying to you. I don't mean for it to be like that, but sometimes I'm protecting you." She turned face to face. "And sometimes I'm looking out for my own interests."

"Yeah. I do feel that way. And it's frustrating. But I also understand you need to look out for yourself." He kissed her. A slow caress that warmed their lips. "I hope you know I care about your best interests as well."

"Yes."

She agreed, but not like she believed it. Graeme turned his attention toward the mission. She was stubborn about some things. Eventually, she would understand. That was his mission too.

He turned on his phone's group communication. "They've tightened security at the front gate. We can get some of the team through there with the Underground team, but we need another gate for exiting."

"We're checking out the alternate," Richie said. "Super sneaky. It comes out the other side of the mountain like our new friends said. The tunnel must be a mile long. All in the dark. But the security seems pretty light. Not many trucks going in and out. And no guards on the outside. When trucks arrive the outside lights go on, so likely somewhere in the tunnel they do the security check."

"Let's get more recon on that," Jocelyn said. "Graeme and I will join you. Let Al know."

"Copy," Richie said.

Graeme and Jocelyn crawled away from the point and stood up.

"Graeme," Jocelyn grabbed his hand and squeezed but said nothing.

"I know. You love me. You just can't say it."

She laughed. "Just get out alive and uninjured, okay?"

He leaned forward and pecked her on the lips. "No guarantees in life, babe."

Georgie and Morgan arrived at the first college on Georgie's list in time for a 9 AM gathering. They had scrambled to contact all the club leaders they could, post-finals. Most students would be leaving tomorrow or Sunday. It was Friday. They needed to wrangle as many bodies as possible.

They brought donuts, bagels, and coffee. To Georgie's surprise there were over a hundred students. She needed to make her pitch as compelling as possible. She opened a folding chair.

Morgan whistled and got everyone's attention.

A club leader introduced Georgie.

Georgie climbed onto the chair and looked at all the faces. Some were probably still eighteen like her and could be in danger if they participated. But would the others fight for them when they were no longer at risk, or just agree with the government that parents' rights were good for everyone?

Her heart thudded too fast. She took a breath.

"The laws don't protect us anymore! Especially here in Colorado where you are now disposable property even at eighteen." She had their attention. "Yeah. Think about that. Your parents have the right to commit you, so beware to all those teens who struggle with puberty, or anxiety, or just lame-ass high school teachers. If you complain too much, you can be subject to scientific testing, imprisonment in a"—she held up finger quotes—"'rehabilitation facility', or ultimately silenced. That's not a joke. So, if you're still eighteen or under, I need to warn you that you are at risk and shouldn't protest with us. But for everyone else, I ask you to think about the fear these laws are meant to invoke in us."

The room was silent.

"A few weeks ago, two of my friends were taken and held at Holliwell West."

Morgan gasped. Georgie glanced at her. Her eyes went wide in confusion.

"The Fibonacci tape is real! My friends witnessed the children. Babies. Toddlers. Teens. Every age. Organized by test group. The scientists are changing their genetic makeup and making them perform tests. When the children or teens fail a test and are no longer useful, they are killed and disposed of. They are mere 'biological waste' as you heard Dr. Dominique Wicker tell us."

She took a breath.

"This is not liberty. This is not the America we want to be part of. Our generation might be the first to lose our freedom if we don't stand up and fight for it. That's our obligation. That's what we do. All humans have the same rights. It's not liberty and justice for some." She took a breath. "It's liberty and justice for all!"

The room cheered loudly. Morgan clapped and encouraged her to go on.

"Tomorrow night we desperately need your help. Dr. Wicker threatened to dispose of the kids. We know from the security tapes there are nearly a thousand. But there could be more we don't even know about. We want to reach as many people as possible and show America that we care not just about words. We care about each other!"

The room gave another cheer. She waited for it to settle down.

A guy in the back called out. "But how? What do we need to do?"

Morgan shouted, as if remembering their plan. "We have flyers!"

She shoved some in Georgie's hand, and they held them up.

"Be there tomorrow night. Spread the word, but only verbally and through paper until the event is over. No email or audio calls. Secure text is okay. I know it's hard but there is constant tracking. It could put everyone in danger, but we have safety in our numbers, and we need everyone. All the directions are on the flyers. Please join us!"

Morgan nudged her. She leaned down and stood up again.

"And there will be a band, bonfires, and other fun!"

Georgie stepped down.

"That was fierce!" Morgan's eyes were lit with energy.

"A band?" Georgie asked.

Morgan brushed it off. "I told you. I know people. Don't worry. I plan all the events at my school. What's next?"

Georgie took a breath. "We go to the next college."

CHAPTER THIRTY-THREE

*J*ocelyn finished checking through their equipment. Al had done a good job. And Luis, who led the Underground in this region, had been preparing for a while.

Now the opportunity was here.

Richie would be at the command station with Luis while Lena, Al, and Graeme would go in with Marco and Avis. Marco was Luis's son that Graeme had met on their previous mission. He drove one of the trucks. Avis was their science expert. She was a nurse inside Holliwell and had provided most of the intel on the children, the experiments, and their location.

At first glance, Luis didn't look like someone who might be leading an underground army. He was stout, balding, and had big forearms. He looked like what he was—a happy baker. His features were a Hispanic and Native American mix. Talking with him, he was steady, and thoughtful; his eyes held the wisdom that comes with love, loss, and living a full life. She understood why he inspired trust.

Marco must have gotten his looks from his mother's side. He was taller with a runner's build, and had a soulful expression partially covered by locks of hair that fell over the right side of his face.

Avis was edgier. She had nervous energy. Jocelyn was surprised she'd passed a Holliwell inspection. Luis told Jocelyn that Avis's daughter had run away and the search ended here. She got a job at Holliwell and found out the truth. Her daughter was 093. She didn't survive the box maze.

There were others that Jocelyn had met. Most were at their posts inside the Holliwell Complex, ready to help if they should need it. Jocelyn was keenly aware, that they didn't have special powers. They were just people trying to help. And if they were caught it could mean their lives.

Luis interrupted her thoughts, updating the team.

"Okay, we have up to twenty luxury passenger buses if we need them. Our guess is twelve should be enough, but...you never know, right?"

"Where will they be taken?" Lena asked.

"We've been building a network across the country for years. We have families ready to take in the children. We just have to get them out and have the time to transport them. We can't bring them back to town. But we've invested in transportation companies over the last several years. We will have kids loaded on every bus with as many volunteers as we can manage for the babies. Each bus will have an administrator who can do the paperwork for the kids. They will go to their new homes and be contacted by a private adoption agency. We have a lot of lawyers who are on our side," Luis shared. "This is organized. Which means we can't make a mistake and get caught, identified, or killed. There are too many people who could be hurt. You have to understand—it has taken us a long time to get people on the inside. We don't want to expose them. This is a long-term game. There will still be a Holliwell after tonight. Our longer mission isn't over.

"We understand," Graeme said. "And we deeply appreciate your trust and help."

"Luis," Jocelyn pulled out plans for the science wing. "This vault. Is that where they keep the science? If we can destroy that, we slow them down." And she also wanted it for herself.

"It's too dangerous. Keep to the primary mission," Luis said.

"We have a chance to cripple them," Jocelyn said.

Avis's expression said she might be interested in crippling.

"Avis, do you know where they keep it?" Jocelyn asked.

Avis nodded. "Yes, I can get into the building, but it's in several layers of security."

"I can get in." Jocelyn was certain she could do anything necessary for a chance to cure Benny.

"It's too risky," Luis said.

"I'm willing to risk it. I'll make sure the kids are out before I go for it."

Luis hesitated.

"I'm with Luis," Graeme said.

Jocelyn turned on him, betrayed. She shook her head. "You don't understand. Stay out of it."

Graeme's eyes hardened. "It's already dangerous."

"They will do this again, and what if they ship the science out of the country? We won't be able to reach it then."

"There isn't much left," Avis revealed. "Of the original science that is. Dr. Wicker was given a small sample to work with and study. The original experiment was called Project Sunday. They terminated it months ago. Supposedly. There haven't been any new samples since then. The original science that was used on Project Sunday is the secret ingredient that no one can replicate."

Jocelyn's heart pounded. Her mother's formula? Greer was right. Her skin flickered with excitement. The cure for Benny was in her grasp!

Lena stepped toward Jocelyn in shock. "Jocelyn." It was a warning. Jocelyn didn't heed it.

She met Luis's gaze head-on. "I am Project Sunday."

Avis gasped.

"That's my blood they're using. That's my DNA making children into slaves—the same way I was. I've got to stop them. You need to understand. I might be the only one who can do this."

Graeme froze. "What's Project Sunday?" He turned to Richie. "Did you know about this?"

Richie shook his head. "Lena did you know about this?"

"Uh, maybe, but not the details," Lena said.

Al put up his hands. "I'm just a bystander trying to make sure y'all don't get your asses wiped off the planet by all these bad guys you keep bringing into our sweet lives."

Avis walked up to Jocelyn and studied her. "We've been told Project Sunday can bio-transmit energy. It's one of the core skills Wicker has been trying to replicate."

Jocelyn turned, raised her hand toward the weapons table and a knife levitated off the surface. A second later it flew fifteen feet into the wall of the warehouse, landing with a hard thump.

Richie spun to her. "Pro-Project Sun—" He stopped, then pulled a brown bag from his pocket and started breathing into it.

Marco gasped, staring in awe and concern.

"I knew it." Graeme shook his head.

"Helicopter. Drones. I tried to tell you," Al said.

Avis was pragmatic. "You can't go in. If they capture you, they will use you. We will be back to where we were."

"I understand the risk, but I'm going in. And I'm going to destroy the science."

Silence.

They all waited.

Finally, Luis nodded his approval. "But the children first."

"Agreed," Jocelyn said.

Avis shook her head. "This is a mistake."

Luis had made his decision. It was done. He answered a call then gave them an update.

"Something is going on. There's a mandatory evacuation of outdoor and public buildings by 7 PM."

"Spraying for roaches?" Al tried to lighten the mood. His pocket vibrated and he pulled out his secure phone.

"No." Luis shook his head. "We need to move everything up an hour."

Marco frowned. "I don't like it, Papa."

Jocelyn didn't like it either.

"It's Brittany," Al said. "She said Georgie has been trying to reach us." He put the phone on speaker.

Brittany's breathless voice came out. "It's a trap. They're going to bomb the facility."

CHAPTER THIRTY-FOUR

*G*etting into Holliwell West was easy. The Underground had that figured out. It was all about timing. Jocelyn counted guards through the window of the bakery truck.

Getting out? *Yeah, A whole other story.*

The three bakery trucks arrived during the evening shift change. The team unloaded the baked goods wearing warm jackets over their Lulu's Cocina t-shirts.

As they brought product into the large food storage area, they were pulled aside and given their new uniform, ID, and security badge. Al and Marco dressed as guards. Graeme and Jocelyn donned white nurse uniforms. Lena was a testing associate—which meant she had access to the maze. Jocelyn knew her friend had her own agenda, but she understood. *Because so did she.*

Avis was already at the nursing station near the dorms. They were going to meet her and evacuate youngest to oldest. The Underground had looped surveillance footage for each location. The babies were easiest as they didn't get up and move around much. No one would be looking at anything unusual. Avis assured that her inside team had all the attendants organized.

The wards were connected, and getting there was easy and direct. The science labs, where they worked on testing and manufacturing their formulas, were on the other side of the complex. That would take skill and timing.

Al handed some papers to Avis in the baby ward when they arrived. She alerted the other nurses and orderlies that it was time for the temporary evacuation. Someone complained that they were early.

"Military efficiency," Al said. "Your safety is paramount." He gave a charming smile.

The nurse agreed. "Thankfully, we were ready." She called to her team to move on out.

"Just follow us," Marco said.

Graeme, Jocelyn, and the others rolled the cribs in a long chain. Fifty nurses and orderlies quickly moved the children toward the buses.

A supervising nurse questioned the buses when she saw them. "I thought we were moving them to another building."

"We are," Avis said. "But it's on the other side of the complex, the underground shuttle is too intermittent, and we need it for staff, so this is the most efficient. They'll go out Mountain Gate and back in South Gate. The temporary beds and team are set up to receive."

"Okay," she nodded. "That's too far to roll this many. Quickly," she instructed the others. "We have fifty more infants and ninety-four toddlers."

Graeme and Jocelyn hustled back with the others. Jocelyn didn't know how many workers were part of the Underground, but everyone followed directions efficiently. The evacuation alert worked in their favor. Avis and Al went to the next three dorms to prepare their dorm leaders and get the papers and attendance signed off with the room keepers. The kids were all old enough to walk and stood by their beds in silence, waiting for their orders, some of them anxious at not knowing where they were going. Explaining anything to them was going to be a hard job. This was the only life the young ones knew. Jocelyn worried about them but hoped they would have a chance at a real life. She counted eight hundred and twenty-five "experiments."

They just needed to get through the tunnel and out the gate...and not be captured, but that was phase three of the plan.

She checked her watch.

Still a long way to go. And not much time.

Dominique wasn't happy about the SOI's plan. Supposedly it was the President's idea. Needless destruction always earned sympathy, but it was incredibly inconvenient. Her heels clicked hard on the floor as she headed toward the maze testing area. If she had to suffer collateral damage, she wanted to get a few more tests out of them.

Unfortunately, the rumblings of opposition in the country were growing from an initial whisper to outright questions. None from the media, but Internet news had become emboldened with recent startups, and until those channels were bought down or brought into line, it was hard to eliminate the pests.

She pressed her badge to the control room. Freddie sat at the panel, a little more nervous and worse for the wear since his interrogation but functioning well with one hand. The other was in a splint. They hadn't broken his thumb. He was lucky Chang was able to prove his innocence before that. His face, however, bore some disfiguring swelling and bruises.

She smiled angelically. "Freddie, love. How are you?"

"Excellent, Dr. Wicker."

He'd learned manners too. "Perfect. Ready for a little fun?"

"Yes, Dr. Wicker."

She pressed the intercom. "Please send our three groups into the mazes. Note the date, test group, subjects, and genetic specialties. This will be a timed test. Thank you for playing."

She released the button. "Freddie, record and proceed."

This spot in the ceiling had become Evie's greatest comfort in the last couple years. The ceiling tile had watermarks where it had once leaked. She took joy in the unchanging quality of those marks. Her favorite water stain was shaped a little bit like a bird flying free, but that was mostly her imagination. The ceiling wasn't anything special. It just meant she had made it through another day.

She closed her eyes just as a commotion began at the other end of the dorm hall. There were gasps from some of the girls.

She jumped off her bed in preparation to fight. At the far end of the hall, a soldier and an orderly dragged their dorm security guard into the dorm hall and laid him on the ground. He was out cold. The female orderly had a short, light brown bob and long bangs. She proceeded down the aisle searching the experiments.

"Evie?" she called out.

Some heads turned to Evie and backed away quickly.

"Evie?"

The woman kept walking, her voice drawing near. The girls could easily take her and the two men, but Evie thought that voice sounded familiar. She peaked over her mattress as the woman got closer. Then she hopped off the bunk and stepped out into the aisle, partially in shock. Had Wicker kidnapped

Jocelyn? If so, why did she have a wig and a fake nose? Evie decided not to say anything.

Let her speak first.

Jocelyn finally reached her but stayed five feet away.

"Evie."

The others were down from their beds, watching, curious.

"We have buses in the tunnel ready to get you out of here if you want to go."

Evie smiled and waved to the iron-framed row of bunks. "Why would I want to leave these luxury accommodations?"

The other girls smiled.

"Because someone in the government is going to drop a bomb or two on the complex and claim it's Americans who disagree with the President."

Evie shook her head. "That makes no sense."

"A video was released of the box maze and some kids being killed in it. People are questioning what's going on here. The planned attack is a distraction to draw sympathy for testing on kids."

"And?"

"And you're the collateral damage."

"What do you mean?"

"Every dorm and facility around you was ordered to evacuate by seventeen hundred hours. It's a little suspicious."

"It's true," a girl stepped forward. "I heard they were moving all the kids—except us. And they emptied out the hospital two days ago." Her voice rang with worry.

"Evie, these girls trust you. I'm risking everything coming in here, and there's not much time."

"I killed Seth."

"You want to have a pity party right now?" Jocelyn had a tinge of anger in her voice. "You think they wouldn't have found someone else to do it? Or they could have replaced your eyes with cameras and equipped your hearing with torture devices to prevent you from leaving your quarantined area. They did that to a friend of mine. He's dead now too."

Evie heard the truth in her words.

"They used you. They are responsible. Not you. You're a victim." She turned to the others around them. "I'm giving you a chance to stop being the victim. You can go free. Return to the world and people who care about you or could care about you if you give them a chance. The world is better than you think, better than you've been told. Don't die here a victim because you're afraid of trusting someone."

"I'm not afraid." Evie stood firm. "I just don't believe you."

"I was captive for ten years at Camp Holliwell in Virginia. I know what's in store for you all. I know the brainwashing. I know the torture. I know the secret missions that 'only you can do for the good of the country.' Ten years, Evie." She pleaded. "I'm not the enemy. Come with us. All of you."

The girls began to huddle in groups. "I want to leave," someone said.

"Me too. Evie?"

They were confused, scared, and uncertain. She had been too. She'd seen the outside world again. And she knew the kind of missions others would have to face. She didn't want that for them, but the clock was ticking. If they were caught, they'd be dead.

As if reading her mind, Jocelyn said the words. "You're already dead if you stay."

That was true. And she hated herself enough to stay. The others didn't deserve the same. There may not be absolution for her—but for them?

A familiar neighing sound caught her ear. *Not the spirit horse. Now?* She hesitantly looked toward their escape route. The horse didn't make eye contact, just walked past the doorway like this was its every day exercise path, then it was gone. *Was this her chance for redemption?*

One of the girls touched her arm, waking her from the hallucination. "Evie?"

Evie took a breath. Pulled herself together. *Okay. She might be crazy.* She studied Jocelyn a moment. *Crazy as well. She was in good hands.* "What's the plan?"

"The surveillance for this room has been placed on a loop. Follow the guard. Don't raise suspicion." She glanced toward the guys. "Guards." The orderly had changed into the guard's uniform and taken his badge and gun.

"Marching formation!" Evie shouted. She and Jocelyn hurried to the front of the room. Evie recognized the Porsche guy now. His hair was dyed bright white with a new military cut, and he had nerdy glasses that did nothing to hide his looks. The other guard was younger and attractive in a sexy Latin kind of way.

"There are buses waiting. They can explain everything there," Jocelyn said.

Evie turned to 021. They'd known each other the longest. "Kasey. Get them out, okay?"

"Aren't you coming?"

"Keisha and the others are in the maze. I have to get them."

"We need to go," the Latin guard said.

An older woman that Evie recognized as a nurse stood outside the dorm waiting. Jocelyn motioned to her. "We'll go with you," Jocelyn told Evie. "It's on the way."

Evie nodded.

"Lena," Jocelyn spoke on a hidden comm device. "Evacuation is complete in the dorms. Set the permanent loops. I'm headed to the maze."

Dominique watched the progress of her young teams. They were doing exceptional. They had adapted and now worked well together. It seemed a shame to end their productivity in an untimely way. She pulled out her pen and started clicking it, irritated.

A call came in and she pressed the intercom.

"Doctor Wicker, there's a crowd that's been building outside the main gate all day. Some protesters."

"And?" This wasn't her problem. Who cared about random people with signs?

"Doctor, it's been building all day long. It's in the thousands, and more are still arriving. We're concerned, but they are on public land."

"Call the Sheriff. That's why he's on our payroll," Dominique told the security agent.

"Yes, ma'am. Am I on a secure line?"

She cut the intercom and picked up the phone on the console. "Yes."

"The Sheriff doesn't have the staff and we're concerned they're in the drop zone."

"I see." Dominique shined her nails on her dress. "That's tragic. Anything else?"

"No ma'am. The evacuation should be complete shortly. We're just waiting on the buses."

"Okay, thank you. Wait—buses?" Dominique pulled up the evac plan on her phone. "I thought we were using the underground tram?"

"I guess someone thought this was faster. Less back and forth."

"Okay." Dominique ended the call, turning her attention to the experiments. "Their group timing is improved."

"Yes, Dr. Wicker," Freddie agreed. "By nearly five seconds in each room."

"Such a shame." She sighed then made a note. "Shorten their success goals by seven seconds in each room."

They looked harmless enough—Avis, Evie, Lena, and herself.

Avis walked with authority in her nursing garb with an experiment—Evie. Behind them, Lena followed, playing with her phone and making notes. Jocelyn, in her white nursing uniform followed last as backup.

The guards didn't think anything of it when Avis swiped her badge and they walked into the maze control room. The door swished shut behind them, securing them with just Wicker and Freddie.

A muffled explosion lit up on the other side of the viewing glass to the warehouse below.

They were seconds too late.

CHAPTER THIRTY-FIVE

*W*icker stood, arms folded, observing. Smoke came through a box in the middle of the maze and a giant Kuka arm moved into place and lifted it out.

"Keisha!" Evie rushed forward in a panic. "What have you done?"

"Seventeen?" Wicker turned. "What—"

Evie swung a furious uppercut to the ribs. Wicker flew backward against the viewing glass so hard the panels vibrated around the tower.

Freddie turned in his seat then shrunk, huddling into a ball. "Don't hurt me!"

Lena ran to the controls. "Stop the game. Freddie! Stop the game or I *will* hurt you."

"I can't." he cried. "It's on a required finish."

"What about a failsafe?" Lena asked.

"Wait," He typed furiously and brought up a settings page on the game interface. "But if I hit the emergency stop they'll be trapped."

"Hit the stop!" Evie yelled.

He hit the stop.

"We can get them out," Evie said. "Pry open the doors from the top?" She wasn't sure. She looked to Jocelyn for help.

"Maintenance Mode," Lena said. "It should stop the game

system and allow for manual door opening. You'll have to walk through their box path, but it should work."

Freddie nodded his head vigorously agreeing. "There are only two teams left."

"You bastard!" Lena grabbed his shaggy hair at the back of his head and pounded his face into the counter. "Murderer!" She pounded it a second time and ripped his security badge from his belt.

Jocelyn turned to Avis. "Are you armed?

Avis pulled out her gun.

"Watch her," Jocelyn pointed to Wicker, slowly recovering. "We'll be back."

Avis nodded.

Jocelyn and Evie ran to the elevator outside the control room.

"Hold the door," Lena said. She dragged Freddie across the floor, and into the elevator, dropping him.

"You're stronger than you look," Evie said.

"I'm angry," Lena said. She took a breath, controlling her temper, then grinned at Jocelyn.

Evie didn't know Lena was wearing a super-suit. It clearly did wonders for her self-esteem.

The elevator went down then dinged open to the warehouse and the start of the maze.

"They were in games three and eleven," Lena pointed out. "One second." She pulled Freddie to his feet. "Time to bug test your game, Freddie." She pressed the manual entry and pulled up the rolling door to the decked-out container.

"Please—"

Lena shoved him in and closed the door. She went to number three and showed Evie and Jocelyn how to open the container doors manually.

Evie and Jocelyn hurriedly began to make their way through games three and eleven—into one box container, out the other side, and into the next. They were almost at the containers with the girls when the lights changed in the warehouse and inside the boxes. Jocelyn ran to the exit of her container as a game alert started.

Jocelyn leaped through a closing door. It locked behind her.

The boxes began to reconfigure.

She scrambled on top of the next container as the one she'd just left exploded.

She started forward, and a container up front exploded, the force sending her back. *Too close.*

She clutched an edge, holding on. The container moved higher. She guessed she was three stories up.

She scrambled to her feet and jumped forward, desperate to reach the box where the girls were trapped.

She pretended to leap forward then stopped and moved in the other direction. The box where she had aimed exploded, confirming her suspicion that someone in the tower wanted to stop her and Evie.

That meant either Wicker had overpowered Avis or Avis had betrayed them.

She gazed at the ever-changing maze—no sign of Evie.

Jocelyn lay flat on the box as it moved, then slid covertly down the side, standing on the edge of the exit door. The container moved forward. Once it was in place there would be no room to maneuver. She needed to jump ahead, hit the manual door opening, get the girls, and hope she wasn't blown up or crushed when the container locked into the maze.

Timing was everything.

She measured the distance mentally and jumped with power, landing hard. She slid down the edge to the entrance door and grabbed the side handle while pressing the unlock button. The previous box moved steadily closer, above them, ready to move into place.

She pulled up the door urgently and met four surprised faces. They stood back frightened, probably from the explosions around them.

"Quickly! Climb out. We don't know which ones will blow next. Evie is here too. We're getting you out of here."

One of the girls understood the scenario and quickly ran to her. Jocelyn pulled her up and out. "Hurry! That other box is about to come into place."

Jocelyn grabbed the next girl, then the third. The box was nearly on top. They weren't going to make it.

"Hurry," one of the girls cried out.

Jocelyn turned to see the three girls pushing back at the incoming box, holding a gap for them. She reached for the last girl and swung her up to safety. The other three girls jumped back, joining them, confused and wide-eyed, as the container squeezed precisely into place.

A box exploded nearby. The girls fell backward and huddled together for protection. Jocelyn shielded them, wondering about their next move. Whatever it was, it needed to be quick.

Lena crouched behind a bearing steal post on the warehouse floor, hands covering her ears from the explosions. She gasped for breath then hurried to a panel, searching for an override option.

Nothing.

Another explosion went off. She didn't have a choice. She needed to stop whoever had taken over the control tower. She went up the elevator. Her stomach tensed at what she might find and who she had to face. She took a full breath before tapping Freddie's badge to access the room.

Dr. Wicker stood at the panel. "You're too late. I've alerted security."

As if on cue, two guards entered the tower. Lena ignored them. She grabbed Wicker and tossed her at guards with full force. The three landed in a heap on the lobby tile outside the doors. Lena slammed the button for the automatic doors, shooting the heap of limbs with the laser gun Richie had modified for her. It kept the guards at bay until the doors closed. Then she shot the security panel three times, forcing a malfunction. It worked.

For now.

She spun back to the keyboard and heard Richie in her ear. "Lena, you need help?"

"Yes! I need to stop the maze. Dr. Wicker put on the death sequence. I can't find the Fail-safe." And if one more box blew up, she wouldn't be able to live with it.

"Freddie probably kept it 'as is'. Did you have one designed?" Richie questioned.

Her mind raced, thinking back to her original design.

"Lena. Take a breath. Slowdown. It would be at a centralized hub in the software, right?"

"Yes. One moment."

She took a deep inhale, typed, and found the fail-safe, holding her breath for the eternity of a single second. The maze stopped. Air whooshed from her lungs. "Thank you." Lena stood, rolled Freddie's chair to glass barrier and took another breath. "Richie." She picked up Freddie's chair.

"Avis abandoned us."

She pounded the glass around the tower, grateful for the extra strength from the suit, though her hands could barely hold onto the chair—a flaw in the suit. Finally, the glass began to fracture. Three more hard swings and she produced a spider crack that quickly webbed outward. One last swing and the chair flew through the shattering window creating an opening. She jumped back as the rest of the glass crashed down.

Lena took a fortifying breath. "Richie. Security was alerted. Tell the others. We're in trouble."

Then she stood on the ledge of the tower window, inhaled and prayed Brittany had sewn enough exo-skeleton into the feet of the suit to withstand a twenty-five-foot landing.

CHAPTER THIRTY-SIX

*J*ocelyn froze, listening. Just as suddenly as the maze started, it stopped.

A crashing sound came from the tower. Glass fell from a large viewing window and Lena stood on the edge a moment before jumping. Her friend landed on two feet, hands out, legs bent like a gymnast, then straightened, as if surprised she had stuck her landing.

Whatever had gone on, Lena had saved them.

"Lena, head to Game Three!"

Jocelyn ran to find Evie, hoping she hadn't been in one of the containers now missing from that path.

"Evie!" Jocelyn called. The maze was four container boxes high and more than twice that long. She didn't know what layer Evie ended up on. She listened for voices.

"Over here," Jocelyn heard a voice. "Evie has them. They're coming out the end!"

Jocelyn, Lena and the girls scurried over the top of the giant collection of container boxes and climbed down at the exit, expectant and hopeful. Until they faced three military escorts who waited, confused at the stopping and starting of the games.

The girls looked at them then at Jocelyn. Simultaneously the last box in row three lifted open. Evie stood there with four girls, a big grin on her face.

The distraction allowed Jocelyn to grab a military escort's gun and tranquilize him. The other two guards were stunned and too slow. She shot them and they stared in shock at the girls before falling to the ground.

"Good night," Keisha said, coming from behind Evie.

Evie grabbed the other guns and handed one to an older girl. "Maria, You're the best shot. And you'll fit in this." The two began to undress a female soldier and take her uniform. Two other girls stripped the badges and smaller weapons.

"Lena," Jocelyn called to her friend. "What's the fastest path out?"

"We can't reach the buses," Lena said.

"What about—"

"Watch out!"

A younger girl yelled a warning. Two armed guards hurried into the game's exit lobby. Maria spun and shot.

Graeme dove for cover.

"Stop! They're with us!" Lena shouted.

The girls looked suspicious.

Marco waited for everyone to calm down then hurried over with Graeme. "We sent off the buses. They're in lock down. I can get us out through the kitchen. We can use the bakery trucks."

Evie raked her short hair, worried. "Everyone," Evie called them together into a huddle. "Walk like you're being escorted. If something goes wrong, do whatever you can to escape. They were going to terminate us tonight—our whole dorm. We have a chance to leave this place. I know that's a little scary too. You don't know anything else…" Evie scanned the others for help.

Marco stepped forward. "There are families who want you, and who will provide everything you need. They will keep you safe, get you into a regular school, you can create any life you want. They are all just waiting for you."

Evie sighed, reassured. "Take a chance. Get out and take a chance."

The girls nodded, albeit anxious, and lined up behind Marco.

Jocelyn took Graeme's hand. "I have to go destroy the science."

"No."

"I have to."

"That was only the plan if things went according to plan. They're looking for us now."

Jocelyn pressed her comm device. "Richie, can you kill surveillance in the science wing?" Jocelyn asked.

"I need five minutes, but I can do it."

"Jocelyn." Graeme's expression was firm and determined. "No."

Jocelyn took a breath. "Graeme, Greer said there was a known formula that might save Benny, but it was confiscated years ago, supposedly from his parents. They have some of it here. If I can get it…" She shook her head. "Graeme don't you want me to try?"

"No!" Then he cursed and grabbed his head in frustration. "Yes. But it's too risky and you don't know for sure."

"I'm stronger than ever. I can do it."

"One bullet can kill you. Seth proved that."

"I'll be careful. But you have to go."

Marco interrupted. "If we want out we have to move." Marco waved the group to the door. The girls took on their marching faces. Maria, the older experiment now in uniform, took up the side, and Graeme and Lena secured the rear.

Keisha hung back, waiting. "Evie?"

Evie's expression filled with concern and regret as she put her hand on the younger girl's shoulder.

Jocelyn caught Evie's eye. "I'll wait by the door."

Evie bent down to her young friend. "I have to stop Wicker. Or she'll keep doing this."

"What if I can't find you?" Keisha asked.

"Keisha," Evie struggled for words. Words had not been welcome in this place. They got you in trouble. Compassion, friendship, hugs—all trouble. Evie was out of practice and she hadn't been good to begin with. "Keisha, you are so smart, and funny, and sweet. And you have other powers that you'll need to learn how to manage in the real world. Most of the time you probably won't even need them, so that's actually a good thing. There's so much beyond these walls. And, I think these people will find you a really nice family. If not, you can get Graeme or Jocelyn's number and they'll take care of it. I just want you to have a chance to be happy. And most of all be safe. I can't go with you."

"Yes! You can! We can go to the same family and be sisters." Keisha argued for the best possible options.

Evie hardened her voice. "I'm not your sister." Why did it hurt so much to say those words? Evie felt her eyes burn despite of her anger and determination. "It's too late for me. I've already…" *Killed two people.* "I've already decided to go out on my own."

"I'll go with you."

"No, Keisha. I don't know anything about raising a kid. I don't have a job. And honestly, I don't want you tagging along."

Keisha scowled, but her eyes filled. "I understand."

"It's better this way. You'll see."

Keisha shrugged her off and turned away before the tears fell. Evie watched, more dejected than ever.

She turned to join Jocelyn. Jocelyn shook her head and gave her a palm to stop. Her expression clearly said Evie was an idiot. Not that she needed it pointed out. Then Jocelyn walked over, impatient.

"Go give her a hug," Jocelyn said. "And hurry!" She inclined her head sharply to Keisha.

Evie turned to the girls getting ready to leave. Her throat tightened. She coughed from the pressure. Keisha turned. Evie swallowed then finally took the first step.

Keisha didn't need a second.

She ran to Evie and wrapped her skinny arms around her waist, squeezing hard enough to crush the organs of a normal person.

"I love you, Evie."

Evie held her friend tight. "I love you too, Keisha. Be safe." She released her and bent down eye to eye. "I'll find you someday, if I can. I promise."

"Okay." Keisha scrubbed her cheeks.

The other girls joined them and Evie hugged them all. It was the first time in years any of them had done something like this—hugged. Or heard the words, "I love you".

It was painful. Freeing. And hopeful.

"Okay. Go!" Evie ordered. "These cute guards look really stressed. Take care of them."

Evie turned back to Jocelyn. The girl had a warrior's face back in place. Evie knew now to respect that look. There was a definitive switch in who she was, but even in battle and chaos Jocelyn showed humanity. Evie had lost that. And she hadn't even mourned it—which was probably why she was having horse hallucinations. Conflicted Crow syndrome. Pretty sure it was a thing.

Jocelyn waited until the girls were out of the game warehouse. Graeme gave them a last nod. He didn't look happy.

"The bleached hair kinda suits him," Evie said to Jocelyn.

Jocelyn gave her a half smile, her thoughts clearly elsewhere.

"Come on," Evie led Jocelyn out of the torture chamber. "I know a shortcut."

CHAPTER THIRTY-SEVEN

*J*erry Ramstein took the call in his office, alerted when he saw Dominique holding a cold pack to her cheek.

"What's going on?"

"You need to move up the demonstration. We're under attack. The experiments have been moved, sir, but not to where they are supposed to be."

"What do you mean?"

"I'm tracking them now. They were put on buses. We believe they're in the tunnel."

Jerry stood up from his chair. "What the hell are you talking about?"

"Project Sunday is here with Greer's deranged offspring. But there's no way they could have done this alone. Someone else is involved. They had to have worked on this for years."

Jerry cursed. "Where's Chang?"

"Directing traffic. There's also about eight thousand people camping and apparently having a protest concert at the border of our property. They started arriving around noon and they're still coming in. It may or may not be related. It's mostly students protesting the age laws."

Jerry took a minute to calibrate. Congress was in session debating the federal version of the age law right now on the Hill. He needed to re-coordinate the timing.

"Okay. The targeted buildings are empty?" He sat back down. This was all very manageable.

"Yes, sir. But I recommend targeting the tunnel as well, to stop the exodus in progress. And," Dominique leaned forward, "there might be value in upsetting the protest. No one likes to see youthful enthusiasm destroyed. Perhaps it's a gift."

"Indeed?" Jerry turned to his wall of displays then pressed for Mercer to come in. "Mercer? Enter."

Mercer walked in seconds later.

"Glad you're back. Get me views on Holliwell West, the tunnel, outside the gates, and over the town. Something is going on. We need to find where Obstructionists might have their headquarters." He leaned back to his video conference. "Hold on, Dominique." He pressed mute.

Mercer pulled up the views quickly.

"Contact the war room, the NSA, and the joint chiefs. I want everyone in that Podunk town covered. I want to hear inside every home, business, street corner, and bar. Wherever there are people gathered, there might be a threat. We have fifteen minutes to find it. Tell them that. Then we're going to—." He took a cleansing breath and smiled. "Take care of it."

"Yes, sir. I'm on it." Mercer strode toward exit.

He unmuted the doctor. "Dominique, I don't need to tell you that this is not good for your career."

"Sir, my science is progressive! This was all fine until Project Sunday got involved."

"It was fine until you went after her friends, Dominique. It's a flaw. Sometimes you need to lose a battle to win the war. You let Texas trash be your downfall. It's a waste." He was very calm about it. Dominique would not have a command role with the science teams again. "I want you to go get the remains of the original Sunday formula and get on a plane to Washington.

"But sir," Dominique said.

He put up a hand. "As soon as Chang has everything on lock down, we'll recalibrate. I'll take care of these Obstructionists. Don't worry. It will be emphatic." He studied his nails a moment then rubbed invisible schmutz off of one. "I think a change of scenery will give you perspective."

Dominique nodded, finally silent.

She looked scared. He clicked off the call.

She should be.

Christmas lights lit up the Capitol Building inside and out. Festive décor announced the coming holidays, and people hustled about with energy.

Brittany checked her watch. It was close to nine o'clock eastern time. She hadn't heard from the team yet and could only pray they were out and safe. If Georgie's information was correct and not a trap they shouldn't have entered Holliwell West at all. And where was Georgie? She had gone MIA too!

Brittany tapped the arm of her seat. It wasn't right. Here she was safe and in style while her friends could be in danger or dead. Why hadn't anyone contacted her yet?

"Brittany, you have outdone yourself. Look at us!"

Brittany's mother, Rosa Beth Walsh sat up straight in the seat next to her, wearing a new dark blue, two-piece, slim-fitting suit that flared at her knees. Matching shoes, scarf, and gold accents completed the ensemble that Brittany had helped pick out. Brittany relaxed a little and grinned at her mom. A year ago, no one would have expected to see the Walsh women as special guests on Capitol Hill. They'd been given a private tour and seats on the floor—not the gallery but a bench right behind the Senators against the wall—and late dinner reservations at the Capitol Club after session ended tonight. Brittany would owe Graeme's mom for the rest of her college days—but it would be worth it. This kind of marketing was priceless!

She straightened as a camera panned their way. Her fabulously designed, purple suit dress with an ultra-wide collar, sharp yellow cuffs, and a tight-fitting pencil skirt would stand out against all the boring blue and black in the chamber. Yellow and purple striped pumps and large dangling earrings complemented her ponytail style hair that she left wild and poofing out naturally behind her.

Her mom reached and squeezed her hand. "I wish Nancy were here. She would have loved this."

"I know." Brittany glanced around. "She believed in all this. In doing the right thing. Someday…"

Her mom turned inquisitively. "Yes?"

"Someday people will know just how brave and wonderful she was."

Rosa Beth smiled. "We know. That's all that matters."

The sergeant at arms motioned. Everyone stood and the formalities began.

Brittany put her hand over her heart to salute the flag. The Senate Chaplain then led them in prayer. She prayed her friends were okay. She prayed she'd made the right choice tonight. And she prayed for her country. It seemed to really need it right now.

She saw her mom wipe an emotional tear away.

Yeah. She felt warmth flood her heart. This was where she needed to be.

Graeme casually put his hand on the tranquilizer gun at his side. Marco led them through two sets of doors and down a hallway through the back of the kitchen. A kitchen staff questioned them as they passed through.

"KP detail," Marco said.

"I don't have any orders about that. We have real work to do. I'm getting a—"

Marco shot a tranquilizer at the man. Graeme and Maria pulled their weapons. Someone called an alert and rushed outside before they could get to the truck. Graeme heard the pounding of boots on the ramp. A lot of boots. Cold fear ran up his spine. The girls huddled in the back with Maria guarding them.

He saw Keisha reach for a cast iron pan and hand another to her friend.

Lena discreetly donned a kitchen jacket that covered most of her clothes. She moved near other bakery staff, blending in.

More than a dozen soldiers burst in from the loading dock, in full gear.

Graeme gripped his weapon and nodded to Marco and Lena.

They would go out fighting.

Graeme didn't wait to see how many soldiers were about to enter. He shot tranquilizer darts at will, unloading on six people. They didn't fall immediately, so he took cover in the bread racks and reloaded.

Marco and Maria were on the other side, taking out as many as they could. Maria fought fearlessly, defending the other girls as they ducked below the counters. Her gun emptied quickly but Lena quickly scooped weapons from the fallen soldiers and slid them to the girls.

A soldier targeted Lena from the loading dock and she rolled, pulling a fallen soldier over her as a shield. She aimed and the soldier went down. Seeing more enter, she lifted the body and threw it at them, knocked two men down and another off balance.

She smirked a little.

Yep. These super-suits were ultra.

Graeme and Marco quickly took down three soldiers, only to see six more arrived. They seemed to come in bigger and bigger hordes.

A kitchen hand fell behind him, dropping a cast iron pan in the chaos. Graeme jumped before it hit his foot. The man fell backwards from a dart. Graeme turned and saw Keisha defending their back. The kid gave him a determined nod, her face tense.

Graeme grabbed the cast iron pan and used it as a shield to cross toward the girls on the other side of the long kitchen island. Some had weapons, others pans and knives they had procured. "Get to the back of the bakery truck, just to the left of the ramp," he told them. They needed to get out of the kitchen.

"Lena, the truck!" He hoped their comms still worked. She looked to the truck and motioned for some girls to move it. They ran out a door next to the loading ramp, and up into the truck. Lena took a spot in the back of the truck and guarded from there. The other girls helped. They still had three girls to get out and Keisha.

A voice called out over a megaphone. "We have you surrounded. Drop your weapons. Come out with your hands up. We have live fire. You *will* be killed."

Maria walked out holding an unconscious soldier hostage. "This soldier is alive, just tranquilized. Let us go, and you won't have any more damage. We don't want to hurt you! We just want our freedom!"

No one in the parking lot moved.

Lena aimed. A body fell from the roof above.

Maria flinched at the thud but didn't stand down.

Lena reloaded and tracked Graeme's eyes for a cue. *They were trapped.* This was going to be a shootout.

Then a voice on a megaphone: Hold fire!

Everyone froze, waiting. Graeme checked the time. He swallowed hard, took breath. This was it. They needed to get to out and get to safety.

Graeme waved to the girls. "Get into the back of the truck." They scrambled behind Maria while Holliwell guards seemed to take cover.

A jet flew overhead.

"Brace yourselves. This might be it!" Graeme watched as something fell on a building behind the soldiers.

He grabbed Keisha, pulled her behind a wall and covered her. And then the explosion. The ground shook. The noise deafened. Thankfully, the wall was still standing when the explosion faded out. His body felt weak. Shock maybe. His stomach felt queasy. He took a breath then checked on Keisha.

Her wide eyes filled with tears. "They really were going to kill us."

Then lights went out at the drop point and spread like a flood sweeping over them. A second later it was pitch black.

Graeme hurried Keisha to the truck and lifted her up.

Lena shut the doors. "Let's go! It's freezing."

There was dust and smoke, and their attackers seemed unsure what to do. He heard a rumbling and guessed a back-up generator was about to expose them again. It did. Some lights went on, and he found Marco lying on top of Maria, gazing at her drunkenly. She smiled back.

Graeme shook his head and snatched the back of Marco's uniform, scooping him up. "Been there. Done that, buddy. Run for your life."

Marco grinned, then promptly fell limp.

Maria jumped up and caught him. They carried him to the truck. "He was protecting me." She smiled broadly, surprised by the act. "Stupid." She got him into the front of the truck.

Graeme ran to the driver's side and hopped in. An armored soldier grabbed his shirt and tried to pull him out. Two strong kicks sent the guy flying into another truck.

Graeme turned in the seat and pulled Marco to the center while Maria climbed in protecting the other side. Graeme had no idea how many soldiers stood between them and the front gates, but he had to try and make it. The bombing wasn't over, but if they were caught the girls would be tortured or killed, and he and Marco would be tried for treason.

Yeah. Not a lot of choices. They needed to get out.

His eyes burned from smoke and dust. His stomach turned with anxiety at another bomb dropping, and his hands trembled on the wheel. If this is what heroes felt like, no wonder there weren't many left.

He revved the engine, strengthened his resolve, and hit the gas.

CHAPTER THIRTY-EIGHT

*G*eorgie felt her secure phone vibrate. She checked it. It was an unknown source. No number noted. Strange. It was a text.

The antique store is not safe. Move your people. Fast!

The antique store?

Georgie called Richie. She didn't have a communication set. "Answer. Answer."

He answered.

"Are you near an antique store?"

"Uh. Why?"

"I just got a strange text from an unknown source saying, 'The antique store is not safe. Move your people. Fast!'" The surrounding noise distracted her. A band played and cheerleaders did routines. There were five bonfires and more pickup trucks than she had ever seen in her life covering the land around them.

"Richie, I don't know what it means, but get out. Wherever you are—"

A noise on the other side of the mountains thundered. Light lit up the sky. A jet flew low toward them, loud and threatening. Something else dropped. This time the explosion was close and visible. A building inside the gates of Holliwell West was bombed.

The students held up phones in shock. Georgie yelled over the noise to Richie. "Richie! Richie! Get out! They're dropping bombs. And they're headed toward town!"

Her eyes fixated on the jet zooming into Little Eagle River. A flash of light lit up the landscape, creating a horizon line. This time a missile launched and whizzed across the sky. The echo of thunder reached them. *No!*

"Richie! Richie!"

Georgie's heart pounded. Just when she thought it was over another sound was heard. She spun back toward the mountain. A second jet appeared. And it seemed to come at them.

Al was on the last bus. They had eleven moving out. The last group of girls didn't make it in time. He stared from the rear of the bus into the dimly lit tunnel. The red lights of the first exit point began to fade as the caravan made its way through the mountain. He hoped Graeme could get the last group out.

Tension built with every rotation of the bus wheels. They still had one more checkpoint to pass.

Al checked his comm device. He didn't have any coverage. Everyone could be dead for all he knew.

One of the girls touched his arm. "Is everything okay?" The others waited, equally curious.

"We're on track," Al said. "The team reached Evie and the other girls. They're going out a different exit." He didn't tell them the front gate. That sounded too dangerous, even to him.

"Evie will get them out," a younger teen said.

"We all have to do our part. It's not over 'til it's over," Al told them. "Stay smart. Follow the plan."

The girls in the front nodded. Joe, the bus driver, gave him a reassuring nod.

Hell. What did any of them know? He took a breath, questioning his sanity for the eighty-seventh time.

"Hey!" A youthful voice called out. "There's someone behind us!"

Al hurried to the back of the bus. Sure enough, white lights were getting closer. "Everyone stay down. Joe! Alert the others."

The administrator for the bus, Tamika, joined him. She lifted the back seat and pulled out cases of equipment. "We have twenty tranq guns. Hand them to the older girls." She looked at the girls nearest them. "Who has experience with live weapons?"

All the girls raise their hands.

"We don't want to kill anyone. This is only precautionary. We'll hand those out if needed."

Al grabbed a belt of ammunition and swung an M240 over his shoulder. He'd carried a similar machine gun during his Army Ranger days. Only he hadn't planned on killing anyone today. It wasn't that long ago that he and Richie had been on the other side of this fight. But then they saw too much, learned too much, and lost too much.

Joe called to the back. "Hold on! We're moving into double formation. So they can't get beside us."

The bus sped up as the one in front slowed and moved into the opposite lane. The others in front did the same. The white lights behind them got bigger. There were solo lights too. Motorcycles. They could get close enough to blow out a bus wheel.

A loud voice from a megaphone, echoed through the tunnel. "Stop the bus!"

"Everyone, down!" Al shouted, ducking below the windows.

The girls ducked too, huddling on the floor in front of their seats and in the aisles.

"Stop!" The megaphone called out. "Or we will use force."

They kept going.

Warning shots fired breaking through windows, shattering glass. Then a container burst through a window.

"Gas!" Someone called. The girls pulled their shirts over their noses. Another girl grabbed the container and tossed it out the window before her friend pulled her back down to safety, frightened.

Something bright shot out of a pursuing truck.

"Hold on!" he shouted.

An explosion lifted the entire back end. The bus landed hard, wobbling, and hitting the bus next to them. The girls didn't scream. It was weird. Hell, Al almost screamed.

Al aimed some warning shots back at them with his M240. It seemed to work. They slowed down.

Joe stepped on it and got the bus moving with determination, but it had a distinct wobble.

The white lights began to fade back—even the motorcycles.

"That's not good," Al said.

"No," Tamika said. "Something's up."

"Everyone put on your seatbelts." He didn't know why he said that. He just had a bad feeling. He and Tamika did the same. Holliwell wasn't going to just let them go. They had a plan.

The earth shook.

Girls gasped.

The earth rumbled.

The girls cried out.

The buses in front slowed. It started a chain reaction. Soon they were squealing to a stop. Al guessed there were tanks or trucks blocking them in the front.

Then he wished it were tanks or trucks.

Instead, rocks and pieces of the walls around them began to fall. Dust and dirt came in through the open windows. Girls quickly put them up.

"The tunnel is crumbling," a girl in the front screamed.

Al ran to the front of the bus. "Open the door, Joe!"

A loud cracking began. Joe opened the door.

Al ran in between the buses until he got to the front. Rocks were coming down on the front two buses as well. The littlest babies would be buried.

"Back up! Back up!" He yelled, waving his hands.

They moved, but not fast enough.

The mountain collapsed and crashed down upon them.

Brittany stretched her legs. The Vice President, Susan Rash, had just given an overly long introduction to the new bill about to be debated, and the vital need for science and research to save our most valuable resources—people. Apparently only some people, as others were to be used as test subjects in the research, but Brittany tried not to look cynical on camera. It was being broadcast live after all.

In the midst of the speech VP Rash also managed to bring up the group of domestic terrorists identified as Obstructionists. Honestly, Brittany was sick of hearing about these people. If anyone dared to disagree with the administration on any little issue they were tagged an Ostructionist. Chill out already.

And…smile for the camera.

Rachel was up next. Brittany was interested in hearing her speak. Graeme's mom looked sharp and powerful in a tailored black suit and crisp white shirt. She stood behind the lifted podium of her desk on the floor of the Senate and started with the thank yous—which were all very polite.

"Before my prepared remarks," Rachel spoke from her seat in Senate. "I'd like to address Vice President Rash's comments on "Obstructionists". There is no new party or movement that has come out and called themselves Obstructionists. That title is only reserved for anyone who disagrees with the President or any aspect of his administration or leadership. Hashtags and labels don't make something real. What is real is that there are many opinions in America and as elected leaders we are all required to listen to them, assess the challenges, seek options and negotiate the best solutions for all sides. 'My way or the highway,' is not a leadership mentality, it's a dictator's mentality."

Brittany sucked in a breath. The Vice President, sitting front and center on the Senatorial throne, looked pissed-off!

Her mom noticed too. She leaned into Brittany's ear, "This is getting good now." She smiled. Brittany relaxed. It's just politics—all for show. *And…an interested nod for the camera.*

"On the issue of the proposed bill to increase the federal 'parents' rights' laws to eighteen—giving parents essentially ownership of their children, their lives, and their life choices—and be required to apply to the government in order to make them legitimate and accepted humans at some government dictated age, I'd like to present the moral and constitutional issues as to why we should not do this, and instead should move to repeal these laws permanently in all states."

Brittany leaned forward interested, as the Senator opened her mouth to continue. Whatever she was going to say was lost in a popping sound.

People gasped then dived for cover.

Brittany didn't move. She watched in horror as Rachel's head slung forward unnaturally then her whole body fell over her desk before sliding to the floor.

Rachel!

Someone screamed.

The Sergeant-at-Arms by the right entrance pulled her weapon but was shot from another direction and slammed into the wall behind her.

Oh-my-God. Brittany's stomach flooded with pain. She got light-headed. There was more than one shooter inside the chamber!

Her mom grabbed her hard and pulled her to the ground as people began to duck and run for cover.

Brittany didn't know where the shots were coming from. She swallowed, then pulled herself to her knees, forcing herself to get bearings. She didn't want to walk into a killer.

A guard at the other side of the room pushed a civilian behind a wall and shot at one of the shooters.

Another shooter walked up the few steps toward the Vice President and shot her twice.

Brittany stared, numb. They killed the Vice President. With no fear. Just like that.

Her hand hit the floor holding herself in shock as her mom pulled her back against the wall. Someone walked past them with an easy stride. *Evil strolling by.*

She took a breath, crawled on the cold floor and peaked around the wall toward the Senators' seats.

Black polished wingtips turned at Rachel's row.

Rachel!

Brittany took a breath and scrambled rapidly on her knees down the main aisle. The wingtips were making their way toward Rachel. Gasping for oxygen to enable her, Brittany stood and tried to run at him, but her body would not obey.

He raised his arm.

Brittany forced her legs to move. She stumbled in her spikey heels but recovered enough to stumble forward, get one good foot plant and launched, tackling him from behind.

They fell sideways. His elbow swung back into her face trying to dislodge her as they hit the hard wood of another desk. She held on, grasping his throat with one hand and clawing his face from behind with the other. Her skirt rode up her thighs and she wrapped her legs around him doing what she could to slow him down.

He half stood, taking Brittany with him, then pounded her violently backward into a desk until she released him. Stunned and breathless, she rolled into the next row of seats but scrambled to recover, only to find him standing over her. He searched for his weapon, then reached for another on his body.

In the corner of her eye, Brittany saw movement.

Rachel stood up!

And she had a gun. His gun.

Without hesitating the Senator shot her attacker in the head. He fell over with finality—dead. Rachel turned at the sound of more shots and fired at the man who killed the VP hitting him in the chest. She fired a third time, sending a bullet through his throat. A guard ran to either finish him off or subdue him. Brittany didn't know. She just stared at Rachel in awe.

A cold, haunting silence fell in the Senate chamber.

Brittany slowly stood, pulling her skirt down. She'd lost a shoe somewhere. She spotted it by Rachel who put her hand out to Brittany in warning.

"Nobody move," a third shooter yelled. "Or this one's dead."

Brittany turned slowly, fear crawling over her skin from the direction of that voice. Then her limbs turned cold, and her stomach flipped to heave.

Fifteen feet away a man dragged her mother up against him with a pistol shoved into the side of her head.

Brittany stared, a distant part of her observing without emotion. Her mother's hair was mussed. There was an arm around her neck choking her. But her mother only stared at Brittany, her face serene and calm. Her eyes full of love, like this was her last message.

Love radiated from her mom. An ethereal warmth enfolded Brittany bringing calm and peace beyond they physical circumstances.

She understood in an instant.

This might be their last moment. No regrets. Never. No regrets.

"I love you, mom! I love you!" Brittany yelled it, eyes glued to her mom's, refusing to look away. Tears streamed down her face. She shouted louder. "I love you! I love you!"

A gunshot exploded.

CHAPTER THIRTY-NINE

*J*ocelyn and Evie fast walked to the science wing.

In her nursing garb, no one questioned her credentials. Everyone was too busy scrambling for cover before another bomb dropped. Military members ran toward the tunnels and outdoors where the "Obstructionists" were supposedly attacking.

She and Evie walked through the hospital and out the other side, across to the large wing that held the science labs. It was suddenly quiet and peaceful. Workers were gone for the day and the area was far removed from danger. The giant lab was pristine with white floors, lots of glass, and rows of counters filled with lab equipment.

A lone scientist working at a counter was their only obstacle.

"We're meeting Dr. Wicker here," Jocelyn said.

"I'm supposed to get a new dose," Evie added.

"That's not the protocol," the scientist said.

"She's been getting seizures," Jocelyn filled in. "We think it's time for...you know." She acted like she didn't want to say it in front of Evie.

The woman understood and nodded, more sympathetic. "It's a normal symptom in the earlier cases. I'm sorry." She said it to Evie. "Do you want to have a seat in the lounge by the kitchen?"

Evie nodded.

"Are the evacuations complete?" the scientist asked.

"Yes, all done," Jocelyn informed. "We'll just wait in Dr. Wicker's office. Thanks,"

The woman nodded and went back to work. The science lab was an open floor, about fifty

by a hundred feet, one side lined with glass-enclosed individual patient rooms. Everything could be seen and monitored.

Jocelyn strode with authority to double glass doors leading to more offices. She guessed the lab's vaults would be further after that. Hopefully, her security badge would work.

A woman turned a corner in front of them and Jocelyn saw her through the glass door. *Avis!*

Avis walked toward them and opened the door, holding it for them. "Come in. Quickly."

Jocelyn hesitated, surprised, but then entered and followed the woman.

Avis hurried ahead of them. "I wasn't able to get into the last vault. I think that's what you're looking for."

Evie gave Jocelyn a questioning glance. Jocelyn shook her head. She didn't know what Avis was up to, but she didn't trust her.

"Why did you leave the tower?"

"I'm sorry. Security was on the way." Avis stopped and explained directly. "I was trapped. I had only seconds to get out. I thought it best to try to get here before we lost our chance."

"Oh," Jocelyn nodded, still not trusting the woman. They followed her through two more secure doors to a vault. "Richie, do you have this? Are we secure?"

"Yes, ma'am," Richie's voice was breathless, like he was on the move.

"What's the problem," Jocelyn asked.

"It's biometric. We need the hand and the eyes of an approved person."

Evie tried to pull the door of the vault. It wouldn't budge. "We need Wicker."

"Richie, any chance you can locate Dr. Wicker in this chaos?"

"Piece of cake," his voice crackled a bit from reception. "She's headed your way."

"How close?"

"About to enter the science wing."

"Got it. Thanks." To the women. "Wicker is about to enter the lab. We need to hide somewhere until she gets here."

"Follow me," Avis said. "There are offices just outside the vault."

The three hustled to an office. Avis opened it, turned the lights off and waited.

"I think we need to go to the lab," Evie said. "What if she leaves before we can get her?"

"Richie, eyes?" Jocelyn asked.

"She's walking west, toward you. With purpose. She's going for something."

"She's in trouble," Avis said. "She might be going to get the formula for herself."

Jocelyn tuned to the surroundings, catching the click of heels unique to Wicker's pace. A minute later, she passed them.

"Definitely headed to the vault," Avis said, triumphant. She opened the door of the office to follow.

"Wait," Jocelyn grabbed Avis's arm and stayed back a little. She wanted the vault opened before they exposed themselves.

"It's going to take time to open the vault. I'll go first."

Jocelyn walked softly on the white tile floor, checking the walls for any reflection that would give her away. She listened as Wicker swiped her badge, entered a code, pressed her hand and eyes to the scanners then entered another code. There was a click, a swish of release then she pulled the temperature-controlled vault open. Jocelyn heard the light buzz of multiple refrigerators and containment units.

Avis came forward and Jocelyn held her back again. "Let her lead us."

Jocelyn needed the formula in her hands. Hope for Benny filled her, but she wasn't there yet. The vault was large. There could be any number of science projects kept there. She listened more as Wicker pressed another code and opened a door to a smaller refrigerated safe, taking something out. *This had to be it!*

Jocelyn moved quickly. "Hello, Dr. Wicker."

The older woman held a black and silver, locked medical case.

"I just can't get rid of you." Wicker smiled at Jocelyn. "Et tu, Evie?"

Evie came up behind Jocelyn. "You were going to kill us."

"That's ridiculous. Where did you hear such nonsense?" Wicker tried to leave the vault.

Evie pushed her chest, forcing her back. "As if your maze torture wasn't enough." She reached for the medical case. "Open the case."

Dr. Wicker just smiled.

Jocelyn grabbed the case. She had to see inside. Hope bubbled. This could be her mother's formula—the cure for Benny that was stolen. She opened the case.

Inside were two small vials—one empty, one a quarter full. It wasn't much, but it was hope. She exhaled quiet excitement and took the vial.

"You can't have that," Dr. Wicker said. "It belongs to the government."

"Actually, you know better, Wicker." Jocelyn pocketed the vial inside a secure medical bag under the waist of her nursing uniform.

"It doesn't belong to anyone," Avis said, standing outside the vault and sliding the handle so the door was nearly closed. "It's an abomination." She took a small device from her supply bag. "All the science must be destroyed," Avis looked at Jocelyn, half apologetic. "All of it."

Then she pulled the pin and threw the grenade into the vault as the door shut.

CHAPTER FORTY

*E*vie leapt for the grenade. *Three.*

Strangely, she wasn't sure that it was the dumbest or most terrifying thing she'd ever done. Which was probably not a good sign about how far she'd fallen. *Two.*

They'd taught the girls that you had three seconds before detonation. A lot of her life on the reservation passed through her mind. Odd how three seconds could be so important.

She slid on the floor, her hand covered the grenade, and she pushed it forward like a puck in air hockey, going for the goal. *One.*

The grenade flew across the floor into the small open space of the closing vault. Only it hit the wall and bounced left toward the closing door. Her heart rate spiked as it looked like it might bounce back in, but then the door hit it, and it spun out of the vault. *Score.*

Evie felt a pull on her shirt then was yanked backward on top of Wicker and dog piled by Jocelyn. The explosion screamed through the hall outside the vault. Or maybe that was Avis? Evie felt a whoosh of heat and movement surround them.

The explosion rocked everything in the vault. Loose items fell off shelves and refrigeration units. But the sound hurt the most.

Jocelyn got up and helped her. They left Wicker to her own devices.

Evie pressed her ears, pounding them. "That hurt."

Jocelyn nodded but looked unfazed.

Evie pressed her eyes. Colors were not clear. "You look a little blue," she said to Jocelyn.

Jocelyn merely nodded again then went to the door of the vault. It was severely mangled and stuck. Jocelyn pushed until there was enough room for them to get through. She slid out.

Evie followed. Then swallowed hard at the scene.

Avis didn't make it.

She shouldn't feel bad. The woman had just tried to kill all three of them. But this was …bad. Evie gagged and stepped back.

The pure white walls of scientific sanctity around them were splattered…with Avis.

Wicker came behind them. "Good job, Seventeen. That bitch deserved it." She stepped around the woman's remains. "I'll get security and someone to clean this up."

Evie stared at Wicker, her mouth dropping. The woman must be in shock, right? She acted like someone spilled their juice in the lunchroom.

"Sunday," Wicker continued speaking to Jocelyn. "Give me the formula and we'll call it all even. Seventeen can go back to her dorms and you can leave."

Evie almost did throw up now. Staying terrified her. She took a breath for control, shaken and seeking Jocelyn's cue.

"No go, Wicker." Jocelyn took off her white nursing pants to reveal winter army fatigues. "Evie, take her down the hall, and hold her. I need to check something here."

Evie obeyed, capturing Wicker's arm with ease. She glanced back to see Jocelyn take off the white orderly top. She

308

had a white t-shirt underneath and used the orderly shirt to protect her hand as she picked through parts of Avis. Evie didn't know what she looked for, but she found something that she pocketed. Then she draped the shirt over Avis's head.

Evie turned back to Wicker too late. She felt a hard prick in her arm and instinctively reached and pulled out the syringe. Very little liquid remained. Whatever was inside the syringe was now inside her! *Great.* Evie punched Wicker in the face without thinking. *Better.*

Wicker fell sideways on a knee then got up.

"She'll be dead in five minutes," Wicker said to Jocelyn. "Unless you give me back the formula."

"No." Jocelyn had no expression. "And she's not going to die, so you should watch your back."

Evie felt numb. She didn't know if it was from fear or if the potion was killing her.

Crazy Wicker wasn't sticking around. She ran for the exit.

"Don't let that bitch get away," Evie ordered.

"We don't need her. We need to move," Jocelyn said. "There's a squad headed our way."

Evie wobbled. "Your eyes are so blue."

A few people in the lab came out from under cover and looked at them.

Jocelyn caught Evie and hurried through the lab. "Stay in your offices until it's safe," Jocelyn shouted as they rushed by. "I'm taking her to the hospital."

Evie smiled, amazed. Everyone seemed as dazed and obedient as she—not her normal state, but at least she wasn't hallucinating horses again.

Brittany cried out.

She felt her life force slip away as she stared into her mother's closed eyes.

Her stomach clenched. She wept out loud. "Mom." The word was a plea.

Then the man fell away and her mom stumbled the other direction. A secret service officer caught her mom and pulled her to safety.

Brittany's first instinct was to run to them but she couldn't move. Her mind would not compute. She turned around to see if there were any more dangers. Rachel swayed, still holding the gun. The Senator had shot the third man in the side of the head. He wasn't dead, but agents grabbed him. She'd saved Brittany's mom.

Another agent came to Rachel's side and took the gun from her frozen grip. "Nice shooting, Senator."

Rachel nodded. "I have a concussion." Then she collapsed into the man's arms.

Brittany reached to help.

"Get back, miss!" The man warned, carrying Rachel to the aisle and laying her down.

"I'm with her. I made her wig. Let me take it off. Please! You can bring it to the doctor. She was shot in the back of the head."

He looked disbelieving.

"Please," Brittany urged. "Let me show you."

He seemed to take a chance and Brittany knelt, gently removing the wig and attached skullcap.

Definitely bulletproof.

She showed the agent the bullet mark. "Bring this to the hospital. The force of the bullet was powerful. She needs an MRI or something."

EMTs hurried into the Senate chamber.

Rachel opened her eyes and tried to sit up.

"Stay put ma'am. We're getting you to a hospital."

She grabbed Brittany's hand. "Get my security detail. Don't let them give me anything."

Brittany nodded. She'd seen the two men earlier. They hadn't been allowed in the chamber. She ran out and found them by the door with Rachel's secretary, driver, and other staff. "The Senator wants her private detail to travel with her," she told the people guarding the doors. They let one pass as the gurney rolled forward then the other joined her.

"We'll meet you at the hospital," Brittany told Rachel.

"My purse," Rachel said.

Brittany ran to the desk, grabbed the purse, and opened it at the sound of a vibrating phone. She saw the caller and answered, putting the phone by Rachel's ear.

"It's Ford," she said.

Rachel smiled. "Hi honey. Stay with me on the drive to the hospital, okay?"

Brittany watched them go then spotted her mom again. They ran to each other and embraced. Her mom held her, strong and firm. Brittany did the same, a lifetime of hugs flooding her, all precious but none as much as this.

"I love you," they both spoke at the same time. They laughed. Tears filled both their eyes. They hugged again. Finally, they pulled apart. Brittany fixed her mom's suit and makeup, then made sure she looked presentable. One of Rachel's assistants found them and escorted them to a car.

They were walking out a side security door when they heard another shot.

Brittany spun.

A woman shouted, "Long live the resistance!" Then another shot was fired.

The three women hurried with secret service to the waiting car, but even when they were safe, Brittany couldn't stop the chills that shook her body.

A feeling of loss and doom came over her.

This wasn't the end. This was just the beginning.

CHAPTER FORTY-ONE

*J*ocelyn carried Evie to the hospital ward and laid her on a gurney in the hall. There was lots of activity. The targeted destruction of a dorm had people panicked and scrambling. Some who had not obeyed the evacuation orders were injured but one glance told Jocelyn all the wounds were minor.

Evie, on the other hand, had been unconscious for nearly five minutes.

Jocelyn rolled her on the gurney toward the original evacuation tunnel. She ditched her wig, and snagged a military cap. She wasn't sure how to get Evie out in her current condition, but figured it was time to improvise.

She'd been cut off from Richie, and Graeme's team was somewhere in the loading bay. No one had heard from Al. Not a good sign. She would head that direction. He might need help. Maybe she could liberate a vehicle.

She touched the pouch at her waist. This was the most important thing—Benny's cure. If nothing else, she needed to get this formula to New York.

Jocelyn pulled up the map on her phone. They had already dropped a bomb inside the front gate. The other dorm targets were next. But the fastest route to the tunnels required them to pass the dorms. She picked up her pace. How much time before the next drop?

Seconds? Minutes? Never enough time.

"Watch out!" she warned some people in the halls. "Coming through."

She skirted some guards and heard one call behind, "Hey? That's her! Stop!"

Jocelyn charged the elevator. She made a quick turn back, and at their raised weapons lifted a hand and blasted enough energy to throw them off target and slow them down. When she turned back, Evie sat up with a gasp.

Jocelyn grabbed the gurney again and took off.

"Am I dead? Everything is white and I'm going fast through space." She put her hands out wide, feeling the air go by.

"You're not dead. Lie down!"

Evie turned around and stared at her, confused. "What are you doing here? What's—"

They reached the elevator. Jocelyn pounded the buttons then helped Evie off the gurney.

"I'm glad you're awake. We need to get out." She dragged the girl into the elevator and pressed to go down.

"Okay." Evie nodded her head trying to catch up. "Wait." She scowled at Jocelyn. "What the hell is going on? How did you know Wicker didn't poison me?"

"I didn't. I just hoped she was self-serving enough to keep you alive."

"Great." Evie rubbed her eyes and focused. "Can you please tell me what is going on?"

Jocelyn shuffled through the security badges she had and picked one. "They are bombing the dorms to make it look like Obstructionists. They were going to let you die. We came to save you. Now we need to get out." She touched the badge to the panel and selected the locked basement level. "I don't know how destructive the bombs really are. We're going lower. Not sure if it's safer. We can pass the dorms then take an elevator up to the tunnel."

Evie stared at her a long moment. "My vision is really good right now. I think I can see your aura. And my skin is tingling."

"Maybe Wicker gave you a hallucinogen. You were out for about five minutes."

"I see." Evie stood ultra-still. "Very clearly."

The elevator opened and Jocelyn pulled Evie out.

Evie pulled back. Her head dropped. "I can't go with you."

"What?" Jocelyn panicked. "Evie, they will torture you and conduct crazy experiments on you if they find you. It's not an option."

"I know where Wicker is going." Evie lifted her head. "There are private quarters near the dorms. She has a suite there for nights when she doesn't go into town or visit the city. She probably has all her duplicate research and I'm pretty sure, more of that formula. I heard her say one time she had a back-up plan. She could take this formula to anyone, any country." Evie shook her head. "I need to stop her. You need to get out… and make sure the others escape."

"Evie, please." Jocelyn knew Evie's odds if she stayed. "It's not worth it. Come with me."

She shook her head. "I have to do this."

"It's suicide."

"Says the girl who attacked an airplane."

Jocelyn gave a resigned smiled. "Just come with me. Please."

"I never planned on leaving, Jocelyn. She's killed thir-ty-four girls that I know of. And now I've killed *for* her. There's nothing out there for me." Evie shook her head. "And I'll never be at peace with her alive. No one will be." Evie took Jocelyn's hand and squeezed it. "This is *my* mission."

Jocelyn struggled. It wasn't acceptable. It wasn't fair. And nothing about it felt right.

But she understood.

She grasped Evie and hugged her hard. "Watch out for bombs, grenades, and crazy-ass scientists with needles."

Evie chuckled a little and hugged back. "I think we could have been friends." She let go. "I mean if I hadn't done all the things I've done and—"

Jocelyn shook her head.

"No?" Evie slumped a little. "Yeah, I guess not."

"Shut up you idiot," Jocelyn took a breath. "I meant— we *are* friends." She held back the tears that threatened and squeezed Evie again. "Now go kick ass like a Crow."

Evie laughed. "So lame."

They fist bumped and separated.

Red sirens started wailing and flashing in the halls. Jocelyn looked back. So did Evie. With a final nod of luck and farewell, they ran like the wind.

Al had a sinking feeling. More like an eighty-pound weight in his stomach.

Eighty pairs of worried, uncertain eyes were on him. Girls from ten to maybe seventeen. They were every race and mix. Some held hands, frightened. Others hugged or clenched the seats in front of them.

He took a breath. He needed to promote confidence. Soldiers were only as good as their leader.

He sized up the situation—tunnel of darkness, collapsed exit, military likely to return, and a lot of girls needing escape.

He modified that. *Girls with superpowers.* He smiled.

"Listen up!" he called out. "We are all going to escape and be safe. You need to know that. But you also need to know that you are the ones who will make that happen. You're smart, you're strong and you're trained to do stuff, right?"

There were some nods.

"You got this, but we need to work together and quickly. Anyone who doesn't have a weapon, stand up and go to the front of the tunnel and help remove rocks. We need to clear a path out of here. This is very important. Make sure the little ones are safe. You are now their protectors. You must get them to safety! We need to move enough rock for one bus. Got it?"

The determined girls nodded and rushed out of the bus. Two others with weapons came to him, faces serious.

"We should go to the top of the bus. We're both sharp-shooters. Top of our units."

"Excellent. Stay low. Do not make yourself a target. And don't shoot until I say."

"Yes, sir." They said in unison then climbed up the door of the roof of the bus.

"Joe, tell the other drivers to turn off their lights." Al turned to the remaining girls. "Tamika, you stay here with Joe and the sharpshooters. The rest of you take position outside along the walls. Stay behind the posts in the walls for cover. When I give the call, you'll fire. But they have armor and most of you only have tranquilizer darts, so you need to find a soft spot—their face, throat, cracks in gear. Don't waste your shot. Wait if you must and get close."

"Yes, sir." The girls hurried to take up their positions.

317

He stopped two of them—a cute, wide-eyed, Asian American girl with a ponytail, and a brown-haired, freckled, mixed-race girl who said she was experienced with live fire.

"What's your name?" he asked the first one.

"Sixty-seven, sir."

Al balked. "Uh. Do you have another name?"

"I used to be called Pepper."

"Pepper. First or last?"

"First."

"Okay, Pepper—and?" he asked the other girl.

"Gemma," she smiled a little.

He huddled them in a circle. "Here's the plan.

Jocelyn heard the soldiers organizing and moving in. She clipped her badge to the outside of her pants and walked up to the tables covered with gear. Most of the guns were for subduing experiments, but other weapons were being employed.

"They're trapped at the end of the tunnel. There's nowhere for them to go," a sergeant informed Chang.

Chang nodded. "How many do we have assembled?"

"Eighty here. One thousand at the ready around the complex. The others are spread out in the front, and we have troops headed to the other side of the tunnel. They should be there in twelve minutes."

Jocelyne counted Eighty-two military with the sergeant and Commander Chang. She assessed her options while casually blending in, grabbing gear, and slipping two loaded tranq guns into her holster. Most of the soldiers were already on open transport vehicles and moving forward into the tunnel. Chang jumped into a big Hummer and followed them. Only Jocelyn and some support staff remained. The last bus still sat to the side. She walked over to it.

"Soldier, what are you doing?"

Jocelyn didn't miss a beat. "Sir, I'm bringing the bus up behind for transport back, sir."

"On whose order?"

"Commander Change, sir. I'll wait for you to confirm." She stood at the ready.

The man nodded. "Go ahead. Grab some body armor, just in case. Even bus drivers can get shot."

"Yes, sir." Jocelyn obeyed then got in the bus. No keys. *Shoot.*

The man came to the door of the bus. "Problem?"

"Yes, sir. No keys."

He held them up. "Never leave keys in a vehicle. Don't know who might drive off with your car." He tossed her the keys.

"Yes, sir." She grinned. "Good advice, sir."

Jocelyn started the bus and slowly moved it out, driving at a slow pace as she tracked the military transport trucks ahead of her. They slowed down and she parked behind them about twenty feet back. They were in the widest part of the tunnel and used the trucks to form a blockade. Did they expect an army? Did they know who they were fighting, or had they been kept in the dark?

Jocelyn crept closer in the dark seeking a better view. A small light came at them from the other end of the tunnel. Floodlights went on, exposing two terrified, skinny girls about Maddie's age. They were covered in dirt and dust, had their arms linked, and were bent over a little, huddled together.

"Please help us." The dark-haired girl cried out. "We didn't want to go. They took us."

Two soldiers with armor slowly came out and grabbed the girls bringing them to safety.

Chang interrogated them. "Where are the others?"

Jocelyn stepped closer in the dark, alongside the wall. She leaned back, casually holding her gun with the barrel pointed down like the other soldiers.

The same girl spoke. "They're dead, and the others are trapped and hurt. The tunnel collapsed on all the buses. We crawled out one of the back windows. Some of the others wanted to come but they're too afraid."

"It's okay," Chang said. "We'll help them and get everyone back. Can you tell me if the people who took you are armed?"

"There's only two people on each bus. I think at least one has a gun, but I didn't see it."

Chang questioned the other girl and got the same information.

"Let's move forward. Slowly," she told her team. "We need the younger ones alive. Tell your units to spare as many as you can." The men and women nodded and dispersed. A soldier brought the two girls back through the tunnel. They passed Jocelyn. She was tempted to take them, but she couldn't risk betrayal. They disappeared into the darkness.

She waited, watching the forward motion. She had twenty darts, and two reloads, so potentially forty soldiers if she could connect with skin. But she had no back up and who knew how many were waiting outside the collapsed tunnel if they made it that far.

Just as she was planning the order of attack, a familiar sound of small feet caught her ear. She searched in the darkness. One of the little girls crawled under a truck making her way back to the front. Jocelyn moved into a corner for cover and searched for the other one. She spotted the girl holding a tranq gun—their escort nowhere in sight. *Al, you're a genius.* She quietly followed them to see the plan.

The familiar sounds of a click then the rolling of a grenade got her attention.

Outstanding plan!

She dove for cover.

CHAPTER FORTY-TWO

The grenade blew up an empty truck in the front of the blockade, and sent it flying upward. Parts hit the ceiling and sailed in every direction. The destruction also broke Chang's defense just enough.

"Now!" Jocelyn heard Al order.

Chang called out a similar order and her soldiers rushed toward Al.

Jocelyn attacked from behind, silently tranquilizing soldiers and pulling them into the darkness. Nearing the front, she spotted the grenade girls hiding under a truck. She rolled next to them, held up a finger for silence and handed them tranq guns. "Come with me."

They crawled out and ran back through the dark toward the bus. Jocelyn started it up and drove it into position. With a little luck they could get through the barricade. "Open the window in the back," she ordered. They obeyed then returned. She gave the tallest one directions. "The bus is in gear. This pedal is go. This one stop. As soon as I clear the path, gas it and go through."

"What about you?"

"I'll hop on as you pass. Don't worry. Just brake before you hit the other buses, okay? I'll come back and take the wheel."

"Okay." The girl looked nervous but nodded that she would do it.

Jocelyn put the smaller girl on the floor of the front seat. "Take cover."

"I'll cover you and Pepper," the girl declared, her face determined.

"Okay." Jocelyn understood that expression. "Give me twenty seconds."

Jocelyn ran back to the front of the fight. Chang, nearby, yelled into her comm device for backup. Jocelyn needed to disrupt Chang's core huddle of power and break up the largest group of soldiers.

She focused on the remains of the grenade-exploded vehicle and took a breath, letting the cold mountain seep into her skin. In close quarters it was easier to sense shape and mass, but she was far from expert. She would need to practice this more in the future.

Since leaving Holliwell and clearing her system of their controlling drugs, her powers had become stronger and her skills more fine-tuned. Her energy now felt more like a natural form of touch. She couldn't feel the truck or the blown wheel or the metal parts the same way her hand could feel them. But, her energy when controlled could grasp objects and she could feel the weight and shape of them, assess the power it took to move them, and she could collect them one by one before sliding them slowly across the road, almost unnoticed.

Finally, the pieces were in position, locked by her focused energy. She moved quickly, sending a surge through her body, down her arms and out. The metal and rubber lifted and she flung them with force to where Chang and others defended their position.

The shock of heavy metal and objects landing and hitting soldiers produced yelps of surprise and panic as Chang and the remaining soldiers, believing they were attacked from behind, ran forward into the Al's small but mighty army.

Al saw Chang and the soldiers run toward them. The girls, making good on their promise, picked them off with a precision that was chilling.

Chang locked on Al, identified him as the leader, and approached fearless, ready for battle.

She swung.

He blocked with ease.

"Hey now! Don't you remember me? I thought we had a moment." It wasn't going to be a fair fight. He was much bigger and he had a flexo-skeleton on. Something sharp cut his arm.

He cursed and deflected the knife, feeling the power of the super-suit deflate where the cut had been made. Damn. Never underestimate an angry chick. Especially not in special ops.

"I really don't want to hurt you," Al told Chang.

"I really want to hurt you," she swung the knife again.

Al high-kicked her wrist. The knife fell from her grip. She put her hands up to fight. He had no doubt she had skills. But he didn't have time to play. He went on attack, kicking, keeping a safe distance. She deflected, backing into the Hummer. He got close enough to grab her. She punched. It connected hard, but he caught her arm in a lock.

Call off your back up. Tell them you have everything under control."

"Never."

He twisted her arm to break it. She whimpered.

Seriously, Chang." He growled in her ear. "Why are you on the wrong side of the war?"

"Quick way up the ladder." She gasped at the pain more pressure induced.

"Bad decision. Make a good one now."

"It's too late."

"It's never too late," Al said. "Believe me. I know."

"It's in the Hummer. My other comm."

Al opened the door and grabbed the device. She squirmed, and he caught her back against him, holding the device to her mouth. Give the order.

"This is Chang." She took a breath. "Hurry!"

Al let go of the comm. "I'm disappointed in you Chang." He shot her shoulder with a tranquilizer. "You're going to pay dearly for all these girls. The ones who died and the ones whose freedom you took."

Chang stared at him. "I didn't do it. I just followed…"

She went limp. He dragged her toward the wall, searched her weapon belt, and found zip ties to secure her. It would slow her down temporarily if she woke too soon.

The girls finished the battle around him and recovered weapons from soldiers who obviously were not used to fighting badass girls.

A moment later Pepper came bursting through the debris in a bus. He stepped back. Then a voice running behind called out.

"Al! Come on!" Jocelyn called. "There's more coming. We only have a few minutes."

Jocelyn! He was never so happy to see her. She sprinted toward the back of the bus. He kept pace and they jumped together, grabbing hold.

"There was a cave in. We're trapped."

"Oh." She sounded worried.

"You can handle that, right?"

"Sure. Piece o'cake."

He turned back as one last soldier crawled out of a Hummer. Al aimed and shot him in the throat. The soldier pulled at the dart in panic, took a few steps then fell.

The bus disappeared into the darkness, slowing down as they reached the other buses.

Al tossed his empty weapon. "Let's go get that cake."

Evie intersected Wicker exiting her suite. The area had been evacuated for safety and two guards escorted her. The three of them hopped onto a green golf cart and came back her way. Evie stood in the path, unmoving. It took Wicker a moment for recognition to set in. Not recognition that it was Evie standing there, but recognition of the fact that Evie hadn't left—instead, she'd come back for her. Evie tilted her head and smiled when she saw that moment of understanding flash across Wicker's face.

It was followed by panic.

"Shoot her!" Wicker yelled.

The soldier driving stopped the vehicle and pulled her gun. The other soldier did the same. They didn't use tranquilizer guns. The sirens in the area had alerted the military to a bigger danger. Obstructionists in their midst. Live fire flew toward her.

Strangely, the bullets didn't move that fast. Evie turned, bobbed, then ran forward, sliding under a stream of lead projectiles with ease.

Whatever Wicker had injected her with gave her *really* good vision.

She jumped to her feet. The soldiers seemed equally slow to respond.

She punched the female who took a few hard hits but fought back. Evie picked her up and flung her at the male guard as he pulled out another gun. Wicker took the moment to put the cart in reverse. It jetted backward into a wall then spun it around.

A bullet grazed Evie's arm and she turned back in time to see the male guard shoot again. She stepped up to the soldier, disarmed him, then shot him in both legs, repeating the same routine with the female before spinning back toward Wicker and unloading the gun. A cry from Wicker let her know that at least one bullet connected before the golf cart whizzed around the corner.

Evie took off after it.

She might not have to kill Wicker herself. The woman drove straight for the dorms and the drop zone.

Evie just had to time their arrival with the bombs and all her problems would be over.

For good.

CHAPTER FORTY-THREE

The President wanted to address the nation from the Oval Office. It was going to be a historic speech. The setting should be right. Jerry planned everything. And it went according to plan—mostly. Colorado was not yet contained, but this next round of jets should take care of that. Senator Winslow-Rochester lived, to his surprise, but he already had an idea of how to make use of that failure.

Most of all, the evening would certainly turn the country against Obstructionists and those who wanted to usurp the status quo. They would be able to quickly pass laws for easier use of military rule, set curfews, and shut down all internet objections before any alternate news sources could get a foothold. And he'd terminated the Vice President. She could never serve as President. She actually believed their ideology. It made her a little dangerous and uncontrollable. The best Presidents were the ones who wanted power and adulation, but knew they needed others to achieve and maintain it. He'd had a good run at picking those people in each party. It was a gift.

The director cued the President. Jerry watched the screen like the rest of America would be doing tonight.

"Fellow Americans, it is with great distress that I share this news tonight." He paused and gazed gravely into the cameras. "Tonight, we were attacked by violent terrorist forces in a combined effort, from within our own country. Civilian and military bases in Colorado, Texas and New York were attacked. We don't yet know the lives lost or the damage done.

Further, here in Washington D.C., in the sacred Senate chamber, at least three known Obstructionists opened fire in a cold and brutal assault on our most senior leaders. There were three deaths, including—". He looked down and paused, gathering himself. His eyes burned with emotion. "Including our Vice President, Susan Rash." He took an emotional breath. "Vice President Rash was a devoted supporter of freedom and liberty around the world. She fought for unity in Congress. She was smart, funny, and had compassion for all. And…she was a dear friend. This loss is personal, but first and foremost, it is a loss to our country."

The President leaned forward, his fist on the table.

"Violence, against any American, will not be tolerated. As a consequence, I am issuing an executive order to put Colorado, Texas, New York, and the D.C. area under martial law. There will be a 10 PM curfew for the next seventy-two hours in those locations. I also urge Congress to immediately pass laws to allow for the protection of our freedom-loving citizens.

We are responding directly to this terrorist group and have launched an attack on their headquarters in Colorado and these other states. We will track down every one of them. We will arrest them. And we will prosecute them to the highest degree the law allows. For anyone who sympathizes with these sick terrorists, we will hunt you too. We will find you in the dark corners and gutters where you live. And we will shine the light of justice throughout this land until we are once again, one nation, under me—civilized, tolerant, and at peace.

We will continue to post ongoing updates as progress is made. Our thoughts are with all who lost loved ones tonight, and with our country and the future. Thank you, and good-night."

"And cut!" the director said. "Great job, Mr. President."

Jerry shook his head.

"What?" the President asked.

"You know what."

The President grinned and shrugged. "You know I don't believe in God. Why would I end with that?"

"Because it works," Jerry said.

The President slapped him on the back good-naturedly. "Come on Jerry. I was good. Did you like the fist?" He lifted his fist, grinning.

"Yes."

"That's what people will remember." They exited the Oval office. The President switched faces for the somber applause in the hall, grasping hands, and nodding gravely to staff and press lining the hallway. His generals waited at the end. He gave them a nod. "Let's go kick some butt."

Georgie stood in the center of the stage, mic in hand. They estimated over eight thousand. She wasn't sure their speaker system reached everyone but the sound guy in the band said it should be okay.

Two bombs dropped in the front area of Holliwell, then one in the city and one in the mountains. She hadn't heard from Richie, but the last communication from Lena was they were at the loading dock and coming out the front. She worried they wouldn't make it in time.

Jets were coming back. Students fed the bonfires, and everyone gathered in the central area, hoping their numbers kept them safe. A few had left in fear, but cameras were rolling everywhere. It would not be an event that could be ignored if something went wrong. But no one believed the government was so evil as to actually drop a bomb on a bunch of students just because they protested.

Morgan ran up the long line of protestors and cued each one to cheer, finally reaching Georgie. Then she pointed to Georgie. Georgie figured that was her cue. Her knees shook at the size of the crowd. A spotlight turned on her, and she couldn't see the crowd anymore from the blinding glare. She pulled her beanie lower. The wind had picked up, and though the stars were out, the temperature continued to drop.

"Hello Colorado!"

A loud cheer sounded.

"Thank you for coming tonight and supporting innocent children and teens who are being victimized and enslaved by our government. They are right over there!" She pointed to Holliwell West. "I know this truth, because two of my friends were victims. They escaped. But just two weeks ago, one of them was shot and killed by a Holliwell agent because they wanted to dissect his body for science. He was nineteen."

"Our politicians and press have lost their way. They would have us believe that because a law is called compassionate that it must be good. It's time we use reason, not emotions to find the truth. These children who have been turned over to the government are not being saved, they are enslaved."

The crowd roared. She shivered, not sure if it was from the loud response or the cold. Morgan was nowhere in sight. The girl had proven resourceful, so Georgie had to trust she was where she needed to be.

"Tonight, is about us," Georgie took a breath. "Our community, our spirit, and a new start to turn the tide of injustice that has been haunting our country for more than a decade. Every single one of us must wake up and fight to keep our freedom." She shouted out her last line so that everyone across the valley would hear it. "Freedom is not just for some, but for all!"

The cheer started, but more important, the lights in the center of the giant ring lit up on top of trucks arranged in the center. From the stage Georgie saw the red letters in LED lights: Freedom for All!

White light from phones and flashlights and work lights filled in a circle around the red letters on the trucks, and the giant ring on the outside was made up of blue light from more than a thousand phones. It was a giant badge of freedom. Georgie couldn't believe it worked. Morgan did it! They'd see that illuminated badge from space!

Georgie handed the microphone to the lead singer, who encouraged them to keep their phones up as he launched into a song that had everyone singing and swaying in unity.

Georgie stepped down from the platform, her mouth open in awe. Yes, they had worked all night to make this happen but she still couldn't believe it!

Morgan joined her. "Awesome! Right?" The girl grinned, excited.

"Where did you get the giant LED lights?"

Morgan shouted over the music. "I used my trust fund." She shrugged mischievously. "Merry Christmas!"

Georgie shook her head, then reached and hugged the teen. Who knew? The girl had promise! Morgan squeezed back, happily.

"Come on," Georgie said. "Phase two."

The flight staff of the stealth bomber had their doubts about the mission. When the President ordered an extra drop on Obstructionists outside of Holliwell, Captain Christine Gonzales called on her flight crew. They could all clearly see the array of lights below, shining into the sky like a beautiful symbol of America's freedom. It's one of the reasons they all joined the military.

"Maybe he can't see what's below," her co-pilot offered.

"Send video surveillance. I'm going to circle."

"It's already on the Internet," their navigator, Slater, informed. It says, "'Students from five colleges abandon their holiday break to send a message to America on a cold Colorado night.'" She showed the co-pilot. "The views are racking up."

"Sir, this is Captain Gonzales. We're sending video of the target. It's a student protest. A mighty pretty one actually."

They sent the video and waited.

The response came back. "Proceed with mission."

"Sir, did you get the visual. This is on the Internet. It's a gathering of college students."

Her commander sounded tense but repeated his words.

"Is the President there?" she asked.

There was a pause.

"Captain, I'm here." The President spoke to them over the secure line. "We have investigated the group and similar organizations have attacked our country tonight. Rest easy that you are serving your country."

"Yes, sir. Making the final loop."

Christine cut off the transmission.

"Are we seriously bombing students on American soil?" her co-pilot Robert asked the question without emotion. They had to take emotion out of their job sometimes, but she knew exactly what he was asking.

Slater piped in. "We don't always have the details. We have to follow orders or we're toast. We won't just lose our careers; we could be court-marshaled…or worse."

Christine nodded. "That is all true." She turned to them. "We have to be in this together. I won't put your careers and families at risk. Thumbs up or down?"

They voted.

Christine turned the transmission back on. "We are coming in for the target. Standby."

Christine circled and saw the bright lights ahead. It created the perfect kill zone. Two missiles were on load. The locking light blinked then went solid.

She banked tight.

"Freedom for all."

The bombs dropped.

CHAPTER FORTY-FOUR

*G*raeme gassed it hard. There was chaos but not enough for them to sneak out because of it. A backup generator activated and lit up the scene. Maria picked off troublemakers. Graeme wished it was dark again so he couldn't see all the soldiers aiming their guns.

He felt a hard thump. *Hell.* Their back tire got shot. The truck slumped, then skid on icy asphalt.

"Hold on!" he yelled to Lena and the girls. He could see the lights in the distance. He just had to get out the gate.

A massive wall of metal began to raise, blocking the exit.

Graeme shook his head, throat dry. "We're screwed."

A soldier ran into the guard gate. A moment later the metal began to lower.

"Yes!" He gassed it. "One of ours!"

The guard jumped out from the guard gate onto the side of the truck, hanging on through Graeme's window, covering them with single-handed fire power as they raced through the exit into the open road.

Graeme spotted vehicles rolling out behind him. They would catch up in a minute. With their blown tire they would never make it. Tension filled him. Marco, Maria, Lena…he looked in the back at the girls huddled. Keisha held onto his back seat.

"I can stop them," she said.

"No."

A jet banked loudly overhead and they looked out the front to see it turn sharply toward mountains further away.

Their truck slowed to a bumpy thirty miles an hour. They were close to the freedom rally. They had to make it.

A thundering blast lit up the horizon just to the left of the rally, but safely away. Then another.

Lena leaned forward, confused. "They just bombed nothing. Do you think they're calling things off?"

Graeme looked east. "I don't know.

A girl stood on a pickup truck near the lights ahead. She waved a flare and the crowd parted. He glanced back again in the rearview mirror—the Holliwell team gained on them. "Come on truck." He pressed the acceleration, hoping the vehicle would hold on.

It did.

They passed the pickup and his head spun when he saw the face-splitting grin on the girl with the flare. *Morgan?*

He drove through the crowd and immediately bodies enveloped the truck from behind, blocking the road and all other vehicles. Georgie waved Graeme to a stop and hurried to open the back. Lena and Keisha stood there with the stunned girls huddled in shock.

"Make room!" Georgie shouted.

People quieted down. The girls crawled out, hesitant, looking around. Suddenly there were thunderous cheers. Graeme and the others helped them out as they gazed, stunned at all the people and absorbing the smiles and getting pats on the back.

They weren't just kids. They were evidence. And now they were seen.

"Quick," Georgie told Graeme. "Luis sent a transfer van." She pointed to the white van with a church logo on it. "They will transfer again in town, and again after that. Obviously, we'll have a problem with photos." She noted the crowd, though some realized it wasn't a good idea and told others to put their cameras away.

"The antique store, bakery, and Horseshoe Saloon all took direct hits. Completely destroyed. Richie is alive but—"

"I'm here!" Richie said, climbing out of the van.

Graeme shook his head at the sight of his friend and felt his eyes tear up. Richie seemed to be dirty and cut up on every part of his body. He limped forward. Graeme strode over and hugged him.

"Not too hard, G." Richie groaned.

"Lena's here," Graeme pulled back. Richie couldn't seem to hear him. "Lena!"

He knew when Richie saw her. He felt the change as he released his buddy. Richie lifted his arms and Lena ran through the crowd and knocked the air out him. Another cheer went up. *Who were all these people?*

He shook his head. "Georgie, how did you do it?"

"I had some help." She pointed behind him.

He shook his head again as Morgan came through and stopped, unsure of her reception. Anger and fear surged. This was not safe at all. His parents were going to kill them!

Morgan struck a pose with thumbs and pinkies out and gave them a shake. "Hey!"

"Don't be mad," Georgie said. "She was pretty amazing."

Graeme shook his head a third time then opened his arms for his sister. He held her tight. But he eyed Georgie to let her know he wasn't done with this.

The crowd gave them space to move the girls to the van, and they carried Marco as well. Maria was very solicitous of him as he was still unconscious. The girls hugged Lena and Graeme as they climbed in. He tried to reassure them, told them to be safe and be happy. Keisha was the last.

"Have you heard from Evie," she asked.

"No. I'm sorry." He bent to her height. "Go and be happy."

"But—"

"Here's a number you can reach me at." He wrote on her arm. "Memorize it and wash it off, okay?"

"Okay." She smiled a little, finally reassured.

Maria took Keisha's hand and loaded her in the van. She gave Graeme a rib crushing hug and brief kiss on the lips, before grinning bashfully and hopping in the van. It took off through the crowd.

Coming from the other direction was a Sheriff's vehicle. Graeme dodged into the crowd so as not to be recognized and grabbed his sister.

"Who's in charge here?" the Sheriff called out.

Everyone turned to Georgie. She raised her hand.

"You're under arrest."

"For what?"

"Obstructionist activity."

Georgie faced the heavyset sheriff. "We're not Obstructionists. We're students. And citizens."

"Well…assembling without a permit. Do you have a permit?"

"Um." Georgie shrugged. "Not on me."

"Then let's break it up. Come on. Everyone! Presidential curfew! Time to go home!" The Sheriff and his deputy waved their hands to scatter everyone.

Georgie turned on her hand mic and shouted. "Good-night, Colorado!" A loud cheer followed with thumping on the ground and pounding of drums of the band from the stage.

The Sheriff put cuffs on Georgie and tucked her into his vehicle.

The lead singer in the band called out to the crowd with some riffs of an electric guitar cutting through the night. "Freedom for all, my friends! Freedom for all! Thank you and good-night!"

Graeme smiled. Now they just needed Jocelyn and Al. No one had heard from them. He prayed that no news was good news.

Morgan grabbed his arm and tugged. She wasn't smiling anymore.

"It's Rex." She showed him the text. "Mom was shot in the Senate chamber! They took her to the hospital. The Vice President was killed. Benny and Poem were watching. Benny—" She broke off choking. "He went into shock. He's at the hospital on a respirator. We need to go. Where's Jocelyn?"

Graeme's throat clenched. "I don't know."

Morgan looked around at the crowd dispersing. "I have to take care of the band and some things. I'll be right back."

Graeme hurried over to Richie. "How far is it to the mountain gate?"

"What?" Richie turned his other ear to him.

"Have you heard from Al or Joss? How far are they?"

Richie shook his head. "I lost him in the tunnel."

Graeme ran to Morgan. "I'm going for Al and Jocelyn. You go straight to the airport. I'll be right behind."

"What about Georgie?"

"I know someone who can help." At least, he hoped Luis knew someone.

"Okay." She gave him the keys for an SUV. "I'll get a ride. Be safe, okay?"

He hugged her tight. "Always."

Graeme, Lena and Richie piled into the SUV, but it took time getting out of the crowd. He maneuvered safely away from the students, his mind racing. They needed to get to the turn off. *His mom was shot!* He needed details. Did someone try to assassinate her? And Benny? If the stress continued to accelerate Benny's disease, they didn't have much time before his condition was irreversible, or realistically—fatal.

He gazed out at the complex as they turned up a mountain road. Was there really a cure inside Holliwell?

He prayed there was, and that Jocelyn had it.

Jocelyn and Al hurried to the front of the buses to assess the magnitude of the cave-in. It seemed like a wall of mountain faced them. No moonlight filtered in. Just cold, dark mountain. The girls had done well, tunneling through on the right side, creating a potential opening.

"Al, you get the babies and their chaperones off this bus and onto the last bus."

She examined the rock pile and tested the top of the opening to see if more would fall when she moved the bottom. It seemed stable. "Everyone back to their buses!"

The girls didn't move. They were confused about how they would get out if they didn't continue. She ordered them again. This time Al barked in support and the adults in the Underground scurried to move all the kids.

While they went to move the babies and children, Jocelyn sent energy toward the wall of fallen mountain, gripping the mountain of rock with her entire being. Then she walked forward, moving it slowly, cautious to make sure it didn't cause an avalanche or more damage. Debris and loose stones fell but it wasn't bad. When moon and starlight could be seen above, she gathered her energy, slid the pile to the shoulder of the road, and with a great force, expelled it over the side. The task left her depleted. She sucked in oxygen and took a knee.

"That was a lot of rock." Al came up from behind her.

"Like a mountain," she half gasped, and half joked.

"Don't be a wuss." He held out a hand. "No time for that."

She agreed, her legs wobbled but recovered. She kept moving and was able to slowly jog back to the tunnel. The buses were already moving around the first bus that had been damaged. It still drove but wasn't safe transport for babies.

Jocelyn hopped into the damaged bus. "I'll catch up."

"I'm coming with you," Al said.

"Al, seriously. You don't want to be in this bus when I'm done with it."

He considered her words and relented. "Okay. I'll be in the last bus. We'll pick you up."

"Wait!" Jocelyn took off her secure pack with the original formula. "Al. Hold this. It's really important. Protect it with your life, okay."

"Sheesh! What—"

"It might cure Benny. Please!"

Al took it. "I'll keep it safe until you get back. Right?"

"That's the hope."

She shut the doors. There was no time for planning. She hit reverse and backed up until the last bus was past and made a tight turn. She could see the military vehicles racing toward her.

Chang's calvary.

She needed to block any vehicles from exiting. Jocelyn squealed to a stop, attached her seatbelt, put the bus in drive, took a deep breath, and accelerated.

She'd never done this maneuver in a bus.

Instinct told her it was gonna hurt.

She could see the security checkpoint. Someone dragged Chang to safety. With the end of the tunnel in sight, she braked hard and spun the wheel all the way to the left, into the wall of the tunnel.

The bus swerved out of control, hit the wall, flipped, crashed and slid. Whatever glass had been left on the bus after the cave in was now on her. The steering wheel came close to crushing her stomach, and metal frame bent around her, the sound of it twisting and crushing loudly in her ears.

The mangled vehicle slid to a stop. Jocelyn choked on dust and unbuckled herself. She pulled metal from her arm, wincing at the pull on the flesh. It was more gross than painful. She tossed it. Her head hurt. She had a bump. Not too bad. Carefully but quickly, she crawled out the front where the windshield used to be.

Giant spotlights were on her. Shots fired. She blasted back with blind protection to create a shield then hurried back down the tunnel into the darkness. She turned back to survey her work.

Not bad.

The bus, flipped on its side, blocked most of the road. Trucks couldn't pass, but they could get motorcycles through. And no doubt they had equipment to move the bus. But it was a good temporary deterrent. She ran back, pressing the cut on her arm, blood streamed to her fingertips. That had been a lucky move.

But they still had to get the buses to safety.

They reached the opening in the tunnel where the last bus waited for her. Al stood at the door.

She heard the jet before she saw it. Searching the skies she waited, wondering how many minutes they had. Then she spotted it high in the sky—a military strike aircraft—the kind used for more precise targeting. It flew toward the complex then would be over the mountain and on them.

Al turned as well. "What is it?"

"Another round."

Then he saw it.

"No time. Let's go!" Al pulled her up on the bus.

Jocelyn stared behind them. Minutes would have been a luxury.

They had seconds.

Evie had less.

CHAPTER FORTY-FIVE

*E*vie raced after Wicker through the second dorm, gaining on her. She lengthened her stride, picking up speed. A rolling I.V. near a bed caught her eye. She stopped and broke off the metal pole. A flash from childhood of playing chunkey on the reservation summer camp shot through her mind. The golf cart was like a moving stone. The metal pole was her spear. She'd been pretty good back then—before life had changed so drastically.

She adjusted her grip on the pole and aimed. Thanks to Wicker, she was stronger than her seven-year-old self. And her aim proved exceptional.

The pole flew through the back of the golf cart, through the front dash, and close enough to the engine to cause a spark.

The cart sputtered, slowing down.

Wicker leapt from the vehicle before it completely stopped. Evie gained on her, jumped, and took her down.

"Evie! Please! We have to go!"

Evie flipped the woman over and straddled her belly.

"Evie!"

Punch.

Blood came from Wicker's mouth. *Strange.* It wasn't nearly as satisfying as Evie thought it would be. She reminded

344

herself of Tatiana and all the others. Worse, she recalled Seth and the bodyguard. She'd killed innocents for Wicker.

Punch.

Yeah. That felt a little better.

Wicker struggled, blocking her face, legs squiggling like a roach on its back.

Pathetic.

The fight went out of Evie.

She looked at the empty warehouse, beds abandoned—so many innocent lives.

Her eyes burned unnaturally.

Let them be free. Please. Let them be free.

She didn't know who she prayed to. If there was a Great Spirit or a Creator, Evie had

been cut off.

"Evie. They are going to bomb us." Wicker gave a muffled cry. "Please."

Evie shook her head. It felt like her own spirit had already left. She stood up, dragging Wicker with her. Wicker's greatest strength wasn't science. It was fear. Wicker mastered the art of fear and used it efficiently and effectively on all of them.

Every girl here had lived with it and felt the power of it. Fear of failing, fear of succeeding, fear of uncertainty, fear of dying, fear of not being good enough, fear of being alone. There were so many things to fear and so many ways to twist it and use it.

It seemed strange to see fear in Wicker's eyes now.

Evie took the bag from Wicker's shoulder and gave her a shove. She'd lived her life in fear and wasted it completely.

Wicker turned to her, surprised. Evie opened the bag and pulled out the silver case. Inside were two vials. She crushed both with her foot.

"It's over."

"You have no idea what you've just done."

Evie laughed. "You better hurry. Bombs, right?"

"You disappoint me, Seventeen." With bloodied face, Wicker abandoned her heels and took off barefoot, at a fast pace, toward the first dorm and the complex's mountain interior.

Evie shook her head at her former captor, her words only for herself. "You were never the one that mattered."

The energy outside shifted. Evie felt instinctively when it was time. She estimated the doctor would have been in the center of the first dorm when the first bomb dropped.

Evie spun for the exit. "What the hell." She ran toward dorm three.

The second bomb dropped on dorm two. The energy sent her through the doors of the third dorm. She rolled to her feet and raced. She wasn't going to make it. She knew that. She'd always known it. But she couldn't give up after all. Even broken, she was meant to fight. There had to be some honor in that.

She counted the seconds of her life. The third bomb was coming.

Three. The doors were so close. *Faster!*

Two. She sucked in her last breath of air.

The ceiling of the building thundered. Metal hit the ground.

One.

She felt the explosive heat and deafening destruction. It lasted a mere second. With it registered her last thought.

Regret.

Jocelyn knew the military could easily detect them, but she had a better chance of defending one location than two.

The curve of the mountain road didn't give them much room and they still had a few miles before reaching the main highway from this direction.

She had to consolidate. She ordered the buses into rows of three, until they were a tight block front to back. They turned off the lights.

They were also an easier target.

She shivered from nineteen-degree temperature. The clear sky and moonlight were probably beautiful, but she had no appreciation for them. They were the enemy tonight. She tossed her hat, pulled off the remains of her disguise, bared her arms down to her tank top. If there were clouds it would be snowing for sure. Goosebumps raised on her skin. She'd had enough snow for this lifetime.

She swung up onto the roof of the bus and ran across two buses to the center of their convoy. Girls peeked out windows. Others huddled in their seats. The drivers and administrators told everyone to be quiet and get low.

"Get away from the windows," she called to the girls.

Fifteen seconds had passed. Twenty seconds.

Al stayed near on the ground and looked to her for reassurance but didn't ask if she had this. He probably didn't want to know the answer.

The jets soared toward them; engines nearly silent to the human ear. Jocelyn braced herself. She needed to detect the missiles visually and physically as they accelerated downward at them. And she needed to counter their velocity and mass enough to push them off target.

She swallowed. Not totally impossible.

Her arms trembled as she held them up, preparing. She wasn't certain if she shook from anxiety, exhaustion or cold. But she knew everything depended on her.

Thirty seconds.

No more thinking.

Her energy locked instantly. Not a bomb—a missile— faster, more targeted. But detectable. She pushed it off target into the canyon. The second got closer. She shot energy, blocking it.

The third got away from her.

She could see it!

Coming down in front of the first line of buses. It would take out the road and the buses with it.

She spun in a wide circle, sending a twirling force of energy from the bottom of her toes to the top of her scalp and out through her skin. The sharp ping of heat felt like an electrical shock through her fingers.

But it worked.

To anyone watching, the missile veered to their left mid-air from an invisible source and hit the canyon bottom with a quake, shaking the road and causing gasps from inside all the buses.

Her vision flickered. She fell to her hands and knees. A feeling of extreme low blood sugar caused a slight nausea and shaking. "Al."

It had only been a whisper, but Al was there. He must have climbed up to the top of the bus already. He grabbed her around the waist and helped her stand. She needed a break.

"The second plane is coming," he said.

"I know." She gasped for air. Then again. She needed time to reload her energy.

"There are a thousand kids on this mountain, Joss. You're it. Whatever you've got, now is the time to give it."

I can't! Tears streaked her face. Fear took hold.

"For when I am weak, then I am strong."

"What?" Attention turned to Al.

"Bible verse. Looked like you needed it. We're not alone. You're not alone. Popped in my head." He squeezed her arm. "That said, I'll pray. You do that power thing you do." He waved his arms about like a demented cheerleader to demonstrate.

She felt a smile move inside her and reach her lips. His words turned her thoughts positive somehow—and that helped her strength physically.

She struggled to inhale but her mind seemed calmer.

"About ten seconds 'til impact." He added, "No pressure."

Jocelyn took a sustaining breath. Al did the same.

At least she had the pacing, assuming the second jet did the same pattern and only sent three missiles and the payload was the same in each. *Yeah. Assuming all that.*

She sucked in more fresh energy through her lungs and into her body. She needed a different tactic. A larger blocking defense. She wouldn't need to hold it for long. She was good at short bursts. That's all she needed—but she needed to time her bursts to work for all three missiles.

She took one more breath and the energy from trees, the earth, and the air soaked into her. The drank it in, absorbing as much as she could.

Suddenly something warm grasped her ankle. A hand.

She felt a hand touch her waist. Someone else grabbed her foot. Al was pushed away as girls climbed up on the bus roof surrounding her.

The girls touching her legs and waist grasped the arms of other girls making a web around her.

"Use our energy," Gemma said.

Jocelyn felt the touch of skin and pulled on them, curious. She felt the power. It felt dangerous.

Could she? Was it safe?

"Do it!" Gemma commanded as the plane flew over.

Jocelyn saw the first missile launch. Then the second. She couldn't wait to see the third. She focused into the sky and sent her power outward, deflecting. She breathed and sent another burst, maintaining her shield. Two missiles swerved away, exploding in the distance. Her energy flailed as the third came and she felt a strong squeeze on her ankle.

Use us.

Frightened, she pulled from the energy around her. It was like nothing she'd ever felt. A powerful charge poured through her and upward.

She directed her energy. It surged strong and yet so intimate she thought she could touch the missile, feel the cold outer shell, even crush it with her hand. Then it was too much. It had to be released.

Jocelyn felt the acceleration of the missile, visualized her energy moving. An electrifying pulse streamed through her cells, manifesting in her skin. Her body lifted off the bus. Hands tightened on her, holding her, grounding her.

She released.

Her power met the third missile and it detonated in the sky. An umbrella of red and blue light exploded over them.

It wasn't the only explosion.

Jocelyn's energy sent the web of girls flying through the air, off the bus, into trees, to the ground, the trees, into rocks, slamming into the mountainside. They scattered amidst the deafening roar above, tumbling, and grasping to hold onto each other or something real.

Her body stretched taut, seemingly pulled in every direction at once until she didn't think she could last another second. Would she shatter? Rip apart? She breathed and held on with every ounce of control she had.

Then the shock was over.

Jocelyn's feet landed hard on the bus. The jet flew further away.

Light faded.

Cold invaded.

She was alone.

She took a breath, searching, then she understood. She surveyed the destruction in the moonlight.

The road was littered with bodies.

CHAPTER FORTY-SIX

*G*raeme pulled as far up the road as he could, making way for the buses coming toward him. That was a good sign. They were escaping!

He waited, tension building in his chest.

"I don't see Al or Jocelyn," Lena said.

Three buses remained parked as they inched closer.

Graeme swallowed his rising panic. There were bodies on the road. *Girls. What happened?*

He swerved to the side, set the emergency brake and ran forward. They were lifting and carrying girls. Some girls hobbled to their feet, helping each other.

"Jocelyn!" He searched the darkness. "Jocelyn!"

"Here!"

Lena and Richie raced with him toward her voice. Jocelyn bent over Al at the side of the road. She was doing CPR. Graeme didn't ask questions. He took the other side and picked up the count. Richie fell to his knees in shock, clutching his friend's calf, bobbing slightly.

A woman rushed to them with a portable defibrillator. "Move!"

Jocelyn ripped open Al's shirt and set the pads while the woman watched the charge.

"Get back," she said. The machine did its work. "Got him. Back to sinus rhythm." She took the pads off Al and put them in the box. "How's his head?"

"Bleeding," Jocelyn said taking the cold compress from the woman. "That's Tamika," she introduced.

"What—" Graeme didn't have a delicate way to ask. "What happened?"

Tamika glanced at Jocelyn then answered for them. "He flew into the side of the mountain." She pointed a flashlight to a spot twelve feet above them.

Jocelyn sniffed and wiped her eyes. "I think he hit the hardest rock."

Graeme, Lena and Richie looked up at the wall of rock.

Richie wrapped his arms around his belly and began to bob forward and back in earnest.

Lena studied the girls being carried to the bus. "Yeah. But…what happened?"

Al groaned. His hand went down to push himself up. Jocelyn helped him. "Go slow. We need to leave, but everyone's okay. The planes haven't come back. We might only have a few minutes though. Can you stand?"

Al stared at her. Then he reached for something at his waist. "The bag."

"I have it," Jocelyn said.

There was something in her voice that caught Al's attention. Graeme glanced at the bag. *Benny?* Now was not the time. No one was in shape to talk, and they weren't safe.

Jocelyn hurried Al along. "Come on. We're not home free yet."

Graeme concurred. "Let's go."

Graeme and Richie helped Al to the SUV. Jocelyn and Lena helped Tamika and others get the girls on the buses. They waited until the last bus left.

Richie connected with Luis once they were in the SUV.

"We're diverting all the buses to safe locations then will transfer the girls," Luis said. "We've got it from here. This is what we've planned for. As long we can get to our first checkpoint before state officers find us, we will be good to go. We have disguises planned. I'll get a message to you when the girls are safe. Get out now and don't speed." The line cut.

"How am I not supposed to speed?" Graeme grumbled.

They drove to the airport. It took over forty minutes and the passengers in the SUV remained silent the entire time. They'd expended energy and adrenalin, but they still needed to get out of town. He could only pray Luis got all the girls to safety. Right now he had his own team to look out for—and all were looking worse for wear.

He alerted the pilot of their arrival. Morgan's plane had left, and he felt a great deal of relief about that. A young man met him at the airport and took the keys to the SUV. He didn't know the guy but was passed a business card. All it had on it was a horseshoe with a red splatter.

The plane took off.

Lena tended to Richie's injuries. He shivered still, seemingly unable to get warm, and his loud comments of thanks made Lena blush.

Al buckled in, not moving much, resting his head on an ice pack. He said he felt fine. "Surprisingly energized other than the concussion. I should get shock treatment every day." Al smiled at Jocelyn as if to comfort her but it didn't change her tense expression.

"Don't go to sleep," Graeme said.

"Yeah." Al closed his eyes then popped one open. "Resting, not sleeping."

Jocelyn sat by the window, across from Al, staring out, holding a bag on her lap. Graeme sighed. Too much to unpack right now.

He got his brother on the phone as soon as possible. Rex's voice came over the speaker, his words terse, laced with anger. Graeme couldn't blame him.

"We don't know who was behind the Senate assassinations," Rex said. "Mom has a concussion but will be released tomorrow if everything looks good. Benny is the one we're worried about. We were watching mom. I was with him. His lungs froze. We had to force oxygen in. He's hooked to a respirator. The doctors said it's not long before other functions and organs give up. Three days, three weeks, three months. No one knows. You need to get here."

Rex hung up.

Graeme didn't move. Three days? It couldn't be that quick. Benny had to fight.

When he lifted his head Lena and Richie were there—arms around him on either side.

Jocelyn didn't move. She hugged the bag crying silently.

"I'm so sorry, Joss." Al said, moving next to her, putting a big hand over hers. "I'm so sorry. This is my fault." He pulled her into her chest and absorbed her quiet heaving. "I'm so sorry."

"No." Jocelyn said. "I nearly killed you and everyone else. All those girls could have died. If I had the bag on me, it would have been destroyed. And I still destroyed it."

Graeme joined them and took the bag in question. "Benny's cure?"

She nodded.

Graeme swallowed. It had been too much to hope for.

"I'm sorry. I'm so sorry." Jocelyn cried. "Everything we did to get it. And now nothing. The vials exploded."

"Hey," Graeme said. "You did good." To Al, "You were amazing. We saved nearly a thousand children and babies. Who does that in their lifetime? We did everything we set out to do. And honestly, we don't even know if this thing would have worked on Benny anyway or if it was the serum you were told about."

She shook her head. The whites of her eyes were nearly all blue, and blue tears stained the napkins he handed her. "Everything is my fault. Seth shouldn't have been in New York. If I hadn't come to New York, Benny would still be healthy. Now he's dying. Evie's dead. Medina's dead. Al—"

Al jumped in. "Seriously, I feel pretty amazing. If not for this bloody lump, I'd be on fire."

"Richie might be deaf—"

"What?" Richie heard his name.

"Jocelyn." Graeme cut her off, frustrated and wanting answers. "What happened out there?"

Jocelyn disappeared inward. "I'm not sure."

Al didn't offer anything up. He took his seat again and gave a warning to give it a rest. At Jocelyn's continued silence, Al snuggled down with a blanket and closed his eyes. "Resting, not sleeping."

Graeme put a blanket over Jocelyn. She merely turned away and stared out the window into the darkness. Her rejection of him hurt. And it pissed him off. And yeah, maybe he was upset about his mom and Benny, and could use a little love right now.

He grabbed the bag in question and took a seat on the other side of the plane with Lena and Richie. Maybe Sabrina could use some of the trace amounts? He opened the bag and felt inside. It was dry and empty other than fragments of glass, shattered into pieces.

Like everything else around him.

Jerry Ramstein needed to update the President and he was not happy. This day just got longer. He would recommend a morning press conference and see what developed overnight. Mercer continued with the update.

"It seems impossible, sir. But the contacts at Holliwell say twelve buses got away. They put local sheriffs on them, but they seemed to disappear before even getting to the highway. No surveillance could find them. We did, however, get this."

She handed him a picture of waving girls in a bus, all wearing matching striped jerseys.

"A Latvian ice hockey team. Their story checked out. Passports and all."

He studied it. Girls posed for the shot, looking crazy, doing American gang signals—one held her hockey stick up like a bat. Still, it was hard to get a good look at any face.

"Run their faces against the experiments to be sure." He pointed to a woman in the back. "Who's that?"

Mercer checked her notes. "Tamika Jean Woodley. Their American liaison and training coach."

Jerry sighed. "What about Luis Mendez?"

"Waiting to confirm dead in the antique store."

Jerry hoped that bastard was dead. He'd been a small thorn for too long. Tonight the man had proven more formidable than anticipated. He tapped down his list. "Wicker?"

"Presumed dead as well. She was in the dorm drop zone. Guards said Seventeen attacked them with the intent to kill Dr. Wicker. Best guess is that the doctor and Seventeen are buried there."

"Okay. Recover her body and make sure any possessions or science are secured. That's enough. Tomorrow, we rebuild. Tonight, we salute the enemy. They showed us our weaknesses. And they were fearless." He was silent a moment. "And patient."

Mercer hesitated.

"Sir, there is one thing. The pilot and crew that were ordered to bomb the student protestors. They said their GPS malfunctioned. The payload dropped but off target. We're investigating."

Jerry waved a hand. "Let that one go. The President made the wrong call. He got lucky. And he won't want anyone on witness stand sharing that information during a court-martial."

Mercer nodded and turned to go.

"Wait," Jerry called her back. "What about the girl who organized the protest?"

"Henrietta Georgiana Washington."

"That's unfortunate."

"Yes, sir." Mercer agreed. "She's Project Sunday's friend. We have taps on her parents. She's been good at alluding tracking. But she's had help."

"Damn if that little group isn't starting to look like a terrorist cell." *Brats.* "She's a Barnard girl?"

"Yes, sir."

"Your alumni."

"They do turn out a lot of activists, sir." She shrugged. "We've hired most of them. We thought we had converted her. She worked on the recent march."

"Hmmm. Okay. That's enough." He grabbed his jacket and shoved his e-pad inside his light carrier. "Tomorrow. We rebuild."

"Yes, sir."

Mercer left and Jerry stared after her. He wrinkled his nose and made the call. "Get me Teresa Mercer's taped conversations and whereabouts for the last week. For my eyes only. Thanks." He hung up.

He would be very disappointed if Mercer had betrayed them.

Very disappointed.

CHAPTER FORTY-SEVEN

*J*ocelyn stared into the darkness. Greer had given her two other possible places to search for the cure. But now she didn't know if Benny would make it through Christmas. Each day brought him closer to the end. She swallowed. He would make it. He had to. The Rochesters would do everything possible to keep him alive. She believed that with everything in her.

Okay. She took a breath. She needed to re-strategize. That's all.

She peeked at Graeme. He was muttering. He knew she could hear him clearly—though he may have forgotten that in his current state.

Richie shivered and Lena leaned into him for comfort, pulling the blanket tighter around them.

Finally, Graeme slammed the bag on the table in front of him and stood up. "Enough!"

Richie startled and began to bob.

Graeme scooted around the table into the aisle, standing over her. "I'm his brother! You don't get to mope right now. If anyone gets to mope it will be me. But I still have hope for Benny. And today we got justice for Seth and for all those girls." He pounded the empty seat next to her once with the meat of his fist. "Do you even understand that?"

Jocelyn nodded, mute, letting him know she heard. He was right. Angry and right. And not done with her.

"Evie made her own choices. She killed Ellis and she killed Seth. Maybe she thought she didn't have a choice about either, but she was still an accomplice to two murders. I give her credit for wanting to make up for it, but it doesn't change the facts. I'm not going to grieve for her. But damn it, I grieve for Ellis's family." His eyes burned red with emotion. "And I grieve for Seth. The stupid, irritating, cowboy dumbass." He smiled through eyes full of tears. "I should have punched the smirk off his face when I had the chance."

Jocelyn laughed. "I'm glad you didn't. He had a mean hook."

Al nodded. "No doubt."

Graeme took a breath, recovering. "We're just a small piece of a bigger fight, Jocelyn. You can't take it all on you. Today was a triumph and a miracle. And there's more life in the world than not, because of all of us. You're not perfect. You never will be. But you should be grateful. We should all be damned grateful we're going home in one piece after doing what we just did."

"We're not home yet," Richie spoke loudly. He and Lena pressed their faces against a window. "But I'll join you in gratitude if that B23 classified jet doesn't shoot us down."

The others ran to the windows.

A scary shadow flying parallel to them lit up, revealing itself to them. Jocelyn's heart raced. There was nothing she could do inside an airplane! They were sitting targets.

She grabbed Graeme's hand. Was this it?

They stared, not breathing until the jet rocked its wings and took off. Its lights went dark, and it disappeared.

Al spoke first. "I think that meant, 'well done.' In military speak."

"There are others out there," Lena said. She turned to Jocelyn. "Graeme's right. We're not alone in the fight, Jocelyn. We just have to do our part."

Jocelyn felt her heart lift a little. A small weight evaporated, not all of it, but a piece. She squeezed Graeme's hand. "I'm sorry." She surveyed the group. "You were all so amazing today. Al, you kept all those girls safe and calm. And you led them like a true general. Lena, you were so genius, saving us in the maze—twice—beating Wicker like a badass then jumping twenty feet like an Olympian."

Richie turned. "You jumped twenty feet?"

"And she kicked ass in the bakery like a ninja chef," Graeme added.

Lena blushed. She pulled Richie back into the seat and put the blanket on him.

Jocelyn went to Richie's side. "Richie, you are always our eyes, ears and brains."

Richie turned his head. "I think you're saying something nice, but this ear—"

"Moment's gone." Al shook his head.

Jocelyn bent over Richie and touched his chest. "Will you let me?"

Richie shivered but nodded.

She pressed one hand against his chest and the other over his back. Gently she radiated warmth into him. The shivering stopped and finally he took a slow deep breath of relief. He relaxed into the seat, closing his eyes.

She released him. "Better?"

"Like a hot sauna of love."

Lena's eyes popped wide, but Jocelyn just laughed lightly. Richie fell asleep.

"We accomplished everything we hoped to do," Jocelyn finished. "Graeme is right. We need to celebrate this together."

"I'll make it happen," Graeme said. He went to his seat, serious and still a little tense.

Al and Jocelyn went back to theirs and buckled in.

"Graeme," Jocelyn called to him softly. He looked across the aisle. She smiled in gratitude and with all the emotion she couldn't express. "I adore you."

Graeme pressed his lips but then they curved into a reluctant smile. He gave her a nod of acknowledgment and leaned back, closing his eyes.

Al winked his approval, chuckling as he too closed his eyes, a big grin on his face.

Jocelyn didn't sleep. She watched the lights of cities as they flew back to New York, and she planned her next move.

Georgie waited for the guard to unlock the outer door then exited to the police counter to sign for her belongings. The police in Little Eagle weren't the friendliest, but they were letting her go. She wasn't exactly sure why until a professional looking man in a dark suit and briefcase presented himself with papers.

"It looks like everything is in order," he said. "Just sign here. The charges are being dropped."

"Next time, carry the permit with you," the officer advised, glaring at her. "And we won't have this confusion."

"Yes, sir." Georgie knew when to agree with good news.

He nodded to the man next to her. "Lucky for you, Mr. Peters here got your paperwork in fast, or you'd be stuck until Monday."

"Yes, sir. I'm very grateful. I hate being a bother around the holidays." She smiled like she appreciated his hospitality.

He grunted.

"Ready to go?" Mr. Peters asked.

"Yes. Thank you." Georgie's body released a massive load of tension. Last night being booked by the locals had not been her most shining moment.

"You have someone waiting for you?"

"I do?"

"Umm-hmm."

She glanced up covertly at her lawyerly savior. He had a slight grin, as if he thought something was funny.

They turned and exited to the lobby. Tension flooded back into her body.

"Uh-oh."

"Um-hm." Mr. Peters put a hand on her back and nudged her forward.

Her dad lifted his head from where it rested in his hands, elbows on his knees. She had no idea how long he'd been there, but he looked exhausted, and his expression said, 'not happy.'

"Dad!"

He checked her for damage then relief took over, and he opened his arms.

She ran into them and hugged hard.

"I can't believe you're here! Why are you here? How did you know? Did Mr. Peters—"

She turned to her lawyer, but he shook his head.

"It was on the news!" Her father informed. "Henrietta Washington, our only baby taken by police and thrown in jail."

Georgie cringed. "They called me Henrietta! Someone's going to be punished for that."

Her dad didn't laugh at the joke. "You've caused your mother and I great anxiety."

Georgie took a breath. That was a bible quote. As in Mary and Joseph just lost Jesus the savior of the world type of anxiety. He only used those lines when he fought for emotional control.

Mr. Peters saved her. "I'll drive you both to the airport. I understand there's a jet waiting."

"A jet?" Her father blinked.

"Miss Brittany pulled some favors. She is a national hero, you know. When she heard you were in trouble, she asked the Senator for assistance."

Her father stared at the man silently, nodded, and got into his black Sedan, tossing a carry-on bag into the backseat with Georgie.

"It's an honor to meet you, Mr. Washington." He started the car. "Your daughter has proven to be very impressive."

"Is that right?" her dad asked.

Georgie cringed. Her father's voice wreaked suspicion.

"And who will be paying your bill?"

"No charge, sir. Just helping a friend." He reached into his pocket and handed her father a card. Georgie leaned forward to see, but her dad pocketed it.

He sat strangely silent the rest of the ride, and nearly as cold as the temperature outside.

But he thanked Peters at the jet.

"Trust me, handing the Sheriff that permit this morning was the most pleasure I've had in months." He winked at Georgie. "Have a safe flight and happy holidays."

Georgie and her father climbed into the warmth and luxury of the jet. A flight attendant waited on hand with coffee as they prepared for takeoff and told them there would be time to freshen up before breakfast. In flight, Georgie gratefully showered and took advantage of the leggings and sweater provided. She returned to the inviting aroma of breakfast and the less inviting look on her father's face as she sat in the leather seat across from him. She felt the lecture coming. She expected it. She was sorry her father had flown out to get her. Even more sorry if he was embarrassed by her being on the news. Her parents valued being respected. And she knew as their only daughter everything she did reflected on them a lot.

Her father flipped a card in his hand, deep in thought. He finally acknowledged her. "You've made some rich friends."

There was no doubt the Rochesters traveled in class. Her stomach grumbled. Even being stressed out waiting for her dad to give it to her, the smell of breakfast enticed her.

"Their son, Graeme, is friends with us. And Al." Georgie swallowed. "And Richie."

"The Senator was nearly assassinated with the Vice President last night." He studied her. He flipped the card again. "Dangerous friends?"

"I—I don't know."

"Well, I know. Freedom is a dangerous game."

Georgie wasn't sure how to take that. "Every generation has to fight to keep it. You taught me that. American history."

He nodded and leaned back. "It wasn't on the news but some sources on the Internet say about a thousand kids were… liberated last night from a military complex in Colorado. I understand they are in safe houses by now."

Georgie swallowed. She didn't know how her dad would know that.

"Your mother and I trust you. You're eighteen now, so even if we are paying for school"—he reminded her—"we aren't responsible for your decisions. But we know we raised you well. Maybe too well."

"You did, dad. I'm sorry about the news—"

He waved a hand at her then flipped the card out from his palm and started turning it again. "That's not what I meant. We love you, Georgie. We just don't want to outlive you. Understand?"

Georgie knew her friends had been taking risks. She didn't want her parents to be the ones to bury her. That would kill them. She knew that. Her throat tightened. "I understand, sir."

He nodded, a very faint, almost sad and gentle smile finally appearing. He placed the card on the table between them and slid it toward her.

"That said, I couldn't be prouder of you."

Georgie felt her eyes burn—part confusion, part gratitude. Then she picked up the card and turned it over. Tears fell when she saw the blood splatter on the horseshoe.

CHAPTER FORTY-EIGHT

*J*ocelyn checked in with John and Kymber as soon as she arrived back in New York. They spent most of the day watching the news, of which Brittany and her butt was a substantial portion. The only news camera in the chamber that night that got a decent recording just happened to be behind her when she jumped a shooter. It was a small piece of good news in the darkness.

The primary focus remained on the death of the Vice President and others in the Senate Chamber shooting. Very little was made of the supposed attacks on military bases except to note collateral damage, and reinforcement of martial law rules in the states affected.

Senator Rochester was also hailed as a hero. Her sharp shooting under pressure strengthened the country's perception of her and many suggested she should be appointed vice president. She was still in a D.C. hospital, and Ford was with Benny at a New York hospital. Graeme had been there all morning with the family. Jocelyn wanted to see Benny, but knew she had to wait. He was stabilized for now.

The Rochesters were flying Mr. Washington, Georgie, Brittany, Al, and Richie, back to Virginia tonight. Mrs. Walsh and Mrs. Washington were eager to have everyone home and safe. Jocelyn wanted to meet Georgie's dad, but Georgie had left him at a hotel to sleep. Georgie said it was safer this way. Jocelyn thought she meant it was safer her parents weren't connected with Jocelyn. It hurt a little, but she understood. And she agreed.

Lena would be leaving from New York for Europe with her dad for the holidays. Jocelyn had an inkling Greer would be joining them. She also hoped Lena would get more insight into what her mother actually did for this international science and technology company.

They were all exhausted, spent, and strangely energized. They'd succeeded at something amazing—they'd connected with a more extensive underground that seemed to share some of their goals. While the government had spun all the news and Internet stories into overcoming evil Obstructionists, there were people fighting for the good who were having some success. And that group would grow. It might be years before there would be a truly free election again, and years before a new administration cleaned up the corruption pervading every government agency, but Jocelyn had hope. Someday, maybe even Holliwell would be stopped.

Today, they had one day for all of them to gather before Christmas. Jocelyn was grateful to Graeme for getting Georgie and Brittany back to New York.

They needed to do this one last thing together.

Jocelyn, Graeme, Richie, Lena, Al, Georgie, and Brittany climbed the steps to Seth's last lair. He always picked the top floor.

"I don't care if I'm a national hero," Brittany complained. "Every time someone searches me, my butt comes up. The only camera that catches me live, broadcasts me with my skirt riding up. How does that happen? And what does it say about our country that my butt got more views than Rachel's speech?

Georgie paused and considered Brittany seriously. "That they have good taste?"

"Aww! You do love me." Brittany hugged her friend.

"You saved my mom," Graeme said. "You're not just a national hero, you're a national treasure."

"Well," Brittany flung her hair back dramatically, hiding her embarrassment at the compliment. "That's sweet, but—."

"You have a good butt," Georgie said. "Own it like a badass, right? And you already have more than fifteen million likes. Look!" Georgie held out her phone. "You can't buy that kind of publicity. It's good for your business."

"I liked it," Al added.

Brittany halted on the stairs. Richie bumped into her as she turned down to Al. "You 'liked' my ass?"

He nodded seriously. "I hearted it too."

Brittany's grin split her face. "Well, okay then." She smoothed her purple peacoat over her backside and continued up the stairs with a new swagger.

"Even better live," Al teased.

A shout from below interrupted anything Brittany was about to say.

"Hey! Wait for me!" Morgan hurried to join them, breathless, then silent at the surprised stares.

Jocelyn looked to the others to see who had invited her.

"She's earned the right to be here," Georgie said.

Jocelyn unlocked the door to Seth's lair with a smile to Morgan. "I agree."

Georgie and Morgan exhaled, relieved. Richie gave Morgan an encouraging pat on the back earning her gratitude.

All of them piled into the lair—which made the small, furnished one-room rental feel even smaller.

A faint scent of old leftover Chinese wafted from the trash, mixed with vanilla-scented soap and a hint of felt and leather. Jocelyn turned toward the source of that last item. Seth's hat hung on the knob at the head of the short, four-poster bed.

Graeme opened the closet. "There's not too much. We'll pack it up."

"There's something under the bed," Brittany said.

Jocelyn got on her knees and pulled out the box. It was filled with Christmas presents.

Graeme joined her and stared into the box. "Ah, hell." He rubbed his jaw.

The top one was for the Morrows. Jocelyn put it aside, then gave the next one to Graeme. "It's for you."

He swallowed hard. "I was going to give him a one-way bus ticket." Graeme reassured, "as a joke."

Jocelyn handed out the other gifts. All of them were the same size and shape. The last one surprised her. She turned to Morgan and passed it.

"There's one for me!" Morgan took it in shock and excitement. "Do we have to wait for Christmas?"

"Hannukah starts tomorrow. I'm opening mine," Lena said, ripping off the paper. She took one look at the framed photo and hugged it to her chest. "Open yours. In case they're the same.

Lena, Brittany, and Georgie all had the same photo. A picture of the girls with Jocelyn, sitting in a booth at Cravings, everyone eating pie.

Morgan opened hers and shared it with Jocelyn. "I was kind of hoping for a naked photo of him. But this is kinda cute."

It was a candid of Morgan and Jocelyn, elbows resting identically on the counter at Cravings during a lull in the night shift. Jocelyn stared at it, wondering if Seth tried to help Morgan see the resemblance between them. Even though they took after different parents, there was something in their faces that made them look alike to Jocelyn. Jocelyn studied Morgan looking again at the photo. *Sisters.* Would she ever know?

"I don't know how he got this. I think we should feel violated." Morgan said.

Brittany took an appreciative look. "He had a good eye."

Al and Richie got a photo of the two of them play-fighting in the War Room.

Jocelyn opened her photo and smiled. It was her and Seth sitting atop the old trailer in the Texas heat, arms around each other's shoulders like buddies, showing off their ice cream for the camera. She wore Seth's hat to protect her bald head, and he sported sunglasses. They looked like kids goofing around. It was a moment frozen in time. One she cherished.

She shared with the others and explained. "This was our rendezvous point after we escaped."

"Um. The infamous RV?" Graeme asked.

"Yes." Jocelyn leaned over and kissed Graeme. "We took one photo, but he told me he deleted it. He was so careful. I can't believe he gave us photos—of all things."

"Well," Graeme said. "I think mine was meant for Morgan." He plucked a blue sticky note off the glass. "It says, 'Something to kiss before bed.'" He showed the close-up photo.

The guys laughed while the girls examined further, confused.

"I believe that's his ass," Graeme explained.

"What!" Morgan snatched it. "Oh-mi-god."

Graeme turned to Jocelyn.

"Don't look at me," she defended. "How would I know? I'm sure it's a self-portrait."

"Seth as an ass?" Graeme teased.

"No! I mean, I'm sure he took the photo himself. You wouldn't really put someone through that, right?" Jocelyn couldn't hold back the grin.

"I'm cracking up," Al said. "Pun intended."

Richie wiped his eyes. "I think Seth got the last laugh, brother."

"Yep." Graeme admitted, "Can't believe I actually miss him."

"I don't know how to say a serious eulogy after that," Georgie said.

"He wouldn't want that." Graeme took the cowboy hat off the hook and put it in the center of the table.

"Richie and I brought something," Lena said. She pulled out some soda and a bunch of little red solo cup shot glasses. "So we can toast him," Lena explained to Jocelyn, prepping the drinks.

Jocelyn smiled.

Graeme reached for Jocelyn and Morgan on either side of him and they all made a circle.

Their humor settled to a more introspective energy.

Graeme squeezed her hand. "Jocelyn, you should say something. You knew him the longest."

Jocelyn took a breath. Unsure. It was silent for a while. No one seemed to mind. Finally, she spoke.

"Seth. Maybe we didn't have much time. Not nearly as much as we wanted. But we had enough. And you were a pain in the ass for most of it. Mostly because you were always annoyingly right about a lot." She glanced around the circle of bowed heads. "You were a friend to all of us. And family to me. Sometimes in an overbearing big brother way, but I appreciated it. You let me share all my stupid dreams and didn't make fun of them completely." She took a breath. "Everyone who knew you misses you. You knew that would happen too. You made sure of it. What you didn't know…"

The words suddenly caught in her throat. She bit her lip hard, but the tears spilled over unchecked. "What you didn't know was how good you really were." Her body shuddered. "No one ever told you. And when they did, you never believed it. But you were good inside. I always knew it." She took a breath. "And I hope wherever you are now, somehow, someway, you know it too." She wiped her eyes. "Because you deserve your Zihuatanejo."

Jocelyn picked up a little red cup. The others did the same. She took a breath. "Cheers, Seth. Until we meet again."

"Cheers," the friends rang together.

It was done.

The group filed out.

Graeme took Seth's hat and put it on her head. "Suits you."

Jocelyn let everyone leave, then took a moment alone. Determination steeled her. "We *will* meet again."

With one last look at the lonely studio room, Jocelyn adjusted the cowboy hat, closed the door on Seth and turned to the life ahead. No matter how short her life might be, she still had much more to give.

Sunshine filtered through the windows in the staircase, casting small rainbows through the icy glass only she could see. Her friends filed down the stairwell and she leaned over the edge memorizing their smiles as they circled around. A warmth filled the emptiness inside her and despite so much loss, something hopeful filled her spirit.

There would come a time when she had to walk alone. But today wasn't that day. Today she would live and enjoy the time she had.

Grinning with mischief, she tossed Seth's hat into the air then hopped over the safety rail to fly after it.

EPILOGUE

*I*t had been a busy week.

Ford wanted to pour a drink and not deal with another family member in danger. Instead, he poured mineral water. The stress had added to his gray hair, and he was pretty sure his blood pressure was not normal. They moved Benny back home but with a full-time nurse on hand. Rachel sat quietly in the chair near him nursing hot tea. Now they had Graeme and Morgan to take care of. He'd wanted to be sure of a few things before reading the riot act.

Morgan stood next to Graeme, innocent and subdued, but looking surprisingly happy. He felt a little guilty about upsetting the mood. Graeme…Geez. Where to begin?

"You were visiting colleges?" Ford asked Morgan.

"Yes, I went to five. Colorado has a lot to offer," Morgan gushed.

"Well, you hurt our feelings by not inviting us to look at colleges with you. Parents look forward to that. Right, Rachel?"

"Absolutely," Rachel nodded. "I'm quite hurt. If it weren't for my concussion, I'd do my wounded routine. I'm just too exhausted."

Morgan smiled. "I'm sorry. There's going to be a lot more colleges though. To visit."

"Uh-huh." Ford pulled out a piece of paper from his suit jacket. "So just to make sure. You didn't go to Colorado to attend this?" He read the flyer. "'Save Our Asses! A Tailgate for Freedom.'"

"That's catchy," Rachel remarked.

"Oh. I heard about that," Morgan said.

"Uh-huh?"

Morgan smiled, beguiling. It worked when she was five. He'd built up his immunity since then.

"Well, just so we're clear," Ford said. "Your flight privileges are suspended."

"But! I was just visiting colleges!" Morgan insisted.

Ford straightened to his full height, took a step toward her so she had to look up, and let his voice resound in the room. "They are suspended because you forged my name and lied to the pilot."

"Oh. That." Morgan shrunk a little. "Sorry. That was definitely wrong."

"Thank you for recognizing it." He rubbed his brows, exasperated, then turned to his son. "And you. What the *hell* is going on with your hair? You look like a North Pole army ranger."

Morgan sputtered, until he gave her the eye.

Graeme touched his short, white spikes. "Just, uh-holiday hairstyle."

His wife intervened. "It's cute, but maybe, color it back before the Christmas photo, dearest."

"And you were skiing?" Ford interrogated.

"Yes, sir. It was great." Graeme said.

He persisted. "I read the conditions were icy."

"It's all about who you're with, right?" Graeme smiled at both of them.

Silence. *What a mess.*

Ford finally waved a dismissive hand. "Get out of here."

They kissed their mom on the head and scrambled.

"Graeme," Ford called out.

"Yes, sir?" Graeme stopped at the door. His son seemed serious despite the easy escape.

"You were supposed to be the easy one, you know?"

His son nodded soberly. "I'm sorry."

Ford sighed and plopped in a chair next to Rachel. Alone again.

She put a hand over his. "They've got too much of you in them."

He straightened instantly. "Me! Me? Who's the crusader in the family? I just wanted to use science to help mankind and make a little money on the side. Easy stuff. Then you came along."

"Don't yell at me. I just came back from a state funeral, and I have a concussion." Rachel moaned and rested back with a smile.

"Sorry love." He kissed her head gently. "I'm extremely grateful you're alive. I'm doubling your security. And I'm going to invest in The Fabulous Brittany Walsh. That young woman rocked an assassin in heels and her bulletproof wig saved your life.

"I know. It was close."

"Too close." He leaned back and took her hand. "Let's just enjoy the holidays. I'll be happy to say goodbye to this year."

John smiled as Jocelyn modeled the new baby blue p-coat Kymber had picked out for her. They had a late lunch and were going to Christmas Eve services. It had snowed the day before, and though it melted, the temperatures were low. Kymber thought it was a good time for Jocelyn to open an early present—which meant everyone got to open one. New coats for all the kids magically appeared.

The doorbell rang and he checked his watch in surprise. It was four-thirty.

A skinny, short-haired, stern-looking woman stood at the entrance, bundled up and holding a briefcase. Kymber came up behind him and slipped an arm under his. There was a taxi at the curb, presumably waiting on the woman.

"Hello. Are you the Morrows?" the woman asked.

Suspicion and concern fired up first. "I'm John Morrow. And you are?"

The woman smiled and handed him a card.

He examined it. "You're a lawyer."

"Adoption. I've come to pick up Star. I understand you've been looking after her?"

"Pick her up?" Panic rang in Kymber's voice. Fingers tightened around the skin on his arm.

Jocelyn came up behind them, obviously listening in. "Let me through." She studied the woman. "How do we know you're legit?"

John looked from Jocelyn to the woman and back again. It was a stand-off.

"Through blood and luck, I make change happen," the stranger said.

Jocelyn nodded. "Where will you take her?"

"We have a good family."

John had no idea what just happened, but it felt like he had been gut-punched. The woman came in.

"No," Kymber said it out loud. She turned to John. He thought she might hyperventilate. He felt the same panic as he gripped the nearest chair.

"Unless of course," the woman studied them quietly. "You wanted to adopt her."

John turned to Kymber. They hadn't really thought anyone would take her away. She reached for his hand, and he nodded.

"Yes."

Jocelyn breathed with relief. The younger kids wandered into the living room, curious.

"Excellent!" the woman said. "I brought those papers as well. Just in case." She popped open her briefcase. "I just need both parents to sign on the spots highlighted. Both copies please." She handed them two pens and proceeded to turn pages for them to sign. "I'll file the paperwork. I'm also a notary, so just let me stamp this."

John and Kymber sat in a daze, signing documents, while the lawyer wrapped up all the paperwork.

"And that's that. Just thirty-nine dollars for the filing fee. Everything else has been covered."

John pulled out cash. "Keep the change." He added another sixty. "And here, for your cab."

"Thank you." She smiled at everyone. "Star Mi-hi Morrow, congratulations. You've been adopted. Merry Christmas!"

Finally understanding, the kids hooted, jumped, and danced in a circle with Star.

John walked the lawyer to her cab then joined his family in the living room. They were waiting by the tree. John plopped into his chair, taking it all in.

Jocelyn handed Kymber a gift. "I think you should open this one tonight. It's from Seth. He had a hard time coordinating it, but…you'll see."

Kymber wiped her eyes and handed the present to John. "I can't."

"Women," he joked and winked at Max. His son came and sat on the arm of his chair. "Do you know what this is?" John asked him.

Max smiled. "Maybe."

John opened the gift. He'd had an idea, but not this. It wasn't Max and Maddie. It was Seth, Jocelyn, Star, Max and Maddie. They were laying on the grass in the yard with all their heads and hands together in a star shape. Kymber leaned in, tears flowing.

"Those are happy tears, Star." Maddie explained.

Jocelyn knelt in front of them. "He wanted you to have at least one picture of all your kids." She squeezed John's hand and reached for Kymber's. "Including the ones you saved."

John nodded, his throat too tight to speak. Finally, he opened his arms to his family. "Best. Christmas. Ever."

Something cold and wet rubbed her nose.

Or licked it?

Evie tried to move her arm. Rubble shifted around her. Everything was gray. Was this hell?

She shifted and pulled herself up a little. Her body ached everywhere but seemed in one piece. She jolted when wet slobber hit her face.

What was that?

Heavy eyes looked up.

The Spirit Horse. It licked her? Was it real?

She shook her head. Dead for sure. Delusional in death too.

Irritated neighs made her turn. Then hooves stomped, impatient.

She heard workers in the distance. They arrived to continue clean up.

Evie pulled her legs free and got to her knees. The world spun around her.

The Spirit Horse nudged then nearly knocked her back down. She grabbed it for balance. Then scratched. It felt real. The horse nudged her again and bent low.

Evie was conceived on a horse and born on a horse—or so she'd been told. She grabbed the mane of the Spirit Horse and pulled herself atop. It made perfect sense that she'd die on a horse.

The horse approved then carried her away from the site into a dense fog surrounding the mountains.

She leaned forward and rested her head. If she wasn't dead, she had no idea where she was going.

Jocelyn had spent a good portion of her holiday tracking Sabrina and figuring out how to break into her house—Jocelyn's former home.

She knew from Graeme that Sabrina would not be home tonight. She'd been spending a lot of nights at the Rochesters to be close to Benny.

Jocelyn took advantage of that news to trespass. She needed a good block of time to explore where her parents' home lab used to be in the bottom floor of the building. Currently it was the least used space in Sabrina's home. It had been refinished and partially furnished as a home gym. Jocelyn had spent the last hour carefully pulling up the wood floor.

But with good cause. Her finger followed an edge in the concrete below. The safe was here. She thought someone would have found it, but it was well-matched with the rest of the concrete.

Her memories were real after all. Her heart pounded with a mix of relief and excitement.

She used some tools to lever the concrete camouflage. Her mother had a remote back then. It raised and lowered the safe. Tonight, Jocelyn applied brute strength and determination.

It sufficed.

The safe.

A vehicle drove near and stopped. Female steps caught her attention. Jocelyn froze. Her super hearing heard the click at the entrance to the building, the security code entered. Sabrina would realize the alarm was deactivated.

Jocelyn couldn't leave. Not yet. Not until she opened the safe. But what if Sabrina alerted the police? Jocelyn turned off her small work light and used her flashlight.

She listened, hurrying to pull free the opening of the safe. She didn't want to hurt Sabrina, but Benny's life was more important right now.

Jocelyn yanked the door of the small safe and pulled out the silver box. It was dented and not closed properly. Her mother had put the vial inside.

Give it to Benny. Save him!

The memory haunted her. She would do this.

Steps froze at the top of the stairs. Jocelyn waited. When Sabrina didn't come down, she opened the case.

It was as she remembered…only not. The vial was cracked. No hint of serum remained. Time had erased and evaporated hope. The explosion must have caused the final damage. Her mother's desperate attempt at saving Benny failed. And now, so did Jocelyn's. There was only one other place where any remaining serum could be—an impossible mission.

She slumped over the hole in the floor, fought back the disappointment.

Lights switched on, illuminating the room. Sabrina was foolish. You didn't try to stop a burglar on your own.

Jocelyn waited for her to turn the corner. She stared at the gun in Sabrina's hand without emotion. She didn't have much left emotionally.

"Why aren't you at the Rochesters?" she asked.

Sabrina blinked. She looked at the hole in her floor, the hardwood stacked neatly, the toolbox, and Jocelyn holding the silver medical container.

"You didn't even call the police. You could be dead right now," Jocelyn chastised.

The gun shook. "What the hell are you doing? Who are you? Really."

Jocelyn took a slow breath. She had a feeling Sabrina already knew.

"You know who I am, Aunt Sabrina."

Sabrina shook her head, belief and disbelief at war.

Jocelyn confirmed it. "I'm the prototype. And I don't have much time."

The End…for now.

TO MY READERS

Dear Reader,

If you liked *Shimmer*, I would love to have you leave a review on your favorite online retailer, book review spots, and social media. Your positive words really make a difference to indie authors.

I hope you will also keep in touch on social media or through my newsletter where I run monthly contests and share early news on books as well things that inspire my daily dreams and schemes. Please visit my website: www.triciacerrone.com to sign up. You can find me on all social media as @triciacerrone.

Happy Reading!

Tricia Cerrone

BOOKS BY TRICIA CERRONE

The Black Swan Files
001: Glimmer
002: Glisten
003: Shimmer

BOOKS BY TRICIA CERRONE
WRITING AS TRISH ALBRIGHT

Keepers of the Legacy
Siren's Song
Siren's Secret

The Time Keeper

Made in United States
Orlando, FL
26 April 2023

32479067R00220